PRAISE FOR LAURIE NOTARO

"Notaro portrays this exciting sliver of time with historical accuracy, providing an authentic glimpse of the era (including photographs), and then adds a pump of adrenaline by including dialogue and drama of her own imagination, creating a captivating historical fiction."

—*Kirkus Reviews*

"[Notaro] leverages her . . . keen eye for human foibles in an ambitious fictionalized account. [An] action-packed, character-rich romp."

—*Publishers Weekly*

"Best known for her offbeat essays on contemporary topics, Notaro breaks new literary ground and demonstrates an intuitive sense of narrative and indelible appreciation for history's ironies."

—*Booklist*

"Fascinating . . . Well-researched novelization . . . A compelling story."

—*USA Today*

THE
MURDERESS

ALSO BY LAURIE NOTARO

Fiction

There's a (Slight) Chance I Might Be Going to Hell: A Novel of Sewer Pipes, Pageant Queens, and Big Trouble

Spooky Little Girl

Crossing the Horizon

Nonfiction

The Idiot Girls' Action-Adventure Club: True Tales from a Magnificent and Clumsy Life

Autobiography of a Fat Bride: True Tales of a Pretend Adulthood

I Love Everybody (and Other Atrocious Lies): True Tales of a Loudmouth Girl

We Thought You Would Be Prettier: True Tales of the Dorkiest Girl Alive

An Idiot Girl's Christmas: True Tales from the Top of the Naughty List

The Idiot Girl and the Flaming Tantrum of Death: Reflections on Revenge, Germophobia, and Laser Hair Removal

It Looked Different on the Model: Epic Tales of Impending Shame and Infamy

The Potty Mouth at the Table

Enter Pirates: Vintage Legends 1991–1999

Housebroken: Admissions of an Untidy Life

Predictably Disastrous Results: Vintage Legends 1991–1999 Volume II

Excuse Me While I Disappear: Tales of Midlife Mayhem

THE
MURDERESS
A Novel

LAURIE NOTARO

Little
a

Published by Little A, New York

www.apub.com

Amazon, the Amazon logo, and Little A are trademarks of Amazon.com, Inc., or its affiliates.

ISBN-13: 9781662512209 (hardcover)
ISBN-13: 9781662512216 (paperback)
ISBN-13: 9781662512193 (digital)

Cover design by Mumtaz Mustafa
Cover image: © Donald Jean / Arcangel; © Myotis / Shutterstock

Printed in the United States of America

First edition

To Sunny Lynn Worel
and
Robrt Pela

PART ONE

CHAPTER ONE

October 19, 1931

The first drop of the rust-colored liquid that splashed on the wooden railway platform in the Union Station was not noticed.

Neither was the second, fourth, fifth, or twentieth. But ten minutes after the porter placed the black packer trunk on its side after the train from Phoenix had come to a stop, the stain began to spread. It leached out beyond the corner of the trunk, seeped in between the planks of wood, and settled in a dark, growing puddle, underneath the smaller gray steamer that accompanied it.

The first porter who saw it ignored it; he had a full compartment of baggage to unload and this was not his car. Another porter stopped for a moment, assumed it was water, and moved on. The messenger from the Golden State Limited train stopped, bent down, swiped his index finger through the small pool, and examined the dark, murky liquid. He took a sniff. It smelled of rot.

He checked the tag attached; the name scribbled on it read "Judd."

"Sir?" he called out to the chief porter. It took several attempts to get his attention.

"I think we have something odd here, sir," he said, holding out his fingertip. "I think we have some smuggling. A deer, probably."

Arthur Anderson sighed and studied the accumulating stain. "We'll need to bring the trunks into the baggage room. Don't let anyone claim them until they see me first," he said, and then wrote the same instructions on the baggage tags.

Together, they shifted the larger trunk, exposing an expansive area of liquid that had gathered underneath.

Anderson wrinkled his nose. "God, that's bad," he said to the messenger, who nodded.

They dragged the trunks to the small office on the platform not far from where they had been unloaded, a telling trail of darkness smeared behind.

They placed them as far away from their desk as they could. The pool was growing with speed, the stench gathering potency as well.

It took twenty minutes for a petite blond woman to appear at the baggage room door. She waved to get Anderson's attention, then handed him her claim tickets. She had a young man with bushy chestnut hair as her companion.

Anderson studied the woman for a moment. She was slight, a smooth complexion and wide, deep-set eyes. A pretty thing. She was clothed nicely, in a clean, fashionable dress and a matching hat, tilted and poised on her head of light curls, which stopped just below her chin. She carried a brown leather satchel in one gloved hand, and had the other in the pocket of her jacket. Her shoes were bright and unscuffed; her lips had a slight tint to them, pinkish. Not gaudy. She didn't look like a smuggler. A little girl like this? But things were different now; several years into the Depression, even prominent, upstanding people were employing all sorts of means to keep their families fed and stop the banks from coming for their houses. You couldn't go by looks anymore, he knew, didn't matter who had nice shoes and who didn't. None of it mattered, even if a lady was wearing gloves. If there was a deer in that trunk, and he suspected there was, he would have no choice but to call authorities.

"Are these the ones you're looking for?" he asked, pointing toward the black and gray trunks in the corner.

She suddenly smiled, brightly. "Oh yes, thank you."

Anderson looked at her again, noted her cheerfulness, then moved his eyes to her claim tickets.

"What was the name on that tag, ma'am?" he asked.

"Judd," she said quickly. "Mrs. Judd."

"Thank you, Mrs. Judd, can you tell me what the contents are?" he asked.

"Medical books," she replied without hesitation. "For my husband. He is a physician."

"Did you pack those trunks yourself, Mrs. Judd?" he asked.

She did not look alarmed, but was clearly taken aback.

"I don't understand," she said, looking him in the eye. "Is there a problem? May I just have my trunk, please?"

"Come with me," Anderson said, and led the woman and her companion into the office to where the trunks stood, the spot beneath the larger trunk dark and wet. "Mrs. Judd, do you notice that disagreeable odor?"

She sniffed briefly, delicately, and shook her head. "No, I'm sorry. I don't."

The chief porter looked at her. The smell was not only palpable—it was overbearing. He couldn't help but notice it, even from several feet away. Flies had begun to gather, buzzing above the trunk, several of them landing on the top.

"You don't detect any smell coming from your trunk?" he asked again.

"I do," her companion said. "That is awful! What could be causing that smell?"

"I don't," she replied, shaking her head, her eyes fixed on the chief porter. "May I take my trunks now, please?"

Anderson shifted his weight from one foot to the other.

"Mrs. Judd, this trunk is leaking," he informed her, pointing to the collection of liquid below. "Are you sure there are only medical books in there?"

"Of course I am," she said, a bit irritated. "I'm just bringing them to my husband. I told you, he's a physician."

Anderson didn't want to get involved with this: calling the police, having her taken away, all for some pieces of meat. He was sure of it; there was a deer in that trunk. Parts of a deer, anyway.

"Mrs. Judd, I am going to have to ask you to open this trunk, please," he said with a deep breath.

She shook her head.

"I can't," she said sharply. "I don't have the key."

"All right, then, who has the key?" Anderson asked, looking at her male companion.

"I told you, these are my husband's trunks, they are his books," she said, becoming more agitated, her eyes widening. "This is not my husband. This is my brother. My husband has the key. I was only to bring them to him."

Her companion looked puzzled.

Anderson knew she realized she had been caught. Was it worth calling the police? Getting this woman in trouble? He doubted she had money for bail, not if she was shipping this kind of cargo from Phoenix to Los Angeles. He felt sorry for her. He had as soon as he saw her wave to him at the door.

"Mrs. Judd, I would appreciate it if you would get the key and open up this trunk for me," he said. "I cannot let you have either of them until you do. I'm sorry."

The woman took in a deep breath through her nostrils and bit the inside of her lip.

"That is all right," she told him. "I will get the key from my husband and then we can get this all sorted out."

"I'm sorry," Anderson said, knowing that he was forcing her to walk away from money that she probably needed badly.

She shook her head sharply, once; this was clearly a bother. She turned and walked down the platform, her companion following her, and was quickly absorbed by the crowd of other passengers making their way into the station.

Anderson shook his head. He felt a bit responsible for what he had forced her to lose. A nice lady like that.

The smell was there, he told himself. *The smell was there.*

When the next shift of porters arrived, the trunks remained exactly where Anderson and the other porter had dragged them. Though October, the day was still warm, and the odor from the first trunk had grown with the increasing temperature.

"I've got these trunks," he said to the incoming porter. "Belong to a woman—she said she'd come back with the key hours ago, never did. I think she's smuggling some deer or something. Got blood or something leaking out from all underneath."

"It stinks," the porter agreed. "Whatever's in there has gone off. I don't want that thing stinking all night. Call the cops."

"Sure," Anderson replied, and stepped inside the office. He had hoped it wouldn't come to this.

The porter grimaced at the smell.

Anderson waited until two lieutenants arrived, Detectives Ryan and Torres, both men in their thirties but who looked like they had seen far more in their lives for their age.

Ryan asked if Anderson had a master key ring, but Torres stopped him.

"I'm not going to smell this while you go through fifty keys till you find the right one," he insisted. "You have a crowbar?"

Anderson nodded, and the night porter came back with it. Together, they kicked the larger trunk over. With one lift of the crowbar, the stench ballooned, rising from the trunk, affronting those not even directly in front of it.

"Oh my God," Anderson said, using the hem of his porter's jacket to cover his mouth. The night porter began to gag, stood up, and ran down the platform until he reached clear air, then stood with his hands on his bent knees, trying to inhale.

"What is it?" he called in between breaths. "What the hell is in there?"

"Deer, I think," Ryan said, his words muffled by his hand as he turned away.

Several porters came out of the office almost immediately and, once confronted with the smell, turned away or sought some sort of protection.

In the trunk was a mass of objects: linens, photos, newspaper, clothes. Whatever smelled lay under them, the fabric and household items simply filler for the other contents.

"Give me that," Ryan said to the night porter, who handed him the crowbar.

It took a while. With equal parts revulsion and trepidation, Ryan lifted out as many of the items as he could with the crowbar—the clothing and linens—and then tossed the books, letters, and newspaper out by hand. He had just moved what appeared to be a dirty brown tablecloth up and out of the trunk when a porter who was looking on sprinted over to the platform to vomit.

Anderson stood back for a moment, not wanting to see what foul thing had been uncovered, but he stepped forward, one foot, then another, and looked in.

At first, he didn't know what it was. Was that fur? Hair? What was it? It looked black. Was it curled up? A hand? What? Was it pushed up, curled into a ball? And then, after a few moments of adjusting to the horror he saw, he was rather sure that he was looking at a girl.

The second trunk was opened next. Only a layer of towels was placed on top; the stench was awful, but not as bad as the first trunk. Torres removed the towels and the porters stood back in a group far enough away from the trunk that they couldn't immediately see what was inside—with that smell, they knew it wasn't something they wanted to see.

In the first trunk had been a woman, a Black woman, dead for days, the detectives surmised by the stench. She'd been shoved into it until she was curled up like a shrimp, her head bent so far forward that it was unnatural. It looked like her neck might have been broken.

Torres called to his fellow officers, who had just stepped up on the platform, and shook his head.

"Jesus," one of the newly arrived officers said after he looked into the second trunk, jerking back simultaneously. Another one shook his head and looked upward. A third walked quickly away, muttering in disbelief as he passed the porters, "Legs. Only *legs*."

A few minutes later, another officer came out of the station and onto the platform, calling, "Ryan, Torres. We've got something in the bathroom, behind a door. A brown leather satchel—there's an arm in it."

CHAPTER TWO

October 19, 1931

When Ruth Judd entered the Broadway Department Store on Fourth Street, she knew exactly where to go. She hadn't been in that store for years, but not much had changed. Walking swiftly, though not so fast as to attract attention, she skirted around men's accessories, veered left toward men's sweaters, and walked through women's hosiery, headed for the corner of the main floor. She pushed open one door, then another, entering the women's lounge. It was a Monday, midafternoon, and quiet in the store. She was thankful. It didn't resemble the panicked scenes when she worked in the toy department years ago, the raging thrush of people screaming for her attention those last frantic days before Christmas. She remembered those mad, endless shifts, twelve, fourteen hours at a time with no break. She'd worked so hard to earn money for Doctor, even with her fever. Then she'd woken up in the hospital, almost dead, and was bedridden for months. She had never been so ill. Everything was so different then, and she was in an even bigger mess now. She went for the closest door in the lavatory, locked it behind her, closed the dull black lid of the commode, and then sat down.

She breathed. They were deep, almost gulping breaths, like she had just broken the water's surface after a long dive. Her injured hand throbbed. A slight line of perspiration cooled the top of her upper lip. She wiped it away with the back of her good hand.

I should have arrived here yesterday, she thought. The smell wouldn't have been so strong then. It would have been much less obvious, and by now, the whole thing would have been over and she'd be dumping the trunks into the ocean. But Jack said no, she needed to be at work on Saturday. It would have been suspicious, both her and Anne being gone from the clinic. People would have checked. They would have gone to the house. "Sunday," he said. She needed to leave on Sunday, get to Los Angeles by Monday. She took her left hand out of her pocket and held it tightly around the wrist, almost as if she were strangling it. It was hot with pain, and she tried to cut the agony off at the base. She thought of the ragged hole in it, the blackened flesh, and what was still lodged in it by her knuckle.

"Are you all right, miss?" she heard a delicate voice call outside the stall. The attendant. *Steady yourself,* she thought, *your breathing is too loud. Too loud. Be softer, be quiet!*

"Yes, fine, thank you," Ruth said after a moment. "Something bad at lunch, perhaps."

"If you need a damp towel, you let me know," the attendant replied.

"Thank you," Ruth answered. "I think I'll be fine."

Ruth covered her mouth with her good hand. She resisted the urge to scream. If Jack was here, he'd tell her what to do. But it was because of him that she was here, hiding in a bathroom stall five hundred miles away. If everyone in this city wasn't looking for her already, they would be soon. There wasn't much time. She had to hurry. She'd been in bad spots before, gotten herself out. *Ruth. Ruth. Ruth.*

She shook her head quickly, stood up, flushed the commode, and wiped off her upper lip again. She smoothed her hair and opened the door quickly.

The attendant had reached for the tap to turn on the water, but before she turned around, Ruth was gone. She slipped through the lounge and headed toward the elevator. On the seventh floor, she walked to home furnishings. When she had worked here years ago, many years ago, and needed quiet after a busy rush or just a moment to think to herself, this was where she would come. Just to hide out for a bit.

The wall of curtains displayed the newest trends in the fashion of 1931. Frilly opaque organza for a bedroom, a heavy jacquard for a living room, lace panels for a foyer. Ruth's own little apartment had light cotton panels with tiny strawberries on them that fluttered when the window was open, and she loved watching them bloom and then settle over and over when there was a nice breeze. She much preferred them to the heavy draperies in the house she'd shared with the girls. Dark, weighty, heavy. She felt a shadow fall on her shoulders. The girls.

Shhhh. Settle now.

When she was alone and knew other people were far away in other departments, looking at sofas and chairs and beds (*Stop! Settle! Don't you think of that!*), and it became silent, Ruth picked the heaviest-weighted wool floor-length panel, opaque and quiet, and slipped behind it.

After the store closed and the sounds of customers and salespeople had dribbled into silence, she carefully parted the drapes. Her hand was burning as if she had stuck it into a bed of red-hot coals. She tried her best to push the pain away and listen. There was nothing: no sounds, no rustles. Lightly, she took several more steps and listened again. The store was dark, the lights switched off. She had little time before the night watchman clocked in and began making rounds, if she remembered correctly.

She knew she must get a letter to Doctor, to tell him not to believe what people would say and to know that she still loved him so. She descended the back stairs to the first floor. It was dark inside, it took a minute for her eyes to adjust to the darkness. She thought about Doctor and what he was thinking, whether the police had come for him, and what they had told him.

When she reached the paper and stationery department, she picked up a pad of white writing paper, but instantly put it down. If she could not pay for it, she could not take it. A cable office used to be in the corner of the first floor, and Ruth made her way quietly to where she remembered it was, and on the counter was all the paper she needed: cable blanks for messages to be telegraphed on. She took a stack; this was not stealing. She pulled one sharp pencil from an accompanying box and started back upstairs.

She could not mail the letter to her sister-in-law Carrie's house in Santa Monica, she knew; the police would be on the lookout for any sign of Ruth there. She decided to send the letter to Dr. Moore, an old friend of Doctor's who had helped him get a new job in an emergency hospital, where he was right at that minute. Dr. Moore would know how to reach Doctor quietly and without suspicion.

In the thickening darkness, she wrote in her long, looping handwriting.

Dear Doctor Moore:

I am being sought by the police and can't get any message to my darling precious husband Dr. Judd. I've got to tell him—

Ruth stopped. Tell him what? The truth of what she had done? Was that what she really wanted to say?

—to please not die of grief. I love him and I hope he won't hate me for being wicked. Thank you and Mrs. Moore for having been so good and sweet to me in the past. One of my hands is about shot off so I can scarcely write. Do me this favor to let Dr. Judd know what happened.

Then she started the letter to her husband.

"Darling," she began, and again stopped.

That seemed so preposterous. What could she say to a man who was so sweet and gentle, and whose life she had just destroyed? Things would never be the same once he knew. These might be her last words to him. She should leave him with something good.

"I have a confession I've kept from you as long as we've known each other, because I was so happy with you and loved you," she began, "so why tell you?"

And then it came out.

Darling: I was working so hard at Phoenix when you went to Bisbee then something went wrong in my head . . .

You know how I cried and cried . . .

I was crazy. You said . . .

Mr. H came out the next evening he had been at the coast and he said what's the matter you look terrible you look crazy . . .

The next morning all three of us were yet in our pajamas when the quarrel began. I was going hunting. They said if I did they would tell Mr. Halloran I had introduced him to a girl who had syphilis . . .

There was no harm introducing this nurse who is very pretty to the men . . .

Anne said before Sammy got the gun Ruth I could kill you for introducing that girl . . .

It was horrible to pack things as I did . . .

*I kept saying I've got to go I've got to go or I'll be
hung I've got to go or I'll be hung . . .*

I'm wild with cold hunger pain and fear now . . .

*Doctor darling if I hadn't gotten the gun from
Sammy she would have shot me again. Forgive me
not forget me.*

*The police will hang me. It was as much a battle as
Germany and the US. I killed in defense.*

Love me yet doctor.

Once finished, she folded the sixteen-page letter and put it in her handbag. She was exhausted. Her mind swam with confusion, her hand radiating pain. It would be hard to sleep, she knew. She had nothing to quiet her down.

Shhhh, she said to herself. *Shhhhh.*

She was so tired.

So tired.

When her brother, Burton, had dropped her off in front of the Broadway that afternoon, he'd given her his last five dollars. Even he had smelled the stench when they went to retrieve the trunks at the station. It was overpowering, disgusting. That fetor. She'd never forget it, never get it out of her head. It clung to her.

He hadn't expected her to show up without warning on the University of Southern California campus. After she got off the train, she hailed a cab and looked for him for some time, not sure where to find a student of international law. She went to the registrar's office to find his schedule and waited for him outside his French class.

He immediately thought the worst as he approached her. Their parents? But then . . . no. His parents were in Indiana; she would have called, someone would have called. She wouldn't be here. Dr. Judd then? Burton knew his brother-in-law had been in bad shape, convalescing at the veterans' hospital in Los Angeles. Relapse after relapse. If anything had happened to him, Ruth would be lost. She needed him. He dreaded the words that would first fall out of her mouth.

Ruth looked panicked. Her delicate, pretty features were drawn and pulled. She hadn't been crying, he could tell that as he got closer. She didn't look sorrowful; she looked destroyed.

"I need your help, Burton," she said quickly, without even as much as a hello. "I need you to take me to the train station. I left Doctor's trunks there and I must get them back."

"Why didn't you tell me you were coming?" he said, somewhat relieved. "I would have come to get you."

"I know, it all happened very fast," his sister replied. "Is it close? Your car?"

"It's not far, but I have a class now, Ruth," he explained. "We can go right after. Find a nice cool place to wait and I'll be back when it's over."

"No, no," Ruth said, a little frantically. "I must go now. It's very important. Doctor needs his books immediately."

"Ruth—" he began, but he saw her face begin to tighten, and if he was right, missing one French class was the least thing he should be worried about.

She said little as he walked her two blocks to his car. She had just arrived this morning, there was no time to call Doctor, he'd just said he needed his books as soon as possible.

Burton opened the passenger-side door of his car and let her in, but then he paused.

"Ruth, will you please tell me what is happening?" he asked her sternly.

She looked at him harshly and then swallowed. "Please get in the car, Burton," she pleaded.

He obliged. He hadn't fully closed his car door when she turned to him and visibly shrank before him.

"You must help me," she said, her voice wavering. "I need your boat."

He hadn't seen her in over a year, and she had come to California to ask for his boat?

"What?" he asked, surprised. "What boat? I don't have a boat."

"I need that boat you have," she replied, almost angrily. "The one you captain. *The boat.* Can you get it?"

"Ruth, that's not my boat," he said with a laugh of disbelief. "I captain the boat, but it belongs to the yacht club."

"Well, I need it, I need you to get it for me," she shot back, her eyes wild, growing wider. "It's very important, Burton, that you get that boat for me."

Ruth closed her mouth tightly and spoke through her teeth, nearly hissing. "I need your help. Something bad has happened. You need to help me *now*."

Burton stood speechless. Nothing made sense. This was ludicrous. He bent closer to his sister and took her by the elbow.

"Are you having an episode?" he whispered. "Does Doctor know you're here?"

Ruth ripped her arm away. "No one knows I'm here," she snapped. "I took the train overnight. *I need your help. Please, Burton.*"

"Ruth," he said firmly. "I need you to tell me what has happened."

"No!" she said, squirming out of his grasp, in turn wrenching her other hand out of her pocket.

Burton looked at the bandages wrapped around her hand, raggedy, bulbous.

"What happened?" he gasped.

"I burned it on the stove," she explained hastily. "It will heal."

"What has happened, Ruth?" he asked again. "None of this makes sense. Did someone hurt you?"

"You are the only one who can help me fix this, do you understand? Will you help me?" Her voice had grown louder, higher. He needed to get her out of there now.

As soon as he agreed, she settled herself; calmer, but still serious. She told him to drive her to the train station to pick up her trunks. He cautioned himself not to read too much into her desperate state; he had seen this before, and it typically amounted to nothing more than a hysterical episode. When she was a child and insisted their mother had given birth to a baby, becoming inconsolable when told it must have been a dream. When she was a young woman and went missing for over a week, finally found walking along the train tracks, half-clothed and insistent that she had been kidnapped. Catatonic periods followed, though short, and then she would pop right back to normal. Burton hadn't seen her like this in a very long time. He'd believed that Doctor had these episodes under control.

When they arrived at the train station, she shoved her bandaged hand back into her coat and walked determinedly toward the porter's office. He hastened his step to keep up with her.

But as soon as they stepped foot over the threshold, he knew this was not simply another episode, and she saw the reaction in his face. His disgust mirrored the bubbling, decaying way she felt inside, the smell that was so wrong that Burton knew he couldn't fix any of it. Whatever was in there, in Doctor's trunks, it had gone so far beyond that.

Then Ruth had scrambled to come up with the line about not having the trunk keys, and despite the mess, the flies, the stench, they walked back to the car, unfollowed, alone. Miraculously, alone.

He could not say it. He could not bring himself to ask her. They sat in the car in silence for a while as he drove through downtown until he finally said, "Is it a man or a woman in there?"

She was quiet for a long time before she turned to face him. "The less you know about those trunks, the better. But, Burton, know that I was justified in what I did, always remember that," she told him.

He found himself nodding as a response.

"Stop here," she said as they approached Sixth and Broadway, a congested intersection, and he did. He fumbled through his wallet and gave her everything he had: five dollars. It was clear that when they saw each other again—*if* they saw each other again—it would be under very different circumstances. Nothing would ever be the same as it once was. Five dollars wasn't going to get her far, but she took it. She opened the door with her good hand, then shoved the five dollars into her pocket, and got out.

"I'll call Doctor and tell him everything," she said.

He nodded, unsure of what to say. "I wish you all of the luck in the world, kid," he finally spit out.

"Burton," she said before pushing the door shut, "I'm sorry."

Then she walked several feet to the busy corner, and melted into the crowd.

CHAPTER THREE

October 19, 1931

The two bodies in the Los Angeles County Coroner's Mortuary were badly decomposed, and had clearly been dead for several days. Detective Frank Ryan already knew that. The stench rising from the baggage was strong.

The bodies were still in the trunks. Inside the large one, curled, shoved, and packed, was a girl, or a woman. It was hard to tell.

The face was a swollen jumble of features that he could not logically assemble into a cohesive landscape of what he knew a face should be. Both eyes bulged like a loser in a prize fight who had taken a savage beating. *She must have been clubbed,* Ryan thought. He moved his eyes down a bit. A dark object was projecting from the profile of the head. He stared at it. Was it a shoe, or the handle of something? Tortoiseshell, celluloid? Was it a brush, a kitchen utensil? He jerked back slightly when he realized he was looking at her tongue—swollen, unnatural, pushing out of her mouth as if it had been pulled there.

Her knees reached up to her chin unnaturally; it was a forced position. In life, she had been small, and now was even tinier, curled up in a ball, made to fit that way by other, stronger hands. She was wearing pink silk pajamas.

The legs of the woman in the smaller trunk, which had already been opened by the porters, were severed below the knees and wrapped separately in women's underclothing. He had never seen such a thing before. Ryan didn't want them to be real, but the smell of a decomposing human, although significantly less potent than the larger trunk's, insisted they were. Layered underneath was her torso from the waist up, including her head. She had suffered the same bloat and decaying facial disfigurement as the other victim, although she was not as unidentifiable. She was swollen and bruised on the face, yet Ryan could see she was not a girl but a woman, larger than the tiny body crammed into the larger trunk. The torso, which was also badly bruised, was wearing a slip, wrapped in a blanket with a delicate pink border. Her arms, which were missing, looked as if they had been cleanly sliced off with a guillotine. Ryan noticed something odd: there was barely any blood, as if it had all been drained out before the victim was packed into the trunk like it was a shipping crate. With little to no blood, there would be less decay, he noted, accounting for the less powerful smell.

Ryan worked his way down to the bottom of the trunk, anticipating the unthinkable, using the crowbar to carefully lift items out of the trunk and onto the floor. A tablecloth, women's clothing, cosmetic items. Everyday objects, tucked in and around the remains of a woman who had been butchered as if she had been in a slaughterhouse. The normality of these things struck him as cruel and appalling, equally as grim as the bodies themselves.

Detective Torres, Ryan's partner, was working to open the lock on an old tan suitcase that had accompanied the trunks when someone supplied a hammer and he was able to smash the lock with several swift blows. Torres waited a moment before opening the suitcase, trying to prepare himself for what he was about to see: the torso, cut from the waist to the knees, still wearing pajama bottoms, also pink, and wrapped in a blanket and a sheet. The legs in the smaller trunk, he understood, belonged to the same person who had once been a whole woman, a white woman. The bladder, intestines, and liver were missing. He moved to the satchel that had been located in the bathroom and found the remaining two arms.

Along with the trunks was a hatbox that contained surgical dressings, an old kit of surgeon's instruments including several scalpels that
showed signs of rust, a Colt .25 automatic pistol also stained with rust,
numerous pieces of women's clothing, forty rounds of Winchester .25
automatic cartridges, and a small empty black leather doctor's bag that
stunk of death.

The larger trunk, which contained the body of the Black girl, was
stuffed with an assemblage of household items, including two women's
handbags, one of which contained a thermometer, and two .25-caliber
shells, one exploded and one unexploded, and the other held nothing
but one .25-caliber bullet and a penny. Other items found in the large
trunk consisted of a bent bread knife with a green handle, a heavily
bloodstained piece of rug approximately three feet long and partially
burned, and an abundance of loose photographs, bundled letters, and a
stack of canceled checks written to a Dr. Packer in Whitehall, Montana.
The letters were addressed to "Darling Sammy," while the checks were
signed by a Hedvig Samuelson. A diploma from the Minot Normal
School listed Hedvig Samuelson as the recipient. There was also a teacher's contract for Samuelson from Whitehall, Montana. At the bottom
of the trunk were a pair of ice skates and an array of Christmas cards.

The photos were of no use to identify either of the victims. They
were the images found in typical photo albums: smiling people on
vacation, signifying moments in time of joy and celebration, moments
that were meant to be captured forever. Most of the backgrounds in
the photos revealed a great deal of snow, while others, by comparison,
were taken in a stark, dry desert. The bodies were "considerably decomposed," the coroner noted, while the body of the girl that was whole
had been distended with postmortem gas: "The eyeballs protruded and
tongue, lips and other parts enormously swollen and putrid."

The letters were addressed to 2929 North Second Street in Phoenix,
Arizona. Police officers arrived at the Phoenix duplex only several hours
after the trunks, suitcase, hatbox, and satchel had been moved to the

morgue from the train station, noting that one side of the duplex was uninhabited and the other had occupants, although none were home. Phoenix police immediately began canvassing the neighborhood. According to neighbors, the women who lived at 2929 North Second Street hadn't been seen for three days, since Friday night.

Two women lived there, they were told: Hedvig "Sammy" Samuelson, twenty-three, a schoolteacher. She'd been stabbed several times, shot in the shoulder and then lethally in the head, and was now scattered across three pieces of luggage at the Los Angeles County Coroner's Mortuary.

But the second victim did not match the description of the other resident of 2929 North Second Street, who was a white woman named Anne LeRoi. It was the coroner who realized that on the train journey from Phoenix to Los Angeles, the trunk had been placed on its side, with the victim's head upside down, causing the blood to settle and giving the skin a deep bluish-purple discoloration. The body, he suspected, was that of not a Black woman but a white woman, and most likely that of Anne LeRoi.

LeRoi, twenty-seven, an X-ray technician, had been fatally shot once in the head and stuffed into the larger trunk. The blood on the soaked carpet piece was hers, as was the fluid dripping out of the trunk onto the railway platform. When she was removed from the trunk where she had been curled like a shrimp, a deep, dark stain on the pajama collar and shoulder became visible.

The coroner listed the date of death as October 16 for both, each "shot by unknown person, unjustifiable."

The neighbors were hesitant to say too much, simply mentioning to the police that the two women who lived at 2929 North Second Street were "of the odd sort."

But a third woman was also missing, the police quickly discovered, one who was always in the company of the other two. Neighbors hadn't seen anyone come or go from the house, which was unusual, they noted. It seemed like there was a party going on every night at the duplex, sometimes straight into the next day.

"Single girls," one of the neighbors told the officers. "With a lot of gentlemen friends who drive fancy cars. You know."

The third woman was a coworker and friend to the two deceased women, and also a former roommate. Winnie Ruth Judd, twenty-six, a medical secretary and wife to Dr. William C. Judd. Known simply as Ruth, she was last seen in Phoenix the day prior by her landlord, Mr. Grimm, who drove her to the local train station and unloaded several trunks and suitcases she was taking to her husband in Santa Monica. Mr. Grimm and his son noted that the luggage was quite heavy.

"Medical books," Ruth had told the men, and then she'd smiled.

CHAPTER FOUR

October 19, 1931

The phone rang at 2929 North Second Street, again. It was 10:00 p.m., and Phoenix police officer George Larrison picked it up; normally, he would be wary of newspaper reporters, but when he and his partner, Officer Frasier, had arrived at the house, a small crowd was already waiting outside, the regular beat reporters the officers had come to know.

After learning that the inhabitants of the duplex hadn't been seen in days and there were no signs of life within, Officers Larrison and Frasier pried a window screen off to enter the duplex; all of the doors were locked and the lights were dark. When the officers flipped the lights on, the men from the *Phoenix Gazette* followed them inside, trying to get the scoop.

"That phone has been ringing for two hours straight," one of the reporters mentioned.

Larrison put the receiver to his mouth and simply said, "Hello?" If someone was trying that hard to reach the residents, it made sense to him that the caller might provide some leads that he could follow up on.

"Anne?" a man's voice replied through a tinny connection.

"No," Larrison replied, and left his answer dangling there.

"Is Anne LeRoi there?" the voice on the other end questioned, sounding puzzled. "I would like to speak to her. Is she available?"

"Who is calling?" Larrison asked simply.

"This is Emil Hoitola, Anne's fiancé," the man replied sternly. "If she isn't there, please give the phone to Sammy. I'll speak to Sammy then."

"Neither Anne nor Sammy is home," Larrison informed him. "Can you tell me the last time you spoke to either one?"

"What do you mean, Sammy's not there, either?" Hoitola said with urgency in his voice. "That's impossible. She can't go out. Who is this? Please put Anne or Sammy on the phone. I must speak to them. You're not the first man to answer this phone, by the way, and I've had about enough of it."

Larrison couldn't tell the man that his fiancé and her roommate were most likely dead and stuffed into pieces of baggage that had just been brought to the Los Angeles morgue, and that his fiancé might be in pieces, too. They had no positive identification on either victim, and he'd have to withhold anything until those were established and next of kin were notified.

"You men and your games," Hoitola said angrily. "You're disgusting. Pathetic. Go home to your wives and leave those two sick girls alone."

Larrison was surprised when the line went dead.

"There's a mattress missing on a bed in here," Frasier called from the bedroom down the small, narrow hall. "Looks to be a bloodstain on the floor, right beneath it. Someone tried to clean it up, but it's there. And a piece of carpet has been cut out."

"It's in the fireplace," one of the reporters answered. "It's singed."

Larrison walked over and took a look. The carpet piece was blackened a bit, but hadn't caught fire all the way. A dark-brown stain covered most of the pattern. He went to the back bedroom, a compact, slim room with two single beds flanking a small night table. The bed to the left was made up nicely, and was very neat. The other was heaped with folded quilts and blankets, which rose as high as the other bed, so at first glance it appeared as if a mattress was underneath. The corner of the carpet under one of the beds had been cut away raggedly; undoubtedly some of it was now in the fireplace.

The rest of the apartment was clean and tidy; books on the library table in the living room included *Grand Hotel, Cakes and Ale,* and *The Care of Tuberculosis.* Women's books, he noted of the first two. Romance and wishful thinking. A new radio sat on the table, too, along with a stack of detective magazines.

There were no signs of a struggle; it was a well-kept house. Except for the bloodstain on the bedroom floor and a spray of blood drops found on the baseboard in the kitchen—signs of death, but not a fight.

In the following days, as the police searched the house, they located dozens of affectionate letters to both girls from as many men. Photo albums that belonged to the victims were seized and scrutinized, mirroring the same type of everyday photos in the trunks. Snapshots, holidays, silly poses. A diary belonging to Sammy was lifted by a reporter and slid into his jacket pocket. A bottle of whisky, almost empty, was on the breakfast table.

Parties almost every night, straight into the next day, the neighbors had informed them.

"You men and your games," Anne's fiancé had said. "You're disgusting."

October 19, 1931

Frank Vance, the landlord of the duplex, confirmed that the residents were Hedvig "Sammy" Samuelson and Agnes Anne LeRoi. He immediately realized his looming loss of income and set out to make it right. Before the police could finish their search, he hammered a sign into the front yard announcing a tour of the murder house.

His strategy paid off as soon as locals saw the headlines the next morning that two young women had been savagely murdered right in the heart of this dusty baby boomtown. The line to surrender a dime snaked around the block and lasted for a week straight. Two thousand people, ten cents a head.

CHAPTER FIVE

October 19, 1931

When Dr. William Judd returned home after a day of work at Santa Fe Emergency Hospital in Santa Monica, he was in a good mood. It had been a smooth day, and he was glad. It felt good to treat patients again; it had been difficult to find a position after he lost the last job in Phoenix. He was being careful this time and was more deliberately following the rules. Today he had seen a man with bursitis in his shoulder, a child with a stomachache, and yet another unfortunate woman racked with tuberculosis. It felt good to be able to help in whatever small way, and he had missed that feeling badly. He was grateful that Dr. Moss, a longtime friend and colleague, had considered him for the temporary position while he was away tending to family business.

Carrie, Judd's sister, was just about to finish up with dinner when he came through the door.

She was shocked, but pleasantly so, at the smile on his face. "You're looking better than I've seen you in years!" she exclaimed. "Dinner will be ready in a little while. You've got just enough time to wash up and listen to the news broadcast."

The last several years had been a struggle with little relief. Overweight, Judd had begun having trouble with his knees, and he walked slower to accommodate the discomfort. His hair, now deeply receding, revealed a shiny, freckled scalp from the sun of Mexico, where he'd last lived. He'd been in Santa Monica with his sister for almost a year now, after getting fired from his last post as a doctor for a mining camp near Mazatlán. When Carrie had seen him upon his arrival, the first thing she'd noticed was how his face dripped in soft folds, like melting wax. Then she'd observed his eyes: tired, sad, weary. His affliction had not only worn him down but had eaten at him, leaving a frumpy, hobbling old man who had little hope left in him.

"I had a very nice day," he yelled over his shoulder as he turned on the bathroom tap to wash his hands. "I think this may really turn into something."

"I hope so," Carrie called back. "I think it's a travesty that a good doctor like you has had to work as an orderly over there. Dr. Moss had some good sense to have you fill in."

Judd could not have agreed more. It was humiliating to be doing so little at the hospital when he could be doing so much good. He had a solid feeling that things might actually start to turn around; if he could prove to Moss that he was the responsible doctor he'd known before, there might be a place for him on the hospital staff not giving sponge baths or emptying bedpans. He kept reassuring himself, despite recent outcomes in his past. The job in Phoenix had lasted only two weeks before he was let go; this opportunity with Moss was a favor he could not afford to destroy. They had worked together in Indiana at the hospital where Judd met Ruth. Ten years ago, twelve, maybe? Moss knew him as a solid doctor, devoted to his calling, careful with his patients, and kind. Above all, Dr. Judd was known as kind. None of his patients, should they have been told, would believe the things people said about him.

Even if they were true.

He turned on the radio in the kitchen and sat down at the set table. Carrie was ladling soup into bowls; he'd smelled the familiar waft of beans, onions, and tomatoes when he opened the front door. Soup was on rotation at least five nights out of seven. Times were hard; there was very little money coming in from his war pension, and the remainder of their income was sourced from a tenant who lived in the larger house attached to Carrie's small cottage. When things turned sour in 1929 and people started worrying about jobs and how to pay the rent and feed their families, Carrie, a seamstress known for her elaborate beading work on elegant dresses and ball gowns, figured her own survival hinged on moving her small collection of personal items out of the bigger house that had been her parents' and into what they called the backhouse. It was small but sufficient; one bedroom, a living room big enough for a sofa and a chair, and a tiny lean-to kitchen. It was all she needed, but when Doctor called to ask if he could stay for a little while—he had lost the last in a series of jobs in Mexico and was going back to the veterans' hospital in Los Angeles—of course she said yes. It was only for a week or two, Doctor assured her, just until a bed opened up. He was going to get well this time, he promised her. Completely well. No nonsense like the other times. He would be by himself, he noted; he planned for Ruth to go back to Indiana with her parents until he was well enough to send for her. Carrie did not mind. She liked her sister-in-law; nearly twenty-five years her brother's junior, she was a nice, considerate girl. But Carrie also bore witness to some of Ruth's . . . oddities, she would say. Living in such cramped quarters might prove troublesome for the three of them, especially if her brother was serious about getting well, and he knew that, shipping her back to her parents. But Ruth never made it to Indiana, and in an attempt to hitch a ride back to Los Angeles instead, found herself stuck in Phoenix and ended up staying there. It was for the best, Carrie knew. Her brother needed some quiet if he was ever going to get well.

Judd turned on the radio as Carrie had suggested to listen to the news broadcast, and it crackled to life as he sat down at the kitchen table.

" . . . are searching for a young man in collegiate clothes and a pale-looking woman with light hair. Detectives say this is one of the most baffling cases they have encountered for years. You have just heard the highlights of the day's news. For further details, see your local newspaper."

"'Baffling,'" Carrie commented as she placed a soup bowl in front of her brother and then sat. "I wonder what qualifies as baffling?"

Judd shrugged and then smiled. "Who knows these days?" he said. "The soup is wonderful, Carrie."

"Someday, we'll break out of beans, I suppose," she replied with a slight chuckle.

"I'll get paid on Friday," he added. "I'm sure we can swing a chicken."

"A chicken. Yes. That sounds wonderful," she said, smiling, and then took another mouthful.

They were making fudge when someone knocked on the door. It was eight thirty; not exactly late, but definitely past the time to receive visitors.

Dr. Judd was cracking nuts as Carrie answered the door. "Bill?" she called a moment later, and he heard the door closing. He looked up to see Burton, his wife's brother, standing in the doorway of the kitchen. He looked pained and worried, and he seemed to be out of breath.

"Burton," Judd said, surprised not only to see his brother-in-law but also to see him in such a state. He was a college boy, involved in his studies, and Judd rarely saw him. Tonight he was nervous, flushed, antsy. This was not like Burton, who was jovial, friendly, and sometimes a bit goofy. "What is wrong?"

Burton had a hard time starting and stumbled to get the words out. He was sure by the time he arrived at Carrie's, the police would have already dragged the doctor away. His name was on those trunks. The police wouldn't have had any problem finding him.

For a moment, this calmed Burton enough to ask, "Have you heard from Ruth?"

"I did not get a letter today, did I Carrie?" Judd replied, to which Carrie shook her head to the negative. "But I did get one Saturday."

"I saw Ruth today," Burton shot.

"You saw Ruth today?" Judd echoed. "Where?"

"Here," Burton clarified. "She's here, in Los Angeles. She didn't call you?"

Judd looked confused. "Ruth is here? Why is Ruth here?"

"She was on campus—found me on campus—asking to use the boat; she had taken the train," Burton said in an incoherent rush. "I told her I didn't have a boat, but she demanded that I get the boat. I didn't know what to do; I didn't know what she had done. I drove her to the train station to collect her bags, but it went all wrong. She said they were full of medical books for you, but—there was something else in those trunks, Doctor. She didn't call you? She promised she would tell you everything. You didn't ask her to bring books? She didn't have the keys. She said you had the keys."

"No, I did not ask her to bring books," Judd replied, trying to follow Burton. "I received a letter several days ago, but it said nothing about coming to California. I don't understand. Where is she?"

Burton tightened his lips and shook his head. "I don't know," he said. "I dropped her off downtown. She said she would phone you. Those trunks, Doctor, they were leaking something brown, something awful. They smelled terrible. Flies were everywhere. It almost made me sick. There was something bad in those trunks."

"What do you think was in there?" Judd finally asked.

Burton was quiet, but pulled out a newspaper that was tucked under his arm. He handed it to Judd and said solemnly, "She told me she was justified in what she did."

Judd unfolded it and stared at the headline.

TRUNKS HIDE TWO TORSOS OF WOMEN

Shipped from Phoenix to Los Angeles by Woman

CONSIGNEE UNNAMED

Employee of Clinic Is One Victim, Other Not Known

Phoenix, Ariz., Oct. 19 (AP)—Backed by a chain of circumstantial evidence found in letters seized in a Phoenix apartment from which the bodies of two women were taken in trunks earlier today and in a constantly growing hoard of other details, police tonight broadcast requests for the arrest of Mrs. Ruth M. Judd, a secretary at Lois Grunow Memorial Clinic, Phoenix, and her husband, Dr. William C. Judd, former first lieutenant, medical corps, U.S. Army.

Judd stared at the paper for a long time. The words came apart, then together. He couldn't get them to make sense.

That was his wife. Ruth M. Judd. She worked at the Lois Grunow Clinic in Phoenix.

That was his Ruth.

The bodies of two women. One was an employee of the clinic.

"Oh no," he said aloud.

"Bill?" Carrie started.

"Oh no," he said again.

Detectives Ryan and Torres had first looked for Dr. William Judd at his place of employment at 9:00 p.m. but found the emergency hospital closed for the evening. When they knocked on Carrie's front door twenty minutes later, Judd let them in.

They were in search of not only Judd, but Burton, too. One officer took Judd into the kitchen, while the other questioned Burton in the living room.

Judd hadn't been to Arizona since the beginning of August, he told the detectives. He went out for a brief visit but things turned out differently than he'd expected. He came back to California almost immediately. It was not a pleasant trip, he added.

"No," Judd said to the officers. "She is not on dope. She does not drink." She was adoring. An adoring wife.

Judd pulled out the letter he'd received only the day before, trying to reassure the officers that they were not looking for his wife. She was in Phoenix, as far as he knew.

In the next room, Burton was battling another volley of questions.

"No, she isn't crazy," he told the police. "I don't think she is. I don't think she is crazy."

Her letters had been incoherent lately, he added. She had an insane temper.

"She wanted to dump the trunks into the ocean," Burton told them. "I don't have a boat."

The police required both of the men to come to the central station.

"Your wife, Winnie Ruth Judd," the police informed Judd, "is wanted for questioning in the murders of Anne LeRoi and Hedvig Samuelson."

Judd took a deep breath, afraid he would collapse, but he had already known and wanted it to be a terrible mistake.

The girls.

Carrie watched as both men were led to separate squad cars, police firmly gripping their arms.

Sirens broke into the air as Burton and Judd were sped to the Los Angeles central police station.

She watched until the lights were out of sight and she could no longer hear the sirens, then went back inside and sat at the kitchen table, which was covered in chocolate bits, butter, and smashed nuts, and waited.

⚊⚊◆⚊⚊

Burton and Judd were taken to two different rooms to be questioned by Ryan and Torres.

Neither man had recently traveled to Arizona and neither of them was on that train, that was true, they insisted. Burton had worked all weekend as a janitor for the university, and he could prove it. He had repaired a roof, dug a trench for irrigation, and painted steps. "Call my boss," he urged the police. "He will tell you."

Judd had been home all weekend with Carrie; he'd worked a full day on Friday and then again on Monday. Neighbors had seen him at least once each of those four days. He had just started a new job at the emergency hospital and could provide witnesses there, as well as a patient list. He had not seen his adoring wife since August 9, when he'd briefly visited her in Arizona. He had seen the girls then, too, both Anne and Sammy. Everything seemed fine; he hadn't noticed a change in their friendship. He was supposed to stay longer, but it was best for him to return.

"Ruth could not have done this," he repeated several times. "I know her. She isn't capable. She is a very small woman, and she has tuberculosis. She is not strong."

He knew her, he did. Of course, he had seen her upset, impatient, unreasonable, even frantic. Desperate, hysterical, angry. There were times that he couldn't make her listen, when she wouldn't stop screaming, sometimes into the night. Nothing but screaming. He had driven all through the night in the empty Arizona desert with her screaming, just so people wouldn't hear it. Times when she was inconsolable and nothing would soothe or calm her. But a murderess? *No.* And killing Anne and Sammy? Her two closest friends?

"There is more to this than Ruth," he heard himself say. "She loved those girls. She spent almost all of her time with them."

Almost, he said.

Then Judd pulled back. He said nothing more.

Ryan put something black and heavy on the table in front of Judd. "Do you recognize this?" he asked.

Judd's heart fell as quickly as if he had thrown it off a roof. He felt his entire life go with it, leaving him stunned and hollow. Now it was true. It was all true. And now everything was gone, slipped away from him just like that.

"That's Ruth's gun," he said, nodding. "I sent it to her because I was afraid for her safety when she moved out of the duplex and into her own apartment. I gave her that gun. I bought it."

The truth, Judd thought, *is so cold.*

"Ruth will be dead when you find her," he said quietly.

Ryan looked at Judd, surprised by the comment. "Why do you say that, Dr. Judd?" he asked. "What can you tell me about her mental state?"

"I don't want to talk about that," the doctor replied. "There are some things too close to me to discuss."

"The police in Phoenix found a twenty-five-caliber automatic shell in your wife's apartment on Brill Street," the detective continued. "That is where your wife lived, correct?"

Judd nodded. "She lived with the girls until several months ago," he offered. "It was cramped; Ruth slept on the sofa. So she took the apartment on Brill Street."

"And she had this gun while she was living in the apartment?"

Judd nodded. "I don't remember it being so rusty," he said weakly.

Ryan pitied the man before him, who'd deflated into a tired, tragic old husk over the course of the night. He took a deep breath and exhaled through his nose. This whole thing was a disaster. A tragedy. This feeble man had no idea what his wife was doing.

"Why were you living apart?" he asked.

Dr. Judd opened his mouth and shook his head slightly, but he could not speak.

He put his elbow on the table, his hand to his forehead, and closed his eyes deeply. He did not open them as he spoke.

"I was injured in the war. Badly. First gas and then shrapnel. Results of which persist still, and follow me," he explained. "Everywhere I go. I cannot outrun them. I came to the veterans' hospital here to recover, again, after my job as the doctor for a mining company ended in Mexico. My sister was here, and it seemed a good place—a good hospital with a record of treating men with situations similar to my own. Ruth was supposed to go to Indiana to her parents', but she had the idea to join me. It was a surprise, a last-minute thing. Sometimes Ruth does not know what is best for her. The car broke down in Phoenix. And she was stuck; then she got a job and stayed there while I was recovering. It was just as well. My sister's place is small, and I sleep on the sofa as it is."

Ryan nodded, his gut telling him that this man, who was shrinking more and more before his eyes, had had very little to do with this spectacle aside from furnishing his wife with what was highly likely the murder weapon.

"Dr. Judd," Ryan said as he leaned forward, "you knew these girls. You are the only one in Los Angeles that knew them. And we need a positive identification before we can send them back to Phoenix and on to their families."

Judd, with his head still resting on his hand, closed his eyes tightly and slowly nodded.

⚬

William Judd had seen so much death that he believed it didn't affect him anymore. On the battlefields of Argonne and Verdun, when he was a soldier during the Great War, men fell to the left and right of him, ahead of him and behind, their bodies landing with small, smothered sounds. He heard those muted thumps in his sleep. Death. The land he walked on, the air he inhaled, everything he saw was soaked in death. There was no relief from it, no respite. It had hardened him in his medical career; it was a part of the job in a medical career. Not everyone could do it. For someone who had seen as much as he had, death had been ground down to a factual matter. Even when he lost his first wife—after trying so hard to treat her for tuberculosis—he wept briefly, mourned for her in his own way, but he also accepted it as simple fact.

But when the coroner drew back the sheet to reveal the corpse that was now lying cold and still in the morgue downstairs from the police station, it was unlike anything he'd ever seen. Not during his days of war, as a doctor, nor as a widower who'd watched his wife die.

This was more than death, more than a torn body, more than a corpse.

This was horror.

The victim's face was distorted, bloated, discolored. Judd covered his mouth but could not move his eyes. He couldn't look at the coroner, Ryan, or Torres, who all watched his reaction carefully. Was that Anne? Her face looked more like a terrible mask, sloppily made, bulbous, out of proportion. The skin was a deep purplish shade, the color of raw meat that had been left out and crusted.

The woman had not yet been cleaned up. Her hair was shaped like a helmet with dried blood, which was black and solid on her scalp. She didn't have the bouncy, light-brown curls he remembered. What had happened to her? How terrible must it have been?

Judd, indeed, had seen death in many forms. But he had never seen murder. And that was a kind of death that made him shake.

"Miss LeRoi had brown hair," he whispered, though he'd intended to speak normally. "But I can't make an identification."

"Did she have small hands, fingernails that were well kept?"

Dr. Judd nodded, his eyes still unable to move at all. "Her nails were always polished," he said. "Her eyes were brown. But I couldn't—I hope that is not Anne."

It was the sound that made Judd turn, a whoosh that lifted the sheet off Sammy, leaving her body bare in the wide open.

Judd gasped, thinking he had already seen the worst of it with Anne. But Sammy—the breath felt vacuumed out of his chest, and he took a step back with a jolt. She was assembled like a puzzle on the table, pieces of her put where they used to be. Like a broken doll.

It was repugnant. He wanted to run. Quickly, out of that room. He swallowed a scream and then focused on standing still.

He had the urge to put her back together, to reach out and attach arm to shoulder, knee to thigh. He wanted to fix her. He shouldn't be seeing her like this, it wasn't right. She was nude—the disgrace of it. As if the parts weren't enough to collapse anyone, the nakedness, the bareness, was insulting. Shameful.

The cuts were clean, so clean. Straight, not wavering. That took a steady hand, Judd knew, and a blade designated for surgery, and not just a blade but a saw. She was separated in the optimum places for the easiest, simplest cuts to take someone apart, below the thighs, right through the femur, avoiding the impossibility of the pelvis. Below the shoulders, one saw through the humerus, a clean cut. He could see the ends of each bone on the torso and on the arm. It looked as if she could be glued back together without issue. And the legs, severed below the knee. He had seen that done in the war many, many times. A thick bone, but a saw would have no problem if the patient wasn't protesting. These were things you learned in medical school, on the battlefield, or in practice. This wasn't Ruth's doing.

Ryan had wanted Judd to see Sammy that way. To understand what his wife had done. What an act of revulsion it was, how merciless, how brutal.

It was heartless.

Ryan had told the coroner to make sure Judd understood the monstrous act of cruelty. A woman Judd had once known when she was vibrant, talking, laughing, was left merely as pieces.

"Please," Judd said in a faint voice. "Please cover her up."

"Is it her?" Ryan asked without sympathy.

Judd nodded. "I'm sorry to say that is Sammy; she had very full lips, like this lady," he said. "Please cover her up."

"We haven't found her intestines, bladder, or liver," Ryan added, to heighten the shock. "They don't seem to be among the contents of any of the baggage." He motioned to the side of the room, where the trunks and bags Ruth had last seen on a railway platform were leaking blood and buzzing with flies.

"That's my army trunk," Judd said in disbelief, pointing to the smaller trunk, which had contained Sammy's torso.

"Do you recognize anything else?" Torres asked.

Judd took several steps and looked. Dried blood was evident on almost everything, either in large stains or on portions of things. He recognized Ruth's nightgown, some of her underthings, and an Indian rug that they'd had woven for them when they lived in Mexico. And then, sticking to a doily and bonded by the blood of one of the girls, he saw a birthday card he had sent to Sammy several months before. She had kept it. Sweet girl. She didn't need to keep it, but she had.

"That tan suitcase," he said, motioning to the luggage that most of Sammy had been shoved into. "I brought that to France for the war."

He turned from the heap of things he recognized, away from the girls and toward the door, where he didn't have to see any of it anymore. He stood for a moment, tried to collect himself, and then cleared his throat to produce a regular voice instead of a whisper.

"I knew both of these girls when they were alive," he said, looking at no one. "Active and without a care. They were gay and happy when I last saw them."

"And when was that again, Dr. Judd?" Ryan asked, seeing if he could trip the doctor up.

"August," he replied, his eyes still fixed on the door. "Early August."

"You're sure?" Torres questioned.

Judd nodded. "I hope my wife is never found alive," he said simply, now looking down. "It is my belief that she will be taken from the ocean. She is frail and delicate; she could never stand the ordeal of a trial. If she were alive, it would prolong the agony. She will be very upset about the girls."

The coroner pulled the sheet over Sammy, and Ryan moved to escort Judd out of the room.

Judd took several steps, then stopped. "But you have not met my wife," he added. "She did not do this. It is not within her. She is small, very small. Not strong. Someone else is responsible for this. I will tell you to look for Jack Halloran. He sells lumber in Phoenix and was acquainted with my wife and the girls. I thought he was looking after them. I was fooled. I suggest you ask him where he was when all of this happened."

Before the police led Judd back to the station, the coroner asked him to sign Sammy's death certificate.

Dr. Judd took a deep breath, held it for several seconds, and then obliged.

CHAPTER SIX

October 20, 1931

It was still dark when Ruth woke behind the curtain wall, and the silence of the empty department store was an instant reminder of where she was and why.

Hastily and quietly, she folded the blanket and placed it, along with a pillow, back in the display. The night watchman wouldn't come to the seventh floor; people did not break into department stores to steal sheets and bedspreads. He would be patrolling the jewelry and watch displays several floors down. Still, an odd noise could set him off, and she needed to think.

She looked at her watch. The store would be open in an hour. Staff would be arriving to clock in, get ready for the day. Check stock, tidy the racks. She needed to get settled now.

In the lavatory, her hand burned like an ember as she carefully undid the soiled wrappings. With each layer, she winced, hesitant to see what the next surface revealed. The stain deepened in color as she got closer to her hand, until it became a dark brown. She let the dressings fall away and gasped at what she saw.

The hand was swollen beyond use, black at the site where the bullet had shot into her palm and lodged in front of the knuckle of the third finger, and she could see the lump of the bullet where it had stopped. She wished it had gone through her hand. There had been no time to attend to digging it out, and it would need to be removed. Infection was guaranteed; gangrene was possible. She had neither the tools nor the skill to remove the bullet with only one hand. She rinsed it with water, sucking in her breath to stifle the cries of pain, then braced herself at the edge of the sink and drew several deep breaths before she patted it dry.

With her teeth and her good hand, she tore strips from the new sheet she had pulled off the shelf in the stockroom and then rewrapped her hand. This was not stealing, she told herself; this was necessary. She gathered the dirty bandages and slipped back into the stockroom and into a small service closet that was rarely used when she worked here, and shoved them behind stock.

Then she slid back beneath the curtain that had hidden her so well yesterday and waited. After an hour, when the store became occupied and bustling, she moved from behind the curtain to the front of it, and, with her good hand, rubbed the fabric between her fingers and smiled, as if she were considering buying it, to bring back to her bungalow apartment on Brill Street in Phoenix.

Then she took the stairs down once again to the main floor. She walked easily, with a careful good pace, and out onto the sales floor among countless other women wearing similar dresses and coats. She kept her bandaged hand in her pocket and tilted her head slightly down.

No one screamed, pointed, or shrieked in her direction, yet they all knew what she had done—she was sure of it. She even recognized several of the salespeople she'd known when she worked there. She walked swiftly back out to Seventh Avenue and made a left, headed to the small drugstore she used to frequent on her lunch break if she needed thread, a scrubbing pad, laundry soap. The place hadn't changed at all, right down to the hollow-sounding bell that rang as soon as the door swung open. She lowered her head and plucked a bottle of black dye off the shelf, along with a comb and a package of brown henna. On the way to the counter, she picked up a box of saltine crackers and then placed Burton's five-dollar bill next to them. Without saying a word, she paid, took the bag, and walked back the forty-two steps to the Broadway Department Store.

When the elevator stopped ringing and the sound of voices had quieted, Ruth stripped off the dress she had been wearing since she left Phoenix and plunged it into the bathroom sink, smothering it in black dye. The dress was cotton and light in color; it shouldn't take too much time, she thought. She unwrapped the paper package of brown henna and mixed it in a bowl she had lifted from housewares with a little bit of hot water from the tap. Carefully, she dipped a comb into the henna, then ran it through her blond hair. She was glad she didn't have the same waist-length hair she'd had when she was a girl; she had cut it into a more womanly style right before she married Doctor. They had left immediately after the wedding and headed to Mexico, where he would be the doctor at a mining camp in Tayoltita; it made no sense to fuss with all that hair in the hot climate. She smiled a little at the smart decision she'd made, then stopped, quickly, when she remembered why she was coloring her hair in a department store bathroom in the quiet of night.

She tried not to think about it, to instead pick up her mind and put it someplace else. *Focus on this,* she told herself. *This moment. But surely the girls—surely, they have been found by now.* She inhaled deeply, and the breath stabbed her in a place she couldn't describe, couldn't even locate. In a place that was both above her and below her, and straight through the middle.

Oh no. No no no. She closed her eyes tightly and she pictured something else: the round, chubby face of John Robert, his coos and babble as he reached for her face. *Pretty baby,* she whispered back. *My pretty baby. My love. Oh, my sweetness.* She kissed his red, healthy face and felt his breath on her. His perfect, perfect breath. Sweet, sweet boy.

But then John Robert was gone and, instead, Ruth was running, running in the dark, down the small hall. She was close behind. She was so close behind. She could touch her. Run faster.

Faster.

Ruth's eyes flew open. A stream of henna was dripping down her forehead, almost to her eyebrow. She grabbed the towel next to her and wiped it off quickly before it could stain.

Enough of that, she told herself sternly. *Do you know that's enough? Because it is. There was nothing you could do about it. What were you supposed to do, not fight back? Just let it happen? There was no choice.*

None at all.

She knew it had to be in the paper by now. *Blond Woman Leaves Two Dead Girls at the Train Station.* They were her friends, the paper would say.

They were my friends, Ruth heard herself say.

Her name must be known now, Ruth Judd. She hoped the police hadn't bothered Burton too much. And Doctor. What must he think? Poor Doctor. With so much to worry about already. He couldn't help her now. Burton couldn't help her, either. Even if he had gotten the boat, it was for nothing. The trunks were never going to leave the train station like that. She had smelled it. She was surprised at how much she smelled it, how powerful it was, how there was no way to not smell it. It was awful. She should have left the day before. She'd told Jack that, even when he insisted it would be fine, that the girls wouldn't go off for a couple of days still.

"I'm a doctor's wife," she had insisted. "I've seen war. I've seen what death does and how quickly it takes over a body."

But he wouldn't listen. Her told her to take the Sunday train, it would be quieter. Not so many people. The trunks were packed well; they'd used blankets, sheets—it was all covered up. It was all going to be fine.

"Take the Sunday train," he said again. "I will send a man down with tickets."

But Jack's man never showed. She waited, and waited, and at the very last moment, she took all of the money she had after paying Mr. Grimm to drive her to the station and bought a ticket to Los Angeles. She had less than a dollar left. Once there, she would fetch Burton, he would come, and they'd get the boat. And then they would take the boat to sea, far out, where no one could see and no one would know anything.

They'd drop the bags in the water and the water would take the girls. The girls loved the water. Neither had been to the ocean in a long time, since they'd lived in Alaska. They'd talked about it so many times. Anne had promised Sammy they would go back, as soon as Sammy was a little bit better. Yes, the ocean was a good place for them to be. The water would wash it all away, and then Ruth would find Doctor in Santa Monica, get John Robert back, and they could start hoping again. Things could be good for them. She just needed to be better.

I want to be good, Ruth thought.

But Jack's man had never showed, the trunks were a mess, and the girls had gone off. They had spoilt. Terribly. There was no boat, there was no money, and her name was surely in the paper.

Blond Woman Leaves Two Dead Girls at the Train Station.

Ruth wiped another drip from her forehead and, looking at the sink, saw that her once-light dress had turned fully and deeply black. In the next sink, she rinsed out her hair and saw that just like every aspect of the life she once knew, her fair hair had become unrecognizable.

CHAPTER SEVEN

October 20, 1931

On Tuesday morning it wasn't only Ruth's name that was splashed across the headlines of the *Los Angeles Times* and other local newspapers, each out to capture the highest number of readers. Dr. Judd and Burton appeared as well, reporters speculating what part they had to play in the grisly discovery of the bodies and where they might be hiding the murderess, the photos of both men granular and stark. Most of the front page above the fold, however, was a large photograph of Ruth, her hair falling in soft, pristine waves about her face, the style in vogue; her large brown eyes showing black in the halftone dots, a slight upward turn of her lips that was only a moment away from a full smile.

Her husband was a doctor, the stories relayed, insisting she must know how to take apart a body; her brother, Burton McKinnell, who had been questioned for twenty-four hours, had recently dug a three-by-six-foot trench at his house in Beverly Glen, which was surely meant to be a grave. At the murder house in Phoenix, the landlady, Ethel Vance, noticed two tracks exactly twenty-one inches apart in the grass, leading from the garage to the house; inside the back door, there were tracks scraped across the wood floor into the living room.

The coroner had concluded the autopsies of Anne and Sammy, and had determined the causes of death. Both had been shot at very close range; powder burns and stippling were evident around the entry wounds to each of the victims' heads. On Sammy, the bullet had entered just above the ear on the right side of the head and exited the left side less than half an inch lower. A small wound near the back of her neck was discovered, most likely from a small knife. Another bullet had been shot through her left upper chest and passed through her left shoulder, traveling upward, but it was not a lethal injury. A third bullet had also pierced her right hand, nicked her ring finger, and passed through her middle finger. The coroner had pieced her back together again, sewing her up with long, looping stitches of black thread, like a quilt.

Anne was shot only once, again at close range, the entrance wound almost mirroring the location of the exit wound on the opposite side of her temple. There were no other injuries on Anne—no bruises, no knife wounds, just one deadly shot to the head.

Both bodies were sent to Peck and Chase Mortuary to be shipped back to their families in Oregon and Montana.

Ruth did not plan on spending another day standing behind a curtain in the housewares department. She had borrowed some bobby pins from the store. People always complimented how neat and exact her waves were; it was one of the things she took great pride in about herself. She was a doctor's wife, she thought. She always must be presentable and put together on all occasions. She checked herself in the bathroom mirror one more time, pinched her cheeks to give herself some color. Her hair was fine and had a little body to it, which made styling it easy. It looked good. It looked regular. She looked like everyone else.

She had decided the night before that she should not involve Doctor any more than she already had. Trying to reach out to him was foolish and put him in a bad light. His name was on the trunks. There was no doubt in her mind that the authorities had already paid him a visit. The only worse thing she could imagine was him being accused of acting as an accomplice. She reached into her purse, pulled out the letters she had written to Dr. Moore and Doctor on the telegraph blanks, and tore them up. She tossed them into the closest toilet and pressed the handle. She heard the whoosh of the suction carry the letters away as the bathroom door closed behind her.

She climbed down the six flights of stairs until she reached the main floor, and headed toward the doors just as she had the day before. Before she reached the entrance, she stopped and left a small bundle of bobby pins on a counter that showcased men's ties. She pushed out into the light of a warm, giving sun as a brunette who did not match the description of a deranged murderess who was hiding out in the streets of Los Angeles, her black dress still damp.

Ruth had realized where she needed to go while she was wringing the excess dye out of her dress.

La Vina.

It made sense; she knew it inside and out. No one would look for her there, and she could get there in a day. Years ago, when her tuberculosis had worn her down and made her weak, Doctor had sent her to a sanatorium in La Vina. She'd spent months there, while Doctor stayed at Carrie's until she got well. When she'd arrived at La Vina, Doctor thought she would surely die like his first wife, Lillian. Ruth was every bit as frail and struggling to live. He never said it to her, but she knew by looking at him that he expected her to go, leaving him alone again.

But Ruth was determined not to abandon her husband, and followed orders to the exact degree. She rested in bed twenty-three hours a day, and was wheeled onto the veranda to take in fresh air for one hour with the other feeble, lifeless patients. Ruth did not make friends there; she needed to focus on her own health. She had once been a nurses' aide when she was young, working in the hospital where she met Doctor.

She understood that following measures and being determined was the only way to get well.

If she made good time to La Vina, which was in the foothills of the San Gabriel Mountains a bit north of Pasadena, she would arrive just after sunset, which was what she hoped for. She was too afraid to take a bus or a streetcar—even with her darker hair, she knew she could easily be recognized. So she would walk. As she swam through downtown Los Angeles with the rest of the crowd, she avoided eyes. They were all watching her, she could feel it.

That's her, she heard them whisper, *the one who killed her friends. In cold blood. She has no heart. If you reach in to find it, there won't be anything there but a cold, empty hole. Who would let someone like that become a mother?*

Murderess. Murderess. Murderess.

What will become of your baby now?

Ruth pulled her coat tight to cover the still-damp dress. She had swung it around her head for what seemed like hours the night before, trying to get it to dry. The hem now clung to her legs.

She saw several policemen scanning the faces of the crowd, and she dodged into a shop entrance and turned her face toward a display window. If she didn't look scared, if she didn't appear to be hiding, she could make it out of town unnoticed, even as she passed the police station.

The road out of Los Angeles and toward Pasadena was well traveled, but Ruth saw that as an advantage. Why would a fugitive walk down a long stretch of road out in broad daylight? She had ten miles to go. The dye, henna, and crackers had taken almost all her money.

Once out of Los Angeles, the road became dusty and grew hot, but she didn't remove her coat for fear of her injured hand being seen. She trudged step after step, her spool-heeled black leather shoes starting to pinch as her feet swelled.

What she would give to rest now. To just lie down and get lost in sleep, not keeping one ear open for the tiniest noise, always being alert and on the very edge of being discovered any minute. She'd rested deeply at La Vina. If Sammy had been able to rest like that, she would have gotten well, Ruth thought, and felt that to be true. She had told both Sammy and Anne about her time there and how it was the careful rest that healed her lungs to the point that the consumption wasn't always sitting on her. She had wished so many times that she and Anne could save enough money to send Sammy there. But Anne wouldn't have it. She said no one could take better care of Sammy than she did, and that she could not bear to live without her. It was Anne who'd saved Sammy from the climate of Alaska, giving up everything they'd established to make the journey to Phoenix, where the dry, hot air was a haven for all tuberculosis patients. Anne had told her that their friends and neighbors had pitched in with what they had to afford the passage for the girls to leave. Even the parents of the schoolchildren in Sammy's class had donated money for the trip last year, before Ruth even knew them. When she got back to Phoenix, maybe they could put together something for Sammy to get to La Vina, and maybe even send Anne, too. She was sure Jack would help. He adored them so. She made a note to ask him when she returned home. It wouldn't take much. Ruth could even sell some of the small things that were worth something—she had some lovely linen tablecloths from her mother, she had some silver pieces from Mexico, and Doctor had sent her that gun—

With a jolt, Ruth snapped back and saw that she was now walking in the road, not beside it. She took several quick steps back into the dust and she felt so heavy.

The girls, she thought, putting her hand to her mouth, and heard herself whimper. She felt a pang slice through her chest, and the gash it left grew wider and wider.

Oh, the girls.

Oh no, the girls.

It would rip her apart.

She wanted to scream, to fall down and scream like she had never screamed before, like a hurt animal, like pain she could not bear for one more second. It was the scream that was pushing her open, open, open. Keeping it in was killing her.

What will become of your baby now?

She kept her lips tight and kept walking.

MURDERED WOMAN TRACED BY PHOTO

One Victim Believed to Be Ex–Portland Nurse

Picture of Local Aviator Found with Corpse

The Morning Oregonian, Portland, Ore., October 20—Strong evidence that one of the women whose dismembered bodies were found in trunks delivered to the Union Station in Los Angeles was formerly a Portland nurse was uncovered last night through Hugh Angle, 27-year-old Portland aviator and jewelry manufacturer, whose picture was found in the gruesome baggage. Angle said that he believed the picture found in Los Angeles to be one that he had given to Miss Agnes "Anne" Imiah, a nurse in Good Samaritan Hospital when he was confined there in 1923 or 1924.

The last record of the nurse reported by the hospital was when she was in Juneau, Alaska. She was then Mrs. LeRoi.

Angle's photograph found in the trunk was said by Los Angeles authorities to have borne the inscription, "Hugh Angle, Christmas, 1923, 20 years old." Angle

said last night that he did not remember whether or
not he had written on the photo given to Miss Imiah.

Dr. Judd stood on the corner of Seventh and Broadway where
Burton had told him he had last seen Ruth. He was determined to find
her. He knew if he scanned every face in the crowd, walked up and
down every street downtown, he would find his wife. She would come
to him. His wife was frail in certain ways, but she was not stupid and
could be very clever. She knew downtown, she had worked here several
years ago when he was in between jobs. She could easily find her way
around and melt within a sea of people.

But that was if she was well, and Judd figured she must be. If
she wasn't together, there was no doubt in his mind that they would
have found her already. When Ruth sank, there was no controlling
any of it.

He had hoped she would contact him, but was not surprised when
she didn't. She knew the police had a line on him and were watching
his every move. They were most likely watching him right now. It didn't
matter to him. He would find her and get them out of this mess, once
she could tell her story. When she did, it would all be settled, but he
still could not imagine what events had caused her two dear friends to
be displayed on a cold table in a morgue. He felt like he had just seen
them. When he'd met the girls this past August, Sammy was restricted
to bed rest, but was always cheerful, talkative in between bouts of
coughing, and clearly caring for Ruth so much.

"Doctor, I don't know what Anne and I would do without her,"
Sammy had told him, just several weeks ago. "Ruth is such a dear part
of our little trio."

And now that sweet girl was lying breathless, motionless,
speechless, in a town she didn't know, her body like pieces of a
broken plate.

And Anne—could that really have been Anne? He couldn't bring
himself to believe that what he had seen was the lithe, charming Anne

who was never without lipstick or her curls. What could have brought both of them to such a dire end, and with Ruth now running for her life?

He scanned faces. Hundreds of them, thousands of them—they all looked the same. Women and men blended together into one endless mass of blurred features, distorted, discolored, bloated, swollen, wrong.

In the distance, he heard his name. *Judd. Judd. Judd.* Over and over, like a mantra. As he listened, it became clearer, and he realized the voice was a young boy's, becoming crystalline the harder he focused, and he took a couple of steps closer to the voice until he realized what the words meant.

"DR. JUDD POSSIBLE SUSPECT IN GRISLY SLAYINGS! WINNIE RUTH JUDD'S BROTHER ALSO QUESTIONED! VELVET TIGRESS STILL ON THE LOOSE!"

The boy swung a newspaper over his head like a flag as he stood next to a stack of them, gathering coins as he sold one copy after another to passersby.

Judd walked closer and saw the cover; there was Ruth, her wide eyes soft and warm in a lovely portrait she'd had taken a while ago, in black and white, an image that covered most of the front page above the fold. Next to her image were his, albeit smaller, and a photo of Burton.

He stood staring at the boy who never stopped yelling and watched in amazement as the stack dwindled to nothing in a matter of minutes. Velvet Tigress? Ruth? This was beyond the surreal. It was insanity. *People want to eat this,* he thought. *They will not stop until there is nothing left.*

He was stunned. There was nothing he could do to help her now, even if he did find her. She was lost to him. She was already guilty; no matter what the truth, she was guilty. The public had already deemed it so.

"DR. JUDD!" he heard again and began walking away until someone grabbed his arm and pulled him around.

"It's Dr. Judd!" a man exclaimed, as Judd pulled his arm free.

"Did she do it? How could you be married to a killer and not know it?" the man shouted.

People stopped and stared.

"Your wife is a devil!"

"Were you in on it? Did you saw those poor girls apart?" a woman yelled.

"Monster!"

"You disgust me!"

The voices came from everywhere, a thunder of accusations, whirling insults, fingers reaching out to poke him. Someone in the crowd came forward and pushed him backward and he stumbled, landing against a brick wall, striking the back of his head when he connected.

His hands were trembling, his mouth went dry. Fear rolled over him. He steeled himself and pushed a woman aside, breaking out of the semicircle that had surrounded him. He ran. He ran as fast as he could, past the faces with mouths forming exaggerated words, their sounds becoming thunder, their forms now blurred. He ran through the forest of Argonne, through the suffocating smoke of gunpowder, bullets coming close and the smothered thuds of men falling all around him.

He ran.

He ran to the only safe place he knew, and as he opened the door to the police station, he turned around.

No one had followed him.

Had Ruth stayed in the Broadway Department Store for fifteen more minutes before she took a chance out on the street, she would have borne witness to the horde of strangers bearing down on her tired, afflicted, suffering husband. It did not cross her mind that he might have gone out looking for her, simply because he wouldn't know where to look. She had vanished, invisible behind a curtain where she could be quiet, tucked within herself. She did not want to see Doctor.

She did not want to answer his questions.

She arrived at the gates to La Vina just as the sun was setting. She had traversed the dusty road in the brightness of day. Several police cars had rushed by her, but none stopped and she kept going. There were no guards to sneak past; La Vina was a sanatorium, not an asylum. Sitting high up on a hill just north of Pasadena in the foothills of Altadena, the refuge for tubercular patients was a working ranch with fruit trees, horses, chickens, cows, and a vineyard. The patients, almost none of whom could afford the cost of a hospital, were fed what La Vina yielded from the gardens and livestock; the simple brown wood bungalows were supported by the sale of grapes and outside donations. The sanatorium also treated soldiers from the war who had suffered lung damage from toxic gassing. It had not escaped Ruth's notice that her husband avoided those men with great care.

The road up the hill was steep, powdered with silky dust and lined with tall palms, yuccas, and prickly pear cactus. Ruth was exhausted and overheated, her feet raw, her lungs heavy, and she was weak with hunger. Her mouth tasted of dirt, and it had gathered in a light film in the creases of her eyes. Every twenty steps—she counted—she stopped to rest on the high embankment on the left side of the road until she summoned enough fortitude to push on for another twenty.

The struggle past the gates and up the road to the sanatorium took almost an hour, but when she saw the lights of La Vina, darkness had crept over the hill and she was relieved. She found a spigot and drank from it like she would never be able to stop, and then splashed water on her face with her good hand, washing the dust from her eyes and nose. The lighting outside the sanatorium was dim, and she slid from one bungalow shadow to the next until she found a bungalow with no light emanating from within. The creak of the screen door hinges was slight; no one would have heard it. She stood, waiting for a sound of occupation while her eyes adjusted to the lack of light. When she was certain the cottage was empty, she hooked the latch on the screen door behind her, then collapsed on the thin mattress of the cast iron bed.

Her insides twisted with hunger, but before she recognized the pain, she was asleep.

TWO MEN RELEASED

Los Angeles, Oct. 20—Burton McKinnell and Dr. W. C. Judd, Phoenix physician and Mrs. Judd's husband, were arrested at the home of Dr. Judd's sister, but were later released from custody when Judd provided an alibi and McKinnell disclaimed knowledge of the killings.

Phoenix authorities learned that at one time Dr. Judd was connected to a Bisbee mining company and during his tenure of service a woman, said to have been identified as Mrs. Judd, appeared in that city and made close inquiries concerning Judd's movements.

Another name entered the investigation after neighbors of Mrs. Judd in Phoenix identified an automobile belonging to J. J. Halloran, a wealthy Phoenix lumberman, as having been seen in front of Mrs. Judd's residence several nights last week.

Diary Is Found

Police declined to say whether they questioned Halloran, but Halloran told newspapermen that he knew of no antagonism between Mrs. Judd, Mrs. LeRoi or Miss Samuelson.

A diary in the possession of County Attorney L. J. Andrews of Phoenix, who flew here to aid in the search and investigation, revealed what he said might be the basis for the theory of intimacies.

He said it told a story of queer affections between the two victims and a sudden change of attitude and actions of Mrs. Judd.

Dr. Judd visited the coroner's office to identify the bodies of Miss Samuelson and Mrs. LeRoi. Judd readily identified Miss Samuelson's body but was doubtful of the other.

Died at the Same Time

Following the inspection at the morgue, Coroner Nance signed and issued the following statement relative to the women's deaths, saying that both "died approximately at the same time."

So far as all of the investigating officers on this case know at this time, it is their belief that the two women died at approximately the same time. The difference in the appearance of the two bodies is due to post-mortem changes and the action of bacteria; but this does not give weight to the theory that one of them may have died some time before the other.

On the seventh floor of the Broadway Department Store, an overflowing toilet in the women's lavatory had been reported to the janitor. When he arrived, water had gathered on the floor in a puddle; he reached behind the toilet and turned the water off and noticed several scraps of torn pieces of paper floating in the overflow.

On one of them, clearly written in pencil—had it been ink, the handwriting would have been washed away—he read the now famous name of Judd.

CHAPTER EIGHT

October 21, 1931

Ruth woke to the uninterrupted song of birds, and she realized that it had been days since she'd heard anything of the world outside. Before that thought could go any further, she was struck by two things simultaneously: her hunger and the constant, agonizing throbbing in her left hand. She didn't dare attempt to move her fingers, too afraid of not being able to. Her hand had become infected, and she suspected that without treatment soon, gangrene would set in. Her legs ached from the walk yesterday, the soles of her feet blistered and battered, her stockings worn straight through.

The light seeping into the bungalow told her she had slept for a long time. Far past midafternoon. She heard people outside, walking, a distant voice calling out to another. The sound of a short, staccato laugh. Now she was here, in that place that had made her well so long ago, when she had been in such a terrible state.

It would have been better had she died then, she thought. Suffocating slowly in a bed just like this one, gasping and reaching for breath. She was so weak then, and yet stronger than she was now. At least then she knew what the next hour, night, morning, would bring. Doctor and Carrie would visit briefly—not too long, the nurse would remind them, she needed to rest. There might be peaches and ham for lunch, maybe soup and a slice of bread for dinner. She would doze, daydream, wonder what John Robert was doing at that very moment. Was he sleeping? Was he playing, rolling on a blanket in brilliant sunshine on a perfectly green lawn, or perhaps someone was singing to him?

But now it was all a mystery. Tomorrow she could be anywhere, discovered, dragged away by the police. Tomorrow was nothing. The future had vanished. She would never see her baby again. All of it was gone, had evaporated, and there was nothing to hang on to.

She curled up into a ball, as tightly as she could, and tried to think, bending her head as far into her knees as she could go.

Tighter, tighter, tighter. Tight until you swallow yourself.

Push harder. Push harder, Ruth. I need you to push. Push until she fits.

Ruth's eyes snapped open and her legs straightened out beneath her like a reflex, her good hand flying to her mouth as she opened it to yell back.

Stop it, stop it. I can't do this. I can't shove her in here like garbage . . . like she was nothing. Why are you making me do this? Stop making me do this!

This is your making, she heard Jack reply. *I had nothing to do with it. This is all yours. All of it. And now I'm all wrapped up in this shit because of you.*

You had everything to do with it! she knew she screamed back. *Every little bit. You're a liar.*

Ruth sobbed. She should have died years ago, when she had tuberculosis, the breath sucked out of her, and she wished she had succumbed like so many others around her had. Why had she recovered, surviving only to face this tragedy?

If she could get a message to Jack, she suddenly thought, he'd be able to get her and hide her in the hunting cabin near Flagstaff until the whole thing blew over and everyone suspected she was gone forever or dead. At once, she was revolted by her own thought, clearly one of desperation and panic. He would not help her, that she already knew. He did not send his man to fetch the trunks as he'd said he would, he did not see her off at the train station. He had abandoned her, left her alone to figure the rest out. He understood nothing could touch him. And he was absolutely right.

⟫⟨

When the new Packard sedan convertible with cream-colored wheels and black fenders rolled into the driveway of the ten-year-old brick bungalow at Lynwood Street and Fifth Avenue, newspaper reporters descended on Jack Halloran before he pulled the car to a stop. They had been camped out on his wide, meticulously kept green lawn, and he did not appreciate it. He could already see when he entered the driveway that they had trodden down the turf so badly it looked like horses had galloped on it.

Halloran resented this swarm of men as they pushed against the car in cheap suits, clutching their pathetic notepads. Scribblers. Men who made a living feasting off the misfortune of others. Humiliation was their game, their livelihood, all too ready to spill the confidences that men with true vocations never aired. They disgusted him.

He made no secret of his feelings when he opened the car door as far as he could, pushing several of the twits out of the way.

"Mr. Halloran, your car was seen at 1130 Brill Street several times last week," a voice shouted. "Do you have an explanation?"

"Mr. Halloran, did you know the victims? Did you have anything to do with the crime?"

"Did you know Mrs. Judd?"

"Did you help Mrs. Judd flee Phoenix?"

"Where is Mrs. Judd? Has she made contact with you?"

Halloran, who was not as tall as he believed himself to be, adjusted his cuff links and smoothed the front of his suit. Slightly balding but fit, neat, and strongly middle-class handsome, he turned and calmly faced the men.

"I'm on the spot and I won't talk," he said in his most dignified voice, which was one octave lower than his actual tone. "Everybody would misconstrue what I might say. I won't tell you a thing and that's final."

The hive did not abate, and the men voiced their dissatisfaction with more questions, pelting Halloran as he walked up the steps to the bungalow's wraparound porch. Mrs. Halloran, petite, dark-haired, and looking weary, opened the screen door, scowled at the reporters, and welcomed her husband home, holding the hand of their small, blond two-year-old daughter, who stood quietly beside her.

BROTHER WRITES FOR "INSANITY PROOFS"

Los Angeles, Oct. 21 (UP)—Burton Joy McKinnell, 20, brother of Mrs. Ruth Judd, tonight wrote a letter to his parents in which he suggested that they attempt to gather evidence of Mrs. Judd's insanity. The parents are Rev. and Mrs. H. J. McKinnell of Darlington, Ind.

Police said they believed McKinnell was attempting to have published a letter which would cause her to give herself up at the same time suggesting that she plead insanity. Also, police said, McKinnell apparently wanted her to know that he had not "talked."

"She has told me nothing and I want to know nothing, unless she is caught by the law or gives herself up and is brought to trial. I want you, Mom, to go through what back letters you have of Ruth's which would be evidence to show her insanity. Many of her letters are incoherent and contradictory. The girl is mentally off-balance, I am sure. x x x"

At 2929 North Second Street, a letter addressed to Sammy Samuelson arrived from her mother. It was returned to White Earth, North Dakota.

Ruth faded back and forth all day in the darkened cabin, coming to for a moment and then diving back into a deep place that released her from the pain. She shook with chills, then became drenched with fever in a loop that blended unconsciousness and the brink of awareness, which rolled her again and again and again.

She was a girl in a white starched dress, looking from the porch of her parents' home to a sea of wildflowers and swaying grasses, and a cool wind blew around her, twirling her long blond hair up like vines; then the wind turned hot and sparked the field into darts of flames. Doctor was there, and she handed him a piece of cool, sugary watermelon, the juice running down her fingers as he laughed and he ate.

"Let's put out the fire," she said in a voice that was not hers. He smiled, she smiled, she kissed him lightly on the cheek, and then she pulled back to see Jack leaning in on her, sheets twisted up, the breeze so hot it began to sear, and there was Doctor behind Jack, standing against a wall, watching it all and knowing. He held a photo of John Robert, showing it to her.

"Look at what your mother has done," Doctor said, the watermelon now a rusty knife in his hand. Jack smirked and kept going. A door slammed, hard and fast.

"Anne, what fell in there?"

The door slammed again.

"Anne, what fell in there?"

I want to be good. I want to be good. I want to be good, Ruth screamed in a voice that she knew was her own.

When Ruth finally opened her eyes without sinking back into the terrible darkness, all of the day's light was gone and she heard nothing; the birds, the crunch of gravel, the faint voices, were all silenced. The mattress was damp and she lay there for some time, struggling to stay alert. She needed to eat; the instinct was now stronger than the pain gnawing at her hand. Pulling herself up to sit on the end of the bed, she tried to understand the location of the dining hall in relation to where she was now. She didn't think it was that far. Could she even make it there? she wondered. She already knew she could not get her swollen feet back into her black leather narrow-toed shoes. Holding the thick, round, cold iron of the headboard, she managed to stand up and instantly felt lightheaded. She grasped the headboard tightly, as hard as she could, and waited for the dizziness to pass.

She stood for what seemed like hours, every bit of her aching and objecting. With the last strength that she had, she took a step. A stabbing pain ran up through her foot, and with a sharp gasp, she collapsed back onto the bed.

Covering her eyes with her working hand, she breathed heavily, and could not help but emit a small, weak wail.

If you don't get up, she told herself, *you are going to die here. You are going to die. You will leave your son motherless. He will never know you. He will only know what they have said about you. He will never know the good things you've done, never. He will never know of the people you have cared for, how you saved Doctor by dragging him through the mountains of Mexico; he will never know how much you loved him. What you gave up for him. He will only know of this tragedy, that he was born of a murderess. And he will live with that mark on him for the rest of his life. He is only a baby now, but someday he will be a man and will never want to speak your name. You will have left him shamed. He will never know the truth if you do not get up.*

Ruth grabbed the headboard again and pulled herself to her feet. She slid one foot forward, moved her hand to the bedside table. She slid the other foot to meet the first. She did it again. After several shuffles across the smooth wooden-plank floor, the initial jolt of agony subsided, becoming only uncomfortable, and for the short distance to the door, she was able to lift her feet and begin to take steps.

She unlocked the door and opened it the tiniest bit, and saw a thin line of blue on the horizon. It was early morning, and if she didn't go now, she would have to wait until nightfall. She unhooked the latch of the screen door and closed both behind her quietly.

If she remembered correctly, the kitchen was at the far end of the bungalows, next to the dormitory that housed the direst of patients. Ruth stepped gingerly, keeping her senses heightened as much as possible to remain hidden. When she reached the dormitory, she moved to the back of the building. It overlooked a valley she'd spent afternoons gazing at while she recovered. She was relieved to know she was right; the kitchen and dining hall were there, just as she recalled, and, as she also hoped, the door was open. It was always open. If anyone was going to steal from indigent tubercular patients, the staff had said, they probably needed it worse than anyone else.

Inside, it took a moment for Ruth to get her bearings, but the first thing that took shape was the white enameled icebox, and she hobbled to it as quickly as she could. Inside were rows and rows of full milk bottles from La Vina's cows, maybe fifty of them, and she stood with the door open as she gulped one bottle after another. She emptied six bottles before she couldn't take in one more. Ruth quickly searched cabinets and bins, finding some bread and a bowl of dates. She ate as fast as she could, crumbs falling to the ground. She filled her pockets with dates, the remaining bread, and a small chunk of cheese that was also in the icebox; there was nothing else in it but milk. She rinsed the milk bottles in the sink and lined them up with the empty bottles near the door. She took two more bottles of milk, tucking them under her arm, and left the kitchen as quietly as she'd entered it. When she returned to the bungalow, dawn was slicing the sky open with brilliant streaks of yellows, oranges, and reds, and she silently vanished back into her refuge, latching the screen door behind her.

CHAPTER NINE

October 22, 1931

After the *Los Angeles Examiner* offered $1,000 for information leading to the arrest of Ruth Judd and several other newspapers followed suit not to be outdone, Dr. Judd felt he had no choice but to plead for Ruth to contact him and turn herself in. He issued this statement: "After years of association with my wife, I have found her to be kind, affectionate, and perfectly loyal and faithful. I know that she has not a violent temper. If she has committed the crime in which she is now charged, it seems without a doubt that it was done in a period of irresponsibility or in an irrational state or condition. I ask her to call Mutual 7235 or Cleveland 61720. I have retained Judge Louis P. Russill and Richard H. Cantillon to care for Ruth's interests."

It was a risk, and he couldn't help but understand that, in part, he had just invited his wife to take her own life. By now, she would be very desperate, in a fragile state, and there was no guarantee that making the statement had not just made him a widower. She would understand that now there was no recourse for her, that this time he could not save her. He could not protect her. She was an open target, and many, many people wanted to get the first shot. He was utterly helpless. A man who could not even help himself was worthless. He had always been.

And he had known that for quite some time.

During the daylight hours, Ruth stayed hidden in the bungalow, remaining still and quiet should she make any sort of noise to indicate that the little brown structure was occupied by a fugitive. When she was certain that the sanatorium had settled for the night, she waited hours more and then snuck back to the kitchen for more milk and whatever she could find, which wasn't much. The gardens and orchard had stopped producing since harvest season was freshly over, and she couldn't do much with the flour, salt, cornmeal, or other dry goods that she found in abundance. She ate a bit of butter on the second night along with a bread heel, and drank as much milk as she could, but even the garbage didn't yield much. The rotten end of a carrot, the peel of an onion. Scraps. She ate the carrot, swallowed the peel. It wasn't enough.

Her hand was terribly infected now. She had no doubt. There must be a supply closet in the medical wing, and feeling braver, she roamed silently until she found it, grabbing a roll of wrapping material and a bottle of what she hoped was antiseptic, and crept back to the bungalow and redressed her hand. She tried to sleep. It was useless. Hiding at La Vina was not sustainable. She could exist on milk and bread bits until they found her, which they would eventually, but it was her hand that would get her first, there was no outrunning that. She was feverish, and her hand was so swollen now it resembled a bear paw. The discharge from the wound was foul, thick, and copious.

She needed another plan.

She smoothed her hair, dusted off her dress as best she could to make it presentable, affixed her hat, stuffed her feet into her shoes, and waited for the lunch bell to ring. She hoped she looked passable and not indigent. When she heard the bell, she walked out of the bungalow as a visitor, not a woman running from the police.

She headed straight for the dormitory where most of the patients resided—at least, they had when she had been there. With staff and the most mobile patients assembled in the dining hall, she walked quickly through the corridor. She entered the first unoccupied room and opened the closet, finding a man's suit, a white shirt, and scuffed brown shoes. The next closet held a shabby day dress clearly made out of flour-sack cloth, and that was not what Ruth was looking for. She needed something of quality, something current and fashionable that would present her as a lady of standing that would not lend her appearance to being questionable. She found it several rooms down: a perfect, clean surplice wool dress in a wonderful rich dark green. Next to it hung a wool coat with a wide fur collar that was far beyond anything Ruth could afford.

She snatched them both, and noticed a handbag at the bottom of the closet. At first, she refused to look in it, but she told herself that just this once, borrowing would be forgiven. She was in the darkest trouble she had ever seen, and sometimes bad things must be done. In the purse, she found a dollar bill and some coins. A tin of Nabisco cookies was sitting on the bedside table. She took those, too.

Slipping into the lavatory a couple of doors down, Ruth ripped off her now shaggy, terribly dyed dress and washed herself as best she could in the sink. She was filthy with dust. Her legs were caked with it, her ankles creased with brown crevices. Her feet were beginning to heal somewhat, the blisters hardening over. She washed them gingerly and was about to dry them when the doorknob jiggled. Ruth froze, her leg still bent up on the basin of the sink. The door shook again, and she was thankful she had locked it. Only when she heard footsteps moving away did she relax her stance. She zipped up the new dress, and although it was a little big on her, it would more than work. In the mirror, she dampened her hair a bit to make it lie smooth. She bundled up her dirty dress, laid it over her bandaged arm, and then the coat over that. She ran a wet cloth over her shoes to shine them a bit, and then opened the door and walked out into the hall.

On her way back to the bungalow, walking in the full sun, she noticed that the driveway in front of the office building had a preponderance of cars, with some men in suits milling in between them, talking to one another. She understood immediately who they were; detectives or reporters had finally come for her.

"Hello," she heard a woman say, but Ruth had not heard her approaching, too fixated on the men and new cars that were arriving.

Ruth smiled and nodded, then turned her head away so as not to give the woman, dressed in a nurse's uniform, a full view of her face.

"Cookies!" the nurse replied, nodding to the tin. "That's a lucky patient!"

Ruth smiled again and kept her pace steady, but as soon as the nurse was ten steps behind her, she quickened her speed and headed for her bungalow, hoping she had otherwise been unnoticed.

Her time at La Vina, she knew, was done.

"BULLETIN" POSTED BY L. A. POLICE IN HUNT FOR "TIGRESS"

Los Angeles Examiner—Mrs. Winnie Ruth Judd, "velvet tigress," sought for the double murder of Mrs. Agnes Anne LeRoi and Hedvig Samuelson of Phoenix, was "bulletined" at police headquarters for the first time since the mutilated bodies of the victims were found in trunks at the central station.

The bulletin reads:

"Phoenix, Ariz., police department holds felony warrant charging Mrs. Winnie Ruth Judd with the murder of Agnes Anne LeRoi and Miss Hedvig Samuelson, committed at Phoenix, Ariz.

"Description: American, age 27, slender build, fair complexion, long, light-brown bobbed hair, permanent wave, blue eyes, very firm chin, is tubercular.

When last seen was wearing a light dress and black Eugenie hat and black high-heel slippers. She may be wearing other clothes now.

"The above suspect is probably acting very nervous.

"In case of arrest in California, notify Joseph F. Taylor, chief of detectives, Los Angeles police department, or chief of police, Phoenix, if arrested outside the state."

October 23, 1931

Ruth left the bungalow before dawn, wearing her stolen clothes and carrying a bundle wrapped in a long sheet of butcher paper she had found in the kitchen earlier that morning. She had reached the end of the stand-alone bungalows when a delivery truck crunched through the gravel behind her. She turned and waved at the driver, who slowed to a stop and rolled down his window.

"Are you all right, miss?" he asked.

"Oh yes, yes, I was wondering if you might be going to Los Angeles," she replied.

"No," the driver answered, shaking his head. "Only to Pasadena."

Ruth nodded. "Would you mind driving me there? I've been up with my mother all night, and I need to get home quickly to my children. Just getting to Pasadena would be helpful; I can take the trolley to the city."

"Of course," the driver said, and reached over to open the passenger door of the truck.

"Thank you so much," Ruth said as she climbed in, and left La Vina for good.

Once in Pasadena, Ruth found a phone booth inside a hotel and made a call to Dr. Moore, who had a clinic there. If he could treat her hand and remove the bullet, she might even have a chance to get to San Diego undetected and then to Mexico, where her life had seen its happiest moments. She and Doctor had lived there on and off for almost seven years while he worked as a doctor for the mines; she spoke Spanish fluently and had many friends who still lived in the mountains where the mining companies were. Then, she thought, Doctor could eventually join her and they could be reunited with John Robert and become the whole family she had yearned for. But she needed the bullet out of her hand before any of that could happen.

The operator patched her through, and before the office girl could say anything, Ruth blurted, "I need to speak to Dr. Moore, this is a matter of life and death and I'm quite serious."

Within moments, Dr. Moore was on the line.

"It's Ruth Judd," she whispered, careful to keep her back to the hotel lobby.

"Ruth—" he started, and realized what he had said in case anyone was listening. "What's seems to be the issue?"

"Can you get a message to my husband?" she said. "I'm in some dreadful trouble."

"Yes, I know," he responded. Then there was a pause.

"Dr. Moore?" Ruth asked. "I've got a bullet in my hand. I'm in Pasadena, not far from your clinic. I need treatment. I don't know what else to do."

"You need to surrender, Ruth," he said very quietly. "You know I want to help you, but I cannot. The best thing for you right now is to go to the nearest police station and end all this."

"No, no, I can't," she said, close to tears. "Please help me. Please let me come to you and treat my hand. It's badly infected and painful. I

won't go to the police. That won't end anything. It will only start something bigger. I won't tell anyone that you helped me."

"I wish I could, I really do," her friend said softly. "But it would
put both of us at terrible risk. Please turn yourself in, if only for your
husband's sake. He must be crazy with worry."

"I have tried to protect him," Ruth said. "But I have only hurt him.
I have to fix this, but I need you to—"

"I'm so sorry, Ruth, but I can't," Dr. Moore finally said. "My very
best advice to you is to surrender. Everyone is looking for you. I read
in the paper today that they have charged Dr. Judd with practicing
medicine in California without a license. They are not going to give up.
They will find you, Ruth, they will."

"Horrible people," she exclaimed. "He's not practicing, he's only an
orderly! What truly awful people. It's not true, Dr. Moore. I did not kill
those girls. I fought and fought and fought. They were going to kill me."

Ruth wiped away the well of tears that had begun streaming down
her sunken cheeks.

"I wish you my best, Ruth," he said.

"Thank you, Dr. Moore, I'm so sorry to have bothered you," she
said finally, and hung up.

Before she got on the streetcar, Ruth passed an empty lot behind a store
and saw smoke coming from a short chimney with a cast iron door on
the outside wall. She had planned on dumping her dress in the trash,
but this was better; she cranked the handle, opened the heavy door and
threw in the dress wrapped in paper and smelled it burning.

She walked to a streetcar stop, and when the next one chimed and
came along, she got on it, headed back to Los Angeles.

CHAPTER TEN

October 23, 1931

Ruth was shocked when she saw the woman in the mirror behind the drugstore soda fountain.

Gaunt, pale, her blond strands beginning to peek out again, wearing a fancy coat that did not belong to her.

Was that really her?

She resisted the panic of being recognized and took a seat at the end of the counter, put her folded coat on her lap, and then realized that if she didn't recognize herself, who else would? With her stolen dollar, she ordered a tuna sandwich and coffee and noticed that the man two stools away was reading a newspaper with her face on it. She dipped her head down and looked away, and then reached for the paper when he got up and left it behind.

She did not want to read the story, but she studied her own face in a myriad of black-and-white grainy dots. *That girl*, she thought, looking at herself, a portrait she'd had taken at least a year ago. *What trouble you have gotten me in. What you have brought me to?* Where would they even have gotten this picture? Had Doctor given it to them? And then she saw his face, under the fold, where it was announced that he had been charged with practicing without a license, as Dr. Moore had told her. What things they said! That he was ill, a drug user, that he had been committed to an asylum in Oregon. Oh, the accusations! How could they say such things? Doctor certainly hadn't given the newspapers his own picture.

She wanted to put the paper down, but her eyes were fixed on headlines: she was charged with murder; the *Los Angeles Examiner* had offered $1,000 for her capture, the *Los Angeles Times*, $1,500; and they were calling her the Velvet Tigress.

Then she smiled. The headline read:

SANATORIUM HUNT PROVES FRUITLESS

Wanted Phoenix Woman Sought in Altadena

Oct. 23—The precincts of La Vina Sanitarium in northwest Altadena were invaded yesterday afternoon by a horde of newspapermen, most of them from Los Angeles, who had been "tipped off" to a rumor that Mrs. Ruth Judd, accused in the Phoenix murders, was in hiding at the institution.

Although a "bunch of police officers from Los Angeles" were supposed to be on their way to round up the wanted woman, no officials, either in uniform or in plainclothes, turned up and two by two, the disappointed amateur sleuths, news photographers and what-not returned to their city editors to report "another bum steer."

It appeared, on inquiries, that Mrs. Judd had stayed at the sanitarium in 1929. Miss L. A. Dunlap, now head nurse, remembered Mrs. Judd during her stay as "a very sweet-natured person, but high strung and nervous," but only met her occasionally.

Ruth stopped smiling when she saw the story directly below it, which included Dr. Judd's statement. Her disbelief amplified with each subsequent word: "I ask her to call Mutual 7235 or Cleveland 61720. I have retained Judge Louis P. Russill and Richard H. Cantillon to care for Ruth's interests."

He wanted her to surrender; he was asking her to turn herself in.

She folded the newspaper and secured it in her lap, underneath the bandaged hand and the wide fur collar of the stolen coat. Her mind flipped like a deck of cards being shuffled.

How could he ask her to do that? Why? Didn't he understand? It meant *the end of everything*. The end of their lives, the end of the future, the end of everything that could be: another little house in Mexico, John Robert playing with chickens and bunnies and learning to ride a horse and learning to speak Spanish. *El pollo. El conejito. El caballo. ¿Quieres aprender a montar a caballo? Yo te puedo enseñar.* They would never have to speak English again; they would forget everything that had happened up until they were safe and together. Didn't Doctor realize that? They could be happy. They could all be a family. They had never been a family. It was his job to *make* them a family.

"More coffee?" the counter girl asked.

She was high-strung. Nervous. Wasn't that what they said? A nurse she didn't even remember. Irresponsible. Irrational. *Oh, Doctor, if you only knew. If you only knew. You left me there, alone. What did you think would happen to a woman by herself, alone, alone, alone in the sweltering Phoenix summer with no money, no family, no baby, and a husband who was too weak to take care of his wife? You sent me a gun. What did you think would happen? Did you not think other men would step in and take care of me and feed me and pay my rent and never ask for anything in return? What did you think would happen? I fought so hard and you think I did a terrible thing.*

Ruth shook her head. "No, thank you."

She heard the rustle of a newspaper behind her and a gasp.

"Can you believe it?" a woman behind her said.

Ruth didn't turn to look or find out what provoked the statement. She left fifteen cents on the counter, took the coat that belonged to another woman, and walked out of the drugstore with the newspaper under her arm.

Within a block, she found a phone booth and opened the door. She picked up the receiver, and when the operator asked for the number, she replied, "Mutual 7235, please."

⋖═◆═⋗

Burton ran his fingers through his thick, chestnut-colored hair. "This mischief is playing with my college work," he said to county attorney Lloyd Andrews, who had called an inquest with the coroner for that afternoon. Both Dr. Judd and Burton had been called as witnesses to determine whether or not the deaths of the girls had been by accident or homicide, and now it was Burton's turn to testify. "I'm afraid Ruth is dead, but if she isn't, I hope she keeps going. She's kept out of the way so far and she's clever."

Andrews did not believe that Burton was telling the truth, and thought he knew far more than what he was saying. Still, Ruth's brother had stuck to his story, never wavered.

"I had nothing to do with the murder," he insisted once again. "I was here, in my classes, at my job, at my house. I can prove I was here, and you've already spoken to those who can verify that. I drove my sister to the train station. Then I dropped her off downtown at her insistence. There is nothing more I can say. There is nothing more that I did."

When Burton got off the stand and sat back down, the lawyer Dr. Judd had retained, Judge Russill, who had been late coming in, passed him a note.

"Keep a straight face and don't tip off the reporters," the note read. "Ruth has called me. I've arranged for her to call again after we get away from here. Whatever you do, keep still until this hearing is over."

Burton retained an expressionless face, folded the note back up, and put it in his jacket pocket. He didn't know what to think. Where had she been hiding? What kind of state was she in? If he was supposed to be overjoyed that Ruth had called in, he was not. He wanted her to remain free, keep running. What would they do to his sister once they got ahold of her?

He couldn't help but feel that with one phone call his sister had signed her own death decree. He took a deep breath and followed Russill and his brother-in-law out of the courtroom when they were excused. As soon as they were out of the courtroom, Doctor's eyes lit up with hope.

For the first time since he had known Doctor, a man he respected and admired despite his deep, unfixable faults, Burton thought he was a fool.

At 1:00 p.m., Ruth called back, and Russill transferred the phone call to another office, afraid his phone was tapped. Ruth immediately said she would talk only to her husband, and when he got on the phone, she spoke to him in Spanish.

"I am close by, Doctor," she told him. "I am downtown. I am in a terrible state. I have been shot and I'm afraid the wound is festering. Is it true that they have charged you for practicing medicine without a license? How could that be?"

"Ruth, do not worry about that at all—it's a technicality," her husband said. "But you need to be treated medically. How bad is it?"

"I haven't looked at it in a day or two but I know it's serious. I'm afraid of gangrene," she replied.

Doctor sighed. He hated to think of his wife in any further distress, and this was so far beyond anything he had ever imagined.

"Ruth, you need to come in," he said as gently as he could.

"I'd rather die out here than cause you any trouble," she replied after a moment. "I'm so sorry for all of it. But you must know, Doctor, that I fought for my life. I fought so hard. I'm so tired."

"Do you want this to be over, Ruth?"

She paused for several seconds, and then answered weakly, "Yes. I very much do."

"Russill says to meet in the lobby of the Biltmore Theatre. Do you remember where that is? We saw *The Passion of Joan of Arc* there."

"The theater in the Biltmore Hotel?"

"Yes. On West Fifth Street."

"I remember. I can find it. I'm not far. Will you be there, Doctor?"

"I will."

"Do you promise? Do you swear it to me?"

"Of course I do, Ruth, of course. I will be waiting."

"I saw the newspaper, Doctor. I wasn't irresponsible. I wasn't irrational. I was fighting."

"I know. I understand. I had to say those things, Ruth, to protect you. You know that."

Doctor heard a long silence. "Ruth?"

"Yes, I know. I know that."

"Ruth: The Biltmore Theatre. Lobby. Three thirty. Say it back to me."

"Biltmore Theatre. Lobby. Three thirty. *Joan of Arc.*"

"Exactly. Be careful, Ruth. Stay someplace safe until then; don't let people see you."

"No, I won't. I will be very careful, Doctor."

"Very well. Till then, Ruth. I love you."

"Doctor," Ruth squeaked out. "It will all be fine, won't it? They will understand that I fought. That I did not do that terrible thing. It will all be fine, yes?"

Judd didn't know what to say. He didn't want to scare her back into running, but she was in a critically dangerous place with her wound.

She knew a bad state when she saw it. If she said the wound was bad, she meant it. He had to have her come in. For her safety. For her life.

"Of course it will," he lied. "I will be right by you the whole time."

—◆—

At 3:30 p.m. promptly, Judd and Russill opened the doors to the Biltmore Theatre and stepped inside. To elude the school of reporters stationed outside the lawyer's office door, Burton had been sent out as bait to wander around downtown. Judd and Russill and one of Russill's assistants took the service elevator down to the basement garage, put the keys into the ignition of a borrowed car, and headed for the Biltmore.

Ruth was nowhere in sight when they entered the lobby, and Judd felt a terrible sinking feeling. The lobby was not crowded, and if she was there, he would see her. If she didn't get help now, she was at risk of blood poisoning, which could lead to only one thing. He didn't want her to die alone, hiding like an injured animal. Even a Ruth behind bars was better than no Ruth at all. He needed her to tell him she didn't do it. She couldn't have done it. But a life full of speculating the worst would have been intolerable. He couldn't bear it.

But then he saw a figure of a woman coming out of the shadows. He strained his eyes to focus. It wasn't her. This woman was even smaller than Ruth, swallowed by an oversized coat with an enormous fur collar. Ruth didn't have a coat like that. Then he realized that he had no idea of what Halloran was giving his wife when he wasn't around. The small woman slipped into a slice of the afternoon sun—she was gaunt with darker hair than Ruth's, wearing a green dress that he also didn't recall. He stopped, looked beyond her, and saw no one else. The woman began running at him with what looked like a dirty oven mitt on one hand. She threw her arms around his neck and kissed him repeatedly, furiously on the cheek, on the lips, on the face.

"Doctor, Doctor, Doctor! Oh, Doctor. I never thought I'd see you again!" she cried, then whimpered and leaned into him as he put his arms around her.

"It's all right, love," he whispered to her, amazed that this tiny bird woman in his arms was his wife. "You're going to be all right."

She went limp in his arms with relief and exhaustion. It was over. He would take her home now, they would send for John Robert, and everything would be fine.

"Let's go," Russill insisted. "We can't risk anyone recognizing either of you in here."

With his arm firmly around her shoulders and his other arm supporting hers, Russill led the group out of the theater and across the street to a garage.

"Where are we going?" Ruth asked, and Doctor replied they were going to have someone treat her hand. She nodded and said nothing else.

Judd helped Ruth into the backseat, where she collapsed onto the floor and began sobbing. He pulled her up and embraced her wholly, as she buried her head under his chin.

"Sammy shot me," she gulped in between breaths. "Sammy shot me. It's an awful mess!"

The car pulled out of the garage and headed up the hill toward First Street, the same way Ruth had headed out of town only several days before. It was also the same route to the police station. Judd held his breath. *They wouldn't do that to her, would they? They wouldn't do that!* He had only known Russill for a matter of days and had no choice but to trust him. Judd felt his heart strike against his ribs in rapid, fierce beats and he felt flushed.

Ruth was still weeping when they passed the police station and kept going several blocks and then turned, pulling into the driveway of a large, looming house, and went around the back. He eased up a bit, but was still uncertain about where they were. Russill got out and hurried Judd and Ruth out of the car, pointing to a large door at the back of the house.

Ruth pulled back. "This is an awful place," she said, "It feels like death here."

Judd assured her everything was fine as they climbed the steps of the back landing. When they entered the back door, a woman ushered them into what looked like a medical room with tables, bright lights and sinks. Judd understood all too well.

"You've taken us to a mortuary?" he asked Russill, and Ruth screamed and began to back away in a panic.

Russill was unfazed that he was standing five feet from a corpse draped under a sheet. "No one is going to look for Ruth in a funeral home," he explained. "We can address Ruth's hand here and then discuss what we're going to do."

"Can you get me a bowl of warm water?" Judd asked the woman, and she nodded as she left the room.

Judd pulled a chair up to an empty table and coaxed Ruth into sitting down.

"Let's take a look," he said, gently lifting her hand up to the table-top and beginning to unwrap the dressing.

"I don't want to look," she said, shaking her head. "It's going to be terrible."

"It's all right, we'll get it all fixed up now," her husband reassured her in a quiet, steady voice. "Now, why don't you tell me where you've been?"

"I'm so tired, Doctor," she said as her eyelids fluttered closed.

He nodded and pulled back the last layer of the bandage to find a handkerchief attached to the wound like a top layer of skin.

The other woman brought in a bowl of water, and he placed Ruth's hand in it. She jerked it back out, with water splashing on her and the woman. Ruth winced, and then slowly slid it back into the bowl.

"Now, Ruth, tell me where you've been," he said again.

She dropped her head so he could not see her worried face.

"I was behind the curtains," she mumbled. "I was so hungry and frightened. I would like some water."

Judd patted her on the arm and nodded to the woman. "Where were you behind the curtains, Ruth?"

"In the store," she answered. "Then I drank milk from the kitchen."

After a few minutes, Judd was able to peel the handkerchief off. Between the first and second knuckle joints he saw where the bullet had entered and was still lodged. It was badly swollen and alarmingly inflamed.

"Who shot you, dear?" he asked, noticing deep bruises under her jaw and on her neck.

"Sammy," Ruth said, drawing her face up to look at her husband, and it took all of her strength to do that. She was exhausted. "Sammy shot me."

"Who shot Sammy and Anne?" Russill asked.

"I fought so hard. They both hurt me," she replied. "Anne hit me with the ironing board, Sammy chased me, and she shot me. I had no choice. I fought so hard and they hurt me so."

The woman brought in a glass of water and a glass of eggnog, both for Ruth.

"She needs to go to the hospital," Judd said to Russill. "I can't remove the bullet without sterilized instruments, it would be too dangerous. But she must get care now."

"I agree," Russill said. "But we'll need to notify the police."

Ruth exploded.

"No!" she shrieked, standing up as the bowl and water tumbled to the floor. "You said no police! No! I will run away and hide!"

"Ruth! Ruth!" Judd cried, trying to grab her by her good wrist. "*Ruth.* Did you defend yourself? Did they attack you and you were defending yourself?"

Ruth began to sob loudly, nodded, and then finally screamed as loudly as she could, pulling her arm out of her husband's grasp.

"Yes! They were both on me, hitting me with the ironing board over the head. Anne was hitting me! I fought them both!"

"If it's self-defense Ruth, we will tell the police that," Russill said in a stark voice.

"We'll get this mess sorted out," Judd added. "Just calm down, Ruth. We cannot hide you, and I can't let you go. Your hand is very bad off."

Ruth backed away from them—her arms crossed, tears falling, her nose running and her breath gulping—until she hit a table behind her. Her cries became louder, echoing off walls and ceilings, bouncing back at her again and again, and she allowed it, she could finally let them out. She screamed for the horror of it, the terror of it, the badness of it. She no longer had to swallow it. She screamed for Anne and Sammy, for what she was forced to do, for what she knew she had done. She cried for everything that could never be again.

And screamed for everything that would take its place.

CHAPTER ELEVEN

October 23, 1931

The police arrived at the hospital just as a nurse was preparing to examine the woman the press had dubbed the Velvet Tigress.

She was so small, very pale and weak, almost feeble. Polite, cooperative, she said nothing until the nurse unzipped the green dress and pulled it over her head.

"It's not mine," the accused said, barely audible. "It should be returned to the woman I borrowed it from."

The nurse was startled. The woman was covered in deep, settled bruises, some the color of wine, others nearly black with a halo of yellow outlining them. It was clear that they were not freshly inflicted; whatever caused them had happened at least several days to a week ago. She had seen similar bruising on men from raucous bar fights, or a victim of a car accident who'd hit something very hard and very fast.

The nurse pulled the sheet around the front of the woman and tucked the end under her arm.

"I'll be right back," she told Ruth, and stepped out of the examining room to hail one of the detectives who were waiting in the hall.

"You're the cop?" she asked the only man in the hall who was not carrying a camera or a notepad. Ryan nodded, reached into his side pocket, and pulled out a badge. "You should see this."

He followed the nurse into the room, where Ruth Judd sat on an examining table, her back hunched and her head drooping, a thick strand of hair falling forward in front of her face.

The detective noticed that her arm was violet, almost none of it the color of her light complexion. Someone had battered this woman, and violently. There was a contusion the size of his palm on the base of her neck, rippling down the vertebrae of her spine and so dark it looked like a shadow. This little thing was what they had been chasing for almost a week, he couldn't help but think. She could hide in a closet, or a dumbwaiter; she was so slight she could have hidden between the pages of a book. This woman, barely bigger than a child, had shot two people and then cut one of them up with such precision that the coroner was able to reassemble the body with needle and thread? He found himself shaking his head in disbelief.

Ruth Judd sat there silently, her eyes fixed on the floor.

"There's more," the nurse told him. "The lower arm on the left is bruised terribly, and her right hip and thigh are very discolored. The inner right knee shows more bruising, and there's discoloration on the upper right leg that wraps around from the front to the side. It's substantial in size."

"What's all this?" Ryan asked, pointing to faded black marks that spotted her skin.

"That looks like dye," the nurse said. "Those aren't bruises."

"I'm going to get a photographer in here," he said, and left the room.

The nurse looked at Ruth, who barely clutched the sheet around her. She was tiny, lithe.

"As soon as we clean you up a little bit, they'll get that bullet out of your hand," the nurse said. "It looks like it hurts."

Ruth nodded.

"Do those bruises hurt?" the nurse asked softly.

Ruth shrugged slightly. The nurse noted that the patient either didn't understand what was happening, or that her mind was somewhere altogether different.

"Don't be afraid," she said to Ruth, trying to console her. "It won't be a difficult operation."

"Please don't say that word," Ruth said, finally looking up and then turning her face away.

When Ruth woke, a clean, pure-white bandage swaddled her hand. It looked like a large cloud. Not dirty, not smudged, but clean. It still throbbed in time with her pulse, but as she surfaced from sedation, the sensation was not as bad as it had once been. Now it was just pain without the feeling of putting it into a fire. And keeping it there.

Doctor was sitting by her bedside; she was in a private room with no other patients. It was quiet and calm, and Ruth felt like she had been buried in a very great sleep. Other men leaning against the wall of the room came into focus, straightening up when they saw she had come to. Did she know them? Ruth hazily asked herself. Jack? Was he here? A woman sat in a chair with a pad of paper and a pencil, a stenographer.

Ruth came to a bit more and recognized the man who had looked at her bruises. He was standing next to her bed with his hands in his pockets. Police. He was here to arrest her.

"Mrs. Judd," he said. "Can you answer some questions for us?"

"Can you let her be for a moment?" Dr. Judd interjected. "She's only just woken."

Ryan ignored him. "Mrs. Judd, can you tell us about the night of October sixteenth? Can you tell us what happened to your friends that night?"

"I really must insist—" Dr. Judd said, and began to stand up, but Russill, who was behind him, placed a calm hand on his shoulder, urging him to sit back down.

"You don't have to say anything, Ruth," Russill advised her.

"Water?" Ruth asked in a dry voice.

Her husband took a glass of water from the table next to him and handed it to her. She took it and drank it all in several swallows.

"This is Chief Taylor, Mrs. Judd," Ryan said, motioning to the stern-looking older man behind him. "He would also like to know how your friends ended up in pieces in your trunks."

"I've had to borrow a dress from a patient at La Vina," Ruth said simply. "And her coat. I hope you will see to it that it is returned to her."

"So you were at La Vina," Taylor said. "Who was helping you?"

"I was at La Vina," she confirmed. "Nobody helped me. No one knew I was there."

"How did you get there?" Ryan asked. "Who took you?"

"No one took me," she replied. "I walked there. I took a trolley back."

"What happened to your friends, Mrs. Judd? Anne and Sammy? What happened that last night?" Taylor continued.

"You don't have to say anything, Mrs. Judd," Russill interjected.

"Listen to him, Ruth," Judd urged.

"Get those two out of here," Taylor ordered Ryan.

"You have the right not to say a word, Mrs. Judd," Russill said, as Ryan pushed both men out the door and shut it.

In the hall, reporters had gathered to eavesdrop and gather any information they could to make their 5:00 p.m. deadline.

"Give me a piece of paper?" Judd asked one of them, and borrowed the reporter's pencil.

"I hereby demand that my lawyers be admitted," he wrote, then folded the note and slid it under the door.

Both Taylor and Ryan ignored it.

"Mrs. Judd," Chief Taylor said in a well-spoken, calm voice. "Would you please tell us what led to you hiding at La Vina while your girlfriends were at the morgue? What happened that night to make everything go so wrong?"

"No, I wasn't at La Vina initially," Ruth corrected them. "I was at the Broadway Department Store for the first night. I hid behind the curtain display in the daytime. Then I walked to La Vina. I walked right past the police station."

Taylor and Ryan looked at each other. That explained the letter that was discovered in the toilet at the store.

"From what we understand, you had a good relationship with Mrs. LeRoi and Miss Samuelson, is that true?" Taylor led.

"Yes, that is true," Ruth said. "They were my dearest friends in the world. I cared for them very much. Without them, I would have been very alone in Phoenix."

"Then something went wrong," Ryan continued. "I saw those bruises on you. It looked like it was a hard fight."

Ruth turned her head away and looked into the distance, saying nothing.

"Your husband told us that you cared for Miss Samuelson when she was very ill," the chief said. "So what could have happened to make such a good friendship end up like this?"

Ruth pursed her lips tight. How did things end up like this? They just did, and now her friends were gone, forever. She would never laugh with them, listen to detective shows on the radio in the living room, cook dinner together, or play bridge again. Those times were now lost.

And they would never again wake up in the morning and not talk about what happened the night before. Secrets they kept and didn't mention. Quiet secrets.

"I know you put up a fight," Ryan added.

Ruth continued to look straight ahead.

"When I was visiting on Friday night, I made an uncomplimentary mark about Mrs. LeRoi that I wish I hadn't," she said, barely audible. "I killed them after Miss Samuelson shot me in the hand during the quarrel. I scuffled with Miss Samuelson and the gun dropped to the floor. Mrs. LeRoi hit me on the head with the ironing board. I fell to the floor. I picked up Miss Samuelson's gun. Then I shot them both."

"Did you get all of that?" Taylor said to the stenographer before turning back to Ruth.

"You shot them both, correct?" he said to Ruth.

"Yes, after Sammy shot me first," she answered. "I fought so hard. You have to understand how hard I fought. She shot me. And then I killed them."

CHAPTER TWELVE

October 24, 1931

Dr. Judd slept for the first time in a week. He had listened at the hospital room's door and heard Ruth tell the detectives that she'd acted in self-defense. He was convinced that the truth would come out and she would be released. He would move her to Los Angeles, or Indiana, or back to Mexico, but he would never go back to Phoenix again. It was a hot hellhole, dirty in every way. Somehow, he would get them a house, and they could start over, leave this mess behind and maybe even change their names to be completely clean. Of course, both of their pictures had been in the paper for an entire week, but after Ruth told her story, people would understand she was innocent of the murder charge, or they would forget. Not Indiana; it was too dangerous for Ruth's health. It was Mexico, he decided. Mexico was the best place for them.

He was sitting at the kitchen table, drinking black coffee. He planned to visit Ruth before they released her from the hospital later today. Then she'd be moved to the county jail. As much as that panicked him, he knew it couldn't be for very long; he had seen the bruises on his wife's body as she lay there in bed after the surgery. It was obvious to him what had happened, and it was exactly as she said. She was defending herself. Yes, he had seen her erupt in frantic episodes that took hours or even days to subside, but she had never been violent. By nature, Ruth was quiet, pleasant, accommodating. In Mexico, she was well known for giving the children of the miners candy and would hug them and play with them when they knocked on the door. She had always wanted a child so badly; how could a woman who yearned to be a mother so much that it tore her apart be the wicked thing the press insisted she was?

It didn't make sense, and the police had to see that. And although Judd didn't know how the pieces fit, he was sure Halloran had something to do with this, if he wasn't behind it altogether. The police, Judd was positive, would unlock that part as well.

He reached for the newspaper, expecting, as he did every day that week, to see Ruth on the cover, along with a salacious headline. He was not disappointed.

VELVET TIGRESS CAUGHT!

City Safe as Slayer Confesses to Murder EXCLUSIVE

Slayer Tells Story of Quarrel and Shooting from Bed in Hospital

Los Angeles Evening Express, Oct. 24 —

"Yes, I shot them—but I was justified!"

Lying in an upstairs room at a local hospital, Mrs. Winnie Ruth Judd told her story of the murders of Anne LeRoi and Hedvig Samuelson to her husband, Dr. William C. Judd, and her attorney, Louis Russill.

It was a story of self-defense.

"Sammy and Anne and I were in the girls' apartment at 2929 Second Street, Phoenix," she began.

"There was a quarrel. I had been talking to Sammy about Anne.

"She must have thought I was angry with Anne—that I was going to say something bad about her friend.

"Sammy grabbed the gun. Things began happening. I don't remember quite clearly. But I can still see Sammy holding that gun.

"Where she got it, I don't know, I think she ran out of the room and came running back in with it. I was so frightened I couldn't see things clearly.

"I tried to scream, but I couldn't. Then the gun went off.

"I felt a blow on [my] left hand. The blood spurted out. I knew I had to get that gun so I ran toward her. We wrestled around. You see, she wasn't very strong, so even with one hand I was able to make her drop the gun. It fell on the floor between us.

"I knew I had to get that gun or be killed. I pushed Sammy back and tried to get it.

"Something hit me over the head. I put up my left arm to ward off the blow, just as my right hand closed over the gun.

"Looking up I saw Anne holding an ironing board with which she was beating me.

"What happened then I could not control. I jumped up to keep out of Anne's reach. She kept coming after me with that ironing board.

"I pointed the gun at her. It went off. Sammy screamed. Then I shot her, too.

"I had to. It was my life or theirs."

And there Mrs. Judd's story of the tragedy ended. She would not touch on the cutting up of Samuelson's body or the shipping of the two bodies in trunks to Los Angeles, though she intimated that she had not been alone in this.

Mrs. Judd then told about coming to Los Angeles.

"You know what happened at the station. You know that Burton gave me $5—that he left me downtown.

"Well I just walked and walked. My hand was throbbing. I bandaged it with my handkerchief.

"I didn't have anything to eat. It was like a nightmare.

"I knew I would be caught if I didn't change my clothes. I had no money to buy more so I went to a drug store and bought dye. In a rest room I dyed my dress.

"Then I saw that you (referring to her husband) wanted me to come to you. You know the rest. I'm here. That ends it."

Judd was furious. "Exclusive"? This was almost word for word what Ruth had told him and Russill. Who gave them this to print? What right did they have to print her statement?

He called Russill's office immediately and was patched through to the lawyer within moments.

"Mr. Russill, did you see the *Examiner* this morning? They've printed Ruth's statement, almost word for word," he said angrily. "What recourse do we have? What right do they have to print it?"

"Every right," Russill said blankly. "I sold the story to the Examiner for three thousand dollars."

"*You* sold the story?" Judd said incredulously. "What gave *you* the right to sell it? I did not give you permission!"

"I didn't need it," the lawyer replied. "I was hired by you to protect Ruth's interests. That's what I am doing. By getting the self-defense story out there, the public plays in our favor. We have to start establishing this now before the police get a chance to get their story out there, whatever it might be."

"Still, Mr. Russill, you didn't even consult with me," Judd argued. "You said nothing."

"Mr. Judd, your wife will be going on trial very soon for murder. There are many costs involved with that," Russill explained. "First, they're going to try to extradite her back to Arizona. And they will win that fight. Then we need to prepare for trial, get our witnesses, our experts, and engage in what may be a very long ordeal. I did you a favor by selling the story, and I'm sorry you don't understand. Trials are a terrible business. But I've applied that sum to the work I've done and the work I will continue to do."

"This is unbelievable! You are treating my wife like a prized cow!" Judd exclaimed.

"You should know I plan to sell a jail-cell interview to the *Los Angeles Times* for five thousand dollars," Russill added. "And forgive me, Mr. Judd, but I've never known a prized cow to shoot her friends and carry their body parts across state lines. I know this is awful for you, but this is what needs to be done."

"Mr. Russill," Judd said firmly before slamming down the phone, "I am no longer in need of your services. Goodbye."

The bodies of Anne LeRoi and Sammy Samuelson arrived in Union Station in Phoenix shortly after 7:00 p.m. on the Golden State Limited, each in a casket made of California redwood.

About one hundred people gathered there to watch the spectacle of the bodies being unloaded, along with two company trucks from A. L. Moore and Sons, a well-established funeral home in the town. The crowd was chattering loudly as a single coffin was placed in the bed of each truck. They were not there to pay their respects but to own a story that they would tell for decades to come. Porters then brought out the two trunks, hatbox, and suitcase on the platform just where they had been placed the previous Sunday when Ruth was about to board the train to Los Angeles with the remains of her friends.

The crowd fell silent all at once, as if the reality of the crime had bared itself. Only the clicks of newspaper cameras could be heard, almost sounding like crickets on a cool summer night at dusk. The gatherers stayed that way for a long time, searching with their eyes for traces of blood, or a bloody rag sticking out of one of the trunk's lids. The trunks were also loaded onto the truck beds to be taken along to the mortuary with the victims, a stark contrast of how they left Phoenix and how they had returned.

Slowly, after the trucks drove away and it was apparent that the show was over, the witnesses to the spectacle trickled back home to their families, where they possibly ate dinner, listened to a radio show, and then slunk into their very own beds for a good night's sleep, eager to tell whoever they met next what they had just seen.

SLAYER LIKENED TO "TIGER GIRL"

Hint of Steel Behind Cold Eyes of Mrs. Judd Told

Los Angeles Examiner, Oct. 24—

Her eyes are drawn in the corners like those of Clara Phillips, tiger woman of another day. Her lips have a little turn in them that criminologists might term "cruel."

Her steady eyes a blue-grey. Her hair is neither blonde or brunette, but brown. Her hands and feet are small, shapely. Her stockingless legs are finely etched. She is of medium build.

Attractive, rather alluring, potentially dangerous.

Such is Winnie Ruth Judd, physically speaking.

She has poise, grace. She seems refined, well-educated. One would never picture her as a woman who placed the bodies of Agnes Anne LeRoi and Hedvig Samuelson in two trunks.

Still, there are those drawn eyes, the warning lips.

At the slightest noise she displays that she is a bundle of nerves.

That her mind is not calm was revealed when she was under gas at the hospital.

She cried and shivered. She talked. Ghosts of dead women came before her and she shouted that she was "justified." The gas wore off. The mutterings continued. The screams and prayers halted.

She regained her poise. She wept a little. She looked adoringly at her husband, Dr. William C. Judd. She called him "Doctor," "Sweet," and "Dear." She appeared to be a normal young woman. Still there were the warning lips, the drawn eyes of the tigress, the hint of steel beneath the velvet of her smooth flesh.

Dr. Judd shuffled through the top drawer of the buffet in the dining room of Carrie's house, and found what he was looking for in an old, long wooden box. He opened it, the hinges stiff with age, and saw the tarnished, deep gray sticks of silver that had once belonged to his mother. Family silver. He did not want to sell his wife in order to pay for her defense if this all went to trial. He had been convinced that once Ruth told her story, everything would snap back to the way it was before last Sunday. He saw now that he was naive. Ruth was already in jail; she might go to prison. She might be hanged. His choices were dwindling, and with sadness but no guilt, he lifted the box out of the buffet and headed to the storefront of a gold smelter he had once passed. He had fought battles before, ended up wounded and scarred and broken.

But he had never fought anything, *anything* like this.

Carrie, he knew, would understand.

CHAPTER THIRTEEN

October 24, 1931

When Dr. Judd arrived at the hospital, police officers stopped him at the door to her room. No visitors, he was told.

"No, I'm her husband," he protested.

"Sorry, sir," an officer said. "She's about to be taken to the county jail."

"She has no clothes," Judd said, stretching out his hand with a bag from the Broadway Department Store in it. "I've bought her some things."

It wasn't a fancy dress, but rather a plain one, a brown wool belted day dress with a pointed collar and long, slim sleeves. He was afraid that the jail might be cold, so he'd picked a black sweater with vertical darts along the shoulder, hitting at mid-thigh, with deep pockets in case her uninjured hand was cold. It wasn't the height of fashion, but for now it would do. With the help of a saleslady, he'd gotten Ruth some underthings, too.

The officer looked at the bag as if he didn't know what to do with it.

"Mrs. Judd has nothing to wear," he emphasized a little stronger this time. "Please see that she gets this. There's nothing controversial in that bag; you are welcome to search it."

The officer nodded and knocked on the door, mumbling something and passing the bag to another man inside. Judd caught a glimpse of Ruth sitting on the bed, looking despondent.

Be patient, he told himself. *You will see her shortly.*

Oh, Ruth, he mourned.

Oh, my darling girl. What have you done?

Contrary to popular belief, the most populous plant life in the desert of Phoenix is not a cactus. Not a prickly pear, ocotillo, or saguaro. It is the creosote bush, a large scraggly thing with short waxy leaves that reflects sunlight and blooms ordinary yellow flowers that are not unsimilar to Saint-John's-wort or any other invasive weed. Its appendages conserve water under drastic circumstances, allowing it to compete aggressively with other plants for resources, and it almost always wins. It thrives in the most meager conditions because it doesn't require much to survive. Whatever genome it was the creosote descended from, it was stock that was brutal, forceful, and undiscerning. It is basic. It will steal from its neighbors, break them down, and forge on to bloom unremarkably.

But when the desert sees rain, the gift of the creosote is released in a slight, fresh perfume that is unlike any other scent on the planet. It is enveloping, seductive, addicting. Its allure remains strong for almost an hour, perhaps two, after a rain, then retracts its magnificence when the desert becomes complete again and not a drop of water is to be had.

The phone at the Phoenix police station rang that morning, trying to alert the authorities that a mattress had been discovered roughly five miles northwest of the murder house. It was just off the dirt road that would become Nineteenth Avenue in the next few years as Phoenix grew.

"Another mattress?" the receiving officer asked. "We've found five already."

This one, the caller informed him, had a large stain at one end and a bundle of sheets with it, which also looked stained. Tire tracks showed that it was likely dragged from a car and then thrown into a creosote bush.

The officer hung up and immediately made another call.

"Where's Sheriff McFadden?" he asked.

Gone, he was told. On his way to Los Angeles to pick up the murderess.

"Train station?" the officer inquired.

"No," the other voice said. "Plane. He *flew. Can you believe that?*"

Halloran finally decided to make a statement. They had caught her, and he needed to make his position clear. He wasn't sure what she would say. Sometimes she was sane and other times she wasn't. Babble, babble, babble, he hoped the police would hear. Nonsense. He had made the right decision avoiding the train station and not taking her calls that Sunday morning. He did what he could, then washed his hands of it—of her. He had hoped that once she got on that train, she would never come back.

Now Sammy and Anne were at the morgue and it was done with.

It was October, and his wife and daughter were back from spending the summer in Flagstaff, where the climate was more suitable for women and children than in broiling Phoenix. He was heading into the busy season of construction in Phoenix, a place where you could keep building year-round if you had strong enough men. Some of them couldn't cut it, out there in the July sun, which beat beat beat down on you and there was no breeze for relief, like being trapped in a tomb. But men were desperate for work—had been—and when there was building to be done, there was a line of them. Those that couldn't cut it fell away quickly. To hell with them. You wanna eat, you gotta build. There were always ten, twenty, thirty more men to take their place. You had to be strong in a place like this. If you weren't, you'd get pushed out, drained, sucked dry.

The police had taken him downtown yesterday, asked him a couple of questions, nothing serious, and then he was out, on his way back home, where he had been every single night for the past week. The police, he was confident, wouldn't bother him again.

But it was time to say something. To set the record straight. Now that she was coming back, it would be a madhouse. He didn't need it, he didn't want it.

"I have not seen, nor in any way heard from, Mrs. Ruth Judd since we left her at home the Thursday before the crime," he told the press. "I have told my story to the proper officials. I have told everything I know. I stand on my statements made heretofore to constituted authorities. The grievousness of my deeds consists of no greater a fault than having been indiscreet. That this indiscretion has become so related to so important a matter is the only reason it has become magnified. The three young women were always on the friendliest terms to the best of my knowledge and belief. At no time did I ever see anything of the contrary. So far as I know, too, they all three were honorable women."

Ruth was wearing the brown dress and sweater when Judd was finally allowed into the jail cell to visit. She leaned into him, covered her face, and began to cry.

There would be a hearing this afternoon, he had learned, about the extradition back to Phoenix. He had decided not to fight it. There was no sense in dragging this out any longer. They were taking her back to Phoenix, and that was that. He couldn't sell enough family silver to stop them.

"I forgot stockings," he said as he held her close and then kissed the top of her head. "I'm so sorry."

She said nothing, and the weeping continued.

He held her there, on the thin, coiled mattress of the jailhouse cot, for a long while. He could not think of another thing to say. He did not tell her about Russill; he was afraid that might push her too far. He let her cry. He did not try to soothe her like he always did. Everything would not be all right, not for some time.

He didn't know how long he sat on the cot with her, and when he heard footsteps and metal doors opening, he realized that Ruth was silent and asleep.

A tall man in a cowboy hat and a tan linen suit stood by the jail cell. An officer came forward and unlocked the gate, swinging it open. The man stepped inside and sat in the chair across from the cot.

Judd gently shook Ruth and her eyes flew open. She looked up and saw the man sitting across from her.

"Ruth?" he said in a warm, soft voice.

"Sheriff McFadden?" she said, startled and sitting up.

"Oh, Ruth," he said with sympathetic eyes. "I'm so sorry to see you here."

"I'm glad it's you," Ruth replied, her eyes still swollen from crying.

McFadden noticed the perplexed look on Dr. Judd's face.

"I know your wife," he explained. "She is the secretary to my wife's doctor. We see each other quite often. My wife is ill."

"Is she feeling better?" Ruth asked.

McFadden smiled slightly. "We'll get there," he answered. "These things take time, I suppose."

"Are you here to take me home?" Ruth asked.

"I am," McFadden answered. "There will be a hearing this afternoon. We can get on the road right after if you don't contest extradition."

Ruth shook her head. "I won't."

"You're in some trouble, Ruth, and my hope is that once we get back to Phoenix, we can sort all of this out," the sheriff told her. "Now, you'll help me do that, won't you?"

"Of course, Sheriff," Ruth obliged.

"I have a feeling you are not alone in this act," he added. "If there is someone else or more than one person I need to look into, you'll let me know, I trust?"

"Yes," she said plainly.

"Dr. Judd, I can arrange for you to follow us in another car to Phoenix, if you like," McFadden said.

"I'd much prefer to sit with Ruth," he replied.

"Not possible," the sheriff replied. "I have a deputy driving us and the jail matron will be coming along to look after Mrs. Judd, I'm afraid. But I'm more than willing to offer you a seat in another car."

"Of course," Judd said, nodding.

"Okay, then," McFadden said, standing up. "An officer will come get you in an hour for the hearing, and we can be on our way. Don't worry, this will all be over very soon."

"All right, I won't worry," Ruth agreed, and then fell back into her husband's arms as McFadden left.

Neither Dr. Judd nor Ruth saw the afternoon edition of the newspaper, which was best. Now that Ruth had surrendered, reporters had nothing to do but hang around outside of Russill's office, mingle on the steps of the courthouse, or park themselves outside of the county jail waiting for a glimpse of the Velvet Tigress. It was a slow day. But for a reporter, a deadline is a deadline for a story due every day, and for those who wanted to keep their editors happy, they dug. Far and wide, they dug.

They didn't expect what came tumbling out of their shovels, and they weren't sure what to do with it. All they knew was that the name Judd was involved, and that's what readers wanted. Some were blowing up over the fact that her father was a reverend or that her poverty-stricken parents were trying to raise the funds to get to her, or running photos of Burton's shack of a house in Beverly Glen. But one had received a tip about Dr. Judd and decided to take a pickax to see what he could find.

There was enough gold there for two or three days' worth of headlines. All it took was a couple of phone calls.

DR. JUDD FORMER NARCOTIC ADDICT

Husband of Murderess Treated in Hospital

Salem, Ore.—Dr. William C. Judd, whose wife is suspected in connection with the trunk murders of Mrs. Anne LeRoi and Miss Hedvig Samuelson in Phoenix, was an inmate of the Oregon State Hospital, authorities said today.

The records show that Dr. Judd was committed from Marion County as a drug addict.

Dr. Judd has served with the American expeditionary forces and his commitment followed his return here. Following his discharge from the hospital, he was said to have been employed as a physician for the Brookings Lumber Company of Brookings, Ore.

Dr. Judd graduated from the Willamette Medical University here in 1906.

At 2929 North Second Street, the police gave Frank Vance, the owner of the murder house, a choice: close down the tour or face charges of disturbing evidence. Vance tried to argue; he had a right to make a living! All it took, though, for him to comply was the jingle of handcuffs.

Those trampling the house were thrown out, and police forced the people waiting in line to see blood in any speck of dirt, grime, or chink in the doorjamb to leave immediately.

The girls' part of the duplex had been terribly disturbed, and the police knew it. Two thousand people had marched through the living room with its brick fireplace, sat on the comfortable mohair sofa and armchairs, traipsed down the skinny hallway to the bathroom and death bedroom, over to the breakfast room and the incredibly narrow kitchen with the wallpaper featuring little Tudor cottages in primary colors, then out to the garage, where the trunks had been dragged through the small yard and into the house.

Despite the public disturbance, the police began another search; they went again through the drawers and closets and looked under cushions and in every cabinet. This time, they found new items of interest: four men's neckties, a half bottle each of barbital and Luminal, a full brown bottle of cocaine, a bridge score sheet that had a note on a torn piece of paper used as a bookmark, on which was scrawled, "Someday someone is going to get you and then you won't be so fresh."

A team of plumbers was brought in to open the traps for the bathtub and basin and examine the cesspool that was located in the yard of the house, in hopes of locating Sammy's missing intestines, bladder, and liver.

The traps, save for some hair, were empty, and the cesspool was dry, producing only a little bit of dirt and a scrap of cloth.

The plumbers were relieved.

Sammy's diary, which had been pocketed by a reporter, was delivered to the police anonymously. It contained a mundane retelling of each day's events, what she did, who she saw, and a very, very long list of prominent Phoenix businessmen and their coordinating phone numbers. Jack Halloran's number was on that list.

After the hearing in Los Angeles, Sheriff McFadden escorted Ruth out of the Hall of Justice and down to a waiting car below. Carrie had packed and brought Dr. Judd's valise so he would be ready to go when the caravan began trekking across the desert. Before Judd and Burton could start down the steps, though, a reporter from the *Examiner* approached them.

"I have instructions from my boss to offer you five thousand dollars for your wife's story, and he will arrange for your legal defense—a topnotch lawyer," the reporter said. "It's a good deal, you should take it."

Judd shook his head and waved the reporter away.

"Don't you want to know who my boss is?" the reporter called after him.

"Who's your boss?" Burton said with a sneer.

"William Randolph Hearst," the reporter said with a smile. "The *Examiner*."

The same newspaper that had published the words, "Still there were the warning lips, the drawn eyes of the tigress, the hint of steel beneath the velvet of her smooth flesh."

Dr. Judd turned around, motioned to the reporter to come to him, and waited for him to catch up.

It was dark when Ruth was led to a large black sedan by McFadden, with the matron of the jail and a deputy sheriff already inside. The second car to make the drive to Phoenix contained Los Angeles County attorney Lloyd Andrews and another deputy sheriff. Dr. Judd rode in the third car, with the *Examiner's* reporters.

Before he left, McFadden had called the California governor, James Rolph, Jr., to advise him that the extradition was taking place. "When we get back to Arizona," McFadden said, rubbing his eyes, not believing the words he was about to say, "we'll hang her, in my opinion. We only have men juries in our state, but we don't stand for vamping. It won't be the first time we hanged a woman."

The *Examiner* published Ruth's note on a full page, in her own handwriting, the next morning. People in Los Angeles began reading it as she was crossing the last miles of desert before pulling to a stop in front of the county jail with an ocean of reporters already waiting for her.

Here it is, my own story in my own words. I don't know what is ahead of me. It may be a long trail, it may be prison and it may be death. A week ago, the name Ruth Judd meant nothing except to the people who knew me. Now I think everyone knows of me. All sorts of things are being said about me. All sorts of people are guessing, judging, condemning. I want to tell the truth that no one else can possibly know. And this is it. This is my story, not hearsay or second handed, just my life as I see it now. My life, my childhood, my mature years—my loves and dreams have been my own. Now that I am before the world, charged with terrible crimes and painted as a tigress and as a woman apart from the rest, my story must be told.

PART TWO

CHAPTER FOURTEEN

Ruth

Look anywhere into the distance to see the mirage. Desert heat is the pitiless dictator of the brightest months, the shimmering wings of a dragon.

The desert has always been a beautiful place, and really, it still is. I've tried to walk away from the desert, but I will never break free. It made me who I am.

In our tiny adobe house that night in March of 1929, I felt alone in the desert, with sounds of the Revolution bouncing between the mountains, shots echoing from one end of the valley to the other. The darkness was both fearsome and solacing.

My dog Bruno whined from the corner of the dark bedroom.

Doctor, my husband, had been sure that we could pay General Escobar's revolutionaries to guard the mine while the rest of his army captured territory from Mazatlán to Nogales, and all of the towns across the Arizona–Mexico border. But he was wrong: yesterday they had taken the mountain pass, stormed the mining camp, and cut the power. Once Doctor treated their wounded, they cut us off from the other camp several miles away.

The bed was shaking so crazy it woke me up. I didn't need the light to know that Doctor was trembling hard enough to bang the bed against the wall, again and again. He was sicker than I'd ever seen him, his moans barely audible. I reached over to him and put my hand on his arm, stiff and strained, clutching his very own body.

I couldn't see before me, I couldn't sense what lay just beyond my reach, inches from my fingertips, but I could sink back deeper into it, curl up into myself until I was almost nothing, and hide.

Years ago, at Christmastime, Doctor asked, "How would you like to marry me and live in a dirty mining town in Arizona?"

I laughed grandly and said the desert sounded wonderful. I was going to make it wonderful because I wanted wonderful. I was determined to get away from all of that mess in my hometown in Indiana.

Mamma and Papa were not delighted at our plans, especially my father. He said Doctor was too old, he was a man of the world, and not for a young girl like me with some of her wild thoughts.

Doctor knew the desert and thought I would like it just fine. He'd been southward to Arizona before. I would have followed Doctor anywhere. I had promised him that I would make him a happy man, whatever our troubles. And I meant my words. I meant them.

He's a good man, Doctor, I promise he is.

I am the one who is at fault.

But I want, oh, I want to be good.

We met the summer of 1923. I was working for the summer at the state hospital in Evanston, trying to earn tuition money so I could return to the missionary college for the next year. I had started out as an attendant but within several weeks I took over for the night manager. They liked me there.

On a melting-hot summer day, I was cutting up watermelon for the patients, and the new staff surgeon asked me for some. I gave it to him. A big, pink, meaty slice. The next day he caught me giving ice cream to a patient who wasn't allowed any. That ice cream cone ran all the way down my arm when I tried to hide it behind my back. But he didn't tell on me.

I didn't think he would.

It didn't matter to me that he was so much older, pretty close to double my age. I didn't mind. I knew Doctor was a nice man, and a good man. And if there was anything I needed, even more than going back to missionary school, it was that. I felt so safe and cared for with him.

He took me to the first restaurant I ever went to. The Elks Club. I was amazed that I could choose what I wanted. I picked a crab salad; it was not the costliest thing on the menu, I made sure of that, but it was something I'd never had before. I didn't want Doctor to think I was grubby or was just there for a showy dinner. I didn't want him to think I was simple, either. I had never really gone very far from home, but I was not simple, I didn't feel. I still don't. The crab salad was very good and cold. It was so different from what I had found in my own life.

Doctor kept saying, "Ruth, I am too old for you! You need a young, strong husband!" And I told him every time, that wasn't what I wanted. I wanted a good husband, a nice man. A husband with a strong heart was more important to me than one with a strong back. I knew I would never have to worry with Doctor by my side. He knew so much, and I thought then he would always take good care of me.

So I kissed him. I did. Not that night at the restaurant, but on Christmas. Mamma and Papa invited him over for a family supper. He took off his coat and I hung it in the closet and I turned around and kissed him. Simple as that. I don't think he expected it, but he let me, up until Papa came around the corner and saw.

Doctor pulled away sharply, was very embarrassed, his face all red and flushed. My father said nothing and just looked at us, until Doctor said, "Reverend McKinnell, I would like to be engaged to Ruth. Would that be all right with you?" And then he said all that about Arizona and it sounded like a dream to me.

Papa flat-out refused to marry us, but he was angry and that was fine. He didn't want me to go all the way across the country, but Mamma talked to him. *The doctor will take care of Ruth,* I imagine she told him. *And then there won't be any more trouble. She needs to go from here. That would be best, even if you can't see it right now.*

It was supposed to be a long engagement, and Doctor went down to Mexico to get things set up. When he came back a couple of months later, he saw I had pink spots on my cheeks and said that we needed to get married right away. *The bloom of happiness,* I thought. My brother, Burton, and Mamma decorated the house in pink and white with ribbons, and we got married in the parlor, April 18, 1924.

It wasn't until after we were married that I knew.

We didn't go to Arizona after all. When the job at the copper mine in Jerome fell through, Doctor took the job with the American Smelting and Mining Company in Mexico.

On the train to New Orleans for our honeymoon, he took up a game of cards with a gentleman. I had never seen a deck of cards before, and I had never been on a Pullman before, either. They were drinking liquor. Mamma and Papa never had any such thing in their house. Doctor's hands were shaking, holding the cards. A little tremble at first, but as the night became longer, the shaking didn't stop. It got worse. And I thought, *Maybe he really is that old. Maybe he was right, I shouldn't have married him. I'd be a widow so young.*

I was not his only wife. His first girl was a poor little thing all choked up with consumption, he told me. This was right after the Great War, and despite his shot-up leg, he was still a strong man then. He brought her to Phoenix to clear her lungs with the dry air, but it was too late for her, and she just went one night. I don't know if he loved her. I never asked. She was even younger than I was when I married Doctor; she was seventeen. Lillian.

Little girl.

When the card game ended, we went back to our train compartment. And I grew quite frightened then. I asked him if he was all right, if there was anything I could get him. Warm milk? Some tea? I was ready to go back to the dining car when he stopped me. And his face was so serious.

"I think you need something to eat," I told him. "You are shaking so badly."

And then he took ahold of my hands and led me to the cot, and we sat down, and by then I could feel it. It wasn't just his hands that were trembling, it was every inch of him. I could feel my heart jumping beats. I tried so hard to stay calm.

"Whatever is it, Doctor?" I asked him, and I was so scared for his answer that I myself started to tremble.

"I have a sickness," he said quietly, and then patted my hand softly.

Oh, when I think of what he must have gone through in France. There were battles at Verdun, Saint Michel, and the Argonne Forest. Shot in the leg, injured badly, and by the time he reached the hospital a week had passed and infection had set in. The surgeons thought they'd have to take the whole leg. But he healed because he was a strong man then; they gave him medicine for the pain and he got better. Healed up so nice that you can barely tell that there's a limp.

But the sickness stays. It doesn't ever go. Doctor cried a little when he told me this, and said he was sorry. As long as he took his medicine, he would be fine, he said very carefully. But sometimes he can't get it when he needs it. And that's when he shakes. And things, sometimes, will get worse. Sometimes, he will become very, very ill.

"Will you die?" I asked. "Will this sickness kill you?"

"No," he answered. "But it can make things difficult. I can never have children."

"Then it is of no matter," I told him. "If it won't take you from me, I will help you and care for you."

He went to his suitcase and took something out of it. He asked me to turn away, and I did because it felt wrong to watch, even though I was Doctor's wife now. When I turned back around, I saw that he was resting and that there was a syringe in his hand. On the small table next to the bed, there was a spoon with small balls of cotton sitting in the well of it.

His hands weren't shaking any longer. I was glad for that, though I didn't know what kind of medicine could have healed him so quickly. Doctor knew best.

We got off in Sinaloa, Mexico. The rugged landscape and the vast open sky took, almost demanded, my love at once.

I learned to speak Spanish very quickly; I was happy to be able to converse with the cultured Spanish upper class. Blind beggars approached us on the streets. I hated to look at the poor things. We gave them a few cents apiece, more than Doctor and I had to spare.

To reach the mining camp where we would live, we had to travel for three days by mule through a narrow mountain pass. When we arrived, all the Americans kissed me on both cheeks because they knew I was a bride. Oh, Mexico was lovely.

The children in the camp flocked to me, and I loved them so, especially the little babies who were so fat and nice to hold. I taught the children a little bit of English, and I practiced my Spanish with them. We played patty-cake and hide-and-go-seek, and for their birthdays, I fried sopapillas, little rolls of flour dough, and poured honey over them. When worried mothers brought their children to Doctor to treat, they always got better.

Our house had five rooms, hardwood floors, and big windows that opened widely and let the night breezes blanket us as we slept. I had never imagined living in a place so fine. And we had servants, mainly men too old to work in the mines anymore. The night watchmen went with Doctor on calls. He worried about me on those nights, but I was never alone.

Our first Christmas in Mexico was magnificent. I had doubted that it would really feel like Christmas, with no snow, no bundling up, and no family, but Doctor made sure that it was one that we would always remember. He had so many packages for me I had to take a break in between opening them all. I made him pajamas that never quite fit, a shirt that did. He bought lights for the tree, strung them with wire, and I painted the bulbs different colors, and oh, how they glowed! We had a real lit-up tree then.

I had a pup named Bruno who loved to fight with goats, a rabbit named Hop. Our horse, Riddle, was always polite when I rode him early in the mornings when it was still cool and fresh, just as the sun was cresting over the mountains, washing the valley in a champagne light. There were four or five yard cats. When an orange tabby had a litter of kittens, Doctor was not pleased. I wanted very much to bring them and the mother inside, away from the coyotes.

"I've said no, Ruth, and that will have to be the final answer," he said harshly, and when I protested that we should at least put a blanket out for them or find a safe place, he said he would take care of it.

But I never saw the kittens again, and when I asked one of the men, he told me that Doctor had him put the babies in a grain sack and taken them away. I didn't ask anything after that. I had to put it right out of my head, that was all, and so I did just that. I didn't think of those kittens for a very long time.

And then the most joyous thing happened. In October, I thought that I was going to have a baby. After what Doctor had said, a miracle came true. I cried when I realized we would have a little baby, Doctor's and mine, to fill our warm house with love, tiny footsteps, and wonderful baby's breath. I was so happy, truly happy. I had never been happier in my life, not even on the day we got married.

I imagined the baby with blond hair like mine and then dark hair like Doctor's, then laughed when I understood he would be born like Doctor anyway, bald and pudgy. I didn't want to tell Doctor right away; I wanted to wait a little bit to make sure I was right. I kept that secret tight for another month, and then I knew my good news was true. When Doctor was at his office or on a call at night, I took out my sewing box and went through the fine cotton fabric I had been collecting to fashion tiny gowns, blankets, and the layette items we would need soon. Although I had a steady hand, I was never much of a seamstress, but living out in the desert was most likely going to make me a competent one, I thought.

I rearranged our bedroom in my mind to fit in a cradle and then a crib, and planned a garden for the spring that would yield squash, carrots, and peas, vegetables I could put up for when the baby was old enough to wean from milk.

I thought of names: William Junior; Harvey, after my father; Burton, after my brother. But after quite a while, I thought that John Robert was a very dignified name, maybe JR for short, maybe Johnny. I hadn't decided. John Robert Judd, if it was a boy, but I knew it was a boy. I could feel it.

One afternoon, while I was sweeping out the front room, I felt the oddest thing, like a tiny little bird fluttering inside me. It was John Robert, still so tiny, I knew, probably not even as big as an apple. I knew he was saying, *Hello, I'm here, I will be there soon and I will love you as much as you love me. I am your baby. I am your son.*

I was so thrilled, I wanted to dance. The day was even more luminous than it had been a moment before, it was all golden and soft and just beautiful, it was like being draped in glory. I knew that this was the time I should tell Doctor about John Robert, and I planned a special dinner with chicken, beans, and rice that I learned how to make from the local women. They called it arroz con pollo. Doctor loved it, but I wasn't always able to get a chicken when I wanted one, so I only made it on special occasions.

When he saw the table set for supper with the arroz con pollo dish in the middle, his smile beamed and made me even more excited to tell him that our baby was on the way.

I waited until we both had a plate full of our special meal. I couldn't wait to see how happy this news would make him.

"I have something wonderful to tell you, Doctor," I said.

"Really?" he said, eating his chicken, which he was clearly pleased with. He was smiling, his eyes were sparkling, and I knew this was going to be one of the happiest moments of our life together. I could barely keep it inside.

"We are going to have a baby, Doctor," I said, putting my fork and knife down. "A baby of our very own."

Instantly, the smiled vanished from his face and he stopped chewing. He was so surprised, it stopped him right in his tracks.

But Doctor was not stunned with joy the way I was sure he would be. He began chewing again and then swallowed.

"Now, Ruth," he said, "do not become upset. It just can't be, and that is all."

"But it is!" I said with a smile and a laugh. "It's true! I felt it, I felt him, like a tiny fish, swimming around. I think we'll have our arrival in May or June. Isn't it wonderful? Isn't it just so wonderful?"

"Ruth—" he started, but I was not about to let him finish.

"I have made clothes, from your old shirts, from an extra sheet; the cotton is so fine and soft it is just perfect for a baby," I said. "I will show you. I will show you what I have been making for him."

With that I stood up, ready to get the trunk where I had been keeping the blankets and gowns in secret. "I sew them in the day when you are at work, I sew them all the time I can spare a minute. I wait for you to go on a call so I can sew more. He's going to have such a nice layette, our John Robert. I have been careful to get better at sewing and making things that will actually fit him! Don't you see? Don't you see how wonderful this is?"

"It's not possible, Ruth," Doctor said, making the chair legs strain against the wood floor as he stood up. "I am too sick. I have been taking a lot of medicine and you know it."

"That doesn't matter," I cried back. "I will take care of everything. I will tend to both of you! I can do that. I can do that!"

"Don't you remember what I told you on the train to New Orleans?" he said. "On our honeymoon? Don't you remember? You are too ill, Ruth. You cannot have a baby."

I was not ill, I was perfectly fine, and I told him that. I was fine. John Robert was fine and I was fine. I did not know what he was talking about. I said that, too.

"You have consumption, Ruth," he said, his voice rising. "The flush on your cheeks—I've told you this! You are tubercular. That's why we are in Mexico. We are here for you. To get better, to get strong. *You know this.*"

"I am not sick!" I screamed. "You are sick! You are the one with illness, and the trouble. It is all yours!"

"Yes, I am sick!" he said sternly. "It wouldn't be right, can't you understand? How is that right?"

And that's why, he said, a baby was impossible. With his sickness and my illness, it wouldn't be right, he said, even when I started to cry. With both of us so bad off, and with him taking so much medicine he said the child couldn't possibly be normal, it would be an idiot, and he told me about medical cases where the babies were born with enormous heads. It would not be a healthy baby and would probably die before it was even born. I couldn't stop crying. Having a child would kill me, he said. It would be motherless and fatherless and no one would take it.

I wanted a family more than I wanted anything. I couldn't wait to be surrounded by beautiful little children and have a happy, laughing household of my own. I thought I could do that with Doctor. I thought he would be a fine father. He was respected, and he knew so much of the world. He had so much to teach a son.

And then that all crumbled in my hand in one second. It went out the door like dirt with a broom. What I would never have, what I would never love, what I would never be. I couldn't help but sob until my throat was sore, until I made no noise at all.

Doctor took me by the wrists.

"Ruth," he said, "if you do the right thing, I will go to a sanatorium and get well, and then we can have a baby. This baby will not be the baby you think it will be. It is already harmed, it is already sick."

Doctor would never say something hurtful to me unless it was true. I shouldn't be so selfish as to put myself before a baby. It wasn't right. I was no longer right to want to have a baby, if having it meant harming it. I did my best to push the desire as far away as I could and quiet down like he said. Even though I was quiet, the tears never stopped coming.

Doctor did his medicine. Then he lay down on the bed and we did not speak of it again that night.

The next day, Doctor took me to his office early in the morning. I did not want to go, but Doctor said what a selfish thing it would be to bring a half-formed baby into the world.

It's not right, he kept telling me.

He promised it was a small operation. To be brave and hold my breath, that it would be over quickly, and I did all of that to show him I could be strong. He gave me a sip of medicine from a small brown bottle to calm me, and another. It was very bitter and hung in my mouth for a long time afterward. Sometimes I can still taste it. Doctor readied the instruments he would need. They were silver, glistening; he kept them always wrapped in gauze. They looked like wicked, evil presents. In some time, I felt dizzy, sleepy, calm. Doctor told me to lie down on the table.

It's not right, it's not right, it's not right, I whispered over and over in my head; it would not leave and stood solidly in my mind. It was painful. I remember yelling out and Doctor telling me to shush. People must not hear. *I must be verystrongnow. Imustbnothinkoftheflutterand-littlefishswimming. Littlefishswimming. Swimmigawayawayaway.*

It's not right.

CHAPTER FIFTEEN

Ruth

Doctor never went to the sanatorium. His work was very busy, and there were outbreaks of cholera, then yellow fever, typhus, smallpox, and influenza. There were so many people to treat that he never treated himself.

And that meant he didn't stop taking the medicine, either, and instead got worse. I could tell. He was sloppy in his demeanor, and spent all of his time sleeping. Maybe it was his way of proving to me that he couldn't be entrusted with the care of a child. I wouldn't trust him with a dead cat. I learned he had emptied the bottles of morphine, heroin, and everything else he could from medical supplies he had access to. This continued for at least a year until he came home early one afternoon and told me to start packing my suitcase and our trunks again. Doctor was out of a job, and we were on our way to Santa Monica to stay with his sister, Carrie, who was a schoolteacher and had a small cottage. I slept on the couch as soon as Carrie and I checked Doctor into the veterans' hospital in Los Angeles for his condition. I can't help but admit that I was angry, because I was. He had always promised he would take care of me; he said that exact thing to my parents before we were married, and here he was now, a feeble, mumbling man who drained the medicine dry out of his own employer's cabinet.

The train trip back to California used up all the money we had. I got a job at the Broadway Department Store as a marker for jewelry and furs, which I liked. It was my duty to inspect them when they came in for any damage and then affix the assigned price tags on them. It was simple work, and I was able to stay in the back stockrooms and I preferred it that way. The jewelry was lovely to touch and look at, even though I knew I could never afford any of it. I began to learn the difference between furs; fox, raccoon, sable, beaver, seal, and mink were the more expensive furs, and even possum! The cheaper furs—squirrel, chinchilla, weasel, and skunk—were so far out of my price range that I couldn't even imagine who could afford them. Would a millionaire wear a skunk? I always laughed at that.

I told the manager at the store to put me down for as many hours as he could, that my husband was sick and I needed to provide for us both. He was a nice man and agreed, and I made many friends there. It was not hard work, but the days were long. When I had an afternoon off, which was always Tuesday, I would go to visit Doctor, who was permitted to come and see me. He said he didn't want me to see him in a hospital, so we always met down at the car line and he would be waiting for me there when I got off. We would have a modest lunch or just go for a walk to visit and talk. I could see that he was getting better than he was during our last days in Mexico. He looked healthier, and the pallor had left his face. He seemed much more like himself, although I had to admit that I didn't know what that was, exactly. Doctor was happy when he wasn't on his medicine, but it never lasted very long. But if the cure stuck this time, I could get John Robert back and we could have a family. He had promised. He had to keep a promise.

As I was leaving one visit and Doctor saw me back to the streetcar stop, I watched him from the window go behind Weaver's Drugstore, which was on the corner of the stop. I didn't understand why he was going that way; the veterans' hospital was right down the street. On my next trip back home after a visit, I watched carefully, and saw he did it again. At the next stop, I jumped off and ran back the three blocks and went around into the alley and there was Doctor, taking a bag from a pharmacist who had opened the alley door. Doctor saw me coming and the other man shut the door quickly. I took the bag out of Doctor's hands and opened it; inside were two bottles of Cheracol cough syrup. I was so mad I couldn't look up at him. I knew what he was doing, drinking it for the codeine.

I said nothing but walked back around to the front of the drugstore and went inside to find that white-coated man standing behind the counter. There were several customers in the store, but I was so angry I didn't care.

"Why are you trying to make a sick man sicker?" I yelled at him with a roar I did not know I had. "Why are you giving a good man who is trying to get well this poison? What kind of man are you? You're supposed to help people, not make them sicker!"

Everyone in the store turned to look at me; I could see them staring at me over the low aisles of cotton balls and powder and hairbrushes.

"Are you a monster?" I screamed. I was not ashamed, even with all of those eyes on me; I felt ablaze. "Are you? STOP IT! I am telling you to stop it! You cannot have my husband. You cannot have my baby! You cannot have those things!"

I saw a bag fly past the pharmacist's head and explode on the wall behind him, dripping thick red liquid down toward the floor like blood rushing out of a wound.

"YOU CANNOT HAVE WHAT IS MINE!" I shrieked. "I am calling the police on you!"

I turned and walked back to the door, seeing Doctor right outside of it, just standing, watching with everyone else. I pushed it open with everything I had, the bell on the door whipping wildly and sounding nothing like a bell but instead a siren.

I walked past Doctor, who said nothing, and I kept walking, two blocks, three blocks, four. When the streetcar came, I got on. I did not look back.

When I got back to Carrie's, I immediately went to the kitchen and called the police.

I went back to Los Angeles the next day, but not to see Doctor. I had looked up every pharmacy and drugstore around the veterans' hospital in the phone book. I went to the pharmacist in each store, showed him a picture of Doctor, and flatly told him, "If I find out that you are selling this man Cheracol, I am calling the police on you. Ask the pharmacist at Weaver's if you don't believe me." I went to eight drugstores that day and did not go to visit Doctor the following Tuesday. Or the Tuesday after that.

I was working very hard, all days of the week. I worked as many hours as my manager would allow. I was tired; Carrie said my clothes were starting to hang on me. She was a very caring person, Doctor's sister, very kind. Soft and cushiony like Doctor, but with a sharpness about her that I suppose a woman who has lived alone without a husband might get. I was starting to understand that. I suppose she was tired, like I was—of working, taking care of everything, and having no one there to depend on for such a long time. She said she enjoyed my company and I could stay as long as I liked and not to feel funny about it. We played cards at night, listened to radio shows until we got sleepy, and shared our morning coffee together. I had not really had a chance to know Carrie until then; when Doctor and I were married, we went straight to Mexico and had been there almost the entire time since. *Isn't it odd,* I thought, *to have a sister for so many years and never know her until now.*

Of course, I helped with the house expenses and food and tried to cook as much as she let me, but she didn't find Mexican cooking as delightful as I did. If we ended up back in Mexico, I told her, she should come for the whole summer. Close up the house and take the train down.

"The women there do their laundry in the river and beat the clothes on rocks to get them clean," I said, to her amazement.

She laughed until she cried and said, "How on earth would that ever get them clean?"

I suppose she had a point.

Some days, though, I was so tired I couldn't even stay up to listen to the radio and went straight to bed after work. I felt bad leaving Carrie alone again, but there were many nights when I could not wait to get to sleep. I developed a slight cough that persisted for some time, and I couldn't shake it. Carrie was sure I had caught a cold and that I was so tired I couldn't fight it off. She called her doctor and asked if I could come to see him, and I went. My cough was deeper by that time, and began to hurt my chest when I couldn't stop. It was winter, December, and I wasn't used to the cold air that swung in from the ocean. I felt silly just to be examined. I explained all of this to the doctor, and he asked me how long was it that my cheeks had been flushed.

"They are a very rosy shade of pink," he said.

I explained that I had had that blush since before I was married, and I thought it remained because I was happy.

He didn't laugh at me, though looking back, I laugh at myself. How could I have not known?

"Mrs. Judd, you have tuberculosis, and it has flared," he said. "I believe you've had it for some time."

It wasn't that I hadn't believed Doctor when he told me, but I just had it in my head that it was something mean and spiteful he said that night when I tried to make us a family.

But it was true. Doctor was being true.

"How sick am I?" I asked, knowing the outcome of consumption was not good.

"You should be in a drier climate, but if you get rest and don't exert yourself, that would be the best thing," he told me.

Doctor agreed with the medical opinion when I saw him several days later, which was the first time I had taken the streetcar out since the incident with the cough syrup.

"You didn't tell me you were so ill," he said as we ate tuna sandwiches at a diner.

"I wasn't feeling that poorly until a little while ago," I explained. "I was tired, but I didn't want to fill you with my worries. I wanted you to get better and recover."

And he had. Doctor promised that he had given Cheracol up, and I did not doubt that after I had made my visits to the nearby drugstores. He had been following the treatment at the hospital, which was basically to not take medicine. He seemed more cheerful, and healthier. I was very happy about that.

"Please do as that doctor tells you," he said. "I believe with rest you can make a full recovery. It wouldn't take much. You have a very slight case."

I nodded and took another bite.

"I promise you a new life, Ruth," Doctor said, almost as an apology. "I know I've put you through so much and now all of that has started to make you sick."

"I hope you don't believe that. It's very busy at the department store," I said. "I've gotten a promotion to the head of the toy department."

"Oh, that is wonderful," he said. "Now you're the boss!"

"No," I laughed. "Not exactly. It's temporary until the holidays are over."

"Well, I'm a little glad to hear that," he said with a smile. "Because I have been writing to the mining company. I've told them I will be released soon, and I am fully recovered."

"Will they trust you again?"

"Well, now, that's the thing," he said. "I would be going back as an assistant in Madera at the Dolores mine, but once they see how well I am doing, I'll be back to head doctor in no time."

"So they would not give you a house, I'm supposing," I said, knowing that assistants and orderlies slept in a dormitory or bunkhouse, not a doctor's house.

"No, I don't see that they would, but that wouldn't be so bad. You can stay here with Carrie; we'd both be working and be able to save up a bit of money. How does that sound?"

"I guess it sounds fine," I said, but I was feeling very worried that, alone in Mexico, Doctor would slip back into his old ways, although as a lower staff member, he would not have the availability to the medicine cabinet that he once had.

"I know you really love Mexico," Doctor said with a wide smile, and then winked.

"I do," I admitted. "I do love the desert."

It was arranged, then, that Doctor would go down to Madera right after Christmas and start his new job. I would stay with Carrie until he sent for me.

The department store was a madhouse during those weeks leading up to Christmas in 1927; people were still spending money like mad then. It was constantly busy; it never slowed down for a minute between opening the doors in the morning and closing them at night, making me wish I was back marking up furs in the cold storeroom. It was so busy we didn't take lunch or breaks and worked straight through for ten, eleven, twelve hours. I was becoming more tired and the cough got deeper. I saw blood in the tissue.

On the day of Christmas Eve, the line to get in the store wrapped all the way around the block. I didn't even know what I was selling; people handed me boxes, I put them in a bag and gave them change. It went on like that for hours, and the store became so hot it was smothering. People were everywhere, like ants crawling all over each other, and the din of all of those voices became confusing, jumbled, and then exploded. I began breathing heavily, the thunder of the voices battering my head. I was so thirsty, I needed something to drink very badly. I left the counter, and when I woke up, I was packed in ice in a tub as long as a coffin.

Both Doctor and Carrie were by my side. I had suffered hemorrhages in both lungs and had a raging fever, and the hospital was trying to bring it down. Doctor held my hand tightly. It almost hurt. Carrie's eyes were red and swollen. I wasn't sure what to think.

"Ruth," Doctor said, now covering my hand with both his hands. "I do not want you to listen to these doctors. With the right treatment, you're going to be fine. I can't get you into Barlow Sanatorium here, but I've arranged for a bed in another one a little farther away. But it's going to take time. You have to be patient and do what they tell you. They will give you excellent care; I've talked to the doctors up there and explained the whole thing. Tomorrow we'll move you to a very nice place up in the foothills. It's a beautiful place. It's called La Vina. Doesn't that sound nice?"

I nodded, unable to speak and so very, very tired, and even though I was floating in a freezing bath, I fell back asleep.

=◆=

I didn't know it then but the doctors at the hospital told my husband and Carrie that I would not live long, three to four months, and only patients with more chance of recovery were given beds. That they should take me home to die.

But Doctor knew better and wouldn't hear of it. Carrie told me later that he was furious that they wouldn't help me, that he had been a doctor for far longer and it was obvious the treatment that I needed and that I was clearly strong enough to pull through. She said he called them "fools." He then phoned a friend of his, Dr. Moore, who practiced in Pasadena and knew the doctors up at La Vina and got me a bed there. It was a place where the poorer people with consumption went, existing on donations and what little the patients' families could pay, if at all. Of course, the treatment there was good, so every now and then a person of means would arrive, but typically, people with money went to Barlow Sanatorium in Los Angeles.

Carrie and Doctor went with me to La Vina. I was very weak and delirious. I don't remember barely anything of that day, but I do know that afterward, Doctor got on a train and headed to Madera. To think that we had once had such marvelous holidays, but that year, I was in a sanatorium as he just got out and was headed to another country.

My days at La Vina were uneventful, but if I was going to take the cure, I had to follow precisely what they said. When the fever subsided after several days, I was strong enough to get up.

I was allowed outside for fifteen minutes after breakfast, then back to the dormitory for more rest. The air was very clean, fresh, and from the hilltop that La Vina was built on, the view was so clear you could see to Los Angeles. Lunch was the same procedure, and so was dinner. After several weeks, when I had recovered enough, I had a pneumothorax treatment, in which air is pumped into the lung, and even though I was given morphine and anesthetic during the procedure, waking up to an inflated lung was so painful I thought they had left a knife in me. It was difficult to breathe, talk, do anything, but when I realized there was a whole wing there full of little children, I shushed myself right away. Imagine being a small little child subject to these treatments, and away from their families? Lying in those beds all day, nothing to do, and all alone? It tore at my heart. I swore that when I got well enough, I would go over to their part of the hospital and keep them company. And I did do that, in time. It made me even sadder to see them, very listless in their beds, crying for their parents. I played patty-cake with them, and was able to get some paper and pencils from the nurses so the children could draw. Some of them had toys with them, and I went bed to bed, trying to cheer them up, telling them to think good thoughts. Sometimes we sang songs, but it was difficult to get that much air into my lungs, so at times, we whisper-sang. We looked out the window at the birds and made up stories about them. The children liked that very much. I loved that part of my time there.

It took me longer than I had hoped to get better; it was spring before I was fully recovered, and before I left for Madera, flowers were already blooming and the gardens at La Vina had been planted. So much was blooming, the colors looked like drops of magic everywhere. In the weeks before I left, the nurses even let me sleep outside, since the winter had been so awful and dreadful. Even yellow flowers, the most ordinary of all, made me feel like sunshine and that I could live forever if I really wanted to.

Carrie saw me off at the train station and told me that if Doctor got into trouble again, I should bring him back to Los Angeles immediately. He had been doing well, he said, and had no issues that lingered. He was able to be with the medicine in his hand or knowing that it was in the cabinet without wanting to so much as even touch it. He was able to get us a house; nothing fancy, very tiny, with a kitchen and a bedroom, and for now, that was just fine. I could not complain. We had both been so sick it was a marvel that we were both alive, and together. I didn't care if he had built a grass hut for us, I was excited to go. So much so that when I left La Vina, the nurses and doctors gathered to say goodbye, and although I didn't want them to take it the wrong way, I told them, "I hope the next time we meet, it won't be here. It is lovely, but I never want to see this place again."

CHAPTER SIXTEEN

Ruth

It was a small, adobe house in Tayoltita, much smaller than our first, but I didn't mind. It was less to clean, Doctor told me, and I wouldn't exert myself so much. It never got cold there. There were cows in a nearby pasture and I loved to listen to them all day. We grew strawberries. Doctor fixed a hammock up right outside the house in the shade of the midday sun and I was to rest there if I was feeling tired. He said the sun was good for me, and the more of it I could get, the better.

One day he brought me a special present in a basket, and as he handed it to me, a little black nose popped out of the cloth that covered it and it was the most beautiful puppy. He had large gentle brown eyes and enormous paws that he didn't know what to do with. I called him Bruno; it sounded like a big, strong name for the big, strong dog I knew he would quickly become. I took him into the hammock with me in the afternoon and we slept for a little while until he got wiry and restless. It was so good of Doctor to do that. I had something of my own to love. Bruno grew so quickly it astonished me. Suddenly he was a dog, a friend, my shadow, protecting me when Doctor was away on a visit or call.

Doctor continued the pneumothorax treatments. They were very painful, and Doctor would only give me the slightest bit of medicine to dull the pain because he said he didn't want me to get his sickness. The pain was indescribable, like an orange-hot poker slicing through my body and then exposing it to air. He promised that each treatment would make me stronger, better, and then we could talk about what the future meant for us, maybe even a family. He had to prove himself to the mines, had to have a secure job and remain without illness. He swore to me he could do it.

And he was right; after that time as an assistant, the mine trusted him enough to become the head doctor, but with the understanding that with one incident, just one, he would lose his job again. They were taking a large risk in trusting him, but the camp manager, Mr. Reyer, had been informed and was to watch everything very carefully.

When I was alone, I would say it over and over again: *Let Doctor be good. Let Doctor stay good. Let Doctor want to be good.*

I kept saying it even when he began to sleep more and became irritable at the slightest thing. I knew Mr. Reyer had his eye on him; nothing could happen. Doctor knew people were watching him. I hoped that I was just being suspicious, after all we had put into him being better in California.

But something in Doctor decided it didn't matter, and it wasn't long before I knew we would be moving again. This was the worst I had seen him. He spoke of despair, of loving nothing, of seeing no future. And then I found those bits of cotton balls rolled up in his coat pocket, and I knew what they meant.

But something even more dangerous was heading toward us, faster than we could see it coming. A war we had nothing to do with, had no part it, but which was going to challenge me in a way I had never been challenged before.

It was a revolution, spring of 1929, and everything was about to change.

While Doctor was shaking on the bed uncontrollably, General Escobar's revolutionaries came through the camp and cut the power, and it was just me and Doctor, as he shook and was sick on the bed. The night was so long, filled with shouting, sounds of shots, and noises that I did not want to imagine the cause of.

At daybreak, with the darkness lifted, I broke out of the stillness. Doctor was still shaking as the battle for Mexico raged on, with us in the center.

"Shh, shhh, there now," I whispered, hoping that I could soothe him, even just a little. But I did know better. This could last hours, maybe even days. The medicine had run out the day before.

We had been in Mexico for the better part of five years, and we should have left days ago. I don't know why we didn't. I trusted Doctor's sense of things, even when the revolutionaries moved in swiftly. Now there was nowhere to go unless we took a narrow mountain pass ninety miles long, the same pass I had taken on mule back when we arrived here.

We had a gun, a small pistol for me because Doctor worried about the nights when he had to make a call up the mountain, but we didn't bring it out. The revolutionaries only wanted our supplies, Doctor assured me when they first arrived; they weren't there to harm us. Now that they had invaded our property, I kept the gun hidden in my night-stand, where I could reach it quickly if I needed to.

Doctor moaned loudly, shaking harder now.

"Doctor, I will get you some warm milk," I offered softly. "Would you like that?"

He groaned, rolling into himself. Bruno crept closer.

The soldiers took our horse, and even some of the laying hens. I had raised Betsy and Coo Coo from chicks, and they flapped wildly when a soldier overturned them and held them by their feet.

I got out of bed and lit the lamp. Doctor was sticky with sweat and his face was pallid, the shade of milky dishwater. As I put my hand on his forehead, gently, he lurched forward and vomited on the floor.

The sun was starting to burn fully. If I could, I would have rolled up the little cotton balls in between my fingers as I had seen him do and gotten the spoon ready. Even though I hated that the medicine made him so sick when he didn't have it.

I sat in a chair across the room and watched him sweat, heave, moan. Bruno stretched across my feet, as if to protect me.

I could do nothing.

I was still sitting with Bruno across my feet when there was a banging on the door. I feared the bandits' return until I heard Mr. Reyer, the camp manager, call, "Mrs. Judd? Mrs. Judd? Are you all right?"

Keeping Bruno close, I shut the door to the bedroom and let Mr. Reyer in.

"Have you been hurt, Mrs. Judd?" he asked. "Is the doctor all right?"

"Doctor took ill last night after the bandits left," I told him.

"Where are your men?" he asked.

"Protecting their own homes," I said. "We're alone here."

He cleared his throat.

"Mrs. Judd," he began. "I must confide in you. Trusting doctors with the narcotics supply has been a problem in the camp, as you know."

I put my hands to my face to cover my flush.

"Yes," I said, hoping that Doctor would stay quiet in the bedroom.

"Yes, well, so I kept the narcotics at my house," he went on. "But with this sudden upheaval, I'm going to get my family to Mazatlán to safety and then return. The pass is still open, the battles are raging in the cities. But I must leave them with you for safekeeping. It's all we have for our own patients. I can't risk the bandits finding them."

He handed me a package wrapped in paper and twine.

I found myself close to tears. I did not want to touch what made Doctor so sick, what had made everything change for us and had ruined

Doctor's want to have a family. But I also knew that if Mr. Reyer was leaving, we should go, too, and I couldn't take Doctor as he was.

Maybe just a little would be enough for him to get well and we could leave here, now, as soon as he was better. Just a little, I told myself, just a little, just enough to get him away and better for good.

"Mrs. Judd?" Mr. Reyer said, thrusting the package in his hands closer to me.

I reached out and snatched it, and put it in the pocket of my dress.

"Please give the doctor my best," he said, nodding. "Hope he's feeling well soon. We're leaving on the trail. You should follow as soon as the doctor is able."

"Thank you, and we will," I said quickly, and shut the door behind him.

I leaned against it for a moment, my hand in my pocket, fingers strangling the package.

I thought about the spoon, the rolled-up cotton balls, and I cried. Bruno came forward and leaned against me, and I slumped down to the floor, holding him tightly and closing my eyes against his bristly fur. I gave Doctor the medicine, saved enough for the trip through the mountains. But he was not getting better, he did not snap back. His breathing slowed and he stopped thrashing about, but he did not surface as I thought he would. Something else was wrong, it was not only his war sickness.

Had he caught any of the diseases he had been treating?

I needed to get Doctor through the mountain pass. I needed to get myself out, too.

We took nothing with us, not even Bruno; I left him with one of the men in the village who worked with Doctor, promising I'd come back for him when I could. We took nothing except the pistol, tucked into the lining of my handbag.

We might both have died in the mountains if I hadn't prepared for what we faced ahead. I ran around the town and gathered men and supplies. Doctor could not ride and could not walk. For ninety miles, day after day, hired men and mules hauled him on a stretcher over the pass. It took four men at a time to carry him, and they tired quickly, rubbing their shoulders raw until they changed shifts. I rode on a mule, carrying blocks of ice to put on Doctor's head. He yelled and was delirious. A runner went ahead to tell the farmhouses to have food for us. In the bushes along the trail were bloody hats and clothing. We missed three battles, each by only one day. At Estación Dimas, we learned that the military had confiscated the trains. The boxcars were filled with soldiers. I found an old man with a truck and gave him my last thirty American dollars for it.

Mazatlán was 125 miles away. I drove for eight hours with Doctor's head on my lap. His fever raged; his breath shallowed. I knew in my heart that he was dying. I stopped the car and I cradled him. I told him that I had been happy with him, that he had made me so happy and I had always been true. I had not even kissed another man in the five years we had been married. And that my only regret was that we had not already had a child together for him to love. Suddenly Doctor sat up and said that he would rather I had a child with any other man but him, and named three men I had never heard of. Young men, he demanded. He was delirious, talking to people that I couldn't see and that existed only in his sickness.

General Escobar would fail in his revolution in several weeks' time, but no one knew that then, and I wouldn't have cared, anyway. I was running through the mountains with my dying husband, who was crying about a baby he had already taken from me, something I would never let him do to me again.

I parked the truck in front of the hospital; Doctor was so taken with fever again that as I got him standing, he ran across a field, wailing and screaming. I had to pull him back, fear burning a hole through my heart. I found an American doctor, Dr. Chapman, and I told him of the doctor's illness, how he had never been so low. After Dr. Chapman examined him, he said that Doctor also had a stomach abscess and that he needed to operate immediately.

As for Doctor's wartime sickness, Dr. Chapman advised that as soon as he healed completely from surgery, he needed to go to a hospital in California for a full recovery, but not the veterans' hospital. A better hospital this time, a place he could not leave without a doctor's permission.

I agreed. It would take all the money I had left, everything that I had saved from working at the Broadway Department Store, except for a train ticket I bought to Indiana to stay with my parents.

CHAPTER SEVENTEEN

Ruth

Doctor wrote that he was doing well. He wrote me near every day.

"Ruth," he said in a letter, "I am getting stronger and better all the time. I want to take care of you again. I am sorry for all I have caused; you are so good to me. To think that I have given you pain and worry is something I cannot bear, but I know it to be true. When I think of how strong you were to get us out of Mexico, I cannot hope enough that you will be rewarded with such happiness after such a frightening ordeal. You have saved me, over and over again. You have such courage, Ruth. More than you know. And I am sorry I failed you, wife, my girl, so many times. Soon, we will be together again, and I have learned of a position in a nearby hospital that may take me on. I feel there is a goodness coming. Yours,—Doctor."

I wanted so badly to believe him.

I just couldn't.

⟞⟝

As soon as I'd gotten to Indiana, I realized that people just don't like to forget. No one said, "Well, Ruth, how are you? How have you been? We hear you have been living in Mexico with dogs and horses and cows in a little adobe house." People were still talking about all of that nonsense all that time ago. Mamma has said over and over again, "She was just a girl then. She didn't know what it was to be with a boy in that way," but people believe what they want to believe, and it's hard to change their minds, even about something that happened so long ago it feels foggy.

Frank Hull was my distant cousin, and he was older. He was more of a man than a boy, maybe because he was taller than other boys his age. I could tell that he liked me in a way that men and ladies like each other. And I thought he was handsome, too, I had always thought that. He had asked me to a dance, and Mamma and Papa thought it was fine, so I went. We had a nice time. There was a fiddle there and a man playing piano out in a big barn by Olney, the town we lived in. There were lights strung up that made everything so pretty, even a barn. I remember that night clearly. We laughed and danced, me and Frank, and then he touched my hand. It made me feel warm and thrilled. We took a walk through the woods on the way home, and I couldn't stop thinking about Frank all night. All of my thoughts went to him.

I waited for him to ask me to the dance the next week, but he never said a word. It wasn't until after the dance that I found out he took my best friend, Beulah, and I went to her right away and told her Frank had asked me to the dance before, and that she should stay away from him. She didn't, though, and we were never nice after that. And when I saw Frank the next time and told him he should have asked me to the dance instead of Beulah, he laughed at me. Laughed right at me. The meanness in his laugh upset me quite a bit.

He said, "Oh, you are a crazy one, Ruth! Plain crazy!" Mamma found me crying in my bed that night, and I told her how awful Frank had been. After he told me I was pretty and we had gone for the walk in the woods and that he had even touched me.

Mamma spoke to Frank's mother, who didn't believe a word of it. She called me a liar. Called Mamma a liar. Said Frank would never touch a girl like me, and that he had only asked me to the dance to make Beulah jealous. I hoped it wasn't true. He told me how pretty I was.

Then Mamma had asked me about my monthly, and I was truthful. I didn't lie. I said it hadn't come yet and Mamma got very red in the face and said, "Why would you go into the woods with a boy, Ruth? You know all the girls that go into the woods like that end up with babies!"

I was very scared. Just thinking about it made me freeze up and stop talking. I could not have a baby by myself. I thought of an idea to make Frank come back to me. I made a little baby dress and I mailed it to his mother and signed it, "Love, Ruth."

I was frightened for a long time, thinking about this little baby, and how I had been so wrong about Frank. And I waited and waited and no baby came, and Mamma took me to the doctor in the next town, who said everything would be all right. He told Mamma that he was sure I was not going to have a baby. He said I was fine.

But no one forgot that I went into the woods all that time ago, and they all acted as if I really did have a baby on my own. Even when the judge said that Frank was not going to jail and the whole case had been dismissed. He called me a fake when other people called me crazy. It should have gone back to normal then. Should have. That place disgusted me, and the people there were so awful I don't know how Mamma and Papa stood it for as long as they did before they moved to a town right on the other side of the state line in Indiana, although the gossip followed That whole place was hollow, mean, and didn't think twice about sucking the life right out a girl like me. All over again.

⟨⟩

I felt that sickness creeping, coming over me, even only after a couple of weeks into my visit. I felt it happen all at once, Indiana's terrible, dark cold seeping into my lungs and staying there, piercing my chest with pain. I knew that the winter might not leave much of me for Doctor to fetch and take me to where I could live and be healthy.

I wrote him and told him how poorly I was doing, and his orders were plain. "Ruth, just leave now before you get so sick you can't leave. We need you to be well to take care of things, even if you come to California for enough time that your lungs clear. You must come at once, and by yourself. You mustn't have anything to take you away from getting well."

Doctor loved me and wanted me to get well quickly. To do that, I had to rest and take care of myself, and I knew where I had to go. This time, it was not only for me.

I didn't tell a soul about the coming baby. Not one person, not even Mamma. What happened once could happen again, but if I kept it a secret, everything would be fine. I would go back to the foothills and rest, then the baby would come and I would at least have that. John Robert, I knew, had come back to me, and this time, I would protect him. What would Doctor do with a smiling, healthy baby? Because I knew he would be. Doctor wouldn't say anything at all, but reach for him and feel joy.

Carrie wired me some money for the train. I didn't argue. I outwardly took it without apology.

I cried the whole way out of Indiana, and a good long way after that.

John Robert was easy to hide with a loose dress and a big coat, and that's what I was wearing when Carrie met me at the Los Angeles train station. Union Station was not a grand place—the tall banks of windows showed the truth about the beat-up wooden benches, the octagonal floor was chipped and some tiles were missing altogether—but it was lit by warm, honey-colored light from the enormous pendant chandeliers, and it felt soothing to be back in California. The station was full of people coming and going, and I wondered what their stories were.

Where had they come from, where were they going? A new start, or a sad return?

Mine was both. Carrie greeted me warmly, as I knew she would, and picked up my suitcase, which Doctor has taken with him to war in France. It was barely filled, as I was wearing almost everything I had left. We took the streetcar back to Pasadena, and a taxi to La Vina, going up the long, twisted drive up the hill to the top. I was tired from the trip, but was almost looking forward to the bed rest, feeling that I had escaped the ordeal of Doctor getting well again and the insufferable gossip in Indiana.

People are hateful, spiteful things, and can be so cruel without a single regret.

I really, really hated that. I felt fury when I thought too long on it and had to bury those thoughts very deeply so that I didn't even sense them anymore. Even one word—

fake

crazy

troubled

liar

bad

dirty

—ignited my temper to inflammation.

I had a lot of digging to do.

The good news at La Vina was that I was not as sick as I had been before. I told the doctors immediately that I was due in several months and that nothing should harm my baby, and that it was something I didn't want known outside of La Vina, including Carrie. I also told them I did not want to talk about it further unless it was a complete necessity.

I rested, I watched the birds. The warm air was a respite from the icy breath of Indiana, and I began to feel better immediately. There were no hemorrhages this time, just rest. I slept outside on some nights, especially when it got warmer, and if it is possible to enjoy a sanatorium, I did. Doctor's letter came, and I wrote him back. He said he was progressing again, but he wanted stay in the hospital longer this time, to make sure he was truly cured when he left. I mentioned nothing about John Robert. I wasn't sure what he would tell the physicians at La Vina, and I was not going to take a chance.

When Carrie came to visit, I wore the big coat, even when it got too warm to excuse it, or stayed in bed with blankets.

"Doctor's orders," I told her.

Doctor was released first, and went straight back to Mexico to pick up his job again. Mr. Reyer had explained to the mining company that Doctor had been sick with the stomach abscess, which was true, but he didn't know what I knew. This time, he was in Mazatlán, which was a bigger town, and the train from Los Angeles went straight there. You could be there in a day.

Doctor wrote that this house was not as cozy as our last; it was above the hospital in a big block building. He was afraid I wouldn't like it much, as it was not as idyllic as Tayoltita has been, with cows and strawberries and horses. That area was still too dangerous for us to return to, although I had really set my hopes on getting Bruno back. Doctor wanted to see me before his trip, but I told him I'd rather have him go down as soon as possible to set our house up and I would be there as soon as I was able.

When Doctor finally sent for me and La Vina cleared me to take a train trip, I felt absolutely fine. I felt wonderful and happy. Carrie saw me off once again.

"Ruth, aren't you just sweltering?" she said, motioning to my heavy wool coat.

"I just can't seem to shake off the chill," I told her, and laughed. I could tell John Robert would not be a big baby, and in those pajamas everyone wore at La Vina, it was easy to cover him up.

Carrie was good. She was always good. I wanted badly to be like her. Instead, I lied to her, even if I didn't say a word. Sometimes lying and saying nothing is the same thing. Had I told her the truth, I knew she would be delighted and happy for me, but I had to do everything I possibly could to protect us. Just like before, I headed into Mexico, and when the train had been jostling on the tracks for at least a half an hour, I took my coat off.

CHAPTER EIGHTEEN

Ruth

I saw Doctor standing on the platform from my seat on the train. I saw him before he saw me. I was wearing a loose cotton dress, the kind with a dropped waistline, which swung around my middle instead of cinching it. Doctor was so happy when he saw me and gave me a big hug, a big kiss.

Mazatlán was a beautiful city, lots of Spanish style, arches, pillars, columns, the ocean breeze blowing in and cleaning the city every day. It was all white, every house, every church, every market. Red tile roofs, window jambs painted sky blue. When I was last there, I was too worried about Doctor to take much notice of the place, but it was bright and lovely and so cheerful.

"You've gained weight," he said as he hailed a car to take us to the house, carrying the suitcase. "It looks very good on you, Ruth. I am so happy."

"I am happy you are happy, Doctor," I said.

"We will do well here," he said, helping me into the backseat of the taxi. "I know we have so many good years to look forward to."

"We shall have a family, Doctor, and soon," I said, smiling.

He smiled, patted my hand, and gave the driver directions to our new home.

Some people might say it was a horrible thing not to let Doctor know outright about John Robert, but I don't feel that's entirely true. I had taken care of my husband, I had soothed him, I had nursed him, I had shot his arm up with poison and dragged him across the mountains on mules to save his life. Those were things a good person would do. I had been a good person. But I knew that lying and tricking and faking was not something a good person would do.

But it was something a mother would do to protect her child and keep him safe.

And I was going to keep my baby safe.

I hadn't intended it to be that way, but that's how it became. I was terrified to say anything for fear of what would happen. I wore the loose dress and bought some dresses at the street market that were not structured and flowed around me. They were comfortable and cool and were brightened by colorful embroidery around the collar and sleeves that puffed in the most adorable way. I liked them very much.

We had a girl at the house to come in to clean and cook so I could rest and not get overexerted. She was a young thing, maybe sixteen, seventeen, and spoke a little English, but that was of no matter since I spoke Spanish. When I asked her name, she replied in English, "I am Beatriz." She did want to learn the language, though, so I have to admit that most of our days together were spent as teacher and pupil. The rest of the time, I went back to making clothes for John Robert; I still had those items I'd made before, stuffed at the bottom of a trunk that Doctor had brought back with him on his last trip.

This time, I didn't have to sew clothes out of old shirts or sheets; the market was close by and I bought yards of muslin and soft linen, even a bit of bobbin lace. Beatriz saw me gathering the fabric and needle, and helped me sew a couple of little baby suits and diapers. Her needle was so swift and she was a much better seamstress than I. She told me she had a baby brother who was about a year old and she would ask her mother if she could bring me some things. It was very kind of her, and she arrived the next day with a bundle of baby clothes.

I took them right away and buried them deep in the trunk.

The first pain came in the dark of the night, and I sucked in my breath but did not cry out. Doctor was sleeping deeply, and my jolt to consciousness did not wake him. I was reminded of my pneumothorax treatment, with a needle armed with that excruciating pain going into my chest and piercing my lung until it deflated. It was a suffocating, miserable experience.

This pain made me shrink inward, but as quickly as it came, it was gone. If it was what I was waiting for, there would be another and another. I hoped I had enough time until daylight.

It was earlier than I thought by almost a month.

I clenched my hands several more times as the shock of it came and went. Finally, Doctor got up to ready himself for work. When I didn't rise with him to have his coffee, I said I was tired from shopping the day previous and was going to steal a few more hours of sleep.

He kissed me on the forehead before he left, and told me to be well.

"Beatriz will be here shortly," I said.

"Have her make you a strong breakfast," he said.

I nodded just as another wave came in to grip my abdomen and twist it like a rag. Doctor did not notice my grimace and left for the day. I exhaled deeply, and in a little while I heard Beatriz come through the door.

I called to her right away.

She came in, gasped, and covered her mouth, and ran out of the room.

Another pain seized me, and this time, I did cry out, as loud and fierce as I could.

I wanted this. I wanted this.

Beatriz reappeared with an older woman by her side and patted my hand and dabbed the sweat off my forehead with a soft cloth.

"Soon?" I asked.

She nodded.

"Soon," I whispered again.

John Robert arrived in the afternoon, a couple of hours after midday. His body was small, but his cry was loud and I felt he roared like a lion.

I held him close, wrapped in one of the swaddling blankets Beatriz and I had made, my hair still stuck to my face with sweat. He was a small baby with a cap full of dark, swirling hair, and he was mine.

I had never felt that way before in my life and I never will again. My love for him washed over us both with a crested wave; I wanted every bit of him, to breathe him in and keep him close to me forever. We were bound together, lashed as one with strings of ferocity, devotion, and elation. In those moments when I first held him, there was nothing I couldn't do; I had the power to vanquish anything. I was almighty and indestructible, and he gave me that. I would give him love, keep him happy, and deliver to him the world.

I vowed it.

I was so tired I fell asleep after holding John Robert for as long as I could. It was a deep, rich sleep, full of the swirls of his hair and every bit of him that I had examined so well. He was an absolutely perfect baby, the one who I had waited for so long, the immaculate gift I was given to have as my own. He was flawless, born clean and guiltless. His cries were song to me, evidence of a beautiful little boy that would be mine forever.

When I woke, I reached for the baby right away, expecting him to be beside me. Doctor's side of the bed was empty, and I thought it was so sweet that he had taken John Robert to see the sunrise, to change him or feed him.

"Doctor," I called out, rising onto my elbows. My call fell into a silent house, no response but stillness.

I struggled to my feet, still weak and tired, and put on my dressing gown that was draped over the footboard of the bed. I was exhausted, moved more slowly than I wanted to, and finally got to my feet. I shuffled into the kitchen and saw Beatriz move past the front window and open the door, carrying a large basket.

"Oh, let me see that little marvel," I said, radiant with happiness, and reached for the basket.

Beatriz handed it to me and I pulled back the swaddling, eager to wrap his little fingers around mine, I wanted to touch him so badly. But there was no tiny, grasping hand. With the cloth pulled back, I saw a loaf of bread.

I laughed.

"Oh!" I said, putting my hand to my chest. "Oh my. I thought that was the baby."

Beatriz said nothing and shook her head.

"Where is John Robert?" I asked. "Does Doctor have him? Has he been fed?"

"Please go back to bed, Mrs. Judd," Beatriz said. "You are not strong enough to be walking."

"Doctor has the baby?" I asked. "Are they outside on the balcony?"

"You need to rest," Beatriz said gently, and took my hand to lead me back to my room.

"I really want to see John Robert," I said. "Then I'll rest."

Beatriz was silent, and we stood in that quietness together for what seemed like hours.

An icy feeling started in my stomach and then ran up my spine like a tongue of fire.

"Where is the baby?" I asked, to which Beatriz's silence continued.

"Where is the baby?" I asked again, firmer this time, in a tone that demanded an answer. *"Beatriz, tell me where the baby is!"*

"No se!" she cried back.

"Does Doctor have the baby?" I said, grabbing her arm. *"Did Doctor take the baby?"*

"No se, no se!" she said again, now looking frightened.

"Did he tell you not to tell me?" I yelled. "You must tell me where the baby is!"

Beatriz stood there trembling, her face awash with fear.

"Tell me where my baby is!" I screamed. I could feel my whole body on fire and my heartbeat pounding in my ears like rocks being hammered.

He could not have done it, the back of my mind raced. *He could not do this. Not again. This can't be. I won't let it be.* My whole body prickled with ice and flame at once and I began to sob.

I grabbed Beatriz's other arm and shook her in my raging panic; this was not real, this could not be true. This was a nightmare, nothing true could be this bad. I had not been this bad.

"You know where my baby is!" I shrieked as dug my nails into her wrists. "You must tell me! You must tell me! You must tell me!"

Beatriz pushed back, struggling to get her arms free. I tightened my grip on them and begged her to tell me what he had done with the baby. *Please tell me what he has done. Please tell me.*

The girl wrestled free and ran out the door, the basket of bread tipped over on the floor. I screamed and screamed and screamed until nothing more came out, and even then I screamed inside for hours, days, years, a century.

My screaming would never stop.

"You had a fever, Ruth," Doctor told me. "It was very serious. If Beatriz hadn't fetched me from the hospital, I don't know what would have happened to you."

"Where is my baby?" I asked him again and again and again, hoping that, just once, he would give me an answer, he would tell me the truth.

"You were very sick," he replied. "A very high fever. By the time I got here, Beatriz and her mother had you surrounded by ice, thank heavens. They saved you from getting worse."

"Tell me what you did with him," I demanded.

"You are not well," he insisted. "You must rest, or you will get worse and have to go back to La Vina."

"I want my baby," I repeated. "Where is the baby?"

"Ruth," he said with a deep sigh. "You were gravely ill. I need you to rest and focus on getting better. This obsession isn't doing you any good. It is harming you.

"Be a good girl," he told me. "Go back to sleep."

"If you want me to be well, give me my fucking baby!" I yelled. *"You monster!"*

He did not respond.

Wherever Doctor had hidden John Robert, he had hidden him well. When I was strong enough to venture to the market, I looked for him everywhere, I saw him in every infant, only to get closer and see he wasn't mine. A bald baby. An ugly baby. A baby with no hair swirls and a stubby nose. A baby that looked ruddy, like a potato. Terrible babies everywhere. My baby was nowhere.

Beatriz never came back, as I supposed Doctor paid her not to, afraid she would finally crack and tell me the truth. I had no idea where she came from; I had never thought to ask. There were a million girls named Beatriz in Mazatlán. No one seemed to know the one I knew. I looked for her face, and that of her mother's, but I never found them. Everything we had made for the baby had disappeared from the trunk as well. Only myself and Beatriz knew they were there. Traitor. She had told him. Betrayer. For a little bit of money, too.

The days pounded on. The smell of John Robert evaporated from my memory, but not after quite some time. Every time I asked Doctor what he had done with him—had he placed him with a different family, did he know the family, was it a good family, were they taking care of my baby?—he would pat me on the hand and make me a mug of warm milk. And then I would sleep, worn out by the awfulness of it all. He wanted me to forget, to heal the wound that had torn me open from the inside out. He wanted to erase it all.

"It was your baby, too," I let him know. "You did this to your very own son."

Those were very dark days. I don't remember any light. I stayed in bed most of the time, weeping, thinking, hiding. Trying to make sense of it, trying to understand why Doctor did what he did. Was I that bad that I couldn't be a real mother?

I was powerless, I realized. I had no money of my own. No resources, nowhere to go. And did I even want to go? What if Doctor had done this really believing it was for the best, that he had done it to rescue the baby from a sick father and mother? Was Doctor sick again and not telling me? Would he be going back to the hospital, leaving me with a baby to care for with no means of support? Had he sent the baby to be with Carrie?

I wrote Carrie a letter asking if she knew anything about John Robert and apologized for hiding the truth from her, explaining that I was afraid and unsure of what to do if Doctor found out before the baby was born. I had every right to be afraid. He took the baby away from me again.

I pleaded with her to tell me if she knew the whereabouts of my son, and if she did, could she help me get him back?

I mailed the letter in secret, pulled together whatever was left of me, and walked down to the market. In several weeks, she wrote me back, saying that Doctor had told her of my sudden illness and that my mind was working against me. She said he was worried, and that I needed a good long rest to get everything straight again. She told me to forget as best I could, and that soon, all would be well. If I wasn't going to get better, she said, Doctor had mentioned putting me into a hospital.

She did not say La Vina.

Doctor got notice in the spring of 1930 that the mine was closing and that he would have to find a new job. After the Crash, jobs—even those for doctors—were becoming more and more scarce. He wrote to Dr. Moore in Pasadena and inquired if he knew of any positions. During that time, I had tried to forget. I tried to erase that little tie I had with John Robert, but I couldn't help but wonder what he looked like now, if he was healthy, if he was a colicky baby or if he was a pleasant, happy child. In some moments, I did break down and sob and demand that Doctor tell me the truth, but he would say, "Oh, Ruth, dear. I only want the best for you," or get up and walk out of the room and bring me a cup of warm milk. I'd feel better for a little while and then drift to sleep.

Dr. Moore eventually wrote back and told Doctor that some new practices and clinics had opened up, but it would depend on how quickly he was able to get there. Financially, the state of the country was tight; the Crash had just happened six months before and it seemed like the state of living was tumbling off a cliff. Dr. Moore told him to get there quickly. Doctor didn't have a license to practice in California, so he would have to be an assistant until that paperwork was finished. We made plans to leave. I packed up our belongings, which weren't very many, and shipped the trunks to Carrie's in Santa Monica.

The day before we were due to take the train up, Doctor said we were going to El Paso first, where the Mexican trains connected with the American trains. I was confused and asked why we didn't take the train to California instead.

"It is almost summer, and I want you to go to your mother's while I get things settled and find us a place," he said. "There is not enough room at Carrie's, and with the state of things in the United States, it might be some time before I can find something we can afford. I won't be paid much. Spend as much time as you can outside so you don't succumb again. It won't be long, maybe a month, before I can get us situated in a place of our own. I've written to your mother; your parents are expecting you. I'll go with you to El Paso, and we'll each go on from there."

At the time, I was worn out. Just rubbed raw. My body felt heavy, my mind numb with distress. I agreed. I really did. Maybe being far away would help me think of other things and allow my head to ease. I didn't know how that would happen, but it might.

It might.

In El Paso, we waited at the train station saying little, which was what most of the journey was since we left Mazatlán. Doctor read a book; I don't know which one. I looked out the window and watched Mexico go by as the scenery became more and more desert. Palm trees became scrub and stubby cacti.

I did not want to go to Indiana. Of course, I wanted to see my family, but I recalled my most recent trip there with much disdain. But it was set, planned and paid for already. I was going. My mother was happy.

Doctor's train left before mine by several hours. We ate sandwiches and drank some hot tea.

I knew Doctor always wanted the best for me, even if doing something hurt him terribly or wounded me. I had begun to understand that although he had done a terrible thing, he did it with me in mind. Had my baby died, and he was too afraid to tell me? Too afraid that I would break, shrivel and die as well? Was the thought that he was out there and happy supposed to give me some sort of hope to tie myself to? Would Doctor send for him once we were settled in California? All of this had run through my mind like ticker tape, over and over, never ending. Did he cry over John Robert when I was asleep? Did he have contact with whoever had him? Did he visit a grave I was unaware of? Would I ever know what had happened to my baby?

After Carrie's letter and the mention that Doctor might send me to a hospital—an asylum, a nuthouse—I stopped asking because I would never find my baby if I was locked up. I told myself that someday he would tell me, when the time was right. I knew my husband well enough to know that if John Robert was alive, he was with people who loved and cared for him. If he was dead, I hoped that he was buried properly and had a headstone that was beautiful and engraved with angels' wings.

When Doctor's train was called, we rose from the stiff, worn wooden benches and walked to the platform together. Before he took the step up to the train, he looked around quickly to see if anyone was watching, and he wrapped his arms around me tightly.

"Ruth, know that I love you more than anything in the world," he said into my ear. "I want you to be safe. I want you to be taken care of. I want you to be well. We will be happy in California, you'll see. My love for you is great. It is the greatest thing I've known."

He pulled away, and I nodded with my face in his hands. For a second, it felt like nothing had happened, like everything had faded away and we had just been married and were boarding the train to New Orleans.

Oh, if I could only have that time back again. Just for a minute of it.

I nodded, and Doctor wiped a tear away from my eye with his thumb.

"I promise everything will be good again," he told me. "Please believe me. I am trying so hard to make that happen."

He kissed me on the forehead, and then kept his right hand cupped around my face for a long time until the whistle blew.

I watched as the train with my husband pulled out of the station and wished that I trusted his hope.

CHAPTER NINETEEN

Ruth

I met Lucy Ryder at a coffee shop right outside of the train station where Doctor and I had lunch only hours before. I was sitting at the counter waiting for my train to arrive when a pretty woman asked if the stool next to me was taken and I said no—it was suppertime, and the coffee shop was very full.

She arranged herself on the stool and smoothed her dress with her hand like a proper lady. I couldn't say I was dressed as nicely. I was not wearing my best dress; I wanted to be comfortable for the very long train ride ahead, as we could not afford a sleeper car and I would have to make do with the journey in front of me while sitting.

"Are you on your own?" she asked with a kind smile.

"Yes—no—yes, I think I am," I said, smiling back. It felt good to smile. I hadn't done it in a long time.

"Lucy," she said, holding out her hand.

"Ruth," I said in turn, and took hers.

"Ah, single girl?" she asked.

"No," I said, taking a sip of coffee. "I just saw my husband off to his train."

"Oh," she said, looking rather taken aback.

"No, no, no," I said, waving my hand a little. "I don't mean like that. I mean that I'm off to Indiana to see my parents and he's off to California to start a new job."

"Really? Where in California is he heading?"

"Los Angeles, Pasadena, around that area," I said. "We lived there before for a short time."

"You don't say?" Lucy exclaimed. "That's right where I'm headed!"

"Hopefully, I'll be there soon," I added. "My husband needs to find us a house and get things ready."

"I see, I see," she said, then ordered herself a coffee.

"Are you meeting your husband there?" I asked.

She raised her eyebrows and let out a tiny laugh.

"Oh, no," she replied. "Not married. On my own. I have a friend out there—she's been living there for a while—and she says it's just a lovely place. Right by the beach, and it doesn't get as hot as it does in Texas."

"That's very true," I said, nodding. "You really can't ask for better weather."

"We're going to start a beauty parlor," she told me, and then smiled to herself.

"Really?" I asked. "Just you and your friend?"

Lucy nodded. "It's very exciting, don't you think? I've been saving my money all year; my specialty is permanent waves. Yours are perfect, I noticed."

"That's very nice of you to notice," I said. "I've been living in Mexico; my husband was a doctor for the mines down there. Sometimes we lived in very small towns, or not even towns, really. I learned to do the permanent waves on my own. I'm afraid I'm not very good at it."

"That's nonsense. They look professionally done. I think you may have a gift for it, Ruth. I surely would have thought your hair had been done by a beautician."

I'm sure I blushed. I wasn't used to anyone ever commenting on my appearance in such a way.

"If you're heading to Los Angeles, I'm afraid you've missed your train. It left about forty minutes ago," I said sadly.

Lucy shook her head. "Oh, no. I have a car. Coming from Houston. I just stopped here for a break before I get back on the road again."

I looked at this young woman and admired her independence. "You aren't afraid to drive alone?"

"Well, I sure wish I had some company with me, but if it's just me, it's just me."

"When I get to California, we should meet," I said, being very brave. "I would love to have a friend in the area."

"I think that would be nice," Lucy said, and raised her coffee cup to her lips. "You sure you've never been in the beauty business before? Like I said, I think you'd be a natural!"

"I'd love to learn more. Maybe I'll take some classes. I've heard of cosmetology schools now."

"Yes!" Lucy cried. "Then you can come and work in my shop!"

"That is a grand idea," I agreed, and we both laughed.

When we stopped laughing, Lucy looked at me and lightly smacked her hand on the countertop.

"Come with me now," she said with a shrug. "I'd love the company; you're going to end up in California anyhow, so let's have an adventure!"

"Oh, I couldn't," I said, shaking my head. "I'm expected in Indiana. They are waiting for me."

"Indiana is boring," she said in a comical deep voice. "What are you going to do there except get bitten by mosquitoes?"

"No, no, it's impossible," I said politely.

"Indiana isn't going anywhere," she pointed out. "And why do you want to let your husband pick out a house? You have to live in it, too."

"Oh, I don't know," I replied. "I am going to miss the ocean. I have grown so used to it."

"Cash in your train ticket. You'll have enough for food, and we'll drive all day, so we'll probably only need one night in a motel. Have you ever driven across the desert?"

"I have," I admitted. "And during a revolution!"

"I like a girl who knows how to drive, and if you can drive with guns blazing, you're my kind of copilot!"

I sat there a moment and actually entertained the thought. Indiana made my stomach churn. Filled me with dread. Of course, I wanted to see my mother and father, but being subjected to all of those bad people was something I could not bring myself do to.

Crazy.

Fake.

Liar.

Dirty.

Crazy.

Fake.

Liar.

Dirty.

Why would you go into the woods with a boy, Ruth?

Oh, you are a crazy one, Ruth! Plain crazy!

Bad.

Bad.

Bad.

Bad.

"Yes," I said suddenly. "Yes, I will. Of course I will. An adventure. Yes. Yes!"

⸻

I sold my train ticket back at the station and put my suitcase into Lucy's backseat. It was an older Model T missing a fender on one side and looked like it had seen better days, like thousands of them.

"Don't let the looks fool you," Lucy said, noticing my survey of the car. "This gal's a champ! She won't let us down!"

With twenty-three dollars in my pocket, I got in, closed the door, and headed to LA with a woman I had known for an hour.

"Tell me about yourself, Ruth," Lucy said as she started the car and headed for the highway.

I thought for a moment, considering my options. I am tubercular. My husband is a doctor who is a narcotics addict. I've lived in Mexico for the past five years when I wasn't in a sanatorium or my husband wasn't in a sanatorium, and I can teach you how to do your laundry on a rock.

"I have a son," I said finally. "His name is John Robert. He is about to turn one."

<hr />

We drove as far as Deming, New Mexico, and stopped for the night. The desert was at its most beautiful, fresh from rains and blooming like crazy. It was still cool that time of year, but not cold, so we drove with the windows open as far as we could stand it as our hair whipped around under scarves. I dropped Mamma and Papa a wire that said,

Please forgive late notice but am joining Doctor in Los Angeles. Will explain more when I arrive.

Love, Ruth

I figured there really wasn't much to say aside from that. Anyway, it was too late. I was in New Mexico, and my train was well out of Texas by now. I must admit I had an odd feeling about the whole thing, as if the floor would just vanish at any moment. But then I realized I had never really made a decision like this on my own; Mamma and Papa always looked out for me, and then I was handed straight over to Doctor. I never had the freedom to do what it was I wanted to do, even if I didn't know what that was. John Robert just happened, I didn't plan it, but as it happened, I lost my voice in that, too. In what happened to my very own baby.

I looked at Lucy and envied her freedom, her ability to pack up her life and start somewhere new without asking anybody for permission. How I wished I had that. The luxury of being alone.

We started out for Tucson very early the next morning, and we talked the whole way about our new lives in Los Angeles and how we would make the whole city beautiful. She was a friendly girl, and I was amazed at my good luck, and being in the right place at the right time. I was on my way to becoming a beautician. At first I would be a trainee, Lucy explained, then I'd get my license and be a true professional. We talked about our uniforms, which would have to be plain white, almost like doctor coats. I laughed about the idea of Doctor and me getting ours mixed up. But, Lucy said, we could brighten them up with our names embroidered on the shoulder or wear brooches for some color. I was very much looking forward to it and found it far more appealing than marking up furs or working in the toy department, which Lucy just laughed at.

We got to Tucson before the sun set, spent the night in a tiny roadside motor motel, and then headed to Phoenix, where we would take the highway over to Los Angeles. Lucy thought we might make it to California by nightfall. I hoped it would take longer. I had never wired Doctor that I was coming, and I didn't want our adventure to end so soon.

Phoenix did not remind me of Mexico; it was hotter, and much dustier. Large modern buildings looked like they had sprung out of the desert floor, and were unnatural-looking, standing alone here and there on the dotted landscape. It wasn't like Los Angeles, which was organized and a real city where everything looked in proportion. This place was different. There was one building that looked a thousand feet tall, and I counted seven floors, topped with a spire of some sort, as big as the Broadway Department Store. This one seemed larger than the Broadway, stretching up against a cloudless blue sky and crowned with the gold brim of the sun like a halo. It was a hotel called the Westward Ho, and Lucy said it looked like a good place to stop and rest for a while. The lobby was grand, with large octagonal pillars reaching at least three stories high to hold up an elaborate Moroccan-style plastered ceiling painted in blues, greens, and yellows. The chandeliers were heavy black wrought iron, spiraling up, forming a large circle and then smaller ones. I wasn't dressed appropriately for such a fancy place, but Lucy grabbed my hand, walked straight past the reception desk across the tile floor, which matched the ceiling in color and pattern, and asked for a table for two.

It turns out that tuna salad is pretty much the same thing no matter where you order it, it just costs double the price when you eat it inside someplace decadently lovely.

"Wouldn't it be nice to eat in places like this for every meal?" Lucy asked, laughing.

"The consommé was fifty cents!" I said, laughing back. "That's as much as a movie ticket!"

"I wonder how many movie stars we'll see in Hollywood?" she asked.

"I never saw one the whole time I lived there," I replied. "Although I didn't exactly expect them to march into the Broadway and buy a doll."

Then we both laughed. We needed to get going again, so she paid the bill, gave the lobby one final look, and loaded ourselves back into the car.

Lucy turned the ignition and the engine made a whirring sound but didn't catch. She tried it again. The whirring struck up again. Lucy seemed undeterred as she got out and opened both sides of the engine hoods.

I got out and stared at it, too.

"Do you know what you're looking at?" I asked.

"No, but sometimes squirrels and mice get in there, and I know those when I see them," she answered.

"If you're staying at the hotel, it has a garage attached," a man who noticed our troubles said as he walked by.

"I'll go ask for a mechanic," Lucy said. "Maybe it's something simple that I can't figure out."

Fifteen minutes later, she came out with a fellow with terribly dirty hands. The heat had begun to make me perspire and I felt sticky.

"Well," he said after poking around a little. "I'll have to have it towed into the garage and take a closer look. Everything seems okay from here, but that doesn't mean anything, really."

"That would be wonderful," Lucy said, and handed him fifty cents and the keys. "If you wouldn't mind, I'd be very thankful. Is there a YWCA close by?"

"You're about two blocks south and two blocks east. Over on Third Avenue."

When he left to line up the tow truck, Lucy looked at me and said, "Get your bag. I think we're going to be staying a couple of days here."

I didn't mind. It was making our adventure last longer, I thought. We got a cheap room at the YWCA and waited for the car to get fixed. We saw *Min and Bill* at the movie theater a couple of blocks away and played several hands of cribbage before we went to sleep.

Lucy went downstairs to call the garage the next morning and came back to the room with a sour face.

"It's going to be another day?" I asked.

"No," she said. "It's going to be forever. I don't have enough money to fix it."

"I can help you," I offered.

"Ruth, neither of us has enough money separately or together," she said, frustrated. "I have to get to California. I have enough money for a train ticket plus a little extra for when I get there. What are you going to do?"

I didn't know. I thought and thought, but I didn't know.

I shook my head silently as she waited for an answer.

"But what about the car?" I asked.

"That's how I got the money for the train," Lucy answered. "I sold it to the mechanic."

"Oh," I said simply.

"You have an hour to decide, toots," she said, throwing her things into her cardboard suitcase. "That train leaves in an hour and I need to be on it."

I couldn't decide. I really didn't know. Right now, right this minute, I had a chance to be as free as Lucy. To make my own choices. To see if I could survive alone. After living my whole dictated life, I could build something here until it was time to go to California.

"I would see you to the train station," I said slowly, "but I should really save the taxi fare back. I'm going to stay. Just for a little while."

Lucy smiled. "Aw, Ruth," she said. "We could have had some real fun. But we still could, you know. Next time you come to Los Angeles, look me up. I'll give you a job."

"Thank you, Lucy," I said, and she patted me on the arm. "I am so happy I met you."

"I'm happy, too, Ruth Judd," she said. "I have to go."

She blew me a kiss, picked up her suitcase, and headed for the staircase.

I sat on the bed, folded my hands in my lap, and looked around. I wasn't sure what to do first.

Well, I finally thought. *I should probably see the matron for a smaller, cheaper room.*

CHAPTER TWENTY

Ruth

We had arrived in Phoenix in May, which was the beginning of blistering weather. And there was no breeze. In Mexico, there was a breeze,
but in Phoenix, it was stagnant and dry, almost as if any living thing
that stayed in one position too long might mummify.

The heat was a fever on the land that never subsided, even after
the sun set. People hung up drenched sheets over their windows, and I
went to bed in my rented room at the YWCA with a cooling wet sheet
over me. I believed the dry air would immediately increase my health,
so I reassured myself I made the right decision. But I needed money. I
needed to find work.

The next day, I took the streetcar to the new hospital to see if there
were any jobs, but they would only hire nurses. A gentleman there did
give me the address of the job registry, so I went there.

I learned that a family named Ford was looking for a live-in nurse,
and a fellow at the job registry let me use the phone. A woman answered,
and I asked for Mrs. Ford, but she said I had reached Mr. Ford's office.
I told her why I was calling, and she said yes, come to the office and he
will see you at three o'clock p.m. His office is in the Westward Ho, did
I know where that was?

I did, I said, I will see you then.

Mr. Ford was not a young man, but he wasn't aged like Doctor, either. He looked friendly but tired, and was wearing an impeccable tan linen suit. Walking to the hotel in the afternoon sun had flattened my hair a little and made my forehead bubble with sweat. I was wearing my nice wool dress but wished I had chosen cotton.

He explained the job to me; his wife was very ill with consumption, and he had three children to tend. Was I able to care for the children and his wife as needed?

I told him my husband was a doctor, about our times at the mines and my job at the hospital in Indiana. I wasn't afraid of tuberculosis, and had been treated for it, but I was now recovered. I knew the disease, I told him; I knew what a person with it needed. I knew only very sick people could pass on the disease, and I wasn't nearly as sick as Mrs. Ford. The children would be safe around me.

That must have satisfied Mr. Ford, because he called his wife right then and told her he was sending me over. He gave me the address and a nickel for the streetcar fare and thanked me for meeting him.

I took the trolley to 514 West Lynwood Street, in what I was to discover was one of the finest neighborhoods in Phoenix. It was a beautiful house, a new brick bungalow with a wide, low porch, and big front windows to let the air in.

The maid answered the door and showed me to Mrs. Ford's bedroom. She was completely bedridden. She was another who had contracted the disease; her room was in the far back of the house, away from the children to keep them safer. There were three children, she told me; twelve, nine, and six.

"I can't do much for my children anymore," she said, "but you look like a sweet girl who could take good care of them." The pay was eighty dollars a month with one day off a week, preferably Sunday, and my own room off the garage. I moved my things in at the end of the week.

It was a family place. The sounds of children playing rang out all day long, until the sun began to set over the rows of newly planted palm trees that lined the street and the lamps suddenly flickered bright. Every time I heard a baby laugh, the sound echoed, bouncing off the walls in my heart. I do admit to tearing up and weeping once or twice.

I wrote Doctor and told him of my change in plans, and how a wonderful opportunity had turned out a little bit different than I had hoped. I told him about Lucy, driving into New Mexico, on to Tucson and Phoenix, and what a jolly time we had. Things had turned toward the worst, but I was making the best of it. I would stay here for a little while until he felt it was time for me to join him, and then I would become a hairdresser when I reached Los Angeles. I signed it "Yours, Ruth."

The Ford children really weren't much work at all. They were nicely behaved, and played often with the little girl next door.

On my first day working for Mrs. Ford, I cut the fullest, pinkest bloom on the rosebush, which continued to thrive despite the oppressive weather, with hearty daily watering. It was lovely in the small crystal vase that I found in the breakfront. I arranged the tray with a doily topped by a delicate china bowl that caught the exact shade of the rose in the pattern around the rim.

Mrs. Ford only took two spoonfuls of the chilled tomato soup before she sank back into her pillows. She was exhausted and warm, with no relief from the heat except for a small electric fan, which she found more irritating than helpful. She brushed me away with her hand and tried to focus on something else besides the agitation caused by the unrelenting temperature.

"Summer will be here so soon, Ruth," she said, exasperated. "Would you mind if we went through the children's wardrobes today? They'll be needing new things for the season and we should donate what they won't use anymore."

I nodded, and Mrs. Ford directed me to start with James's clothes first; he would be the last of the Ford children, so whatever he had grown out of was no longer useful.

"Think of all of those families now that have nothing at all," Mrs. Ford said. "These clothes can help them, certainly."

She called Rosa, the maid, to the doorway and asked her to bring the children's clothes in to her.

"Of course, Mrs. Ford," Rosa said, and then left the room, returning minutes later with a heap of children's clothing in her arms.

When I held up the most elegant baby dress of gossamer cotton with hand-stitched lace around the collar, Mrs. Ford couldn't help but be struck. She remembered her last child, her infant son, in it when she could still hold and care for her children. When she could still nuzzle them without worry and deeply inhale their perfect fragrance without fear of spreading her disease to their flawless little bodies. When she was still a mother.

But it was I who suddenly burst into tears.

"Why, Ruth," Mrs. Ford cried, reaching forward to touch my arm.

I shook my head and covered my mouth with my hand, tears running over my fingers.

"Please tell me," Mrs. Ford implored, concerned over the sudden outburst. "Whatever is the matter?"

I struggled for breath and my crying slowed a little. I had surprised myself with the suddenness of it all.

I shook my head again; I wasn't sure whether to force the words out or keep them in.

"I just—" I began, then emitted a small cry and drew in a large breath.

I paused, wiping the streams of tears from my face, and took another breath.

"It makes me miss my own baby," I finally blurted.

Mrs. Ford was stunned.

"You have a baby, Ruth?" she asked softly.

I nodded. "I have a son," I told her. I was trembling slightly, my face still red and streaked. "A baby boy."

"I didn't know, Ruth," Mrs. Ford said after a pause. "I'm so sorry."

I nodded, trying desperately to wind everything back together, to push it away and calm myself.

"John Robert," I said. "But I can't have him with me here until my husband finds a steady job and we can all be together."

"Where is the baby, then?" Mrs. Ford asked. "Who looks after him?"

I looked down. I didn't know what to say.

"My parents," I lied, which somehow calmed me. "In Indiana. I had to leave him behind."

Mrs. Ford nodded, her lips tight with sympathy. "I do understand the ache of it," she said quietly. "Of being a mother unable to care for her child. We have much in common, you and I."

I looked downward, my hands crumpled in my lap atop the baby dress.

Mrs. Ford looked at me for a moment and said, "It is hard enough only being able to talk to my children from the distance of the doorway; but I can't imagine being thousands of miles from them, not being able to soothe them when they cried, or missing the moments when they cooed with happiness."

I said nothing but held my breath tightly inside me, too afraid to let anything out.

"I think you should take some of these baby clothes," she said. "Send them on to Indiana for John Robert."

"You're too kind," I finally said. "I couldn't."

"I insist," Mrs. Ford said with a smile. "If your baby can use them, by all means, we should send them!"

"Thank you so much, Mrs. Ford," I replied, gathering several pieces of clothing. "I'll post them tomorrow."

The following week, I am sure Mrs. Ford blanched when Rosa, the maid, showed her. I was in the hallway when Rosa brought her the whole basket and said she didn't touch a thing, but saw it and took it in right away. The maid recognized it instantly, the fine cotton, the beautiful stitching on the lace collar, shoved all the way to the bottom of the wastebasket and covered up with trash to hide it. She remembered Mrs. Ford's little boy in it.

The beautiful little baby dress, tossed away, pushed all the way down, as if it were just a rag.

CHAPTER
TWENTY ONE

Jack

From his bedroom window, the Fords' next-door neighbor noticed the striking girl at their house. Their new governess. He was intrigued by her fresh beauty, enormous dark eyes, vitreous face, and opaline skin. She often sat on the front porch to watch the Ford children, her perfectly waved hair impervious to the long, sweeping gusts of her linen fan.

As a lumberman who had a thriving business despite the financial crash the previous fall, Jack Halloran liked to decide things. Phoenix was shedding its rugged trappings of a western saloon town, and although the economy had crumbled, construction—for now—was not slowing as other businesses had. Due to its status as a health destination for the tubercular, new residents continued to flow in. But the frontier ethic— heads turning to close backdoor deals; fingers pulling strings to grant favors—held in full force. There was a brotherhood in charge, and those powerful few ran the town behind closed doors.

That selected coterie included Jack Halloran.

He had a nice wife, two older children who were creeping into their teens, and a little daughter named Susan who he and his wife had adopted after finding an infant in the passenger seat of his car with the note "Here's your baby. You take care of it" pinned to the blanket that swathed it. His wife picked the baby up and never asked a question. Neither did anyone else in town.

In the sweltering months, Halloran was a summer bachelor, who, like many other men of his prominence, sent his wife and daughter north for the summer, beginning in May. The laboring classes, as well as invalids, like his neighbor Mrs. Ford, had to struggle through months of vindictive heat that turned all of Phoenix to brittle and bone.

Local working girls who had no husbands to put them on a train stayed behind in the grit and the sweat, relying on their ingenuity to devise distracting entertainments. These were the lively and beguiling local women Jack and his friends called the summer wives.

As the new Ford girl swept the small fan back and forth—looking beyond the lawn of the house, beyond the unblemished, newly poured cement curb, beyond all that was in front of her—he realized that she was waiting for something.

She looked thirsty, he decided.

He brought her a cold glass of iced tea in the warmest hour of a brutal, merciless July day.

Her name, she said, was Ruth Judd.

She was a beautiful girl, perfect, spectral, and breakable.

CHAPTER TWENTY TWO

Ruth

Doctor sent me a package that held a letter and a little box of candy. It would not be long before he could come to join me, he wrote. He just needed to earn a little money first to get us a nice place to live.

At the bottom of the package was a small item wrapped tightly in flannel, and when I took the fabric off, I saw it was the pistol from Mexico. "You should have this," he wrote in a note attached to the handle, "a woman all alone in a strange place."

A woman all alone in a strange place. Was that what I was? That night I settled into my small bed with a pillow so flat it felt like a napkin, and I thought of how wonderful things could have been. I pictured Doctor playing with John Robert on the floor of a living room with curtains made of lace, and the phonograph playing a happy song. I saw my baby gurgle with joy, Doctor laughing, too, and our nice family, happy, warm, and together, and I thought about it so hard I burst out in tears. I was soaking with them, and soon, not even the thoughts of us listening to the phonograph could soothe me. It was too much.

I tried to make myself feel better by holding the beautiful dress Mrs. Ford had given me, and imagined my baby in it, but I was overwhelmed with sadness and I could not find one single cheerful thought. The empty dress became something full of sorrow and so grievous that I could not bear to hold it in my hands for even one more second. It was searing me with grief. I left my room and entered the kitchen, where I stuffed it down into the trash, far down, to the bottom, so that I would never cry over that dress again.

I spent my Sundays outside of the house on Lynwood; I could take a streetcar downtown so I often did, to see a movie or do some window shopping, even though most of downtown was closed on Sundays. It was good to have some time by myself. On one of those Sundays I ran into Mr. Halloran, the Fords' nice neighbor. He was just coming from a meeting at one of the hotels downtown, he said, and asked me to join him for lunch at one of the little drugstore counters down there.

He was not a stranger to me; I had talked to him many times during my stay at the Fords' and I knew him to be a nice, considerate gentleman of good reputation. He was respected. Mr. Halloran was one of the few people who had even spoken to me since I came to Phoenix. I found him to be kind. So I said yes, I would join him for lunch.

We sat right at the counter on those stools that swiveled a bit, just like the place where I met Lucy. The drugstore was mainly empty except for the people who worked there and Mr. Halloran and me. I ordered a turkey sandwich. The lettuce was a little wilted, but otherwise the sandwich was good. I didn't want to make a fuss.

Mr. Halloran—Jack, as he asked me to call him—was very kind to ask how well I was getting along in the Ford house, and I was honest. I said they were good people but that sometimes I did get a little lonely. I told him I liked working for the Fords a great deal, but I wasn't making enough money. I was grateful to the Fords for giving me a place to live, but I did want my own apartment.

Jack asked me what it was that I wanted to do. I don't recall anyone ever asking me that question before. I told Jack that I enjoyed working at the hospital, and that was where I met my husband. Jack asked me if I had looked at the new clinic on McDowell Road. Grunow, it was called, across the street from the new hospital. I didn't know of it. The next day, Jack said, he'd make a phone call. He knew the fellow who owned it, and would see if there was a position that would be good for me. He was sure he could help me, he said, and that the clinic would pay far better than the Fords.

I was so grateful, and when the ticket came for lunch, I did not pull out the fifty cents I had planned to pay for my turkey sandwich. I would not like Doctor to know that another man had paid for my sandwich, even a nice man like Jack, but he had been so kind and kind to me. I didn't dare insult him.

I didn't see Jack for several days after that, and, with that silence, understood that there was nothing for me at the clinic, either.

The Fords were good people. They welcomed me into their home, and this position would do for a little while. I loved the children, and that's really what made me stay. Rosa was difficult to get along with. She would not talk to me; I tried to speak to her in Spanish and tell her how much I loved living in Mexico and that I hoped someday Doctor and I would go back. I told her the dishes I made and what a beautiful life we had there. She didn't want to listen, and I thought perhaps she was homesick for Mexico, too.

As I was returning from walking the children to school one afternoon, Mr. Halloran came out of his house to say hello.

He had good news, he told me. He had called the man at the Grunow Clinic, and he said that, right away, as soon as I could manage it, a doctor there wanted to see me about a job.

PART THREE

Sammy and Anne

CHAPTER
TWENTY THREE

February 1930

The girl the orderly rolled into the X-ray room was so weak and frail Anne could almost see through her. Suddenly, the tiny body lurched forward, erupting into a cough that shook the gurney and rattled it like bones in a jar.

The girl's face bloomed scarlet.

Anne rushed forward and steadied her, trying to keep her sitting as the fit racked her lungs. When Anne looked up, the orderly had vanished, happy to deposit the young girl, maybe twenty-three or twenty-four, into her care.

The coughing finally quieted after a minute or two, but the girl's eyes teared at the pressure of the hacking, and Anne couldn't help but feel a rush of pity toward her.

"You won't burn me, will you?" the girl said, droplets now running down her face. "I knew someone who was burned in one of these machines. You will be careful, won't you? Please don't burn me!"

Anne had seen this panic many times before, and it was not misplaced. With careless training and a machine with inaccurate settings, patients could be injured. The radiation burns were brutal and painful, as if the patient had leaned over a blazing stove; she had once seen

X-ray burns so extensive the skin became charred, bubbled up, and then peeled away in sheets that exposed raw flesh.

"I've been working on X-ray machines for years," she said, trying to soothe the girl. "And this one is my best friend. We know all of each other's secrets and habits. We fit better than my oldest pair of shoes."

The girl looked at her doubtfully, but her panic had eased.

Anne smiled at her. "My teachers trained me too well," she added. "I can't even burn toast in this contraption. I've tried! But it does make an excellent grilled cheese sandwich."

The girl broke into an easy smile.

"Does it also warm up soup?" she asked.

Now Anne laughed. "I'll tell you what," she said, helping the girl off the gurney and onto the X-ray table. "After your X-ray, how 'bout I cook us up some lunch? I keep my cauldron in the supply closet."

"Since we're in the middle of an Alaskan winter, I'm inclined to accept," the girl said as Anne positioned the machine over her lungs.

The day after Anne LeRoi arrived in Juneau, Alaska, at the beginning of winter, a brutal blizzard dropped three feet of snow in the span of two days; the roads were treacherous enough that only delivery trucks were allowed on them. Anne skidded and slipped the four blocks to St. Ann's Hospital, determined to arrive on time for her first day. She had thirty seconds to spare, after she ran up the three flights to the X-ray room, the ice and snow that clung to every part of her melting in a trail.

She did not care. She was out of Portland, Oregon, and beginning again in this faraway gold-mining town, and she felt untouchable. At thirty-one, she had married once and divorced. Then married a second time and divorced. No trouble, just the wrong fit, she supposed. She even kept the middle name of her last one—Leroy—as her surname because she liked how it sounded.

Anne LeRoi. A little French. A little sophisticated. A little unexpected after such a plain first name.

She had a new name. All she had to do was create a new story behind it.

And that's what she had come to Alaska to do.

Her last story had ended with four bars of purple bruises finally fading around her arm and her leaving her apartment in the blackest hour of the morning. She'd bought a ticket for a steamship headed north with her rent money. She couldn't forget the words the chief doctor had thrown at her, hitting like a bullet.

"Remove yourself from the premises at once, Miss LeRoi," he had yelled, loud enough for the whole ward to hear. Nurses, patients, all of them. "You should be wary. But I already knew what you were. *Degenerate.*"

She had only defended herself when he questioned her work, he, the chief of the hospital, unable to properly read a simple X-ray. But she had not expected the rawness, the volume, the exposure.

Within a moment his hand was curled around her upper arm, his compressed fingers squeezing so tightly a thread of alarm shot through her abdomen into her jaw. Suddenly he shoved her violently away and demanded that she leave. It was not about her work, and she knew it. She had heard the rumors about the time she spent with a nurse on the floor below hers. There had been whispers, and Anne had refused to address them. That had been private, secret, tawdry. She chose not to feed the allegations by adding to the volume.

But the moment she stepped off the boat in the harbor at Juneau, her past melted from her like snow on a warm coat. She went to the hospital immediately, leaving her one suitcase at the front desk. After Anne demonstrated that she knew what to do with an X-ray machine, the head radiologist replied that they'd be happy to have her, and didn't ask for a reference.

That was lucky, Anne thought. She didn't have one to give.

The coughing girl on the gurney was in for an extended stay at the hospital, under strict confinement to bed as the symptoms of pneumonia continued to rack her fragile frame. When she passed by the girl's ward on the second floor, Anne would duck in to give a wave and a smile. The ward was long and sterile; two rows of chipped white iron beds lined each side of the hall, though there were not enough to absorb the sound of clinking medical instruments on steel trays or the whimpering of a patient overdue for a painkiller. It was a dire place, orderly, static, and lacking hope.

The thought of the girl spending endless hours in her bed by herself, bound under the white sheets, nagged at Anne. There was no harm in chatting a bit; it might help pass the time for her. It was either that or they'd sit in beds by themselves, Anne told herself, the girl in her ward and Anne at the Alaskan Hotel, where she was still living, paying by the week for a room with a sink. They could both use the company.

"You still owe me a grilled cheese sandwich," the girl said the first time Anne stopped by her bed after her shift was over, and she laughed. Anne laughed, too. The girl's name was Sammy, short for her last name of Samuelson. Anne thought that suited her. Sammy was a friendly, electric sort of name.

"And your given name?" she asked, to which the girl rolled her eyes.

"Hedvig," she replied with a defeated sigh and a giggle.

"That is quite possibly the most Norwegian name I've ever heard, Hedvig Samuelson," Anne chided, pulling over a worn, pocked wooden chair from the next bed. "Are you sure you're not the captain of a fishing vessel?"

Sammy rolled her eyes. "Personally, I think it sounds like a skin condition," she said with a laugh.

She was clearly improving; she was no longer the frightened, pitiful patient Anne first saw in the X-ray room. Her wavy golden hair was neat and smooth in a stylish bob that rested just below her chin. She had more color now, Anne noticed, and her cheeks had filled out a little. Her eyes had risen from the sockets they were starting to sink into, taking their natural form, which was wide, bright, and delicately sloping at the sides, making her appear wise and childlike at the same time. Sammy, she realized, was a beautiful girl.

In full health, Anne imagined, she'd be lovely.

Anne noticed the rattle of her pneumonia was not as deep as it had been, and within a month, it had trailed off into a manageable, almost regular cough. She was rising back to life, Anne thought, from a near corpse into a bubbly, shining girl. She quickly became Anne's favorite hobby, and Anne delighted in checking in on her, staying until the ward closed to ensure that the girl was never lonely, being the first visitor in before she started her shift. Anne brought a deck of cards, and the two played vigorous rounds of gin rummy until visiting hours were called and Anne was shooed away.

Anne first enjoyed Sammy's company, then savored it. Longed for it. She was bright, witty, funny, and, as she improved further, could be wicked.

"Do you see that nurse with the mole on her cheek?" she whispered to Anne from behind her cards one night, nodding at the woman sitting behind the nursing station down the corridor. "I am fairly certain that there is some hanky-panky going on with the ward doctor. I've caught them in several 'knowing glances.' I believe he pinched her bottom once. Or twice."

"Ooooh, how tawdry!" Anne whispered back. "And to think they look so respectable!"

"I believe they rendezvous in the laundry room. Every time she takes a clean sheet off of a bed, she's gone for an hour."

"Hmmm, maybe he's helping her fold," Anne replied with a stifled laugh as the nurse looked their way and stared for a moment.

"I'll say he is," Sammy said under her breath, and then they both burst out laughing, and the nurse left the ward in a huff.

This move, this place, Anne thought, *it was right for me.* Never mind the moth-eaten room she called home, or that she hadn't made any friends in Juneau yet except one. That the snow piled up like she had never seen it before, like miniature mountain ranges made from sugar. That some mornings, her teeth chattered until they ached, and that the meals included in her rent at the hotel were just a level above slop. None of that concerned her.

She was comfortable here, and oddly content.

It was only the thought of what would happen when Sammy was released from the hospital that gave her a chill.

Night after night, Anne laughed at Sammy's stories of her students at the Juneau elementary school where she had been teaching before she got sick: which ones were allowed to run about like animals and acted the same way in her classroom, which ones tried to butter her up for grades they had not earned, and which ones wanted to learn and work at something better than swinging a pickax in a gold mine like the generations before them. The boy who had lost his father in a mine explosion and was pulled out of school to work at the dairy because the family needed the money. Sammy tutored him and his brother when they weren't working, hoping they wouldn't fall too far behind when they were able to return to school, even though she knew they probably never would.

In turn, Anne divulged her own name change, her attempts at marriage and at a traditional life.

"I don't think I was meant for that sort of thing," Anne said, drawing a card from the pile and discarding a seven of clubs. "I tried twice. Both perfectly nice men; it just wasn't right for me. I'll be a spinster after all."

Sammy scrunched up her nose and playfully hit Anne on the leg. "That is absurd. You're young, nice, and pretty. It will happen."

Anne shrugged. "I really don't think I want to get married again. It seems I'm not very good at it."

Sammy let out an exasperated sigh. "I'm not talking about marriage," she said as she laid down a set of spades and hearts. "Rummy! I'm talking about love."

Two years ago, Sammy told Anne, she had answered an advertisement for teachers that promised good pay and free housing. She didn't hesitate to answer, despite the protests of her insistent fiancé, Howard, who was precisely why Sammy was answering the ad in the first place. She had said yes to his proposal only in a moment of mercy; Howard had laid his feelings bare and, in a wave of benevolence and charity, she had agreed, knowing already that it was not what she wanted.

In the summer of 1928, Sammy landed in Juneau, in awe to discover that her new home city was built into the side of a towering mountain. Wooden staircases linked one level to the next. On Main Street, at the base of the precipice, the architecture was a mix of Victorian and newer buildings dating to after the Great War, bay windows peeking out from second stories and facades topped with intricate molding and cornices. In this monumental, narrow valley, hugged on one side by the mountain and laced at the other by the sea, she felt hidden.

She felt released.

She treated her first winter like a warm, restful hibernation, reading the stash of books she had collected, immersing herself in lesson plans, and organizing indoor activities for recess. If the roads were clear, the other bachelorettes from school would join her for supper and a couple of rounds of bridge. Before long, it seemed, spring had arrived and Sammy could finally feel the warmth of the sun on her skin.

In the fall, she got sick, just a cold caught from one of her students with a perpetually runny nose. She'd improve, then relapse, growing sicker. By January she was weak, fighting a fever that spiked like an alarm every afternoon. She just needed rest, she protested to her friends, even as they helped her to a neighbor's car and drove her to the hospital. And then the confirmation that yes, she really was that sick.

Later, when she was feeling improved and boastful, she bragged to her friends that she had an X-ray of her lungs. She saw right through her skin, she described, straight to the ribs, then even further into the deepest part of her.

I, she told them proudly, so proudly she almost had to whisper, have seen my own heart.

And I think, she added, it looked full.

<hr />

When Sammy's pneumonia had cleared enough for her to go home, Anne clasped her hand and told her it was wonderful news.

"I still can't return to school, I'm too weak for that right now," Sammy continued.

"I agree, you need as much rest as possible before you are turned loose to those little heathens," Anne told her. "Give it a couple of weeks, and you are going to be amazed at the difference in how you feel."

Sammy opened her mouth, about to say something, and then closed it.

"Sammy?" Anne said, looking at her quizzically.

"Have you found a place to live yet?" Sammy quickly blurted. "Or are you still at the Alaskan Hotel?"

Anne laughed. "I am, actually. It's small, a little dingy, but it's affordable, and I get dinner there, too. It's not really dinner. I've never really been sure what exactly it was I was eating."

"I have a house," Sammy continued, and then caught herself. "It's not big, it's not fancy, but it is in town and not only do I need the company, but I'd like it, too."

"Oh, I don't think—" Anne began, and Sammy immediately interrupted.

"Don't feel obligated," she interjected. "I'm sure it's not the most inviting proposition, taking care of an invalid in an awfully tiny house! Don't worry, I do understand. That was very forward of me."

"Oh, Sammy," Anne replied, and then laughed heartily. "I was going to say I didn't think there could be a better idea!"

They both smiled, Sammy giggled a bit, and then Anne gave her the grilled cheese sandwich she had just gotten from the diner next door.

Anne moved another little bed into Sammy's bedroom and hung her two day dresses and her uniform in the closet. Evenings, she cooked dinner, then helped Sammy into the living room and settled her comfortably, warm by the fire. They drank tea and tuned in to radio mystery plays, *Sherlock Holmes* their favorite of all. Sammy read letters from lovelorn Howard aloud and in a dramatic radio-play fashion that Anne sometimes felt compelled to act out, and they would fall over themselves, laughing.

Sammy, dear Sammy. Anne would take care of her forever, just to be near her. The companionship was something that Anne had craved. She had never found it with either of her husbands; she'd had nothing in common with them. The evenings she had spent with the nurse in Portland, even if those hours felt truer than anything she had ever known before, were not this. In Sammy's company, she had found something worth defending.

She dearly longed to lift Sammy's chin with her hand and hold her cheek next to her own, just for a moment. Just for one moment to be that close to her. To risk anything more would be disastrous. She could not ruin Sammy in the way she had already ruined herself. Sammy was too loved for Anne to put that word upon her. *Degenerate.*

If that was what Anne was, if that was what was said of her, she would take it. She would suffocate under it. But she would not bring it to Sammy, who had done nothing wrong, who in her sweetness had in no way encouraged Anne.

She had already lost so much more for so much less than the touch of cheek against cheek.

One night, as Holmes solved his latest crime, Anne looked over at Sammy, curled up in a blanket, the flicker from the fire dancing behind her in shadows on the wall, Sammy's eyes softly gazing off into the distance, her lips turned into the most perfect, slightest smile.

Years from now, Anne thought, *I will remember this moment in our tiny, flawless world, and understand what happiness was finally like, and that I felt it. That I held it in my hands and it belonged to me.*

━◆━

When she was sure Sammy was up to it, Anne surprised her with a little vacation for the summer. Just a brief cruise to Vancouver and back, nothing grand.

The first night, heading south from Juneau, Sammy and Anne snuck out of the ship's dining room before dessert service and had the whole western-facing deck to themselves. They watched as the sun dropped slowly into the ocean, leaving swaths of red, orange, and pink ripples in the wake of its departure. The ship was sailing slowly; the currents of fresh air blew gently against them and fluttered Sammy's bangs over her forehead, making her look even younger and more girlish than she was. The last light from the horizon reflected on Sammy's face, making her almost golden. Sammy looked back at Anne and smiled, then softly slipped her small hand into Anne's, and kept it there for a long, long while. Anne felt everything inside her swell to the point of bursting. She felt her eyes turn hot and then blur. Wrapped in an embrace of hope and comfort, for the first time she could ever remember, she knew she was loved.

Did she know what this meant? Anne wondered. Did she know what people would say if they knew, once they discovered the wrong in them? Should she tell her?

In the next moment, however, Anne pushed all of those thoughts as far away as possible, dropped them right into the ocean, and instead tightened her grasp on Sammy's thin, sweet hand.

The day after they returned from Vancouver, Anne found Sammy in the bathroom, slumped over the tub with the water running. She borrowed a neighbor's car and raced Sammy to St. Ann's. She thought back to their time on the ship, about the sudden onset of Sammy's sweating during the night, and the ache in her joints. She had willfully attributed those to the change in climate.

Anne took the X-rays herself and passed them over to Sammy's doctor.

"I think you should do a sputum test," she added, and waited with shaking hands for the results.

Regardless of her suspicions, she felt a jolt in her bones when she heard them.

"You have tuberculosis, Miss Samuelson," the doctor told Sammy quietly, Anne holding her hand tightly. "I suggest you get to Phoenix for immediate treatment."

Sammy stared blankly back at the doctor, and Anne read her thoughts all too plainly.

Tuberculosis. Consumption. The shadow of death. Known as the corpse disease, it was infectious enough to wipe out entire families. Both Anne, in her hospital work, and Sammy, in the school population, had witnessed how the disease broke a body down, first tearing at the lungs and then traveling like a stain over every remaining system. The suffocation. The bones. Joints growing thick with suffering. The muscles. Hemorrhaging. Draining the life out of its victims in sparse increments until there was nothing left but a coughing, shuddering shell, even the muscles in the face atrophying, the slighter parts of the jaw hovering over the teeth, settling into a final grimace. There was no cure, only treatment. Sanatoriums were known as the waiting rooms for death.

Get to Phoenix, their doctor told them. Dry air. Latest treatments. It's your best chance.

Friends of Anne and Sammy's from the school and hospital collected two thousand dollars for their passages, first a cold, wind-whipped ferry to Seattle, followed by the train to Southern California, then across the dusty bleached desert to Phoenix.

The specialist at Good Samaritan Hospital, Dr. Randolph, examined Sammy thoroughly but quickly, checking off all the signs he was looking for. Then he turned to Anne.

"I can make sure that both of you are in the same ward," he told them gently.

"No, no," Sammy interrupted. "I am the one who's sick. Anne is fine. Anne is not ill."

The doctor stood quietly for a minute.

"Miss LeRoi, you are flushed, and the spots on your cheeks have not dissipated in the time you've been here. Have you had X-rays done?"

"No, that's ridiculous, I'm an X-ray technician," Anne said, almost laughing at the poor diagnosis. "I don't have symptoms. I'm fine."

"Please submit to an X-ray, at least," the doctor said patiently. "Just to be positive."

Anne nodded, and Sammy put her hand to her mouth to quiet her sobbing.

Anne's consumption was likely just beginning, the doctor continued; it was now barely discernible, but in the right climate, she would be spared treatment because it was detected so early.

The girls looked at each other, and Sammy took Anne's hand. She held it so tightly both hands turned white. They both knew how Anne had caught it.

CHAPTER
TWENTY FOUR

September 1930

After a week of diligently scanning the *Arizona Republican* newspaper,
Anne found a rental ad for the empty half of a duplex at Second Street
and Catalina less than a mile from the hospital where Sammy was getting treatment. The yard was barren, just a large plot of silky dirt that
whirled into tiny tornadoes when the wind swept in, and it was one of
four houses built on an otherwise empty street. But that barely mattered
to either Anne or Sammy; they just needed a place to live for now. The
house was new, just finished, and the fresh rooms welcomed their first
tenants with their scant belongings.

Anne set up two twin beds in the room toward the back of the
house. Two walls full of windows made it brilliant with sunshine and
would aid in Sammy's recovery. The windows swung open and let the
dry air in during the day and the honey-scented desert breeze at night.
Sammy was not doing well, but Anne reminded herself that they had
only been in Phoenix for a week and it would take time for Sammy's
shabby lungs to heal.

The trolley stop was one block away from the house, the hospital
mere minutes away, if Sammy got worse—and that proximity was what

Anne had in the forefront of her mind as she handed over her deposit and three months' rent.

They were, without a doubt, facing an unsteady future. At least they were taken care of for the next three months. They'd have a place to sleep, for Sammy to recover while Anne looked for a job. It hadn't been easy. She had made inquiries every day since their arrival, but was met with a picture that looked bleaker by the hour. Because the pink blush on Anne's cheeks had vanished almost upon their arrival, she was at a loss to explain her inability to find employment until a nurse pulled her aside.

"All of the jobs go to men, even if they aren't as qualified as women looking for the same work," she said to Anne in a whisper. "They have families to feed. Been like this since the Crash. If I were you, I would start mentioning that you have children."

"But I don't," Anne replied.

"I'd suggest you find some fast," the nurse advised. "Otherwise, you're the last rung on the ladder."

Anne nodded. It was up to her to keep them afloat. Sammy was still too ill to get out of bed some days, let alone find a job. Her treatment was going to be both more extensive and expensive than either of them had initially believed. The fear of not being able to pay for it nested in Anne's stomach like a stone. With no money there would be no treatment, and the only solution would be to admit Sammy to a sanatorium, which everyone knew was a death hotel. It was a thought she couldn't imagine, let alone bear.

"I can get some children," she said to the nurse. "Do you know of any place that would be willing to hire a mother with a hungry family?"

"The Grunow Clinic is about to open. At McDowell and Tenth," the nurse told her. "I would get there as fast as you can. Before a man walks in with a hungry family of his own."

Anne and Sammy sat in the doctor's office, waiting impatiently for the results of the tests Dr. Randolph had run. The room was chilled and terrifyingly quiet, aside from the whistling from Sammy's breaths.

"It's going to be fine," Sammy whispered after a while, squeezing Anne's hand as they sat side by side on a wooden bench so worn it looked polished.

Anne turned to her and gave a tight smile.

"The doctor's going to say that you are fine," Sammy insisted. "You look so much better already."

Anne nodded, but her own health was not the thought that weighed so heavily on her. Although they had only been in Phoenix for a short time, Sammy had not improved, not even by the smallest increment. Anne's fear was that the doctor would reveal there was no hope of any recovery; that Sammy was so ill she was beyond healing. It was a future that Anne didn't want to face, the vision of it turning the heart of her into a hopeless, vacant vacuum.

When the door opened and Dr. Randolph walked in, Anne instantly wished him away. She wanted one more moment before her world turned bleak and empty. She didn't want to understand how sick Sammy was, she didn't want to give the illness any more of either of them than they already had.

Instead, the doctor cleared his throat and stood in front of them like a minister about to deliver a sermon. He began with Anne.

"Mrs. LeRoi," he said. "Your improvement has been remarkable in the short time you've been here."

Anne almost emitted her nervousness as laughter. Instead, she nodded. "I felt no symptoms, so I'm not very surprised to hear you say that."

Dr. Randolph looked at her and shrugged slightly. "Had you stayed in Alaska, your condition would have become much more apparent, and quickly, too, I would think."

"I'm much more concerned about Sammy's condition," she interjected. "She doesn't seem to be getting better at all."

Dr. Randolph was undaunted by Anne's sudden outburst. "I'm afraid Miss Samuelson needs a great deal more care than you do, Mrs. LeRoi. Her degree of illness far surpasses yours. Had you not arrived when you did, I'd think that the outcome would have been quite dire."

"But now that we're here . . . ?" Anne asked.

"I think there's hope for Miss Samuelson," he said, and Anne finally exhaled a bit.

Sammy smiled. "I hope you're right, Dr. Randolph. I'm anxious to get back to Alaska and my students."

Dr. Randolph looked at Sammy as if she hadn't heard him.

"You can't go back to Alaska," he said bluntly. "We will get you well here, and it will take extensive treatment and some time. But Alaska, no. It's out of the question. You'd relapse within a week of your arrival. Your condition is poor, Miss Samuelson. Very poor. I want to stress that to you. You need to live in a dry climate, like Phoenix, not only to heal, but to sustain good health—for the rest of your life."

Both Sammy and Anne were stunned.

"But our friends are in Alaska," Sammy stuttered in protest. "Our home, our jobs. I'm tutoring students there who need me."

"You won't be much good to them in a wooden box," he pointed out. "If you go back to that climate, I'd give you a year."

"Oh, Sammy," Anne said. She had suspected this might be the case, but clearly, Sammy had no idea how ill she really was. Anne's only wish was to get Sammy better, while Sammy had hoped to be well enough to return to the life that had just been pulled from them.

Sammy looked at Anne and saw her lack of shock. She understood then that Anne had known how sick she was but had never told her.

"What is our next step?" Anne asked, bracing herself for even more terrible news.

"Pneumothorax," he continued. "We artificially collapse the lung to let it rest and heal. The injection of air into the intrapleural space closes tubercular cavities."

Sammy bit her lip and Anne reached for her hand.

"It's not without its discomfort," he admitted. "But it really is the best and newest treatment. You'd need a weeklong stay in the hospital for monitoring. It's your best option."

"Yes, we should do this," said Anne, pasting a comforting smile on her face to hide her mounting panic.

Sammy was waiting in the hallway when Anne gently tapped the doctor on the arm.

"I'm an X-ray technician by trade," she told him. "And I'm looking for work. If you hear of anything. Anything at all."

The doctor nodded, then moved into the hallway. "The treatment for your sister will be costly, Mrs. LeRoi."

"Sammy is not my sister," Anne corrected, then immediately regretted it.

The doctor nodded again.

"We can come to terms," he said, then began to walk away before Anne touched his arm and stopped him.

"Do you know anyone at the Grunow Clinic? The one that's just about to open?" she asked.

Anne put on her plainest day dress, smoothed her hair, and then walked the block to the trolley.

The Grunow Clinic was just finished and, much like her duplex, sat on a bare plot of dirt that had yet a single hint of green growing on it. The kind of dirt that pours from the hand like water. It was a grand building; ornate bas-relief friezes stretched across its Spanish Colonial Revival facade, replete with intricate stone carvings, elaborate and elegant. Anne walked up the three steps to the front door, and was impressed by the sweeping, open lobby that mirrored the exterior of the building with its stonework stretching up two stories, topped with murals and golden windows that let in the afternoon light gracefully.

In what was clearly an attempt to ensure payment for his services, Dr. Randolph had given Anne a phone number and she then arranged for an appointment the next day. The clinic was the first of its kind in Arizona, she was told, a collective space where doctors and medical treatment were accessible separately from a hospital, with Good Samaritan directly across the street.

She didn't waste time in telling the director of the X-ray department what machines she was proficient with; when she mentioned the model she'd worked with in Alaska, his eyes opened wide.

"We just ordered that very one," he told her, with an approving nod.

"It's a reliable machine," she told him. "It's fast, safer for patients, and produces clean, clear images."

"That's good to know," the director replied.

"It has been difficult to obtain a position since I came here to aid with my cousin's health," Anne didn't hesitate to say. "I know that positions are in short supply, but I assure you I know this machine inside and out."

"Thank you, Mrs. LeRoi," he said. "I will let you know as soon as possible when we are ready to fill this position."

"I'm a widow," Anne lied. "With three children and my cousin to feed."

The director stopped, looked at Anne sympathetically, and said, "We wouldn't need you for six more weeks until the clinic opens. And there may be times when you'll have to stay until all the patients are attended to. I can't officially offer you the position until the machine arrives and I can see how well you perform on it. Do you understand? I need to make sure you can do what you told me you can do."

"I can accept those terms," Anne said quickly before he could add any more caveats. "When the machine arrives, I will be happy to show you my qualifications."

Anne left the building with a lighter step, still nervous, but she sensed a slight thread of hope.

PART FOUR

Ruth

CHAPTER
TWENTY FIVE

November 1930

Sometimes, riding in a car was like riding a horse at a full, wild gallop.

The horizon was endless and broad, streaked with hues of oranges and reds that faded into purples and blues ripping across the sky as if someone had just dragged a paintbrush over it. A bank of clouds crested upward like waves in a downy row, framing the view with what resembled lashes of feathers. The mountain range that surrounded the valley was shadowed, turning it into a border of deep amethyst.

The sun was a golden, twinkling star that hovered over the landscape like a guardian, producing the kind of light that is so magical and consuming you just become part of it, blending and melting until it all shimmers, inside and out.

Everything fell away in that Packard convertible as Jack drove through the desert on the newest paved road out of Phoenix with no other care around coming or going. It was just us. It was silent as I sat up on my knees, holding on to the windshield and the side of the car, the wind blowing, turning, running through my hair as I lifted my face up toward the sun, catching the last rays that were beaming at us. I closed my eyes as he drove on, farther and farther, as far as that road would go. I could smell the desert, sweet, fresh, dry, breathing it in as deeply as I could in this ethereal moment.

My hair whipped around like a meringue, and I didn't care as the long, sleek nose of the car sliced through the air and it flew over us, soft and smooth like an embrace that has been longingly anticipated.

I felt so free. I felt so free. I felt so free, wanting to ride to the end of the Earth.

I had never felt like magic before, but there it was, in the passenger seat of Jack's car, my head lifting, my whole self smiling.

I could keep it like that for always as long as I never opened my eyes.

I never wanted to leave that moment and would remember it forever.

We were standing in the front yard between the two houses and I had just come from taking laundry off the line when Jack asked me to dinner for the first time.

I asked if his wife wouldn't mind.

"Of course not," he laughed. "We're celebrating your new job at the clinic! One neighbor helping another. What is there to be jealous of?"

"Oh, I don't know," I said, feeling a bit embarrassed. "Just checking. And I don't have the job just yet."

"But you will! Where would you like to go?"

"I hardly know Phoenix at all," I stumbled.

"That's all right," he said. "I know everybody."

"I've only been to the Westward Ho, but that was for lunch," I said. "It was awfully expensive. The consommé was fifty cents."

"Then I bet it will be a dollar for dinner," he said. "Let's go slurp on expensive soup. Wear your best dress. When is your next night off?"

"Sunday," I replied.

"Then Sunday I will pick you up on that corner at seven p.m.," he said, pointing to Fifth Avenue.

I didn't have a best dress to wear, exactly, but wore my newest one that showed the least wear. Even though I didn't have to pay for food and rent, I was trying to send some money back to Indiana because I'd heard from my brother, Burton, that Papa wasn't doing too well and their bills were piling up. Ministry was not an occupation known for reaping great profit. We had lived simply when I was a girl, but our town was beginning to shrink, with the younger people off to cities to look for jobs. There was basically little you could do in Indiana for work during the Depression but beg if you weren't a farmer, and even they were in terrible spots. What little I could afford to put aside I did, and I sent it to them monthly to help them out.

To make up for my lacking dress, I did my hair very carefully, waving it and making it smooth as glass. Not one stray hair. I put on a little face powder and some rouge on my cheeks, then a little on my lips. I didn't want people at the Westward Ho thinking that Jack was taking his maid out to dinner; a distinguished man like that should be seen with a lady who took great care with herself. If he knew everybody like he said, he was sure to meet someone there who knew his name.

I waited at the corner at seven as he told me to do, but he came around from the opposite way, right behind me, and then honked the horn in a playful way. When I turned around I saw his face drop a little, and then I became very embarrassed; I had done too much.

Then he smiled bright and wide and said, "Oh, Ruth. Do look at you! I don't know when I've seen a prettier girl!"

See, that was the thing about Jack. He was always there to liven things up, to make you laugh, and to make you feel like there was nothing in the world that could touch you when he was right next to you. I felt electric when I was next to Jack, a buzzing inside my chest that I could not control, and everything was light and sensitive to the touch. The buzzing got stronger and more powerful the closer his hand got to mine, the nearer our legs were to one another, the way he would lean over and whisper something into my ear and make me smile.

When I was with him, I felt very much alive, almost wanting to explode and let out all of this life that had been bottled inside me for so, so long. At times, it was too much to bear and I wanted to laugh boundlessly, crazily, uncontrollably. I had never felt excitement like that before; it was as if I had just been plugged in and told that this was what being alive meant.

No, I had never felt that way with Doctor. He was a kind man and that's what was most important to me. That he was good, gentle, did not raise his voice all the time. He was made happy, or at least satisfied, with little effort. I never cared about making Doctor laugh.

But I wanted to make Jack laugh all the time.

I burned for it. I wanted him to know that I was smart, knowledgeable, valuable. That I was distinctive and interesting, that I was a whole person. I wanted him to ask me questions, and I wanted even more to answer them.

Yes, I told him, I was married, I was not a widow. I told him about Doctor trying to secure a permanent position in Pasadena or Los Angeles, and the time we spent in Mexico, and how we escaped the revolutionaries.

I did not tell him about Doctor's illness, or mine. I did not tell him how Doctor could not keep a job and kept breaking into medicine cabinets. I did not tell him that to get over the mountains while escaping the revolutionaries I had to stick a needle in my husband's arm to keep him as quiet as possible. I did not tell him about La Vina. I did not tell him about John Robert.

I wanted him to know me as a happy, bright, enchanting girl who had never shed a tear in her life. Whose story had been one delightful turn after another and would always continue to be that way. I wanted to be perfect for Jack. I wanted to be unbroken.

So when he reached out and took my hand that night after dinner, I let him. His fingers were slim, strong, the hands of a man. And the next Sunday, after he took me to the cinema, stopped the car a block away from our houses and leaned over, cupped my face into that hand and came in to kiss me, I did not stop him. I was never going to stop him.

I wanted it.

I took it.

CHAPTER
TWENTY SIX

I started working for Dr. McKeown on Armistice Day, a holiday that Doctor took very seriously, of course. While it represented the end of the war, it also signaled a new beginning for the world, and that's how I saw if for me, too.

I was to be a medical secretary, typing patient histories from the doctor's notes, managing the telephone messages, making appointments and receiving patients as they came in, and keeping the books. I enjoyed the work, and was talking with people most of the day, so much so that I often had to take the histories home with the typewriter and work on them at night. That was fine; it kept me busy when Jack wasn't visiting, as he only came by several nights a week.

Jack had helped with the rent money on my new cottage apartment at Eleventh and Brill Streets, unit C. I had my money saved, so I only needed a little bit. It was a new little Spanish-style stucco apartment that looked just like a real house but smaller, sharing a courtyard with the apartment next door, which was attached by one wall of the bedroom. Two steps guided by a black iron railing led up to the door, with small dark-wood awnings over every window topped with red tile, like in Mexico. I even had a doorbell. The apartment had a full but small kitchen, and a brand-new icebox and a two-burner gas stove. I had four kitchen cabinets and two drawers, plenty for me. Mrs. Ford had an actual refrigerator, but I couldn't expect something that fancy in a little place like this. It was all mine. I had never had a place to myself before, and it came furnished, so all I had to do was unpack. It felt like a little dollhouse. I was thrilled. I even had my own telephone.

I had already written to Doctor to tell him about my move, so he was expecting it, and I explained every detail about the new apartment to him. I told him I was very busy, bringing home my work every night to catch up. I was also packing up Dr. McKeown's office, as we were moving to the Grunow Clinic in a couple of weeks' time. My new place was so close—only about three blocks away—that I could walk and even come home for lunch. I saw it almost every time I went somewhere, and the building was so grand and stately. It had a Spanish feel to it, like so many of the missions I had seen in Mexico. It had beautiful plaster work with scrolls, Moorish arches, and rosettes and black wrought-iron lamps on either side of the matching double doors. I would be making seventy-five dollars a month—less than I was making at the Fords', but I would have every night to myself and a whole extra day with Saturday. I wrote to Doctor that maybe someday he could get a position there, knowing that was an impossibility. I would never try to make that happen. If I did, he'd lose his job and I knew I would, too. Doctor could not keep his fingers away from opening the doors of medical cabinets.

On the nights that I wasn't working, Jack would drop by or visit if he had time or wasn't at a business dinner and showing his clients a nice time. He ran O'Malley's, a hardware and lumber supplier that was one of the largest in Arizona, so he was very well known in political and social circles. Imagine that! A "social circle." I had no idea what that was until Jack explained that it was the most important people in the city, all of the bosses who knew how to get things done and did it all their own way. If you knew the right people in the right places, he told me, you could make anything happen. Or make it go away.

He was the only person I knew socially in Phoenix, so I never minded when I heard the Packard pull up in the gravel outside the apartment. In fact, I waited for it, sure that every time I heard a car drive up it was him. I'd run around the apartment trying to make everything nice and perfect. I tried to keep it very tidy at all times because I never knew when he was coming over. Sometimes he'd show up late at night after he'd been drinking with people in the social circle. He never asked me to go with him, and that was all right. I knew why. He was a married man, and I was a married woman, after all. It wouldn't look right and he didn't want people getting the wrong idea.

But of course they wouldn't get the wrong idea. They would be right thinking that two married people were spending the time together because it made them feel good and happy and it was not like anything else they ever felt before. With any other person. It made the world shine, it made colors brighter, it made smiles bigger. It made everything so beautiful, made it all delicious. I hadn't known how fine the world could look, because I had never seen it that way before. It was always so regular. And Jack wasn't regular. He made everything as bright as a spotlight.

So that's why, I suppose, I didn't stop things when he came to kiss me again. Jack close to me brought a kind of magic that fell all over everything, and I liked that feeling. I wasn't ready to let it go. I wanted just a little bit more, because however much I got, it was going to have to last me the rest of a lifetime.

I couldn't bear the thought of going back to a life without it.

⟶✦⟵

I could not get the time off of work to go to California for Christmas, with Dr. McKeown moving offices the next week into the Grunow Clinic. I was busy up until the afternoon on Christmas Eve, packing up files and instruments, wrapping them in gauze the way Doctor did. The movers had already come for the furniture and the medical equipment, and we were tying up the remnants of the things we needed up to the last minute. Dr. McKeown let me go at three to start enjoying my holiday, but there was no holiday to be had. It was going to be a quiet night; Jack, I was sure, would be spending it with his wife and daughter. I had no plans to see him.

At seven or so, I had changed into my pajamas and was writing a letter to Mamma when I heard the wheels on the gravel, but paid it no mind. My next-door neighbor was a friendly single girl who often had visitors. But I knew this set of tires in the gravel was for me.

A knock came at the door, one, then two in quick succession. It was Jack's knock. I didn't know what to do; I was not dressed or prepared for him to come over. I reached for my robe, put it on, then cracked the door a little so he could only see my face.

"I heard there was a girl from Indiana here with no family of her own to spend Christmas Eve with," he said, with his trademark smile that looked a bit impish.

I just stood there, too embarrassed to let him in but wanting desperately to let him in.

"Oh, Jack, I'm in my pajamas, I didn't expect you," I said, trying not to let him past the door. "I'm not dressed."

"What color are they?" he asked, suddenly serious.

"What color are what?" I replied in turn.

"The pajamas," he said.

"They're pink," I said. "With a little lace collar."

"Then I think that's perfect," he said with a nod. "Now let me in before your Christmas Eve dinner gets cold!"

I still don't know how he got away from his house that night; probably mentioned the social circle and that he had to do some business. But here he was, at my door, with a large paper bag in his hands.

I laughed and opened the door. "Oh, you didn't, Jack!"

"Oh, but I did, of course I did," he said, and came into the house. "Let's see what the Westward Ho thinks is their very finest dish. Get it while it's hot!"

I had lobster that night for the very first time. Jack showed me how to twist the tail—he said that in fancy restaurants, you're supposed to cut it elegantly with a knife, but to heck with that and we should use our hands with brute force—and also crack the claws with what looked like a nutcracker, which he pulled from the bag, then reach in with a thin fork that was also in the bag, pull out the meat, and dip it in golden melted butter.

It was like eating velvet.

We laughed as the lobster squirted out what I hoped was water, and then Jack took the claw and pretended to pinch me with it. It was all wonderful.

He brought champagne, which I hadn't had since my honeymoon, but this one was crisp and sweet and not bitter the way I remembered it. *This is why people drink champagne,* I thought. The tiniest bubbles burst and tickled my nose, and I laughed more. And I got happier. And I felt like warm honey inside, and everything was soft and shimmering wherever I looked.

Jack swept me up in his arms and kissed me, and I'd never felt so safe before as I did in that moment. My robe slipped off, and I kissed him this time. It became dark, darker, darker, and I felt the back of my head touch the pillow on my bed. Time slowed down; every second was surreal and was stretched like taffy. The kisses lingered, quiet and warm. I fell into a flawless abyss, a lovely dive into resplendent delirium.

We are the only ones, I remember thinking, *the only ones who have ever known this kind of purity, this moment of confluence.* I had never known this kind of peace before. No one else could have ever known it, because they would have stayed there forever and never reemerged.

On Christmas Day, I lied to Doctor for the first time. I wrote to him that my eve had been unremarkable and consisted of me drinking hot chocolate and reading a book. But it wasn't. It was the most spellbinding thing to happen to me in my life aside from John Robert. I could not erase it from my mind and did not resist playing it over and over in my head, touch by touch, second by second. I became consumed with it that day, wondering how something so marvelous and entrancing could have ever happened to me. Could this have been my whole life if I had waited a little bit longer and not married Doctor so young? I knew in my heart that what connected me and Jack was not ordinary, it was not regular, and that somehow we would have found each other if I had not been so hasty in taking that step with an older man who had secrets. When we were together and even apart, he was what kept my heart beating, my lungs breathing, my legs walking. We shared an invisible tie to each other, a cord or rope that bound us, from deep within me to him. He made me feel so electric and so necessary, but at the same time it was dreamlike and imaginary, like swimming through clouds of ether.

I never felt that way with Doctor, and I am ashamed to admit it. There was never an ember that burned so fervently within me when I thought about him. I did care for him and I did love him, but I never felt so bound to him that I knew I couldn't live without him.

I did not like lying. It made me want to squirm out of myself.

It made me bad. And I knew I could never atone for such a horrible thing. I would pay for this. Someday, it would come.

And Jack came over later that night, after midnight, and, wearing my pink pajamas, I took his hand softly, and led him to my room.

When the Grunow Clinic opened on January 2, 1931, it was a spectacle rarely seen in Phoenix. It was the first time doctors had their offices under one roof—there were thirteen of them—and the clinic included a laboratory and an X-ray clinic. There was a ribbon-cutting ceremony with a hundred or so people gathered on the sparkling new steps to watch.

I met Anna Stevens that day, the medical secretary to the doctor across from Dr. McKeown. After the festivities were finished up, we went back to our offices and began to get ready for our first patients to arrive.

"I'm Anna," she said after opening the door and poking her head in. "I'm across the hall working for Dr. Feeney. Does your office take a lunch break at noon?"

"I'm Ruth Judd," I said, standing up behind my desk. "Nice to meet you. Yes, noon is our break, we close for half an hour."

"Lucky for us there's a coffee shop on Tenth and McDowell, a block from here. Would you care to join me?"

"I'd be delighted to. I eat at that place all the time," I replied. "They have a good tuna salad. Yes, I'll meet you in the lobby at noon!"

"Perfect," Anna said, and then closed the door.

The morning was so busy I lost track of time, with the phone ringing, patients coming out and in, and trying my best to keep up with the histories. It was Dr. McKeown who came into the office and told me to go and take a break. He also had a suggestion.

"I know you can't do shorthand, Ruth, but I think it would really help both of us with these cases," he said. "I've heard of some classes you can take. I think you should go."

It struck me a little odd that he was bringing this up; he had never been dissatisfied with my work before.

I smiled and I nodded politely; after all, I was able to learn Spanish fluently in a relatively short span of time, and I didn't see how shorthand could be any different.

On our block-long walk to the coffee shop, I asked Anna if she knew shorthand and how difficult it was to learn.

"Oh, it's not hard," she said with a laugh. "You'll have it down in a couple of months. It's two or three nights a week, I can't remember. You'll pick it up in a snap!"

Three nights a week, I thought, feeling very sour on it, and I didn't know how I would pay for it. What if Jack wanted to come over that night—what if I wasn't there? He liked surprising me, and we didn't have a regular schedule; he arrived with his one knock followed by two quick ones, announcing that he'd been able to break free from his house or that a business engagement was over and he wanted to see me.

I loved that he wanted to see me. It filled me with so much joy that it poured ever.

When we opened the door to the coffee shop, Anna exclaimed happily, "Oh they're already here!" and proceeded to introduce me to three women who were already sitting around a table.

"This is Ruth Judd, Dr. McKeown's secretary," she said as the women moved their chairs closer together to make room for us. "And, Ruth, this is Mary Jenkins from Dr. Abbott's office, Bea Barton from Dr. Schroeder's office, and this is Anne LeRoi, from the X-ray department."

I shook hands with each of them, saying, "Nice to meet you," after each one.

I kept a smile on my face and listened to everyone talk about how exciting it was to work for such a new and wonderful place. It would be on the front page of the afternoon edition of the paper, one of the girls said, complete with a photograph of the ribbon cutting.

While Anna, Mary, and Bea had lived in Phoenix for a while, Anne was another newcomer.

"Where are you from?" I asked her as we finished our sandwiches—tuna all the way around.

"Oregon mostly, but really, I feel like an Alaskan the most," she said. "I just moved here from Juneau with a friend to improve her health, and we miss it terribly."

"Alaska?" I marveled. I had never even thought that girls like Anne—girls like me—even considered going to Alaska. It seemed so distant and rugged. I thought of gold miners and igloos.

"What made you go to such a wild place?" I asked, but then Anna tapped her watch.

"Five minutes to get back to work, ladies," she said, so we paid our bills and hurried back to Grunow.

I ran into Anne LeRoi later that afternoon as we were leaving the clinic for the day.

We greeted each other with a smile, but before I knew it, I blurted out, "So Alaska? Really? What was it like?"

"Oh, it really is a marvelous place, if you like snow!" she said, laughing, as she walked briskly to the streetcar stop on the corner. Even though I was supposed to be going the opposite way, I kept up with her steady pace.

"How did you end up there?" I asked. "Did your husband get a job there?"

Anne laughed loudly. "I'm not married," she said, looking behind at me. "But my streetcar is here and I've got to get on. See you at the clinic tomorrow?"

"Of course," I said. "I'll see you then."

That night, during Jack's visit, I lay next to him in the bed and told him about the oddest thing I'd heard that day.

"A girl in my office lived in Alaska!" I said, my fingers intertwined with his. "Have you ever heard of such a crazy thing?"

"Oh, Ruth," he said. "Women are everywhere. Otherwise there would be some pretty dull places."

"I know, but Alaska!" I marveled. "With icebergs and polar bears! I can't imagine what I would do there. It seems so dangerous."

"And fighting with revolutionaries wasn't dangerous?" he said, laughing.

"I didn't *fight* them," I corrected him. "I *ran* from them."

"On a mule over mountain ranges with the dead all around you," he said, kissing me on the forehead. "That takes a miracle of a woman. *Alaska*. Sheesh! Just a bunch of snow if you ask me."

I smiled and I laughed. And then I kissed him back.

Several days later, I looked up from my typewriter after I heard the door open and saw Anne LeRoi standing there with a bright, friendly smile on her face.

"I heard you're a single girl here in this new town," she said to me. "I told my friend Sammy about you and she wanted me to ask you if you play cards."

I smiled back. I had not noticed how handsome Anne was during lunch, there was so much going on and new people to meet. She had definitive features that were all perfectly proportioned and together presented as striking. Her hair was the lightest brown, and she was slim, but with bright eyes and a strong jaw that didn't detract from her features but framed them all together in the most flattering way. She looked like someone who could be very determined, but her rose lipstick and delicate curls gave her a soft look.

"I love bridge and cribbage—and rummy. And hearts. I love hearts. It's my favorite," I answered.

"Well, I don't know if you have plans for supper tomorrow night, but we'd like to invite you over," she said. "Please say yes. Sammy is desperate to meet new people."

"That sounds lovely," I replied. "I accept!"

"That is wonderful," Anne said with a clap of her hands, and her smile got bigger. "Everyone around here is married and has families. It would be nice to meet someone our own age, like us."

"I haven't made very many friends, either," I admitted. "But I am married. My husband is in California working."

"It's so hard to find work anywhere," Anne said. "I had to tell the gentleman who runs the X-ray clinic that I had children! Otherwise, I wouldn't have gotten the job. It would have gone to a man."

I nodded. I had not told Dr. McKeown about John Robert, but then again, I had Jack to help me.

"What line of work is your husband in?" she asked me.

"He's a doctor," I said. "Hard to believe, but even those jobs are hard to come by if you're not established like our doctors are."

"Maybe they'll have a spot for him here?" Anne suggested.

"Maybe," I said, trying to look hopeful. "I keep my ears open!"

Anne paused for a moment, and the look on her face made it clear that she was trying to decide whether to tell me something.

"I need to let you know," she began, picking her words carefully, "that my friend Sammy has consumption. Now, I know that it's very contagious, but she is recovering and is not active. She had tests done several weeks ago to confirm that. I don't want to frighten you."

"I've been very ill with tuberculosis myself," I confessed. "I nearly died."

"Is that why you're here in Phoenix?"

"Partly," I said. "I had rather a fateful landing, you could say. I spent several months in Pasadena at a sanatorium there. I'm recovered now, but the dry climate is best."

"I also have TB," Anne confessed. "But it's very mild. It looks like we arrived in Arizona just in time for me. Sammy, though—she's getting better but it's been very hard. She was a—"

A patient opened the door and came in, and Anne looked flustered.

"How does six sound?" she said quickly.

I nodded.

"It's an easy address," she said on her way out. "2929 North Second Street. See you then!"

With that, Anne LeRoi slipped out the door, and I checked Dr. McKeown's next patient in.

CHAPTER
TWENTY SEVEN

The house at 2929 North Second Street was a quaint little bungalow, a bit of a combination of Spanish and Tudor details; it was an odd-looking little place. The gables were hipped, but arches appeared here and there; one was the entry to the duplex on the opposite side of Anne and Sammy's. It sat on a barren dirt lot without a single living thing on it. It reminded me again of Mexico, but a bit more desolate.

Other houses dotted the street, some finished, others under construction. I was always surprised when Jack mentioned that the lumber business was brisk; who could afford to build a house these days? Then again, the clinic had just opened, funded by a wealthy philanthropist and named after his daughter, Lois, who had died as a child.

I stood on the porch and knocked; it was getting a little chilly and the desert cold could cut you right in half. With no moisture to cushion the lower temperatures, the cold sliced at you and made you shiver in a way that five below would in Indiana. In Phoenix, it only needed to be in the forties to come after you and shake you by the shoulders.

Anne opened the door to a warm, cozy living room with a fire roaring in the brick fireplace. The house was fairly new, but almost everything in Phoenix was fairly new. It was a baby boomtown. You'd never see a house from the Civil War times or earlier along any of its dry, brittle roads. Here, it was old if it was considered Victorian, built only twenty or thirty years ago.

I'd brought some muffins I had baked last night with things I had in the house: pumpkin and cinnamon. I wasn't much of a baker, never was, but I hoped as I handed them to Anne that they would be passable.

Anne took my coat and laid it across the arm of a maroon mohair sofa with a low back and wide, curving arms trimmed out in oak. It was a lovely piece. The whole place seemed very warm and homey. I felt comfortable immediately.

"Sammy, Sammy," Anne called toward the back of the house. "Come meet Ruth. She's just arrived."

Anne turned to me. "Poor Sammy. She's been on bed rest for months now and you're the first new person she's met in quite a while. She wants very much to make a good impression," she said in a quieter voice.

I heard light footsteps in the hallway and from the shadows emerged a beautiful girl, taller than I was but with lovely dark hair, bouncy with curls, and an opaline complexion that was accented with the red flush of consumption. She had full lips, warm eyes that sloped the smallest little bit and made her look kind and gentle. I liked her instantly.

Anne introduced us, and Sammy immediately took a seat in the sofa's matching chair. I came around and sat on the couch.

"Now," I said, slapping the palms of my hands on the tops of my legs, "I want to hear all about Alaska."

The girls, as I began to call them, were wonderful company. They relayed all about their time in Alaska until Sammy got sick and they had to move south.

I was amazed at what a devoted friend Anne was, uprooting her entire life to help a friend in need. That told me so much about her. Only a gentle and good person would do such a thing. Of course, I had pulled up stakes many times for Doctor, and when I recounted those moves all across Mexico for the girls, I realized how many times I'd had to start over. It was not a surprise to me then that I wanted to stay in Phoenix. I felt stable there, and very accomplished that I was building a life for myself, one brick at a time. A new apartment, a new job. New friends. And, of course, Jack.

But Doctor was my husband, and I'd almost always gone wherever he went, until now. A wife follows her husband; that's the rule. But for a friend, even a devoted one, to move across the country with a friend required a very big sacrifice.

"How many children did you say you had?" she asked me the first night I had dinner at their house on Second Street.

"None," I said quickly, and then added, "with me. I have a baby that lives with my mother in Indiana."

"Do you really?" Sammy asked, leaning forward. "A baby? Boy or girl?"

I nodded quickly. "Yes," I answered. "John Robert."

"Do you see him often?" Anne said with a sympathetic look.

"No, not as often as I'd like," I replied. "With my husband in California and me here . . . well, being with my mother is the best thing for him."

"How old is he?" Sammy asked.

"Eighteen months," I said simply.

Sammy reached out and softly took my hand.

"I can see that pains you a great deal," she said. "I am so sorry."

"I am, too," Anne said. "I know I invented my children, but Sammy and I do love babies. We each have nieces and nephews."

"We would love to meet him one day," Sammy added.

"That would be nice," I said, and tried to smile. "Would you like to see a photograph?"

Both girls excitedly said they did.

I pulled a small photo of Mrs. Ford's youngest child, James, which I had taken with me when I left. He was chubby and full, with wide, dark, gorgeous eyes, wearing a little straw hat that was almost comical.

"He looks just like you!" they squealed.

"Do you really think so?" I asked, and I smiled.

I saw Anne with much regularity at the clinic; I had to bring many patients to her for X-rays, and felt very comfortable telling them, "You are in very good hands. Anne is the best X-ray operator you'll find!"

We often had lunch together, maybe two or three times a week, and when we couldn't afford to go to the coffee shop, we'd walk over to my little bungalow on Brill and I'd make us omelets or tuna sandwiches. It became sort of a habit after a while, and we started planning out our entire week of which days we would go where and what we'd have. Sometimes Anne would bring something from her house, sometimes we'd make something in my kitchen, and on paydays we'd hop over to the coffee shop for something special. Having lunch at my apartment saved us a lot of money, and it was no secret that we were all struggling with paying bills. We were truly happy with our jobs, but it was clear that the men in the clinic made almost twice as much as we did, and I don't mean the doctors. I mean the lab employees or the fellow who was an X-ray operator right along with Anne.

Likewise, the girls and I saved more money by eating together almost every night at their bungalow; Sammy wasn't able to travel any distance unless it was to see a doctor, and my kitchen could only fit two people, anyway. Those times were very tight. Very lean. I was happy that I had found friends who understood exactly what I was experiencing during the Depression, and were willing and even eager to share meals and company.

It was hard for me to pay my rent, buy food, and send Mamma and Papa money every month like I used to, so I had to pare that down and scrimp when I could. There would be times when I'd be getting ready for work and I'd find a five-dollar bill on the kitchen table that Jack had left the night before. He always told me not to thank him, that he liked taking care of me. With that money, I could afford to buy chicken or pork chops for me, Anne, and Sammy, and then the next night, Anne would find a piece of chuck and we'd make a pot roast. It was easier and better to share things among us.

The girls loved radio shows, and we'd listen to *Amos 'n' Andy* every night while we were making and eating dinner. Sammy and Anne particularly liked detective broadcasts that could be a bit spicy at times, and their favorite was Sherlock Holmes. Sammy was so taken with those shows that she would often write lines down from them on any old piece of paper nearby, tearing it off and sticking it in some odd place, like a book or under a doily. She said she loved coming across these little quips that she had usually forgotten about and they would make her either laugh or get excited all over again about them.

On Mondays, the *Maytag Dance Orchestra* was on, and the first time I heard it, Anne snuck behind me, twirled me around, and started to dance.

"Come on!" she laughed, moving both of my hands while I stood there stupidly, not knowing what to do.

"Dance, Ruthie, dance!" Sammy shouted from the sofa.

It was a crazy enough thing, but I had to admit it.

"I don't know how," I said, a little flustered.

"Oh, you do! Don't be shy, Ruthie!" she said, moving her feet while I stood still like a tree stump.

She dropped my hands and put them on her hips.

"Now, Ruth Judd, I need a partner and can't count on Sammy over there, so you'll just have to do. Come on, Black Bottom?"

Anne slapped her knees, looked like a cow struggling to get out of mud, and shot her arms up twice in rapid motion.

I shook my head and laughed.

"All right, this one is easy," she said. "Charleston? Everyone knows the Charleston."

She kicked backward, then came forward and was doing all sorts of nonsense with her hands.

"Anne, I was living in a Mexican mining town for the last seven years," I said. "It looks silly."

"Then the basic foxtrot?" she said, grabbing me with one hand around the waist and the other hand held out and high. "Two steps backward, one step to the side. I'll lead."

I tried to follow her feet, but I couldn't quite get it, and I stepped on her foot. She made me try again.

"I feel ridiculous," I said, but tried again, with Anne leading me slowly, calling out the steps: "Back, back, side, side. Back, back, side, side."

"Did I do it?" I asked, after I realized I hadn't stepped on any part of her.

"Yes! Ruth, you danced! You know how to dance!"

"I know how to dance?" I said, throwing my arms around her neck and laughing with her as Sammy cheered us on from the couch, and then we both began jumping up and down. "I know how to dance!"

That night, Jack mentioned what a cheerful mood I was in when he came over. Sammy and Anne went to bed strictly at 10:00 p.m. and I would be home just as Jack was pulling into the driveway. Sammy needed her rest and could not settle in the room by herself. She said she needed to hear Anne breathe to be comfortable, so if Anne wasn't tired, she'd read a book by a tiny lamp on the table that separated their two little iron beds.

"I learned how to dance tonight," I told Jack with a giggle as he took off his hat and set it on the hook I had nailed up especially for that.

"You didn't know how to dance?" he asked unbelievingly.

"Not a step," I said. "Anne taught me the foxtrot."

"These new friends of yours seem like girls about town," he said with a smile.

"Oh no, not really," I said. "They are very nice girls. They don't know anyone else in town, either. They're from Alaska. I don't know how wild you can get in Alaska."

Jack nodded. "Plenty wild," he said as pulled a bottle of something from his coat pocket.

Sometimes, it was true, he would come over after he had been drinking. I could tell; his speech would be a little sloppy and he would be more playful, or what he thought was playful, at least.

"Why don't you join me, Ruthie?" he said as he walked into the kitchen and came back with two glasses. "It's a frigid desert night out there. This will warm us up."

"I'm fine, I don't need warming up," I said, curling into the sofa, my knees tucked under me. He sat beside me and put the glasses down in the side table with twin thuds.

"Just a little to warm you . . . *up*," he said, pouring the open bottle into two glasses I regularly used for milk. He handed me one and kept one for himself.

I shook my head and tried to hand it back.

"Have a little fun—you've been dancing all night, finish it off with a toast to living," he said as he raised the glass. "Ruth loves living. She's been dead for too long, that Mrs. Judd."

I didn't say anything and kept the glass in my hand.

"Drink up," he insisted. "It's only a little. It won't hurt you. Just shoot it back and let it settle in."

I tipped the glass to my lips; it was only a little, he was right. But it burned going down, not only my throat but my nostrils. It was strong, medicinal. It did not taste like champagne. But soon I felt a small ember begin to warm inside, and it felt good. It felt cheery and comfortable.

Jack poured us both another. We drank together, glasses raised at the same time. It was just a plain glass bottle, no markings, no label. I suspected that's how it all came nowadays. I had no idea where he got it from. Social circles.

"That's my girl," Jack said, smiling, then poured us another.

When that round was downed, he stood up and extended his hand.

"Dance with me," he said, and I put my hand in his and rose.

"Foxtrot, right?" he asked as his hand slid around my waist.

I nodded.

The ember burned brighter, I felt luminous and light.

"Back, back, side, side," I said quietly, and we glided in the tiny living room, Jack humming a song I had heard on the radio but didn't really know. I leaned in closer and rested my head against his shoulder, and he drew me in tight to him.

CHAPTER TWENTY EIGHT

I was on the phone with Jack when Anne came through Dr. McKeown's office door dripping water.

"Well, you should see who just popped up at my desk," I said to him coyly, nodding hello to Anne. "It's my friend Anne, the prettiest girl in all of Phoenix, wearing the most adorable red rain slicker!"

Anne giggled.

"Well, I'd sure like to meet her," Jack said. "It's about time I met your friends."

I smiled. "We'll have to arrange that then," I said. "Call later?"

"You can count on it," he said before he hung up.

Jack often called during breaks in the day to tell me that either he would be over that night or he wouldn't, depending on his business dealings and whether he could get away from the house. It gave me something to look forward to, and if he didn't come over, I'd either stay later at Anne and Sammy's or spend the night altogether, sleeping on the maroon sofa, which was enormous.

"Who was that?" Anne asked wryly, her coat still dripping. "Was that Dr. Judd calling from California? How fancy!"

"No, no," I laughed. "It's a friend of mine, Jack. He'd like to meet you and Sammy."

"I've never heard of this Jack," she said with an odd smile. "What are you not telling me?"

"He was a neighbor of the Fords when I worked for them," I explained. "He helped me get this job."

"Sounds like a fine fellow," Anne said. "Does he happen to have any friends of his own?"

"Oh, Anne," I said. "You are a card!"

"Okay, then meet my friend Lucille," she said, looking behind her, and sure enough, there was a tiny girl in very high heels. The first thing I noticed about her was the amount of makeup she had on. I had never seen a person, aside from in the movies, wear that much. She looked like a gangster's moll in a James Cagney movie. Her fashionable cloche was pulled close to her head and almost covered her eyes, as if she was hiding.

"Hiya," she said in a very high-pitched voice. She extended her hand, which emerged from a thick cuff of fox fur from her wool coat. I knew it was expensive.

"I'm Ruth," I said, shaking her hand, which was a bit limp and slid backward as her fingertips left my grasp.

"I met Lucille when we were taking our certification exams," Anne explained. "She's back in town and is hoping to get a job here. I'm showing her around. I told her she needs to have at least a dozen children."

The three of us laughed.

"Or maybe meet your friend Jack," Anne added. She was the only one who laughed.

"Well, I hope you do get to join us here at the clinic, Lucille," I said, trying to break the silence.

"Lucille is coming over for dinner tonight," Anne said. "Maybe we can get a rousing game of whist in afterward."

"I'm a nurse," Lucille added voluntarily, and in a sly way, as if that put her in a place higher than a medical secretary.

I nodded. "That is wonderful. I'll keep my ears open, of course."

"Okay, Ruthie, see you tonight?" Anne said as she turned and walked out of the office with Lucille following. "Meet you at the car stop! Oh—I'm taking Lucille for lunch at the coffee shop—you okay on your own?"

I nodded and smiled. I needed time to think.

I had never told the girls about Jack. There was no need to, I didn't want to, and I felt stupid about making that comment on the phone to him about Anne. *Why did I say that?* I cursed myself. It was a frivolous and innocent comment because I was in an incredibly happy mood, which I always was when Jack called, and it made me careless. His voice buoyed the day, and he was my secret, which made him something that was entirely mine and that I didn't have to share with anyone. Now I had ruined it. What a foolish thing to do.

My bright mood paled for the rest of the day, and became darker once I knew I would have to explain Jack later that night at the bungalow. Maybe, I thought, I had been wrong by not telling the girls. We had grown so close and they were quickly my dearest friends, even after only a couple of months. But this was a secret that could destroy so much. It made my love for Jack a little less mine, a little less special. Because I did love him, and I knew that. There was no doubt in my mind. I never felt as full and whole as I did when I was with him. I liked being "his girl." *He had chosen me.* Of all of the secretaries in his office, in his business dealings, he had picked *me.* And that gave me a sense of place that I had never achieved before. It was a place I wanted to keep for as long as I could. And once I had known this place, now that I had lived here, I wasn't sure if I could survive without it.

Lucille was already at the bungalow when Anne and I arrived. She was smoking a cigarette in the armchair while Sammy engaged her in conversation from her place lying on the sofa. Her hair was waved but flat, although I could tell she had made a point of trying to fluff it up.

That's exactly what your fashionable hat will do to coiffed hair, I said only to myself.

The smell from the kitchen told me we were having vegetable soup and it had likely been simmering all day. Anne made her greetings and vanished into the kitchen, and after I kissed Sammy hello on the cheek and said hello to Lucille, I followed her.

"Ruthie, do you mind making some noodles and peas?" she asked me. "We have just enough butter and milk for it, and I have a can of peas in the cupboard. I'm going to get some cornbread going."

I nodded and went to work; this was how we usually made dinner, Anne in charge of one part and I taking another so we could feed ourselves and then settle into a nice radio show.

The kitchen was incredibly narrow, almost as small as my apartment kitchen, but theirs was a galley, which made it almost impossible for two people to be in, let alone cook in, at the same time. Anne and I always joked that the architect must have been a man who'd never cooked a meal in his life. We made a game of it, and when she needed to get where I was or vice versa, we'd call out "Left!" or "Right!" or "Behind!" to let each other know which way we needed the other person to move. It was like a Marx Brothers movie. Sometimes we'd crash into each other, drop an egg on the floor, spill some flour. We'd laugh hysterically, because we still laughed a lot then.

"So Ruthie," Anne began, as I knew she was going to, "tell me about this Jack fellow."

"Oh, not much to tell," I lied. "He was a neighbor to the Fords and his little girl Susan used to play with the Ford children and we were on friendly terms."

"And he got you the job with Dr. McKeown?" she pushed.

"I suppose, yes, in way," I said. "Jack knew the clinic was opening—I'm sure he had something to do with the building of it—and he put in a good word."

"A very good word, I'd say," she replied. "Are you sure you're not keeping a big secret all to yourself? I've never had a man call me at work before."

I suddenly got flustered.

"It was really nothing," I insisted. "Just calling to say hello. Like a friend."

Anne grinned and tilted her head and bopped me on the nose with her index finger. "Oh, Ruthie. You are a sly one."

"Stop lollygagging in there and bring out my supper! I am a starving invalid!" Sammy called from the living room, and we all laughed.

I had a feeling she found Lucille Moore as tiring as I did.

I waited up for Jack until midnight, and then gave up and went to bed. It was usually like him to slip away and call me if he wasn't coming by, but I didn't mind really, and he had a key to the apartment, so if he wanted to come in, he could. He was paying for part of my rent, so I felt that was the right thing to do, and I was never unhappy to see Jack.

I'm not sure how long I had been asleep when the light in my bedroom came on and Jack was at my bedside leaning over me.

"Ruth," he whispered loudly, although he could already see that I was awake. I could smell the whisky on his breath. It was thick and potent.

"Jack," I said, sitting up. "What time is it?"

"Come have whisky with us, let's dance," he said sloppily.

"I'll make you some coffee," I said, looking at my alarm clock. In three hours I had to get ready for work. I got out of the bed just as he sat on it with a flop, and I was reaching for my robe when a man I did not know was standing in the doorway of my bedroom. He was young, dressed in a suit but disheveled, and I could tell he was drunk, too.

"Is she the one?" he said in a gruff, slurring voice. "I like her."

Then he was on me, his hands all over me. Up my pajamas and trying to put his mouth on mine. I struggled and screamed and tried to get out of his grip.

"Oh, you're a fighter, huh?" he said, increasing his hold and hurting me. "A whore who likes to fight. I like that. You will do just fine."

Then Jack was up, pulling this man off me, and pushing him away, out of the bedroom.

"Come on, Happy Jack," I heard the man say. "You promised me a good time, didn't you?"

"Not her," he said, leaning against the bedroom doorjamb.

"I'll take her," the man argued. "She's fine. A little old, but a whore is a whore. I don't care about her face. I'm not going to paint her portrait!"

"I said, not her," Jack repeated.

"Listen, Jack," the man said louder. "You said we'd have a good time, right? Didn't you? You want my account. Now give me a good time."

Jack left the bedroom, told the man they were leaving; I heard a small scuffle, then the front door shutting, the Packard engine starting, and the spray of the gravel as they drove off quickly.

I was breathing quickly, and my whole body was shaking. *Who was that man? Why did Jack bring him here?*

I could not stop trembling, terrified the man would find his way back here without Jack. I locked the door, put a chair under the doorknob to brace it.

I never went back to sleep and watched the door until the sun came up and broke the night sky.

I waited all day for Jack to call me at work, but he didn't. I was restless, tired, and couldn't focus on anything, the events of the night before playing over and over in my head. I couldn't make sense of it, and it bothered me a great deal. I even begged off going over to the girls' for dinner, saying I had a headache and I needed to rest. I made mistakes in some of the histories; Dr. McKeown was not pleased and asked me again to take the stenography class, saying that I needed to be more accurate in my reports or he would hire someone else. That made me more nervous, and I couldn't wait to get home, go to bed, and wait for a new day.

But I couldn't sleep, even though I was exhausted. At ten, I heard the key in the lock and heard Jack come in. I hoped he was alone. I thought about slamming the bedroom door shut and locking it, but he was standing in the doorway before I got both my feet on the ground.

"I'm sorry about last night," he said first thing. "That man is a problem, can't hold his liquor. And that wasn't cheap stuff, either."

"Who was he?" I asked, feeling the panic all over again.

"Oh, he's a guy from Tucson, building a hotel," Jack said. "It's a big account. I promised him a good night."

"He attacked me, Jack," I reminded him.

"He was so drunk he didn't know up from down, passed out in the car on the way back to his hotel. I had to have the bellboys carry him up to his room," Jack said, shaking his head and seeming disgusted.

"Is this what happens when you go out with your customers? They want . . . a girl?"

"He got confused, Ruth, thought we were somewhere else," Jack explained. "I just wanted to stop by for a drink. Things got out of hand."

I nodded. "They did," I agreed. "I've been upset all day. Dr. McKeown said I made so many mistakes he may fire me. He mentioned stenography classes again. I'm very worried, Jack. I can't lose my job."

"Then take the classes," he said simply.

"I can't afford the classes," I almost yelled, my nerves tingling with agitation. "I don't have the money. I don't have any money!"

"Don't worry about the money, Ruth," he said, trying to calm me down. "I'll take care of it. And in the meantime, I want you to take a drop of this."

He pulled out a small brown glass bottle with a dropper on top.

"What is it?" I asked.

"It's called sweet dreams," he said, unscrewing the top, squeezing the rubber top of the dropper. "Open wide."

"One drop," I said, knowing all too well what happened when medicine got ahold of you. "Just one drop."

"Just one," he said, and I opened my mouth. The dropper smelled sweet and strong, but the liquid was very bitter. I winced.

"Maybe next time we'll put it in some warm cocoa," he suggested.

I lay back against my pillows, and then, without another panicked thought, I was dreaming.

CHAPTER TWENTY NINE

The next Saturday, Jack and I stood at the door to Sammy and Anne's bungalow and knocked. I was trembling like a leaf.

I had already advised him that the girls knew I was married to Doctor, and that I considered him a friend who'd helped me in a time of need. And that was all. He was not to indicate that there was anything more between us beyond that, and if he could remember, he was to call me Mrs. Judd.

We brought over a pie I made that afternoon from the strawberries that were just arriving in markets in early spring.

"Anne, this is Jack Halloran," I said, "And Jack, this is Anne, and that is Sammy on the sofa."

The first thing Anne said after introducing herself was, "Is that a Packard?" leaning to her side to get a good look at the car parked in front of the house.

Jack laughed.

"That's a very fine car," Anne said. "I hope someday to go for a ride in it. Top down!"

The house was very tidy, neater than I had seen it before. Every doily was in its place, all the pillows fluffed and full on the couch and chair. I smiled at Anne and I winked.

She smiled back.

I was surprised to see that Anne had made a roast chicken with potatoes and glazed carrots. Chicken was not in our regular rotation of dinners; we rarely had money for such luxuries. She must have spent an entire week's worth of grocery money on it, and I felt terrible, making a note to myself that Jack must take her for a ride in the car sometime soon, top down.

During dinner, Jack chatted about how Phoenix was growing so quickly that the town just might build its way out of the Depression. "Not even Los Angeles is growing this fast," he told us.

The girls regaled us with stories from up north: the glaciers, the icebergs, the blizzards—Anne had once been trapped in a hotel for several days because the snow was piled so high against the door—but also of Sammy's students having snowball fights and being brought to school in the winter by a team of dogs and a sled.

They had once been on a cruise and it sounded so lovely, to be floating on a huge ship right in the middle of the ocean without the sounds of anything but the boat charging through the waves.

"I've never seen more beautiful sunsets than on that ship," Sammy added. "The ocean gives a tint of magic to everything."

After dinner, we settled into the living room with me, Sammy, and Anne on the couch and Jack in the matching armchair to listen to the 7:00 p.m. broadcast of *Amos 'n' Andy*; the "Breach of Promise" serial of that show was nearing its conclusion and we couldn't wait to tune in every night. Andy was trying to wiggle out of his promise to marry Madam Queen, a beauty parlor owner.

We had been listening for almost ten minutes when the sound went loopy and faded away until we couldn't hear it anymore. Anne jumped up and hit the radio several times to bring it back to life, and when that didn't work, Jack got up and took a look.

He held his hand to the back of the radio and said it felt very hot. He took a sniff and then made a frown.

"I'm afraid this radio is headed to the repair shop, ladies," he said sadly. "I smell a melted tube."

"Oh no," Anne cried, and I knew what that meant. If she had any spare money, she had just spent it on a chicken.

"Don't worry, Anne, we'll figure it out," I said. "We'll get it fixed."

"We're going to miss the rest of the show," Sammy said, despondently. "I can't figure out how Andy is going to save himself from Madam Queen."

"Well, there's nothing a good round of gin rummy can't fix," Jack said. "Who has a deck of cards?"

Sammy clapped, and Anne helped her get off the couch.

"Dearest Anne," Jack said. "May I have the liberty of getting something from your kitchen?"

"Of course," she said. "It's so small you'll find what you're looking for in the opening of two cabinets."

I couldn't figure out what Jack was doing until he came back with juice glasses.

Anne and Sammy were silent when they walked into the dining room and saw him put the glasses on the table and pour a nice amount of whisky in each.

I looked at them; Anne's mouth was open in shock.

Oh, this is terrible, I thought, and rushed in to pick them up.

"Ruth!" Anne yelled. "Don't you dare! I haven't had a good stiff drink since we left Alaska! I never thought this day would come!"

The next day, I was doing my usual Sunday cleaning—washing, dusting, sweeping—when the phone rang. It was Anne, and she sounded so excited she could barely spit out a sentence.

"He is a wonderful man, a wonderful man!" she said as soon as I uttered the word "hello."

"Did Andy marry Madam Queen?" I asked, laughing.

"No! He brought us a radio, Ruthie! A brand-new radio that is so clear and big and working!"

"Who did?" I asked.

"Jack," she replied. "Your friend Jack. He just dropped it off. Do you hear the music? We're listening to it right now!"

She insisted I come over that night to listen to *Sherlock Holmes*, which was our favorite show; we loved it even more than *Amos 'n' Andy*. Sammy was devoted to detective stories and found them "scintillating." She read all day while Anne was at work, sometimes poetry, but gobbled up tales of wayward women. Viña Delmar was her favorite writer, and she had read both *Bad Girl* and *Loose Ladies* several times, and blanched once when Anne suggested she loan the books to Lucille for some steamy reading.

The radio was beautiful. The case was made from a bird's-eye maple and gleamed with newness. We didn't even eat at the dining room table, but sat in the living room with bowls of soup on our laps and listened to the sparkling clearness of the voices, which made the story even better, as though the characters were right in the room with us. Sammy even made Anne turn off the lights to make it seem more real, and then made her turn the lights back on again when a character said in a raspy voice, "Someday someone is going to get you and then you won't be so fresh."

"Oh, that's so good!" Sammy squealed. "I have to write that down! I have to write that down! Anne, where is a pen?"

Anne found one directly and handed her an envelope as well to write on the back of. Sammy, purely delighted, tore what she had written off and stuck it in a book that was on the side table.

Then we turned the lights off again.

⋘══⋙

On Monday when I arrived at the office, Dr. McKeown mentioned we had an emergency patient coming in—a little girl had possibly broken her arm—and the mother was bringing her in shortly.

"Doctor," I called out to him as he turned to go back to his office. "I'll be signing up for stenography classes soon."

"Very glad to hear that, Ruth; it will do you lots of good," he said with a nod and shut the door.

I had thought he would be more pleased, and was disappointed in his response, but I sat back down and started work on my histories and was very careful not to make mistakes. I was finishing up my third one when a well-dressed lady came in with a little girl, her arm in a sling. She was quite a handsome child, with very light blond hair and crystal-blue eyes. I was struck by her looks immediately and knew that this little girl was the one Dr. McKeown had told me about. I also realized who she was, but was hoping that the recognition would not be reciprocated.

"You're here to see the doctor," I said. "He let me know you were coming."

"Thank you. This only happened last night, poor thing," the mother said. "Dr. McKeown was so good to let us—Ruth? Is that you?"

"Oh, it's so good to see you, it's been so long," I said, forcing a smile. "And Susan. I'm so sorry about your arm. Let's get you in to see the doctor right away."

I walked to the doctor's door and knocked on it.

"Dr. McKeown?" I called. "Mrs. Halloran is here."

While the doctor examined Susan, I heard her cry out several times in pain, and felt terrible. I was also panic-stricken. I hadn't seen Jack's wife for over six months, since I left the Fords'. She had been pleasant to me. She did not know. Women are not pleasant to women they know are seeing their husbands. Taking time away that belongs to their families. I couldn't shake the fright. I breathed deeply, trying to bring myself together, and I needed to. I couldn't type; I was making mistakes all over the place. My heart was beating as fast and hard as a fist punching inside my chest. Over and over and over again. Pound punch. Pound punch. Pound punch. My palms were clammy and I wiped them on my lap. *Steady yourself, Ruth. Steady. She knows nothing. She knows nothing about you. You are just the nanny.*

You are just the nanny.

I wiped the ridge of perspiration from my upper lip just as the doctor opened the door and Mrs. Halloran and Susan came out.

"Ruth, I'd like you to take Mrs. Halloran and Susie down to the X-ray clinic to see if we do indeed have a broken arm," he said. "And Susie, I want you to stay out of very tall trees, even though they look inviting to climb."

She nodded, and her eyes were red. She had been crying.

I didn't have to make much conversation as we walked down the hall to X-ray. Mrs. Halloran was scared for her daughter, and nervous chatter took us all the way to the other side of the building.

"I've told her so many times to stay out of that tree," she said. "You know it, the one in the backyard that doesn't look very tall, but it must have been the way she fell. I've never heard a scream like that in my life, and Ruth, I don't even know where it came from, me or Susie! How long does a broken arm take to heal? This is just terrible timing, you know, we're leaving Phoenix for the summer in about three weeks and I just don't think this will heal by then. Poor baby. All summer with a broken arm. I hope not. I hope not. What misery for my girl. I hope we can find someone up there who can keep checking on her; we won't be back until September, when summer is over. Are you staying in town for the summer? Oh, I don't know how you do it. The heat is dreadful. Unbearable. I did it once and I won't do it again. I just told Jack to send us up to a decent climate or I would just go mad with the heat. You can't sleep, can't eat, it is with you all the time. I can't cool down. I'm one of those people who just can't cool down once I've reached that point."

"Here we are," I said as we reached the X-ray clinic. I opened the door and called as mother and daughter came in and stood before me.

"Mrs. LeRoi?" I called, and Anne came out from the back. I gave her a stern look and shook my head very slightly as I said, "This is Mrs. Halloran and her daughter, Susie, who we are afraid has broken her arm. I used to live next door to them when I was a nanny."

Anne popped a smile on her face, looked down, and said, "Hello, Susie. Let's see what we have here."

"Will it hurt?" the little girl asked.

"Not one bit," Anne answered as I slid out the door and closed it behind me.

At the girls' that night, Anne pulled me into the kitchen almost as soon as I got there.

"I know that Jack is not just a friend to you," she said. "I knew it before, but now I know it for certain."

I looked away and said nothing.

"Ruth," she said sternly. "Messing with another woman's husband is never a good idea. He has a family."

"I know," I said reluctantly. "I know. It's a terrible thing. I want to hate myself for it, but I can't seem to. I only see him late at night, I promise you. It doesn't interfere with family time."

"That's not the issue," Anne insisted. "You have to stop this, Ruth. It isn't right."

"But it doesn't feel that way," I replied. "All of my life, I've done what people told me; I've had very little choice in the course of what happened to me. Where I lived, how we lived, why we lived like that. This is the first time ever I've had something that is mine, Anne. Do you understand? I know it's wrong and I know I'm bad for doing it. But I can't help it. There is something there that I have never felt before and it fills me with life. It makes me want to get up in the morning, it makes me happy to make him happy. I know it's a terrible thing. But for right now, it's what I have, and when I see him I melt. I have never melted before. I thought that love was something you did out of duty and circumstance. But it's not true. Love is something that happens when it happens, and it doesn't care if I'm married or he's married. It exists despite all of that."

Anne was silent for a long time.

"I do understand what it's like to love someone you're not supposed to love," she told me. "When what you have with someone so dear to you has to be a secret, even though it makes you so happy you want the world to know. I do understand that, Ruth. I truly do. I'll just ask you to be careful, because this could be very dangerous."

"Thank you, Anne," I said, giving her a peck on the cheek. "Thank you for understanding."

Anne drew a deep, serious breath.

"There's one more thing I want to talk to you about," she continued. "I got a letter from my brother-in-law in Oregon when I got home today. My sister is very ill. She's going for tests in Portland; they are not sure what is wrong. I'm hoping it's not consumption. She has three children. He's asked me to come and take care of them for a while because he needs to work. But I can't leave Sammy alone, especially not at night. I'm so worried. I don't know what to do. I don't know if the clinic will give me leave for that long."

"Well, you have to ask," I said. "If she's really that sick, you have to go. Don't worry about Sammy. I'm here. I can fill in."

"Would you? Would you really, Ruth? Sammy is so easy, I just worry about her staying here alone and not having help if she needs it. I'm so worried I feel sick."

"I understand, and please don't worry. I can move in here for a couple of weeks, and it will just be like usual, just missing one friend who will return shortly. I'm happy to do it. I'm happy that I can help you."

"I'm going to wire him tomorrow to see if things have changed. If not, I'll take the train up to Portland as soon as I can, if I get leave."

"I'll take very good care of Sammy," I told her. "It's the least I can do."

There was a letter from Doctor when I got home that night. It was written with a steady hand; I always checked for that. If I wasn't there with him, his handwriting was a good way for me to tell if he had strayed and was in trouble again. I was glad to see that Doctor was doing well, and the letter was filled with ordinary details: he'd found some work as an orderly, another job in a lab, another job as an assistant. He filled in for people who had taken ill or went on leave, so he wasn't getting a steady paycheck. Still, it was something. He mentioned the possibility of the Copper Queen mine in Bisbee needing a doctor in several months, as the current one was retiring. The mine was one of the richest in the country, if not the world. If Doctor could keep himself straight, there was a good chance we could stay there for a long time. It would be steady work. It would be a regular life.

His letter filled me with dread, dripping like a black syrup into my heart as I read to the end, and it sunk me. I did not want a regular life. I had found the life I wanted, and I was not anxious to relinquish it, to walk away and forget that I had taken care of myself, that I had experienced real love with a man and the bond between friends that was so dear to me. The thought of just listening to the radio every night with Anne and Sammy was enough to push me through the day, and the reward of Jack coming to me most nights was a refuge I knew I would never find again. I didn't want to lose what I had built on my own. I didn't want to walk away from the happiness I had found here to become a doctor's wife in a small, dusty mining town all over again.

I wrote back that night, telling Doctor about Anne and Sammy's new radio, the stenography classes I planned to take, and how the weather was turning from cold to warm again. The desert was about to bloom, the spring rains had ended, and I was very busy at work. I did not ask him when he planned to visit, and I did not mention visiting him. I signed it "Affectionately, Ruth."

When Jack arrived later, I told him that Mrs. Halloran had brought Susan in to the clinic to get her arm checked by Dr. McKeown.

"It's broken, all right," he said, placing his fedora on the hook by the door. "Poor kid. She'll be in a cast for a while."

"Jack," I started. "I have to confess something. Today was the first time I really thought about your wife and children. I have been so selfish. Isn't it cruel what we are doing to them?"

He reached out, took me by the wrist, and pulled me close. "She doesn't know anything, aside from having a beautiful house, a fur coat, and the best clothes to dress her children in. She loves the name Mrs. Halloran. She loves having a maid to do her laundry and a cook to make her meals. She knows nothing other than that. She knows I have to entertain for business, and that's what keeps her in that beautiful house and fur coats. She's a kind, good woman. A wonderful mother. But I choose to spend my personal time elsewhere. That's all there is to it."

"She said she and the children were going to Flagstaff soon," I said. "Is that true?"

"Oh, yes, all the wives go to Flagstaff the moment it hits ninety degrees," he said. "That's when I get most of my business done; it's the busiest season. We'll have a very good time this summer."

And then he kissed me.

The clinic granted Anne leave for three weeks, and I packed a suitcase and was going to head over to the girls' on Saturday. Jack thought it was a good idea, and that it was the kind thing to do. He knew that Anne could not afford for a nurse to come in, and neither of us wanted Sammy staying by herself. He offered to drive Anne to the train station, which made me very pleased.

We arrived a bit early; Anne's train was leaving at 5:10 p.m. and I didn't want her to miss it, so I insisted that we have enough of a time cushion so there would be no worries about arriving on schedule.

I ran up the steps to the girls' door as Jack opened the Packard's tailgate for Anne's things. She had a small trunk she was taking with her, no bigger than a footlocker, and it was waiting on the porch. When I walked in, I heard voices in the kitchen, and I entered the dining room to let the girls know we were here.

Anne and Sammy were in a close embrace, and they were locked in a deep kiss. I stopped immediately. I hadn't noticed the voices had ceased, and they hadn't heard me come in. I knew that kiss. It was not a goodbye kiss. It was not a friend kiss. I knew that kiss. It was the kind of kiss that can only be born out of a deep devotion.

I backed up silently on the balls of my feet and hoped that Jack wasn't right behind me. I crept out of the house and closed the door behind me as Jack just reached the porch.

"What's the matter?" he asked.

"They are . . ." I started, still in disbelief of what I had witnessed. "They are saying their goodbyes. I don't think we should interfere."

"Oh, nonsense," he said, rapping on the door once, then twice in quick succession, and then opening the door. "Girls! We're here! Anne, are you ready?"

They both emerged from the kitchen smiling, although I could tell Sammy had been tearful.

Jack noticed and took her hand. "We're going to take very good care of you, Sammy," he said as she smiled. "We're going to do nothing but have fun. Parties every night! How does that sound?"

Anne nudged her playfully. "Parties every night, huh? How does that sound?"

"Wonderful." Sammy laughed, and then wiped her eyes.

CHAPTER THIRTY

Anne was right to go; her sister was more ill than her husband had let on. While it wasn't consumption, she had a severe case of pleurisy and pneumonia, which had left her completely bedridden, unlike Sammy, who could easily get up and walk around if she needed to. In her letter, Anne feared that her sister's recovery would take more than three weeks, and she had notified the clinic as such.

I settled in very quickly at the girls' house. For the first several nights, I slept in Anne's bed, but after a week or so, Sammy said she felt comfortable with me just being in the house, so we moved the bed into the dining room and put a little sheet over the archway that separated it from the living room. I was glad about that. When Jack came over for supper or after doing business, we would stay up later and retreat into the space behind the sheet.

I wasn't sure what I'd seen in the kitchen, but somehow, sleeping in the same room with Sammy felt funny, almost like I was trying to take Anne's place. Of course, I'd heard of those kinds of attractions before— men liking men—but I had never heard of women like that. I didn't think there was such a thing, and I was confused. I never mentioned it to Jack; what I'd seen was private and not for my eyes, and to be honest, I found it so strange I was sure I was mistaken.

I was due to start my stenography classes soon, and I told Jack I was worried about Sammy staying alone at night, she fretted so. He told me to ask around at the clinic to see if we could get a nurse to come in and watch over Sammy while I was gone, and I thought that was a grand idea. He told me of a nurse named Evelyn Nace who might be available, and who worked at Good Samaritan Hospital during the day.

Jack sent groceries over regularly, almost every day, so I was able to make some wonderful dinners for Sammy and myself, and Jack on the occasions he could get away. I made meat loaf, fried chicken, a pot roast—food we hadn't seen in a very long time. As the weather got warmer, Sammy was getting up more and even took to resting in a hammock in the backyard to get some sun. I asked Dr. McKeown to come over and examine her, and he said her breathing was sounding clear and she should walk a half mile a day in the sun. In return, we made him a nice roast dinner and had a lovely time. He admired the girls' radio, and commented on how clear it sounded.

"Thank you," Sammy replied. "It was a wonderful gift."

Jack called me at work one morning and asked me what was my favorite dinner to cook. "Chili," I said immediately; it was a dish I'd learned how to make in Mexico, and Doctor loved it. Said it was the best chili he ever had.

"That may be too exotic," Jack said. "How about something like sausage and potato hash? I'll have the groceries delivered this afternoon."

"Sounds good to me," I said.

"I'm bringing a guest," he said. "I have a man in from out of town and I said I'd treat him to some home cooking."

I was quiet. "Oh, Jack. It's not the man from Tucson is it? Please don't bring that man over."

"No, no, this man's name is Dixon, from Los Angeles," he said. "Could be one of the biggest accounts we've ever had. I'll send over a pie, too."

"All right," I said cautiously. "As long as there's no funny business. I can't scare Sammy like that."

I rushed to the bungalow right after work and started getting ready. I told Sammy to stay in bed to rest and that Jack was bringing a business associate over for supper to impress him.

"Oh, this place is a disaster," she said, getting up. "I'll tidy up."

"Don't wear yourself out," I scolded her. "I'd rather have your bubbling personality than you feeling out of sorts."

Besides, the living room was not that much of a mess; Anne had left a couple of books and detective magazines around, but that was it. I picked them up in a stack, but the top one fell onto the floor while I was walking to the bedroom to stash them. I picked it up, only to see it was Sammy's diary.

I saw the words ". . . not wait for her to return. I do love my Anne so. She takes such good care of me and it is hard to believe we have only been together for one year. I feel like I have known her my whole life, and I know we shall be side by side for the rest of our days." I stopped. I didn't want to read any more.

I walked into the bedroom while Sammy was freshening up in the adjacent bathroom and shoved the pile under her bed.

<hr />

Mr. Dixon was a very pleasant man. He was older, probably about Doctor's age, but he was quite polite and complimentary about my cooking.

"I wish you could come back when Anne is here," Sammy said. "She is a spectacular cook."

I wasn't sure how to take that, but understanding what I now knew to be true, I agreed wholeheartedly and said so.

Jack was right, Mr. Dixon wasn't anything like the man from Tucson. He even brought us a bouquet of daisies when he arrived. Jack broke out a bottle of what might have been gin and poured us all a round. Sammy loved it, and after her third glass, she became very cheery and giggly, and was asking Mr. Dixon all about Los Angeles like she had never heard of the place before. I had told her about my time there, working for the Broadway Department Store and how big the buildings were there. She acted like I had never said a word about it and made such a fuss you'd think Mr. Dixon was talking about China. She became very sleepy after a while, and excused herself to go to bed, but not before she invited Mr. Dixon to stop by whenever he was in town because he was such delightful company.

He and Jack left soon after, and on their way out the door Jack whispered to me not to expect him later, and I understood. Mr. Dixon was an important businessman whose night ahead did not include two tubercular women, one of whom couldn't stand up for five minutes straight.

Letters from Anne came the next day, one for me and one for Sammy. Mine read:

> *Dearest Ruth:*
> *How are you coming, honey? I hope you are not working too hard. You've been so sweet to us and such a very good friend, Ruth. Ruth darling, I'll never thank you enough for all the things you've done for me, but Sammy and I will love you always for them. Write me all concerning my baby (Sammy) because I do worry so about her.*
> *Love to Jack and your sweet self,*
> *Anne*
> *You've been so sweet to us and such a very good friend, Ruth. You did look tired when I left.*

The letter made me smile, and I hoped that she would be back soon to cheer Sammy up and we could return to our friendly trio, listening to the radio and having lunch at my little apartment, which I was dying to go back to.

I did not mind taking care of Sammy; she was my dear friend and such a thoughtful person. In many ways, I saw Sammy as pure; she never had a bad word to say about anyone, was always cheerful and in a good mood even if she felt awful and was having the life coughed out of her. I was very happy that we were companions, and that I had two good friends to count on. I had never had that before.

Sammy's letter, however, upset her quite a bit. She had been laughing while reading it when she burst into tears and began sobbing. I went to the sofa and put my arm around her, asking what was wrong, but she said she couldn't tell me.

"Anne said she would write you," she said, slamming the letter right side down in her lap.

"What has happened?" I asked. "Is it something terrible? I just read her letter; it said nothing of bad news. Are you sure you read it correctly?"

"She told me not to tell you just yet," Sammy said, sniffling. "She's not coming back."

"Of course she's coming back," I said. "Of course she is. In about a week's time, she'll be back home, right here with you."

"She's not coming back for another month, maybe two," she said. "Her sister isn't improving, and Anne says she needs to stay."

Two months, I thought. *That can't be. Why didn't she tell me? And how is Sammy supposed to pay the rent?* I tried to calm Sammy down as much as I could, even giving her a small glass full of Jack's clear moonshine, or whatever it was. She drank it, and we moved her into her room. She fell asleep within minutes.

I sat down at the dining room table, now shoved into a corner, and wrote to Anne. Was what Sammy said true or had it been misunderstood? Two months was a long time, and I couldn't keep paying for my apartment if I wasn't going to live there, and how was Sammy supposed to pay for the rent on Second Street? I begged her to be honest with me and let me know so I could arrange things the best I could; otherwise we'd all start getting in a lot of money trouble.

I mailed the letter the next day, and I told Jack what I had learned when he came over that evening.

"Sammy is getting much better with the heat, but I can't stay here forever," I told him. "The rent on Second Street is due next week, and I have to pay my own rent. I don't know what to do."

"Is Anne sending money?" Jack asked.

"Anne has nothing to send," I told him. "I suspect they are behind on their rent as it is. Sammy was so upset I had to give her some of what was in the bottle. If she gets worried, she's going to start to relapse. I wish Anne would just tell me what was happening."

Jack reached into the pocket inside his suit jacket and pulled out his wallet. He pulled out thirty dollars and handed it to me.

"Pay their rent, and let me know if you need more," he said. "I'm going to be bringing another associate over for dinner tomorrow. Tell Sammy we'll play some cards or something, but to do herself up."

"All right," I said. "I have what I need to make meat loaf."

"Perfect," Jack said. "But if Anne's not coming back for a while, you should leave your apartment for a bit; there's no sense paying on a place that's sitting empty. I'll see you tomorrow."

And then he left, just like that. No goodbye, no kiss. Just started the Packard and drove away, but not in the direction of his house.

The young man Jack brought over was from Tulsa, never having been to Phoenix before. His name was Louis and he kissed both my and Sammy's hands, which I thought was a little silly but nice. Sammy was very impressed, I could tell, and was wearing a sweet dress with puffed sleeves and a strawberry print that I had never seen before. I mostly saw Sammy in pajamas and a robe, but it was ridiculous of me to think she didn't have more than one dress. She did have a life in Alaska before she got sick, and was sure to have one after she got well. Of course she had clothes! And with her hair done and makeup on, she was a stunningly beautiful girl.

After dinner, Jack said he had a surprise for us and went out to the car. He came back with a big wooden box with an electric cord, and I was stunned.

"Is that a phonograph?" I asked.

He laughed and placed it on the side table, dragged the table to the outlet, and plugged it in. The motor began to whirl.

"But we don't have any record albums," Sammy said, to which Jack opened the lid and revealed a whole album, Duke Ellington.

Sammy screamed. "Oh, can we play it now? Please, Jack! Please, Jack!"

"Oh, but wait!" Jack toyed with and pulled not one but two bottles from his suit jacket, which was hanging on the coatrack.

It was a glorious time. Sammy and Louis danced one of the newest dances to "Cotton Club Stomp" until she needed to stop, and Jack and I danced the foxtrot to "Mood Indigo." After we all rested some, we drank a little more and danced a little more until it was way past Sammy's bedtime.

<hr/>

I started stenography school that week, and Evelyn Nace came over to look after Sammy. Taking a streetcar, I went straight from the clinic to the class, which was held in an office building downtown. The class seemed very nicely paced, and I was looking forward to learning more so Dr. McKeown wouldn't fire me and find someone else.

When I got back to Second Street, Sammy and Evelyn were up, listening to the radio and drinking lemonade and engrossed in what sounded like a terrifying detective story. Sammy pointed to the dining room and told me that letters had come from Anne and Dr. Judd; she had placed them on my pillow.

Anne reported that what Sammy had said was true; she wouldn't be back for at least a month. She didn't know how to tell me, but her sister was very ill and wasn't responding well to the medication she was taking.

I dropped the letter on the bed and didn't want to read any more. I wanted to go back to my apartment, I wanted to go back to the way it was before, when Jack came by at night and we had time alone. He rarely stayed longer after Sammy went to bed, and I missed our time together.

Doctor's letter was the same letter he had been writing me three times a week every week since I landed in Phoenix. He was looking for a steady job. Nothing had come through yet. He was picking up odd positions here and there. He had not gone back to medicine. He was doing well. He missed me and hoped he could come out to visit soon.

After the radio show ended, Evelyn left and Sammy went to her room. I could hear her crying, and I knew she was upset about Anne. I thought about going in to comfort her, but I was very tired. It was late. I didn't think Jack was coming over. I changed into my pajamas and went to bed.

The next morning, I called Mr. Grimm, my landlord at Brill Street, and told him I would be leaving the apartment for the time being. I said I was very sorry and didn't want to do it; that I liked living there very much, but a friend needed care and I had to stay at her place for a while. He said he understood, but asked me if I could pay through the end of the month. I agreed, and told him to keep me in mind if another apartment became available in the next couple of months. I said I was hoping it wouldn't be longer than that.

CHAPTER
THIRTY ONE

Sammy cried almost every night, and I wanted to join her. Jack hadn't been over for almost a week, although he'd sent groceries twice. I hoped he was just busy with O'Malley's and all of the accounts he was handling. Sammy and I struggled through the week in sour moods, listening to the radio when I wasn't in stenography class. Evelyn was a great help, and when I told her this, she shrugged and smiled.

"Jack has me do this for everybody," she said.

"Oh," I replied, not sure exactly what she meant, but I figured that Jack had connections all over the place, so if there was someone in the social circle who needed a nurse, he knew of one to send over.

Jack called the next day; I told him that Sammy wasn't getting out of bed and that she was despondent about Anne's delay in coming home. I told him about the crying, and how her appetite had shrunk to almost nothing.

"I'll be over tomorrow, and I'm bringing friends. I'll send over a chicken; do you have another friend that can join us? I have two men that will be arriving, and I'd hate for one of them to be without a dance partner."

I wasn't sure exactly who I'd invite over, but I figured I could lure someone from the clinic over with a chicken dinner.

"Yes, I can get a friend," I said, excited that I would be able to see him. "What about Evelyn?"

"Good idea," he said. "Can you ring her? I'll bring something over for Sammy to help her sadness."

"Wonderful," I said. "Will I see you tonight?"

"Not likely," he answered. "I have a lot of work to get this account ready for tomorrow."

"I understand," I said.

"My family has left to go up north," he told me. "We'll have plenty of time this summer, Ruth."

Evelyn agreed to come over for dinner and a "bit of dancing," as I told her, and she said she had noticed the new phonograph. The three of us pushed the dining room table into the living room so all of us could sit down. I made the chicken, roasting it to a golden brown, and it was ready right on time for Jack and his associates to arrive. I made introductions to Sammy, Evelyn, and the men, and then Jack ushered me into the kitchen.

He pressed a brown bottle with a dropper into my hand—very much like the one he'd given me at my apartment—and told me to give Sammy a little drop before dinner.

"Just a tiny one to get her up and going," he told me.

I nodded, and as Jack put on a new record he'd bought, I called Sammy into the bedroom.

"Jack just gave me this medicine that would help you feel not so blue," I told her. "Would you take one drop?"

"What is it?" she asked.

"Well, I'm not exactly sure, but Jack would never give you anything that would hurt you," I tried.

"I don't know," she said, shaking her head.

"He said it would make you happy," I told her. "Don't you want to be happy? How about if I take one drop and you take one drop?"

She thought for a moment. Then she stuck out her tongue.

I put one drop of brown liquid on her tongue. She pulled back immediately.

"That's tart," she said with a grimace. "Now you."

I drew up the liquid again in the dropper and put a drop on my tongue.

She was right, it tasted awful. I put the dropper back in the bottle and took Sammy's arm in mine and squeezed it a little.

"Let's have a happy night," I said, and together we joined the rest of the party.

Dinner was wonderful. The conversation was lively, and the two gentlemen Jack brought over were funny and charming. They were from Colorado, Utah, I can't remember, but as soon as we finished dinner, we piled all of the dishes into the sink, pushed the table back, and Evelyn tried to teach us the Lindy Hop. Sammy was the first one to get it, and one of the fellows Jack brought already knew it. Jack and I tried, but he got disgusted quickly and started the drinks going. Sammy was delightful; her scowl had disappeared and I'd never seen her laugh that much. The new record Jack brought over was one of the best songs I'd ever heard, and I insisted that we play it again and again. I couldn't seem to get enough of it. I did get so brave that I kissed Jack on the lips right in front of everybody, and we all laughed. The liquor Jack brought didn't seem to taste as awful this time. It seems like we laughed the whole night long, and the party went on far longer than we intended it to. The next morning I was exhausted and had a splitting headache, but I forced myself to go to work. Sammy was still sleeping when I left; I didn't wake her, figuring if I was that tired, she must be beat.

I received a letter that day from Doctor, saying that the position in Bisbee was looking very good and that he would be out in August to go and talk to the hospital administrators there. If I was still at Second Street, he said, he would find lodgings for the two of us. I folded the letter, put it away, and told myself I'd write him back tomorrow.

I should have felt elated that Doctor was about to secure another job, but dread settled in my stomach. Bisbee was more than a hundred miles to the south, basically on the Mexico border, and it was a small mining town. What would I do with myself there? I felt so settled in Phoenix; I had a job, friends, and Jack. All of that would be gone if Doctor took the job. I would be expected to go.

Sammy, on the other hand, came to me almost running, waving a letter in her hand, completely joyful.

"It's Anne! She's coming home! She's coming home!"

Her sister was improving, Anne wrote, and she was returning to us next week. Sammy was beside herself with happiness. That was great news. I called Mr. Grimm immediately to ask if I could move back into my apartment, but told me he had already let it.

"The lady in unit E is moving out in September," he told me, which was months away. I sighed, disappointed, but said yes, please put me down for that one. I might even be in Bisbee by that time.

"If anything becomes available in the meantime, please let me know," I told him.

A moment after I hung up, Jack called. "I'm bringing the fellows from last night over and one of their friends. Get the phonograph ready! Call some more friends, would you?"

I didn't have any more friends. I asked Sammy if Lucille's name might be in her and Anne's phone book.

I suppose you could say Lucille Moore added an ingredient to the party we had never had before: she was a squealer. In front of men, she squealed after almost every sentence she spoke. She squealed after every sip of Jack's stuff she took. It was like a needle in my ear. She was a good dancer and liked to take up a lot of room, so we pushed the couch and chair to the sides of the room to make a bigger dance floor. Sammy was trying hard to keep up, driven by her jubilance at Anne's coming home. But after a few songs, she flopped on the sofa, catching her breath.

"Ruth," she called to me, and motioned me over. "I want to dance more. I need a drop!"

I went to the dresser in her bedroom where I had put the bottle, and called her in. Lucille suddenly appeared in the doorway.

"Whatcha doin', friends?" she said with a big grin.

Lucille hopped around like a grasshopper for the rest of the night, she was unstoppable. It finally got so late that I asked Jack to take her home with his pals, because I could not bear to hear her squeal one more time.

When Anne came home the following Friday, we decided to have a big party that night to celebrate. Some of Jack's associates from the social circle came over. Evelyn called some girls she knew, and although I tried to avoid mentioning Lucille Moore, Sammy had already called her.

It was the biggest party we ever had and was a very nice welcome for Anne. Evelyn brought over some new records and Lucille began squealing almost immediately. The men from the social circle, Mr. Hughes and Mr. Evans, were not associates of Jack's, but I had the sense they were important Phoenix men. They sat on the sofas, drank out of our juice glasses, and smoked cigars with Jack. They were older than Jack but not as old as Doctor.

I didn't know how we'd ever get the smell out.

We had fans on, but it was still very hot, even after sunset. Sammy and I both took drops, and then we included Anne, too, who was eager to see what Sammy was talking about when she was referring to her "happy drops." Lucille managed to squeeze herself in, so we looped in Evelyn and her girlfriends so we'd all have an extra good time.

To our surprise, Mr. Dixon came by, all the way from Los Angeles, and Sammy introduced him to Anne immediately. I think he was quite taken with her. Jack had made sure there was plenty of liquor for the whole night, but it disappeared quickly. I was serving the cake to everyone when I heard one of the older men say to Jack, "This is quite a collection of summer wives you have here, Halloran."

I saw Jack laugh and heard him say, "I do my best, you know."

"You do know how to have a good time," the other man said, and then they all chortled, sucking on their foul maduros.

I noticed I hadn't heard any squealing in a while, and looked around. Lucille had vanished, which meant for a much more enjoyable evening.

Anne took me aside a little while later.

"Word to the wise," she said to me. "If you want to keep your man clean, keep him away from Lucille. She's syphilitic."

The next day, Mr. Dixon called for Anne and then came by to pick her up for a drive. I tidied up the mess from the night before: glasses everywhere, smashed cigarette butts, and ashes from those cigars as big as coins. I was disgusted and wished that my nights with Jack could go back to the way they were, just the two of us in my little apartment on Brill.

When Anne returned later that afternoon, Sammy had just woken up and Anne announced that Mr. Dixon was coming by that night to visit. He had already called Jack, she finished, and it was all arranged.

I didn't know half of the people that were in our living room that night. The music was loud and I was very glad there were no neighbors living on the other side. I was sure someone would call the police. Jack saw me standing in a corner and told me not to ruin it for everybody, they were all having such a good time.

"Lift it up," he told me firmly. "These are important men, which means good business for me."

He was angry with me. I didn't want him to be angry. I was feeling his distance and I wanted him close to me again. I went to the bedroom and opened the drawer, and found there were only two drops left. After that, the bottle was empty. I handed it to him when I came back into the living room and said, "We're out of happiness."

Anne was suddenly wearing a new dress that I hadn't seen before on her first day back at the clinic. Initially, the clinic didn't want her back because they had hired someone to take her place. But after she agreed to a shorter schedule, she was back at the X-ray machine. She hadn't been working for a while.

"It's pretty," I told her as we walked to the streetcar stop. "Is that from Portland?"

"No, it's from Goldwater's," she said, showing it off. "Mr. Dixon bought it for me."

I stopped. "Mr. Dixon, Jack's business associate?"

"Yep," she said.

"Why did he buy you a dress?" I asked.

She laughed and said, "I traded a kiss for it," and got on the streetcar.

Mr. Dixon, who was apparently in town all week, took her to dinner every night. Anne paid the rent in full two months in advance and had a new dress for Sammy, too.

Jack hadn't come by or called for days, which was unusual. I thought maybe he had taken a business trip and forgotten to tell me. Finally, I got up enough nerve to call him at his office, which I had never done before. He was out, I was told, so I left a message. I sat at my desk all day, waiting. Every time the phone rang, it wasn't him.

He did ring that night at the house, and he sounded cold and far-away, like he was talking to a shop clerk.

"I don't understand what is happening," I said. "Why haven't you called or come over?"

"It's fine, Ruth," he said quickly. "Business is very busy during the summer. You know that."

"What, have I done something to anger you?" I asked.

"Ruth," he said. "Stop this."

"What have I done?" I said, and unable to help it, my voice cracked.

"I'll be over tonight," he said, and the line cut.

When he arrived, Sammy and Anne fawned all over him. They sat on either side of him on the couch and I brought four glasses out and we all had drinks. Then I asked Jack if we could go for a ride in the Packard, and the girls said they wanted to go, too.

We drove all the way out to Nineteenth Avenue, as far as we could go, with Anne and Sammy yammering in the backseat, telling Jack to go faster, faster, faster. The hot wind whipped around us like a scorching tornado.

"Faster!" Sammy yelled.

"Go all the way!" Anne added.

I said nothing, and just looked at the desert as we drove through it. The sky was a searing orange, the wind so burning it hurt. The scrub was dry and brittle, and I wanted it to catch fire, burning all the way down to the dirt, and then blistering that, too.

I didn't sleep that night, restless on the sofa in the living room; Anne had taken her bed back to her room beside Sammy. The air was still, stagnant, and suffocating. The heat seeped in everywhere, got under my pajamas, lay on my skin, made my scalp damp and itchy. It snuck up beneath my eyelids. I got up and ran water on my face, put my slip on instead of pajamas, and tried to rest.

The heat never ended; it never went to sleep. It covered everything with a heavy blanket.

Everything was dry, so you could hear things crackle, the life being drawn right out of them. If you listened closely, even blood vessels were breaking like tiny twigs, snap snap snap. You could hear leaves shrivel on the trees, the clouds being decimated from moisture.

The life of everything was draining.

CHAPTER
THIRTY TWO

I came home late one night after stenography class; the instructor wanted to rehash mistakes I made on my last assignment. I could barely keep my eyes open, and the heat had not abated.

I wanted to go back to the bungalow and try to sleep. I stopped at the drugstore and picked up some Veronal tablets to help me. I could not spend another night in the dark stillness, wretched and sweating. It made me queasy to even think about it.

But as I walked up to the house, I could hear it before I even saw it. The music, the laughter, and I knew where it was coming from. Every light in the house was on, and shadows of people bounced in the windows as if they were puppets.

I didn't know some of the people who were dancing in the living room, but there, on my makeshift bed, was Jack, and on his lap was Anne, her arms around his neck, whispering in his ear. It was enough to make me stop right where I was until a dancing man bumped me from behind and I almost fell over. Jack looked at me from the corner of his eye but didn't move a bit. I felt sick. My breath left my lungs. I did not see Sammy. Lucille Moore was with a man I didn't recognize, necking in the armchair, and several girls I did not know were dancing in only their slips, their bodies shiny with sweat, their bodies beating with Jack's liquor.

I turned around and walked out the front door. I went around to the rear of the house to sit on the back steps, but there were another man and woman there, groping each other in the dark. They sounded like animals.

I went to the empty side of the duplex and sat on the front steps, where I didn't have to see so much of what was happening. I opened the Veronal bottle and put a tablet in my mouth, sucking its bitterness away until it was dissolved. I sat there for a long time, not sleeping but numb, until I realized the music had stopped and cars were driving away.

When I went back to the other side, the lights were still on but the house was empty. After I turned off the lights and ignored the mess, I took another tablet and lay still on the sofa.

⸎

I went in to the clinic early, not waiting for Anne to take the streetcar with me. I called Mr. Grimm the next morning to see if my apartment was possibly available yet. I wanted to go back home very badly. He said it wasn't but the lady in H was moving out the next weekend, and did I want it?

I said I did and I would bring my things over on Sunday. He said that would be fine.

I did have to bring a patient down to the X-ray clinic that day, but I avoided seeing Anne. I was boiling with anger. I couldn't even hold a pencil; twice it shot out of my hand. I was queasy, and even though we had several fans in the office, it felt like the sun was directly overhead, broiling me like a tomato in an oven. I stayed in the office at lunch and did not meet Anne in the lobby as I usually did, and she did not come looking for me. When the office closed, I dreaded going home and took a later streetcar to Second Street.

Anne was in the kitchen when I came in; the house was in better shape than when I had left that morning. The bedroom door was closed; Sammy was in there resting, I was sure.

Anne came out to the living room when she heard me.

"Did you see a small brown bottle on the table?" she asked me without saying hello. "I swore I left it there and now I can't find it."

I shook my head. "But I did see you sitting on Jack last night," I said.

"Oh, we were just playing," she said, waving her hand. "You can't think that was anything!"

"It didn't look like play to me," I replied. "You were whispering in his ear. With your arms around him."

"Oh, come on, Ruth," she said, brushing me off. "Jack is just a friend. You know that. We were goofing."

"Are you sure? Because I think Mr. Dixon is a friend, too. I think your friend card is full."

"Mr. Dixon is very kind. And yes, he is a friend, too. He's a harmless old man."

"With a lot of money. And you've just gotten a new dress and paid the rent up for months."

"Ruth, don't be daft. He wanted me to have that money. He told me so. He's very generous."

"What are you doing for that money, Anne? Doesn't that hurt Sammy?"

She shot me a glare that I had never seen on her face before.

"I would never hurt Sammy. How can you even think that?"

I stopped myself for a moment and a voice said, *Don't say it, don't say it,* but before I knew it, it was out there. I wanted to hurt her, sharply and pointedly. I wanted her to know what that kind of hurt felt like, what I felt like last night.

"Because I know you and Sammy are funny. I know that. *I saw you.*"

"You didn't see anything! Don't lie, Ruth. You didn't see anything."

"I did. I did see it the day you left for Portland. I saw you together standing right in that kitchen saying goodbye. It was unnatural and you know what I'm talking about!"

Anne narrowed her eyes and bit her upper lip.

"You'd better be careful about telling people what you saw, Ruth. There might be *some* friends of ours who would not be so pleased to know that you have *a baby* that you can't even take care of," she said almost in a growl, pointing at me.

"Don't you dare," I said, taking a step toward her. "Don't you dare say anything to him."

"Then you keep whatever you think you know to yourself," she said. "I'm the one who takes care of Sammy, and whatever I have to do to keep her well and fed is what I will do. Or your secrets won't be secrets anymore, either."

I heard the bedroom door creak open and Sammy came into the living room, her hair a mess.

"Hello, Ruthie," she said pleasantly, almost like a sleepy child. "What are we having for dinner?"

The letter I received from Doctor that day surprised me, but it should not have. He wrote that he had an appointment the following week with the Copper Queen Hospital in Bisbee, but wanted to stop in Phoenix to stay a couple of days before he went down south. I would be back on Brill Street then, and I was quite relieved.

The girls and I had sandwiches for dinner without incident, and I let them know that Mr. Grimm had invited me to take unit H on Brill Street and I'd agreed; I was moving back there on Sunday. Sammy scowled and said she would miss me, but Anne didn't say a word and kept on eating.

No one came over that night, and there was no word from Jack.

I had Jack's home phone number. I'd had it since the day Mrs. Halloran came to see Dr. McKeown at Grunow with Susan. I had it tucked away in my handbag along with the brown bottle I had found the night after the last raucous party in which Anne was lying over Jack like a rug, whispering in his ear, or could it have been nibbling?

I had never toyed with calling him at the home number, but now my mind was urging me to. Mrs. Halloran and her children were still in Flagstaff, of that I was almost certain. None of the doctors from the clinic had seen their wives return yet. There was still another month before the heat exhausted itself.

I picked up the phone and called. The phone rang and rang, and then, to my surprise, a woman answered, "Halloran residence?"

I was shocked. I stumbled, not knowing what to say, and I heard myself ask, "May I speak to Mrs. Halloran, please?" thinking suddenly that if she was there, if this was her, I had a reason to call: Dr. McKeown wanted to check and see how Susan was doing.

"I'm sorry, she won't be returning until next month," the woman replied.

"Very well, I'll ring back then," I said, and quickly hung up.

It was the maid. I should have known they would keep the maid on during the summer.

I bit at my cuticles, which were getting dry and tough with the relentless, scorching heat of the place. I chewed on one piece of my finger that was tough enough to be leather. I felt a quick sting, and when I pulled my hand away, I saw a blooming bubble of blood fill the divot around my nail, like water rushing through a broken dam.

I wrote to Doctor that night, letting him know I would be in my own apartment when he came, so he should not worry about lodging. We would have our own place. "I have found it so hard to rest in this very hot time here," I continued. "Please be prepared and bring a light jacket and shirts. Otherwise you will roast like a chicken. You cannot imagine the heat."

The next day was hotter than the day before, and having lived through one summer in Phoenix already, I knew the peak was still ahead. It seemed like the sun never left. There was no escape. It beat on you pitilessly, and there was nothing to be done but bear it. I even left earlier than usual to travel to the clinic so it'd be cooler, but that offered little respite. The sun basted everyone golden; I noticed that my upper arms retained their regular color while my lower arms were changing. My face was darkening, too, and my lips were so dry there was a split in the lower one that forced a metallic taste in my mouth when I ate, which I didn't do often. All food looked inedible, floppy with rot or stiff with desiccation.

My stenography was not going well. My head was cloudy, and it was hard to pay attention in that hot classroom, even with the windows raised wide open. I tried to work on my assignment as the instructor dictated to us, but my finger was so sore when I pressed down with the pencil. It was dark around the edges, and when I touched it, the side against the nail was scabbed over and rough. *It must have been the cuticle I bit,* I thought, then realized that finger I'd bitten was on my other hand. There was a black U around the nail beds on both hands.

When I returned to the house, the lights were on and music was playing. I saw the Packard out front. Jack had not called to let me know he was coming. He was not there for me. I knew that. I couldn't go in the house. There was no place for me to be. I went to the back steps, and there were no animals pawing at each other this time. I sat there for a while until I heard the record needle bump into the label again and again and again until someone finally picked it up. I only went into the house when I heard his car leave. The engine sounded like a lion bellowing at me, threatening me, showing me its teeth.

I couldn't understand why he didn't want me anymore. I didn't know what I had done. Maybe Anne had told him about John Robert. I didn't know. Maybe she said horrible things to him about me. Horrible things. Horrible, horrible things.

I put on my pajamas, got a sheet to lie on, and took three tablets. I couldn't stop the tears if I wanted to. They ran all night long.

Dr. McKeown noticed my sloppiness and brought it up the next day and asked me if I wasn't feeling well.

"I'm just so tired, Doctor," I complained. "I'm sorry. In this heat, I can't sleep. It keeps me awake all night long."

He went into his office and came back with a blue glass bottle.

"Try this, Ruth," he said, handing it to me. "My wife has the same problem; the heat keeps her agitated. Be very careful with this—only a little bit when you truly can't sleep. It will help."

"Thank you, Doctor," I said, quite grateful. I looked at the label before I put it in my bag. I had seen it before, many times before. I'd found it in my husband's hands while he was sleeping. I had found it in his bags, in his coat pockets. On the floor. It was barbital.

That night, sleep was like warm milk, and I drank and drank and drank it.

I packed up my things on Sunday morning, and that didn't take long. I had very little that was mine. There were new things on Second Street that I had never seen as I was going through the house, including a silver-plated vase with roses shoved into it that were drooping; no one had put water in with them. There was a candy box, open and empty, with little brown paper cups spilling over the edge. Six cut-glass tumblers in the kitchen sticky with a light-brown residue at the bottom in a perfect circle. Two packages of silk stockings were on the dining room table. There was a bottle of perfume.

Was it Dixon? Was it Jack? Was it other men that I didn't know?

There was a pain going through me, sharp and vibrating, like someone had threaded a wire from my feet through to my head and was plucking it over and over and over and over and wouldn't stop. As I threw my shoes, my slips, my dresses, my compact, into the tan suitcase I felt a scream start in my stomach and race up to escape, but I swallowed it before it did and bit me back.

I was almost out the door when Sammy came into the living room, wearing new pink pajamas and matching fluffy slippers.

"Oh, Ruthie," she said, her arms wrapping around me. "I'm sad that you are going. You've taken such good care of me. Please say you'll come by to visit us."

"Of course I will, Sammy," was all I managed to say.

She kissed me on the cheek. "Please come back and see us," she said again. "I know Anne can be not so nice as other times. She's just flirting with Jack. She doesn't mean anything by it. I know that, I promise it."

CHAPTER
THIRTY THREE

Unit H looked just like unit C but the kitchen table wasn't the one I had eaten lobster on. The sofa was not the one that I had settled in with Jack and drank whisky. The door was not the one that he knocked once, then quickly twice on. There was no hat hook that I had nailed into the wall with the heel of my shoe.

The bed was not the one he had been in.

And for that, I was thankful. I couldn't stand the thought of Doctor being where another man had been with me, and the dirtiness that ground in all over it.

I didn't put away my clothes. I opened my purse, pulled out the blue bottle, and sipped it as if from a holy goblet. Then I lay on the bed that was not ruined, and I screamed until my blood became quiet and that wire was finally still.

Anne came to Dr. McKeown's office a few days before Doctor was due to arrive. She brought a bottle of Coca-Cola, the glass beaded up with coolness. She handed it to me and I held it to my forehead. It felt so calm.

"We shouldn't fight," she said. "I miss you, Ruth. Sammy misses you. Will you come over for supper tonight? I bought a small chicken and a cabbage, and it will be a fine time. Will you? Please? I was so terrible and unkind to you, after all you've done for us. I'm ashamed."

"Will Jack be there?" I asked.

She shook her head. "No, no, just us girls. The way it used to be."

I did miss them, and that was the honest truth. I missed our nights together, listening to the radio and playing cards. Laughing at *Amos 'n' Andy* and having our wits scared out of us by Sammy's favorite detective shows.

Maybe now that we had space from each other, it could be good again, I thought. So I agreed. I'd go to dinner for chicken and cabbage and make things right for the three of us.

And maybe because I wanted so badly to turn everything back to the way it was, to feel that happiness again instead of the plucking wire, it seemed like nothing bad had passed between us. We ate, laughed, played cards, and I took the streetcar back to Brill Street, just like the hottest part of the summer had evaporated and never happened. They were excited to meet Doctor, and insisted I bring him over for dinner when he arrived.

Poor Doctor. He was not prepared for the heat as I had told him to be. He arrived in a serge coat, wool trousers, and a bowtie, his face already strawberry red when he got off the train. The front of his shirt was dark with perspiration.

"I've never felt anything like this," he said, fanning himself with his hat as we walked to the streetcar. "I feel like the flames of hell are licking at me."

"Yes," I said. "I know exactly how you feel."

⋙══⋘

I brought him to Brill Street, unit H, and turned my only fan on him as I helped him change out of his drenched shirt. He seemed so much older than he was the last time I saw him in El Paso; there was less hair, his eyes were lower, and he seemed stiffer, almost like a toy soldier that could not bend.

I looked at him carefully as he tried to cool down and catch his breath, handing him cold water that I had kept in the icebox. I was relieved that he was not shaking, his hands were steady, and he was not pale or jaundiced. He was not using medicine, his letters had insisted, and looking at him then, I believed him.

Maybe Bisbee could be good after all, I thought, but for only a second. I wasn't sure if I could do it all over again, especially now that I knew I cared for Doctor, but didn't love him.

I made good on my promise to bring him over to the girls' so he could meet them, and he was excited, too, after all of the things I had told him in my letters: how they were my first real two friends, and about taking care of Sammy when Anne was away. They welcomed him warmly. Anne had made a pot roast with potatoes and it smelled wonderful.

They asked him about Los Angeles, and what a city that big was like. He told them tales about Mexico, and said that they should visit us down in Bisbee once we got settled.

"That would be wonderful, for all three of you to be together again," Sammy said. "Although I'm sure Ruth's mother will be so sad not to have John Robert with her anymore."

Doctor was still for a minute. He looked at Sammy and then at me.

My mouth went dry and my mind stalled.

"Well, of course," he picked up after the silence. "It will be good to have him back with us."

"Doctor, do you play bridge?" Anne asked.

"It's been a while since I played, but I do love the game," he replied.

The sentence hadn't died yet when I heard something I never wanted to hear again. One knock. Then two quick ones.

The table went quiet, and neither Sammy nor Anne got up. But it didn't matter, because the door swung open boldly, and there stood Jack Halloran.

"Well, look at this," he said, grinning his best shining smile. "You've started the party without me."

⋖═▸═⋗

Jack didn't seem to mind at all that he was playing cards with my husband; in fact, he seemed to revel in it. It took but five minutes after he sat down to pull the bottle out of his jacket pocket and tell Anne to get the glasses. She put five of those cut-glass things on the table, and as Jack started to pour, I pushed mine away, and then pushed Doctor's, too.

"Now, Ruth," Doctor said, pulling my hand back. "A man should be allowed to have a drink every now and then."

I put my hand in my lap and I felt that wire begin to vibrate, to shake, ping, ping.

"*Sherlock Holmes* is almost on," Sammy cried, and jumped up to turn on the radio.

I looked at Jack, but he had his eyes focused on Doctor, pouring him another after he drank the first.

"So, what business are you in, Mr. Halloran?" Doctor asked him.

"Oh, Ruth didn't mention it?" he replied. "I'm in lumber. We're having a boom here in this town, and once this financial thing clears up, there's not going to be stopping this Phoenix from rising sky high."

"I don't know about that," Doctor said, laughing. "I can't understand how anyone can live somewhere that's as hot as the surface of the sun."

"Oh, men can do it," Jack said. "You just bear down."

He poured Doctor another drink, and another. The front of Doctor's shirt was beginning to darken and he kept wiping his face with his handkerchief. Jack didn't produce a bead of sweat. I wasn't sure what Jack was going to say, what was going to come tumbling out of his mouth. They just kept talking.

Ping, ping, ping.

"Ruth, come listen to the show," Sammy begged. "This murder is *terrible!*"

"I think we should go now, Doctor," I said quietly.

"Nonsense, Ruth, we're having a fine time, aren't we, Mr. Halloran?" Doctor replied, saying the name sloppily.

"It's too early to go home," Jack said. "Besides, someone calls my house all night long and it's impossible to sleep."

"Ruth, I'm scared to death!" Sammy called out again.

"We certainly are," Jack said, grinning.

"I want to go," I said, standing up. "I think we should go."

I stood by Doctor's chair and held out my hand. "Please," I said. "I'm not feeling well."

"One more drink for the Doctor!" Jack chortled, and produced a full pour, almost overflowing the cut glass.

"One more!" Doctor yelled, and downed it all.

When he stood up, I took his arm as if he were my father and he shuffled to the door. I kissed both Anne and Sammy on the cheek before we left.

I said nothing to Jack.

I was turning on the fans at Brill Street when Doctor let me know he was not pleased that I'd made him leave.

"You are not sick, Ruth," he said, slurring. "You just don't want me to have a good time."

"That was not a good time, Doctor," I shot back. "That man was trying to get you drunk on purpose and make you look like a fool."

"That's not true," he said, falling into the sofa. "Mr. Halloran is a fine fellow."

"He is *not* a fine fellow," I replied.

"He helped you get a job, he was friendly, and he looks out for you and your friends," he slurred.

"He is not a good man," I repeated. "Don't let him fool you. He is a liar."

"I know a liar when I see one," Doctor said, raising his voice. "Like you. Like you, Ruth. You lied to those girls about the baby. So this baby is going to live with us, is he? Is that what you've been telling people? You're the liar, Ruth, it's you! You know that's a lie!"

"Stop it!" I yelled. "Stop it! You did that! You took him! You are the reason I have to lie!"

"You are the liar," Doctor said again.

"Do you want the truth?" I said, everything rising up in me, everything pouring over because it would not stay in for one more minute. "Do you? You like the truth that much? Do you want to hear some truth? That man? The one you think is so fine and honorable? I have *been* with that man. Not once, not twice. Many, many times. *I have loved that man.* And he loved me. *He loved me, your wife.* Is he so honorable now, Doctor? Are you having a good time now?"

Doctor looked at me, and it was quiet. He was slumped there, his shirt drenched, his cheeks drooping, his eyes staring, the lower rims a shiny crimson. He looked like an old, tired soldier who'd been shot and couldn't understand how to get himself back up.

Doctor left the next day. He was due to stay several more, but that was no longer possible. I watched the taxi leave, headed for Union Station, where he would catch the train to Tucson, and then to Bisbee, to a job he would get and then probably lose.

I opened the blue bottle and walked back to my bedroom and drained it, so I went and pulled the brown bottle out of my handbag and opened that one, too.

I wanted to kill all of the hurt that was swollen and pushing on me from the inside, and that included what I had done to Doctor. I wanted it all to wither and dissolve, like a flower that loses its life petal by petal, dropping to the floor.

CHAPTER
THIRTY FOUR

I got to the clinic early the day after Doctor left and went into Dr. McKeown's office to tidy up before he came in. I placed everything in neat piles, straightened out his instruments and sterilized them, then dried them off. I didn't hear anyone else in the hall or in the building.

I opened his cabinet, quickly, searching, and found it. I opened the full barbital bottle, poured half into my empty one, and filled the rest of the once full bottle with water, shaking it before I put it back. There were also several bottles of Nembutal, so I put one in my pocket and moved the rest of the bottles around to fill the space.

When Dr. McKeown came in, he was pleased to see his neat office, and that he would not have to sterilize his own instruments that morning.

"Thank you, Ruth," he said. "Thank you so much. You seem like you are in a calmer mood this morning. I'm glad to see it."

"I got some good rest, thank you," I replied.

That night, I put wet sheets up over the windows and swallowed several of the Veronal tablets I had left from the drugstore, plus one Nembutal from the doctor's cabinet. I did not eat. I knew I could starve the pain away. If I did not feed it, it could not exist. I was almost asleep when I heard John Robert cry, and I sat up immediately in the dark, my chest running with sweat, the sheets damp underneath me. I ripped the sheets down from the windows and looked outside. Had Doctor brought him back?

Had he now realized what he had done, that I wanted my baby so badly that I told my friends he was going to come home someday?

I heard him again. Crying louder this time, he knew I was near.

I flew out of bed and ran out the front door, looking around. Everything was still.

"John Robert!" I called out into the shadows.

A cat came out of the darkness, flicked its tail, then sat down and watched me.

I picked up a rock and threw it at him.

Had Doctor gone to Bisbee to see the baby? Was that where my baby was? It was very close to Mexico, and this business about getting a job was a lie because it was hopeless. It was hopeless. Everything he dragged me into was hopeless.

That was how he was going to get me to Bisbee, I realized. He was going to lure me down there with my baby, who wouldn't even know me by now. My baby, who was calling another woman Mamma, reaching to someone else for comfort, for songs, for safety.

My baby.

They had probably already poisoned him against me, telling him that I didn't want him and that was why he lived with people he did not belong to.

Do you know what your mother does? I know they told him. *She goes with bad men. She left you so she could do bad things. She didn't want you around.* They told him that every day.

"John Robert?" I called again, listening, wishing, praying for an answer, desperate to hear that cry again.

The silence swarmed. It buzzed. It swallowed everything.

Someone out there has him, I knew. *Someone is keeping him quiet so he doesn't cry out. Someone who is* right there, *hiding.*

"I'm here!" I shouted. "I will find you!

"I am coming for you," I whispered, in case anyone who wasn't supposed to hear was listening. "I am coming."

It was early afternoon by the time I got there. It wasn't hard to find; it was the biggest building in town. Three tall red towers, red tiles, like a palace. Like a castle. The main street wound around in a slow curve and it rose and rose and grew out of the ground until it was as high as the mountains and was right in front of me. The Copper Queen Hotel.

I just walked up to the desk and asked if Dr. William Judd was there. The man told me that he was, did I wish to ring him?

"No," I said quickly. "I'd like a room, please."

I pushed the money across the counter and told him I wanted a room across from Dr. William Judd.

He asked for my name.

"Is that Miss Lucy Ryder or Mrs. Lucy Ryder?" he asked.

"Miss," I said. "I want the room across from Dr. Judd."

"That room is not available, but I have one adjacent," he told me.

"Yes," I said, and held my hand out for the key.

"May I take your luggage?" he asked.

"I don't have any," I said, taking the key from his hand, and headed to room 27.

I listened quietly to hear him. I was so still. I crouched right by my door, knowing that if he was going to the lobby, I would see him through the keyhole. For hours I heard nothing, just the sounds of other people, people I did not know. I did not hear John Robert.

I wondered if the front desk had told him I was there and waiting for him to come out, and that's why I heard nothing. I was going to have to draw him out. Like a little fish.

I went across the street to a garage and used their phone to call the hotel. I asked for Dr. Judd's room. He answered and I was very quiet so I could hear any baby sounds in the room. I heard only Doctor's breathing, and him saying, "Hello? Hello?" again and again.

The baby must be sleeping.

I had to pull him out.

"Dr. Judd, please help me! I am right outside and my baby is having convulsions! Help me!" I cried in a high-pitched voice, then hung up and thanked the man at the garage for the use of his phone. I ran around to the side of the garage and waited for Doctor to come out with John Robert so I could steal him back.

But Doctor did not come out. I waited for ten minutes, and then I went back to use the garage's phone again.

I called again, and asked for Doctor's room. He answered it again, and I was dead quiet.

"Hello?" he asked. "Who is this? Hello?"

I said nothing but listened.

"Lady," the garage man said. "Lady, hang up the phone."

I didn't want to, but he took it out of my hand and hung it up.

"I don't have time to play games here," he said. "Go on, go. Get out of here."

That's fine, I thought. I shrugged at him.

"I'll just wait. You'll see. That man has my baby," I told him, and walked back across the street to the Copper Queen.

I dragged a chair from my room in front of what I was sure was Doctor's and stood on it so I could see over the transom. All I could see was the far side of the room, the window facing the street and nothing else. I tried to lift myself up with my fingers on the lip of the transom, but I wasn't strong enough.

There were no baby sounds. Maybe Doctor had drugged him. Maybe John Robert was just very tired.

I dragged the chair back and put it against my closed door so I could look out my own transom and see when Doctor left his room. I was there for hours. He never left.

It was dark when I heard all of the noise. There was someone trying to open my door; there was a key in the lock and it was jiggling. I opened my eyes just as a crack of light cut across me, and I covered my eyes. I heard the sound of the chair banging against the wall, and then the light went on.

It was the man from the front desk, and next to him was Doctor.

I drew myself up on the bed and crawled backward.

"I know what you're doing!" I shouted at him. "I know you have my baby and I am here to get him."

"Ruth," Doctor said softly, and held out an arm.

"Don't you dare," I said, scurrying as far back as I could. "Don't you dare. Don't you dare. I am not yours. I am not yours. Get away from me!"

He came forward and took my arm, and I began to scream.

"You can't have her in here like that," the front desk man tried to say over my screams as Doctor grabbed both of my arms and was trying to get me down on the bed.

"I am not your wife!" I screeched.

"Ruth, calm down," he said crossly, fighting with me.

I kept screaming. I wasn't going to stop. I couldn't stop. I didn't know how to stop.

"Be quiet and I'll take you to John Robert," he finally said, and then I was able to stop.

Doctor kept driving through the desert, the two car lights shining on the dirt road, running through the dust as it came at us in the night. There were no houses. It was only scrub and the two lights and a brown, choking mist.

"I want to see my baby," I told him.

"I know," he said. "Calm down, Ruth."

"You know where he is," I said. "Take me there."

"You have to stop this, Ruth," he said. "This has to stop. Who is Lucy Ryder? Why would you call yourself that?"

"You said you would bring me to him," I argued.

"Ruth, please stop," he said, and I saw that he was crying.

I didn't care. He didn't care when I cried and begged for him to bring the baby back.

Monster. Bastard. Devil. Soulless.

"You're no father," I said, and I knew he had lied to me again.

He needed to feel what I felt. He needed to know what he had done.

It unraveled in that car, came out of me like a ribbon, a red, never-ending ribbon that twirled around the inside of that car and filled it up so tight that we couldn't even move anymore, a red ribbon of everything that had been rolled up so tight inside of me, finally unraveling.

He just kept driving.

CHAPTER
THIRTY FIVE

Doctor brought me back to Phoenix and called Dr. McKeown, saying I would be out for a couple of days because I had the flu. I was to take a Luminal and a Veronal tablet each night before bed, Doctor told me, but no more of the brown bottle. He asked me where I got it. I said I didn't remember. No more bottles of anything, he reminded me.

He stayed with me on Brill Street until he felt that I was better. It was only a couple of days. He called Anne and told her that I had a terrible fever and if she could look after me for a while, that would be very helpful. He had to get back to Bisbee, he said. He was afraid he had stayed too long and the hospital would be upset.

Anne came over and brought me some soup and juice.

"Doctor said you went to Bisbee, and you got sick there," she said. "What happened?"

I remembered driving through the desert and night and being choked with dust. The rest of it seemed like a lingering dream that disturbed me and I didn't want to think about it anymore.

"I don't know," I told her.

I heard a knock on the front door. And then two quick knocks.

"Surprise," Anne said with a smile.

Jack was kind again. He brought me things to take care of me. He said he was worried. He said he was sorry. He said he never meant to make me so upset. He said to remember that everything was going to be good and he was going to promise that.

He came over every night for short little visits, bringing flowers and a tiny box of candy. I had lost almost a week of work and was worried about money, but he paid my rent and I felt better about things.

We went over to Sammy and Anne's just like we used to, listening to the radio, playing cards. Only Mr. Dixon came over, none of Jack's other associates. That was very nice.

It reminded me of how fun things used to be, and I was glad that the good times had returned.

Mr. Dixon took Anne to Los Angeles for a week, so I went back and stayed with Sammy on Second Street. I told her how much I had missed her company when Anne had come back from Portland and things became so sad. She agreed, and then she said something I didn't expect.

"You mustn't think poorly of Anne for doing the things that she does. She only does them for me, you know. I'm sick and can't work. So Anne makes the sacrifice for both of us. Without her, I'd starve. When she was in Portland, four different men proposed to her. But she turned them all down. She came back to me."

This stunned me. Sammy wasn't stupid, but I didn't get the impression that Anne was sacrificing anything. Anne was having the time of her life. I felt terrible for Sammy. I knew that I had to be extra kind to her, and when I would hear her cry at night, I tapped her on the shoulder and gave her one Luminal and one Veronal and told her that everything would be okay.

Anne returned with an exquisite wardrobe and a fur coat, and even though I didn't get close to it, it looked like an inferior fur from a distance. Raccoon, maybe nutria. Nothing to strut about like she was.

"Sammy," she said, stopping and twirling, "I might let you borrow it before I sell it."

The weather was getting cooler and much more tolerable, but I still kept the windows open at night because the breeze felt so good after such a hot summer. Jack said that was dangerous and that he would make sure I was safe, so for the next two weeks, he stayed over almost every night. He paid Mr. Grimm ten dollars for my light and gas bill; I had been worried about that, too. He had mentioned that before the wives came home, he was going to go hunting up north with Mr. Dixon and some other friends for one last bachelor's hurrah.

Doctor wrote; his job at the Copper Queen Hospital was over and he was going back to Carrie's to pick up a job at a clinic called the Santa Fe Emergency Hospital while the regular doctor was away. He also said that he was to "blame for the whole situation during the past year or more."

He asked if I was still taking the Luminal and Veronal and said that if I was, to stop. "You are in danger of getting yourself into a serious situation. You want to get ahold of yourself. Those pills will knock your nervous system to a fare-thee-well if you don't cut it out. Try to exert a little self-control."

I threw the letter aside. I felt fine, I felt steady. The wire inside of me was gone, and I was happy.

I was happy. And I was going to stay happy.

Mrs. Halloran and most of the wives were returning home now that the brutality of the summer months was over. I knew my time with

Jack would be limited, so I tried my very best to savor what was left. One night, I waited and waited, and he never came, so I went to sleep; it was very late, I waited until 2:00 a.m. I woke up when I heard the door open, and Jack walked into my bedroom very drunk, and he had another man with him.

I was afraid this was the man who attacked me before, and I was terrified.

"Jack!" I cried. "Are you crazy? Why did you bring him here again after what he did?"

"He's the taxi driver," Jack mumbled. "I promised him a drink."

I was furious. I had to be at work by seven, and I had spent my entire night waiting up for him. I was tired and angry. I was not going to stay up all night while Jack and his new crony drank and caused a commotion until morning.

"No," I said adamantly. "Please go. It's too late to be coming over. Please. I have to get some sleep."

He looked at me with eyes I didn't like. I had seen them before.

But he didn't argue. Instead, he pushed the man out of the apartment, and before he slammed the door he said, "Fine. I'll just go to Anne's."

My hands shook. *He didn't mean it*, I told myself. *He didn't mean it.*

But I knew that right in that same second, he had just told the taxi driver, "2929 North Second Street."

I took a Luminal and another and couldn't stop myself from crying. I don't know how I fell asleep. I eventually did, but was still so tired when I woke up.

Anne stopped by the office and asked if I wanted to come by for supper. I didn't think Jack would make an appearance, so I agreed, and went home with her on the streetcar even though I had histories I needed to type up because I was so far behind. She didn't say anything about

Jack stopping by the night before, so I put it out of my head. He was bluffing.

We had just finished dinner and were settling in to listen to a radio show when, without a knock, Jack came in, swooped me in his arms, and kissed me, like nothing had happened. I was relieved, I was so relieved. I went to the kitchen to get Sammy a root beer, and when I came back into the living room, Anne was giving Jack a back rub, not only on his shoulders but then running her hands down the front of his shirt, on his chest. Like she had touched it before.

I handed Sammy the bottle and told Jack we should go, but he didn't get up, and stayed in the armchair.

"Go ahead," he said. "I'll come by later."

I felt a cold thread inside me pop, like a tendon.

I got my handbag, took the streetcar home, and waited.

I reached for my bottle and shook out several tablets.

He never came.

I was furious with Anne. Right in front of me, right there in front of me. That was not playing, or whatever she called it. She was jealous, just as she had been before when she started fooling around and ruined everything. I wasn't going to let that happen again. She had Dixon; what did she need Jack for? Why did she need Jack? Why did she want to rip him from me?

I had a dream that night that I took the last streetcar out to Second Street, went into the dark, silent house, and sat on the couch, waiting for her, waiting for Anne to come out of the bedroom with Jack, with my hand in my purse, my fingers wrapped around the gun Doctor had sent me for my safety.

When I opened my handbag the next morning to get my key and lock the front door, I felt something cold and solid instead. I immediately pulled the object out, and found I was holding the pistol from Mexico.

"Are you all right, Ruth?" Dr. McKeown said to me. "You look very far away. Lost in thought?"

"Yes," I said suddenly, looking at him. "I'm so sorry."

"Not to worry," he said. "I'll need the rest of these histories as soon as possible."

He dropped a thousand pounds of files on my desk; the thud of them hitting made me jump.

"Oh, Ruth," the doctor said, putting his hand on my shoulder. "I think you need some coffee."

"Yes," I agreed. "I'll get some."

There were no thoughts. I don't know where I was; I was nowhere, nobody, floating in a timeless place. I didn't know how long I had been there. I dragged myself back and looked at the histories piled on my desk. I started typing. I wasn't even sure that I was hitting keys.

Jack called at 4:00 p.m. He was drunk and singing into the phone. I couldn't talk to him in Dr. McKeown's office, so I went into another office and called him back. He was at the Luhrs Hotel with Scott, the man who had thought I was a pool hall girl and said those unpleasant things to me. I told him not to bring Scott over, and he said he wouldn't, just he would come over that night after I came back from Anne and Sammy's.

And then the funniest thing happened. I went to Second Street, and kept remembering my dream about sitting on the sofa, waiting to shoot Anne. It seemed so real, and I recalled how frightened I was. I walked to the front of the house, one step up, and stopped. I looked through the window and felt an earthquake in me happen all in one moment. It left me weak and dazed.

I took it as a warning. I couldn't go in. I turned back around and came home.

The Packard was at the apartment when I got home, far earlier than I thought he would arrive. Jack and Scott had started a fight at the hotel with another man and the hotel manager threw them out. Scott got a room at another hotel and stayed there, drinking. I was surprised that Jack was not as drunk as I expected, just a little wobbly. There was a slight bruise on his jaw. I touched it with my thumb and he pulled his chin away.

I took him inside the apartment, and he had some tequila with him that he wanted to drink.

"Let's eat first," I said, and made an omelet with my last three eggs.

"I'll send groceries over tomorrow," he said.

"It's of no mind," I replied, putting it in front of him, my hands shaking, but I don't think he noticed, and I put them behind me.

I had all kinds of thoughts going through my head about the night before, jumping from one corner of my mind to the other like fleas. Bouncing, bouncing, I heard it, ping, ping, ping.

"Have you been with Anne?" I blurted out.

He shoveled a forkful of omelet in his mouth and ate.

"She's a flirt," he said. "She's got Dixon all tied up. She doesn't need me."

"What if Dixon tires of her?" I asked. "And she needs another man to pay her rent?"

"I've already paid her rent, remember, and I never asked a thing for it. Not that I'd need to ask."

"I don't trust her," I told Jack.

He laughed. "You shouldn't."

I sent Jack home after dinner. Our conversation had worked me up and I couldn't come back down, and I started to cry. I did not want him to see me cry, so I asked him to leave.

"Take it easy, Ruthie," he said, giving me a peck on the check. "Here's some happiness for you."

I knew before I looked into my palm and saw a brown bottle.

My dream was different that night. I walked over through the dark streets to 2929, went to the back door, through a tiny patch of grass that was finally growing after the death of the summer, and went in through the narrow kitchen. A flicker from the fire was still going, but just barely, and I saw the figure of someone sleeping on the couch, wrapped up tightly in a blanket. Was it Jack? I walked closer. It was too small to be Jack, and then I noticed the hair of a woman. I had the gun in my hand. I walked closer, put my face down close to the hair, and saw it was Sammy's bouncy curls. I withdrew immediately, left the house the way I came, and walked home.

When I woke in the morning, I had a blister on my heel, and as I was trying to buckle my shoe, which was difficult because of my vibrating hands, I found a blade of grass on the sole.

Anne stopped by that afternoon and asked if I wanted to come by that night.

"I can't," I said. "I have histories. I'm very behind. I need these all done by tomorrow."

"Ruth," Anne said. "It's Friday."

"It's Friday?" I asked.

She nodded. "Sammy's all excited about the finale of the *Sherlock Holmes* show tonight. She can't stop talking about it. I'm making some pork chops and scalloped potatoes and I found some of the last lemons for lemonade. Please come by."

"Well," I said. "I can come over after I get some histories done, in time for the show."

"I will see you then," she said.

A tiny little fire started burning in me, in my belly. It was just a small burn, nothing big. It did not hurt.

I headed over to the girls' after I finished several histories, but I felt a buzzing inside that I couldn't shake and I was unable to concentrate. I took the streetcar over to Second Street and resisted the urge to go through the back kitchen door and went up the steps at the front of the house. Sammy saw me coming and opened the door before I got close enough to knock.

"You've almost missed it all!" she said, and I noticed that Evelyn Nace was there, too. "There's only five more minutes left!"

I sat on the couch after I said hello to Evelyn and Anne, who greeted me warmly. I wasn't listening to the show, so I didn't notice when it was over.

"We have four, let's play bridge," Sammy suggested, so we moved over to the dining table and started to play. We had played four or five, maybe even six, rounds, when I heard a car horn, and I was terrified it was Jack.

"That's my brother," Evelyn said as she got up and gathered her things and kissed us all goodbye. "Thank you for dinner. Ruth, good seeing you!"

She had barely shut the door when Anne looked at me and said, "Did you know that Dixon and Jack had been talking to Lucille Moore about their hunting trip?"

I shook my head. I didn't.

"Who gave Jack her number?" Anne questioned. "Did you do it?"

"No, but if I did, I know they are going to the White Mountains and I think she's from there," I replied.

"Ruth, you are so stupid," she shot. "Do you know what this means? She has syphilis. Do you want syphilis? I don't."

"I didn't give Dixon or Jack her number," I reiterated. "I don't know why you think I did."

"I guess you don't care who gets it, Jack is done with you," Anne hissed.

"Anne, please," Sammy said, reaching for Anne's hand. She pulled away harshly. Sammy sat quiet.

"You are so selfish, Ruth Judd. You already have a husband that can't support you, but you want more."

"I don't want Dixon." I laughed. "That bag of bones is all yours. Get as many squirrel coats as you can off of him."

"That coat paid for Sammy's treatment!" she yelled at me. "Do you think I like spending my time with half-dead men? He's older than my father. I do what I have to do."

"I don't care what you do!" I yelled back. "But keep your hands off of Jack, front and back."

Anne was quiet for a minute. She was seething. I felt that little fire in my belly roar all the way up to my shoulders, up past my neck, into my scalp. I was tingling with embers.

"Do you think he's going to marry you, Ruth? Do you? Leave his pretty wife and that little girl for you? Are you going to be a mother to little Susie when you don't even care about your own baby?"

"Shut up, Anne," I warned.

"Anne, please don't say such things," Sammy pleaded.

"I know Jack doesn't know about your baby," Anne teased. "And do you know how I know? He said you'd be a terrible mother, with all of that craziness that goes on inside your head. Calling his house all night long when he wouldn't come to you. Was that supposed to make him want you? Do you know what it made him do?"

"Don't," Sammy said, close to tears.

"It made him call you 'cuckoo, cuckoo, cuckoo,'" she said, imitating a clock.

"You're a liar," I said. "And a whore."

"He doesn't love you, Ruth, never did. Just uses you like I use Dixon," she said. "You're only a thing to him. I can make you even less than that. I can make you nothing."

"Go to hell," I said. "You tell Jack about my son and I will tell everyone, including Dixon, about how you really are. About what you are. I will tell everyone at the clinic and you will be on the street. I will tell everyone what you do in secret. So you shut your mouth, Anne LeRoi. And you keep it goddamned shut."

Anne swung her arm back as if she was going to hit me, and I started to raise my arm to block her. The only thing that stopped the swing was Sammy screaming.

"She won't say it, she won't say it, will you, Ruth?" Sammy begged, sobbing. "You won't say anything, will you, Ruth? Please, Ruth. You won't, I know you won't ruin us."

I stood there, thundering like the engine of the Packard. I was lying. It was a threat, only that. I could never hurt Sammy.

Anne looked at Sammy and stormed off to the bedroom, slamming the door.

"I'm leaving," I said, exhausted and buzzing and trembling.

Sammy was quiet for a few moments and said, "You should stay, let Anne sleep it off. I'm afraid if you go now, you'll never come back. We'll have breakfast in the morning and make up. And then everything will be fine."

"No, I need to go," I said quietly.

"You can't, anyway, it's too late. The streetcar isn't running anymore. You can't go home. It's too far. You can't walk in those shoes."

"I've done it before," I replied.

"Please don't go, Ruth," Sammy said. "I want to fix things. We can do that in the morning. Just stay here, I'll get you a pillow and a blanket. We'll make up in the morning, I promise."

I was done arguing, I was exhausted, and I could not fathom the two-mile walk home in the darkness. I was so tired.

When Sammy came back into the living room, I took the pillow and blanket from her hands, took off my shoes, and lay on the couch, and Sammy turned the lamp off.

"Good night, Ruth," she said softly.

"Good night, Sammy," I said back, and reached for the brown bottle.

I couldn't sleep. I felt a storm coming upon me. I heard her words over in my mind, circling like a wheel, faster and faster.

You're only a thing to him.

I can make you nothing.

a terrible mother

craziness in your head

doesn'tloveyou

usesyou

thingnothingcrazy

cuckoocuckoocuckoo

crazynothingterriblething

thing

thing

thingthingthingthingthingthingthingthing.

The storm was here.

It was so dark.

So dark, like there was nothing beyond me, behind me, anywhere. It was a void that had eaten every speck of light, every sound, every moment of life. I didn't know if my eyes were open or closed, it was all opaque, the blackness, and then there was thunder.

There was a noise, a loud pop, but just a pop. Not a bang, not a boom, just a pop.

I heard Sammy call out, "Anne, what fell in there?"

I was frozen but then realized I was running, terror-stricken, I ran, not seeing, not hearing, running, running. Panic was biting me, I had to run, run faster, now. A bite at my thigh, a punch to my side, a burn on my shoulder, a push. A pounding on the back of my head. I cried, I yelled, I heard nothing. I fought, I grasped, I defended.

A battle.

I charged. I clawed.

Then, a burst. Then, a howl.

Like an animal, a howl, long and mournful.

He picked up on the fourth ring. It felt like days.

"Jack, come over to Second Street quickly," I said, sobbing.

"Ruth?"

"Please, please come quickly," I spit out between gasps of spittle and mucus sliding from my nose.

"What has happened? Are you all right?" he asked urgently.

"Sammy's dead," I cried. "Sammy's dead. I don't know what to do."

CHAPTER
THIRTY SIX

My mouth was covered with my hands—still in the spot where I had slid down the back door and crumpled onto the floor, my knees drawn up to my chin—when Jack came in. The sun was rising, casting weak, fragile shadows across the kitchen.

"Oh my God," he said when he saw the body on the floor before me. "Oh my God, Sammy."

He came into the kitchen and crouched down, reaching for her cold wrist.

"Oh my God, Sammy," he kept saying again and again, and then he saw the gun in between us.

"What have you done?" he asked me in a whisper.

"I don't know," I sobbed.

He gently moved the blood-encrusted hair away from her face with his finger, then drew it down the side of her face to her jaw and kept it there for a moment.

"Where is Anne?" he asked, looking at me. He reached across Sammy and pulled my hands from my face. "Where is Anne?"

"I don't know," I said shaking my head.

He got up quickly and left the kitchen. I could not get up, stayed still where I was and could not look at Sammy.

"Anne!" I heard him call. "Anne?"

I heard his footsteps in the hall, the only sound in an otherwise still house.

"Oh no, God no," I finally heard him say.

=◆=

"Did you do this, Ruth?" Jack said, standing over me, his heels planted in the drying pool of Sammy's blood.

I said nothing but shook my head and cried.

He grabbed me by the arm and pulled me up.

"Do you know what this means?" he asked me, his voice guttural. "Do you want to hang?"

"No," I sobbed.

"Get in the bathroom and get all of that blood off of you," he said, and I didn't know what he was talking about until I looked at my hands, which were now stained a brownish maroon. He made me step over Sammy, and pushed me into the dining room.

"We have to figure out what to do," he said, his hand now covering his mouth. "Oh my God, what have you done? Why, goddamnit?"

"Are you going to call the police?" I asked feebly.

"Do you really think I can call the police?" he asked. "This is more than looking away, Ruth. You killed them. They are both dead, Ruth."

I had nothing to say.

"Go clean yourself up," he told me. "I need to think."

I went to the bathroom and washed my hands; it took very hot water and tough scrubbing to get Sammy's blood off. It was under my fingernails, in every crease of my knuckles, in the U of each fingernail. Caked around my wedding ring.

I made the water hotter, hotter, hotter, until it was scalding, and I kept scrubbing. I needed to get it off of me. I needed it all off of me. My hands were steaming, and I wanted the blood to evaporate off of my skin.

I heard the kitchen door close, and I ran to the dining room to see if anyone had come in. Through the kitchen window, I saw Jack go into the garage. A minute later, he was dragging Doctor's trunk across the yard. He dragged it as far as it would go into the kitchen because of Sammy's body, and then he left it there.

"Help me lift this," he said, and had me lean over Sammy to grab the handle on the side. We carried it into the dining room and he dragged it into the living room.

"You know where all of the bedding is?" he asked. "Sheets, towels, blankets, pillows, anything."

I nodded and started with the blanket and pillow I had slept with last night.

"Put that at the bottom," he instructed, and I did as he told me, pushed it all the way down. "Go get everything else you can find."

I emptied the linen closet of tablecloths, dish towels, sheets, blankets. I piled everything onto the sofa.

He left the room and I did not follow. I heard him strain and huff, and he came back into the living room carrying Sammy, her arms limp at her sides, flopping, and her neck stretched far back. It bobbed a little with every step he took.

He lowered her onto the sofa, onto all of the linen I had just put there. Then he went back to the kitchen and dragged the trunk into the living room. He lifted her into the trunk, her knees bent over the side until she was just sort of sitting there, her mouth open and head to the side. I could see a reddish brown stain on her chest, on her left side, and blood had dried all down the side of her face.

"Pull her legs," he told me, and I did, and he pushed her, as gently as he could, trying to get her to lie on her back. But she didn't fit. Her shoulders were too wide.

"It's not going to work," he said, strain and perspiration on his face. "Take her legs. We have to move her back to the sofa."

He pulled her up by her arms and was able to get her out, while I carried her knees.

"We have to hurry now," he said. "They are going to get stiff soon."

He went down the hall and got Anne, and this time, put her in the trunk sideways. Only a little trickle of blood was visible on the right temple. Her mouth was only open a little bit.

"Push her knees up, Ruth," Jack said, and I took her feet and tried to push her knees up that way. She was too long. He reached in and pushed her head forward, her chin touching her chest. "Push. Push harder. Harder. You need to push harder."

Touching her cold feet was awful. They were like fish from the icebox. But they were Anne's.

"You're not pushing hard enough," Jack huffed.

"Stop it, stop it. I can't do this. I can't shove her in here like garbage," I cried. "Stop making me do this!"

"This is your making," Jack replied. "I had nothing to do with it. This is all yours. All of it. And now I'm all wrapped up in this shit because of you."

With his hands, he pushed down on her left hip with all of his might, and then she was in the trunk, all of her. I put a sheet over her and tucked it around her.

"Get her clothes," he said. "Get anything you can and fill this up. You still have blood on your legs. Go get it off."

I went back to the bathroom, and ran the water over my legs in the bathtub. I didn't know there was blood there, but it ran down the sink in pink swirls, like the meat you'd drain in the sink first before cooking.

I dried off with the towel in the bathroom, and when I came out, Jack took it from me and shoved it in the sink.

"Fix your hair, it's a mess, and brush off your dress. Get rid of this," he said, handing me the pistol. "I don't care what you do with it. Go to work. I have to call somebody. Don't come back until the afternoon."

I didn't say anything and did what I was told. I went back to my apartment and fixed my hair, put on a clean dress, and soaked the one I had been wearing; a little pink came out at first, but not much. I did not know it was on my dress.

I knew I had to clean that gun. There was matter at the nozzle, sticky and tacky, and I needed to get it off. I took a cleaning brush and, with soap and water, scrubbed it vigorously until I felt it was clean. I was drying it off with a cloth when I heard a loud, dull noise, like a crack of a bat.

I heard Sammy call out, "Anne, what fell in there?"

Then I felt it, first a pang and then an explosion of agony. It ripped my breath out, and I doubled over, my hand pushed against my stomach, my other hand holding it. The gun had tumbled into the sink.

I couldn't breathe, the air did not come back, and I gasped until it became a dry groan, and I fell backward onto the floor.

I sat there for a while trying to breathe, trying to ease the pain. I knew I was shot in the hand, but I did not know if I still had fingers. Grimacing, I pulled the cloth away and saw all five were still there, but the bullet, it seemed from the blood, had lodged in between my knuckles. There was no exit wound on the other side. I knew that was bad. I did not dare to try and move my fingers; I was too afraid.

I stumbled to my feet and got my hand to the sink to run water over it, see exactly what I had done. I needed to see through the pain, but it was difficult. It was raw and stinging, and my vision was blurry. With cold water running over it, the torture did not subside, but as soon as I saw the wound as clearly as I could, I pulled my hand away and tried to pat it dry.

I poured antiseptic on it, cut a piece of my top sheet off and wrapped it around the hand. Once I got to Grunow, I could dress it properly.

I still had to get to work.

I walked to Grunow, my hand throbbing, up the steps where I always waited for Anne, and opened Dr. McKeown's office. I dropped the keys twice; he wasn't in yet.

I quickly dialed the number to the X-ray clinic, and lowered my voice some. I did not recognize the voice of whoever answered and told her I was Mrs. LeRoi and that I would not be in today, adding that Sammy's brother had come to town and we were going to take him to Tucson.

"Well, if you had to change your plans, why didn't you let me know at eight o'clock and I could have arranged a replacement?" the woman said nastily and hung up.

I dressed the hand in Dr. McKeown's office; it was already bruised and black around the edges of the wound. He came in just as I was securing the bandage closed.

"What happened, Ruth? Let me take a look!" he said, very concerned.

It was almost impossible to speak.

"It's just a burn, a bad one, but just a burn from the stove," I explained. "I've dressed it. That's what I get for not paying attention."

I do not know how I sat there until noon, checking patients in and not bursting into tears. The wire running through me was fully live, vibrating everything, making me jump and causing confusion. The hand would not silence itself, and kept banging with alarm that I could feel in my teeth as they rattled. It matched my heartbeat. I wanted to slam the hand in a door to make it quiet. I kept it in my lap so no one would see.

When I finally got home, I sipped a tiny bit out of the blue bottle just to ease the throbbing, just a little bit. I brought the dress I was soaking out to dry, trying to handle it with one hand.

The pain did not stop.

The phone rang later that afternoon. It was Jack, telling me to come back to 2929 North Second Street after the sun set.

"I'm shot," I told him. "The gun went off when I was cleaning it."

"I can't do anything about that," he said. "I have enough over here."

"I want to go to California and have my husband take care of it," I said. "I can't go to anyone here."

"Ruth," he said impatiently. "Stay put until dark. Don't talk to anyone. Don't go out until then."

"I won't," I promised.

"Bring a suitcase and whatever else you have," he said.

I did not go through the front. I went to the backyard and saw one of Sammy's fancy slippers in the yard. I picked it up, and then tried to open the back kitchen door; it was locked, but I still had the key. I opened it, expecting to see Sammy's blood still seeping and running over the floor, but even without the lights on I could see it was gone.

"Jack," I whispered.

I heard someone in the living room, and there were Jack and Dr. Brown, a man I barely knew from the clinic. Dr. Brown looked blanched and nervous. His sleeves were rolled up, as were Jack's. He looked like he had been painting something red; small flecks of scarlet dotted his shirt. Jack had a dark stain smeared across his chest. I knew it was from Sammy. Two trunks, our big trunk and Doctor's footlocker, were placed by the front door.

"Give the suitcase and the satchel to Dr. Brown," he told me, and I handed them over.

Dr. Brown took them to the bathroom without saying a word.

"You're going to go to California, and you're taking these trunks with you," Jack said. "They are medical books for your husband."

"No," I said, shaking my head. "Take them to the desert. Out where we would drive, farther than that. Leave them there."

"Someone would find them. I'm not taking that chance of anyone seeing me dump bodies in the desert. You're taking them on a train to Los Angeles," he said. "A man will meet you at the station by the name of Wilson. He will find you. You let him take the trunks and you go to your husband's. And you don't come back."

"I don't come back?" I asked.

"No. You stay there," he said. "You never come back."

"What should I tell Doctor happened to my hand?"

"We went on a hunting trip last night in the White Mountains and you had an accident," he instructed.

"What will this man do with the trunks?" I asked.

"It doesn't matter, he will take care of it," Jack said sternly. "Just claim them at the depot, and he will take care of the rest. And you don't come back."

"Drive me to California," I said. "We could go now."

"I can't fit what we need to in my car, it has to go by train," he said. "Now come and help me roll this mattress up."

As we passed by the bathroom, I saw the door was closed. I helped Jack roll Anne's mattress tight, the sheets off of it. There was a large bloodstain that had soaked all the way to the bottom on one end, where her head had been, and had stained the rug underneath.

"Get a knife or something and cut that part of the rug out," he said. "We need to burn it."

I got a knife from the kitchen, but it wasn't sharp enough; I ended up bending it in half. I could not do it with one hand, so Jack got a bigger knife from the kitchen, more like a cleaver, which Anne used to cut up chicken. That one worked better.

I was trying to burn the piece of rug in the fireplace when Dr. Brown came back with the satchel and then the suitcase. There was also a hatbox that I knew Anne had brought back with her from Los Angeles.

"What is in there?" I asked, seeing that the two trunks were already by the door.

Jack was tying the rolled-up mattress up with twine.

Dr. Brown didn't say anything but looked at Jack.

"Sammy had an operation," he said quickly.

"What do you mean?" I asked, not understanding. She was already dead. Why would she need surgery?

"She could not fit in the trunk," he said, and said nothing else.

My hand flew to my mouth. I ran to the kitchen sink and vomited.

Jack had called the Lightning Delivery Service to bring the trunks and bags to Brill Street at 10:00 p.m. He told them we were moving books and that the parcels would be very heavy. Two men came to pick them up.

"Did you just varnish the floor?" one of them asked. "It's sticky."

"It's on my hands," the other one said.

Jack handed them a ten-dollar bill.

"Just load it up there, fellas," Jack said. "It's just a spill."

Following the delivery truck, Jack drove me back to Brill Street with the mattress packed in his backseat, along with the sheets.

"What about Dr. Brown?" I said. "What if he talks?"

"After what he just did?" Jack said with a sneer. "I wouldn't count on it. Besides, I have enough on Brown to send him away for a good long time. I learned my lesson once, and that was enough. I never want to find a new baby in my car again."

I didn't say anything.

He pulled into the driveway at Brill Street and parked the car, but did not turn the motor off.

"I'll send the delivery men over at nine to pick things up and take you to the train station. I'll be there to buy you a ticket," he said. "And what do you do when you get to Los Angeles?"

"I wait for Wilson and he takes the trunks, and I go to Doctor's and I never come back," I said.

"And you never come back."

I got out of the car, and he said nothing else, just drove away.

I opened the door to the apartment, and the delivery men dragged the trunks and baggage inside without a word and left me alone with things I had never thought I'd think about.

I gathered a few things of my own and opened the hatbox to put them in, but shut it just as fast and shoved it away from me as hard as I could.

It was 9:10 a.m. and the delivery truck had not come. The train to Los Angeles was at 10:40 a.m. and I was getting frantic. 9:20. 9:30. 9:35. My hand hurt so much.

I tried calling Jack. There was no answer. 9:40.

I called him again. The phone rang and rang and rang.

I didn't know what to do.

I had fifteen dollars. That was all. That was it. I had no other money in the world. I could not call another delivery truck, it would not get here on time.

I had one idea.

"Mr. Grimm!" I said as I knocked loudly on his front door. "Mr. Grimm, it's Ruth Judd!"

Mrs. Grimm came to the front door and I was so relieved. I was afraid they'd be at church.

"Mrs. Grimm, I'm in some awful trouble," I said, and I couldn't help but feel tears welling up in my eyes. "I ordered a delivery truck to take my trunks to the train station, and it hasn't arrived yet. My train leaves at 10:40 and Dr. Judd needs his instruments immediately! Might Mr. Grimm be able to drive me to the station with my things?"

"Of course he can, Ruth, I'll send him right over. What happened to your hand?"

"Just a burn," I said. "I was being careless."

But Mr. Grimm could not load the trunks himself, and called for his son to come and help. Between the two of them, they loaded the trunks, suitcase, satchel, and hatbox in the back of Mr. Grimm's truck and I sat in the middle as they drove me the mile to Phoenix Union Station.

"What is in those trunks, Ruth?" Mr. Grimm remarked. "It felt like you had concrete blocks in there!"

"It's medical books and Doctor's instruments," I lied. "He's starting a new position this week and needs them urgently."

They unloaded the trunks and baggage and I looked around for Jack. There were not many people at the station; I could not have missed him.

"Thank you, Mr. Grimm," I said, and gave him five dollars, saying goodbye. I did not want him to see me with Jack.

10:10.

10:20.

10:25.

10:30.

The porters would not load my trunks on until I had a ticket in hand. I went to the ticket counter and bought one, $5.50. The porters complained about the weight of the trunks; I gave them a dollar. I kept my handbag, satchel, suitcase, and hatbox with me. My hand ached, my body trembled; I was freezing with fear. I wanted to be sick.

I took one last look around for Jack.

10:38.

I started for the train, and got on.

He had not come.

He had not come.

For hours it was just the desert, brown, dry, passing by as a dusty blur. I sat and did not move. I did not want to think. I wanted a sip from the blue bottle, but I realized I had left it all at Brill Street. I hadn't packed anything. I even left my dress drying out on the line. I wanted it all to be gone. Over. Behind me. I should just jump off this train and run into the brush, live like a little animal and dig a hole for myself in the ground. I could stay there forever and be quiet, and the wire would stop sparking and I would not have to believe what had happened and I could chew my own hand off and be fine. Animals do that, when they are in a trap. They chew off parts of themselves and they are fine. They live on. They survive. They don't remember the past or what happened before. I could do that.

The train was not full, there were few passengers, and I was glad for that. I didn't want to talk to anyone, tell them my name was Lucy Ryder and that I was going to start a beauty parlor in Los Angeles, or that I had once outrun a revolution in Mexico or that I had a baby and my husband made it disappear. I sat on the rocking train, not seeing, not listening, not talking, not breathing.

When the car was dark and the few people in my car were sleeping, sliding sideways or spreading out over the whole row, I took the hatbox down from the luggage rail above and opened it like I had the night before. Last night I had unwrapped it, but I couldn't understand what was in there. I wasn't going to do it again. I opened the train window. I picked the bundle up out of the hatbox, wrapped in pillowcases and towels, and threw Sammy's intestines and bladder out to the desert beyond.

The train pulled into Los Angeles the next morning. I scanned the platform for a man who looked like a Wilson, someone who would give me a sign or a tip of the hat to signal he was Jack's man.

I saw no one.

I left the train with the satchel and hatbox, and calmly looked around, moving toward the waiting area. I stopped and waited for a while, hoping someone would approach me, let me know it was fine and they were ready for me to claim the trunks. I waited for an hour, and no one came. The panic rose again in my throat, the wire tightened, and I wanted to run. I tried to calm myself down.

Breathe. Breathe.

I couldn't go to Doctor. I couldn't explain any of this. Even if he came, what would I do with the trunks? Just leave them? With my name on them?

I went to the women's lavatory and tried to think. Why had I not expected this? Why did I think Jack was telling the truth? Why hadn't I come up with another plan, just in case? I took a towel from the attendant and patted my face with it using my right hand; my other hand was in the pocket of my coat.

"Would you mind," I said to the attendant, handing her a dollar, "if I left my hatbox and satchel here for a moment? I have to make a phone call and want to make sure they are safe."

The woman took the dollar, and told me to place them behind the bathroom door.

I walked out of the train station into the sunshine and the Los Angeles air, the bustle and city noise immediately apparent. I found the taxi line and got into a cab. There was only one person who might help me.

"University of Southern California, please," I said.

My brother, Burton.

PART FIVE

CHAPTER
THIRTY SEVEN

On April 13, 1933, fifty engraved invitations were sent out to a carefully selected band of politicians, public figures, and those who expected to be awarded the status of being witnesses.

The cardstock was a thick, pure white; the script was as formal and impeccable as it would be on the invitation to an outstanding occasion—a ball, gala, or wedding.

And like those events, it was a marked occasion; it wasn't every day that Arizona hanged a woman.

YOU ARE RESPECTFULLY INVITED TO WITNESS THE
EXECUTION OF
WINNIE RUTH JUDD
AT THE
ARIZONA STATE PRISON, AT FLORENCE,
BETWEEN THE HOURS OF 12 AND 5 A.M. A.D. 1933
SIGNED,
AG WALKER
WARDEN

The last woman to be hanged in Arizona had been Eva Dugan in 1930, convicted of murdering a chicken farmer with a hatchet. She'd climbed the steps to the gallows before sunrise, and at 5:11 a.m., the trapdoor had sprung open. The force was enormous, and as the rope was pulled tight by the weight of her plump body, she was decapitated and her head flew several yards, rolling to a stop at the feet of the spectators. It was reported that blood shot out of her neck as her heart seemingly beat several last times, spraying in a wide, generous arc. Five audience members, two women and three men, fainted.

⋙━◆━⋘

After being extradited back to Phoenix from Los Angeles, Ruth was arraigned on November 3, 1931, and pled not guilty to two counts of murder. A trial date was set for six weeks later. Photos of Ruth, Sammy, and Anne were already being hawked on the street as postcards for a nickel and the spectacle was fully underway.

The trial, which began on January 19, was never going to be anything but a farce; the public demanded it. With Ruth's lawyers retained by William Randolph Hearst, it was a mirage, engineered to feed the voracious appetite of spectators across the country who bought his newspapers in every edition, morning, afternoon, and evening. She was a cash cow, an investment well made for a paltry sum of $5,000 after Dr. Judd fired Judge Russill for selling a story without his knowledge. Hearst, in the interest of feeding the public for months and months to come, provided her defense.

She would be tried for the murder of Agnes "Anne" LeRoi first; a separate trial would then take place for the death and dismemberment of Hedvig "Sammy" Samuelson.

Witnesses who lived on or about Second Street testified in God's honest truth that they heard screams at ten o'clock Friday night; no, eight o'clock Saturday morning; yes, eight o'clock Saturday night. Sounds of gunshots were reported by four different neighbors, none of which heard the same number of shots. Evelyn Nace testified about playing bridge with Ruth and the girls that night; Lucille Moore was brought to the stand to describe their parties, detail by lurid detail. *What songs did you dance to? Who was there? What kind of liquor? What time did you go home? Did you go home?* There were headlines that insisted drugs were involved; others stated drugs weren't involved. Ruth was a lovely woman to Miss Marshall, her neighbor on Brill Street, but a monster to Mrs. Reed, who had a daughter Ruth had once scolded for throwing bricks in a vacant lot. It was a three-way love triangle between Sammy, Ruth, and Anne, fueling competition and jealousy; Ruth was running a prostitution ring for her own financial gain; Ruth was caught up with mobsters involved with narcotics. Everyone had a story about Ruth; everyone wanted to be important. Everyone needed to have their own piece of it.

Ruth never said a word, not even in her own defense, on advice of counsel. In her jail cell, she changed her story daily: she had done it alone, she had cut up Sammy, she had killed in self-defense, Sammy and Anne had both attacked her, and Sammy had shot her first.

She spent most of her murder trial looking at nothing in particular, unwrapping and rewrapping the bandage on her left hand, her right leg crossed over her left, constantly kicking as if it was held by a wire.

Jack Halloran attended the trial every day, expecting to be called to testify. He never was.

The jury found Ruth guilty on circumstantial evidence and lore. A key piece of evidence was the letter she had flushed down the toilet in the department store. So long ago.

On February 8, 1932, the Supreme Court of Arizona decided that Ruth's payment for Anne's death would be her life. Prosecutors were satisfied with their win and did not pursue the second murder charge.

Her conviction was immediately appealed, but that was dismissed. Her new lawyers, acting pro bono, were Ernest McFarland, who would become governor of the state of Arizona in twenty years, and H. G.

Richardson; they filed for a hearing with the Arizona State Board of Pardons and Paroles. After a lengthy debate that lasted several weeks, the commutation to life imprisonment from the death sentence was denied.

In December, the State Supreme Court sentenced her to hang in six weeks, on February 17, 1933.

⟨═⟩

Florence, Arizona, was little more than a dot of an outpost on the way to Tucson. It was known then, as it is known now, for two things and two things only: the state prison and the courthouse where Ruth's trial was located. The industry there was nothing but crime and punishment, save for several saloons that helped populate the prison.

Ruth looked forward to visits with her parents, who had moved from Indiana to Florence to be closer to their daughter while she was still alive. The matrons were kind to her, getting accustomed to Ruth singing Spanish songs to them in her cell. It helped break up the dismal, hopeless pallor of death row and the atrocity that hung over the young woman who had killed two of the people she loved most in the world.

She was thin, frail; she had arrived that way, soft-spoken and thankful to whoever gave her a moment of benevolence. How had such a gentle girl ended up spending her last days waiting for a noose? It didn't seem possible. She was harmless. Sweet. She asked after the matrons' families and if they had children. This girl belonged at tea parties, married to a man who treasured her and provided her with a nice life. An easy life. How had she fallen here, notorious, dishonorable, a murderess?

Their fears hidden away, because they did not show it, Ruth frightened them. She was terrifying. They were accustomed to guarding reckless women with ill morals who were deplorable and, often, vicious. If a girl like Ruth was now their charge, behind bars and waiting for her doomed fate, what was their assurance that it would never happen to them? She was not like the others they had seen in this place. She was like them. What lay dormant in any woman, ready to spring forward and put them in her place?

Her mother, Carrie McKinnell, brought her clean dresses every week; her favorite was a blue gingham with a velvet bow at the collar, and the warden allowed her to wear it. It was a silent agreement: for her remaining time, as a kindness, she didn't have to wear the gray prison dress uniforms worn by the other convicted women could be spared for this one.

> *Duérmete, mi niño*
> *Que tengo quehacer*
> *Lavar los pañales y sentarme a coser*
> *Este niño quiere que lo duerma yo*
> *Duérmalo su mami que ella lo parió*
> *Este niño quiere que lo duerma yo*
> *Duérmalo su mami que ella lo parió*

Her lithe voice was airy, almost ghostly, trailing through the hall of cells, wrapping itself around bars and escaping out windows. Some of the matrons didn't understand Spanish; to them, the song was comforting and pleasing. Those who understood the words focused on the melody instead.

> Sleep my child
> I have to wash the nappies and sit down to sew
> This child wants me to put him to sleep
> His mommy put him to sleep, she gave birth to him

Arizona State Prison warden A. G. Walker allowed Ruth to have a black cat, who she named Egypt. The cat nested in her lap, curled and tucked. Ruth ran her fingers over the mink-like fur, shiny and glistening, head to tail, for hours, singing, singing.

Este niño quiere que lo duerma yo
Duérmalo su mami que ella lo parió.

After Ruth's verdict was announced and the invitations to her execution addressed and mailed, Jack Halloran was indicted as an accessory to Anne LeRoi's murder and brought before a grand jury. Ruth entered the courtroom first, and Jack passed by her chair on his way in. He made no notice of her—not a look, nothing of acknowledgment. When Ruth was called to testify in her blue gingham dress with the velvet bow, she looked at him once, then glanced away. As she spoke, he leaned forward in his chair and stared at her intently, watching every movement of her mouth.

The courtroom was overflowing; reporters circled like lions around an injured animal. It was so full that seats were removed in order to provide more standing room.

It was Jack who packed the bodies, she told them.

"He told me Sammy has been 'operated' on," she testified.

He did not take his eyes from her, and even though she did not look at him, she knew it. She felt the direct line of him to her; it was there, it was strong, and it burrowed in her chest and made her cold. With each question it wormed itself deeper and harder into her. He still had her, and he knew it. The cord was not broken; it beat with its own heart and struck her repeatedly, with every question. Time moved as slowly as she had ever known it.

"I'm not here for the purpose of clearing Jack Halloran," she blurted, responding to the escalating trembling that surged through to her fingertips, the top of her head, the heels of her feet. "He had an opportunity to clear me at my trial, but he didn't. He is a coward."

Halloran openly laughed at her.

"He is signaling to me. Make him stop talking to me," Ruth cried. "I don't want him to talk to me. He's talked to me too much already."

The deputy county attorney asked the judge to instruct Halloran to stop communicating to her in any way. The judge replied that he had not seen the defendant make any overtures to the witness.

"When he came into this room, I wanted to scream at him," Ruth said in a shaking voice. "The longer this case goes on, the bigger a coward he is."

Halloran smiled widely.

She couldn't bear it. She could not bear one more second of it.

"He doesn't care that Anne is dead and Sammy is dead, or that I am going to die," she shouted. "He just sits and laughs about it. He is responsible for the deaths of three girls in this state. I have only four more weeks to live."

Ruth did not hear the Halloran's lawyer object, never knew the judge was striking her words from the record.

"I hope you've suffered as much as I've suffered, as much as my mother, Anne's mother, and Sammy's mother have suffered," she railed. "You're a coward! A coward! A coward!"

The judge halted the cross-examination and court was postponed for two hours. The prison matrons charged with Ruth came and removed her gently, and she sobbed, unable to breathe, spittle flying.

"Coward!" she screamed hoarsely as she passed him, but Halloran kept smiling.

The following day, she refused to answer any questions after Halloran's lawyer tossed Dr. Judd's pistol from hand to hand like a ball and then handed it to her, telling her to hold it in her right hand.

"No," she said simply. "I don't want to. I won't."

The case against Halloran was dismissed, three weeks before Ruth was due to arrive on the gallows.

=⬧=

Spanish lullabies no longer trailed from Ruth's throat. Instead, she climbed up into the window of her cell and sat there, like a monkey in a cage. She laughed in one moment and sobbed in another. She continually took off her slipper and beat herself on the back of the neck with it.

"Coward!" she would scream from the window. "Coward!"

She had stopped asking after the matrons' children and left her food untouched.

She began sawing through the bars of her cell with a small blade someone passed her—everyone suspected Burton. She had completed two of them before anyone noticed. Ruth's mother began to cry when she saw her daughter's raw and bleeding hands.

H. G. Richardson, Ruth's most recent attorney, saw only one way to spare her. He requested an insanity hearing with the Arizona Board of Pardons and Paroles. After her behavior at Halloran's inquest, he was hopeful he might be able to save her life.

"Ruth," he told her. "I need you to write down in this letter exactly what happened. I need you to tell everything. What you were thinking, what you were feeling, what medicine you were taking. Write down what drove all of this to happen. Can you do that?"

Ruth nodded. The possibility of escaping her execution had brought her a little back to life, and the chance to tell her story to people who might listen ignited a belief in her that she would live through this.

She wrote a letter to Mr. Richardson, as he requested, with everything she wanted to say. Her husband was a good man. She had truly loved Jack Halloran. She had never sold her love. Anne taunted her. Anne was using Jack for money. Anne never cared for him, she just wanted to take. Ruth never wanted to hurt Sammy, she loved Sammy, she still loved both of the girls. She never even thought of Sammy being hurt. She was taking Luminal. It made her crazy, she didn't know her own mind. She couldn't sleep, couldn't sleep. She kept thinking of Anne's taunts. She couldn't sleep. The thoughts rolled and rolled and rolled around in her head, at night, always at night. The hatbox. The train station. Portions of Sammy. Then the shot to her own hand.

It was down. Finally, it was down.

But not all of it. Not the parts that would make him guilty.

He was free now.

And maybe, she thought, if he was free and she could be free . . .

Richardson read the letter, all nineteen pages in Ruth's long, looping handwriting. When he was done reading it, he folded it and placed it a safe-deposit box where he kept important personal papers.

Then he went back to Arizona State Prison and asked Ruth to write another one.

At the insanity hearing, Ruth repeated much of what she had told at Halloran's inquest: that Jack had aided her in disposing of the bodies and told to her to hide the crime. She broke down and sobbed. She talked about moving parts of Sammy from the large trunk to the smaller trunk, afraid that it would weigh too much. She was angry that she had never been able to tell her own story at her trial.

Witnesses were called, many of them the same as at the murder trial. Mr. Grimm, her landlord; Sheriff McFadden; and Burton McKinnell.

And then they called Jack Halloran.

"I would like to take his head and break it against the ceiling and spatter his brains like a dish of oatmeal," she said, laughing, then clapped her hands like a child and broke down into tears.

Halloran testified that the last time he saw Ruth was the night before the killings, October 15, 1931, and he had not seen her again until her trial in 1932.

"I never saw Mrs. Judd after Thursday night," he proclaimed, "and I was not the last to see her at that time. She was escorted to her door by another man as I sat in the car outside."

Had he gone to Second Street on Friday?

"I did not."

Had he seen any bodies there?

"I did not."

Had he cut up a body at Second Street?

"I certainly did not."

Did he arrange to have it done?

"I did not."

Did he see Ruth Judd on Saturday?

"I did not."

Did he aid Mrs. Judd in leaving on the train to Los Angeles Sunday morning?

"I did not," he answered firmly. "I was playing golf at the Phoenix Country Club."

Ruth was still. She had waited on Brill Street, panicked, 9:10 a.m., then 10:00 a.m., then 10:10 a.m.

She had called. It rang. And rang. And rang.

He knew where she was. He knew she was waiting. He knew everything.

And he was playing golf.

Dr. Judd took the stand, lighting a cigarette as soon as he got to the witness box, and proceeded to chain-smoke through his testimony.

Does he believe Ruth dissected Sammy?

"No, she couldn't cut up a chicken. Knowing something myself of the difficulty in disarticulating a spinal column, it's impossible that she could have done it. She has no experience in surgical operations."

Does he believe Ruth Judd is a woman of sound reasoning?

"No, I do not."

What is his medical opinion of the state of his wife?

"My wife is suffering from dementia praecox," he told the jury. "God in himself could not cause that woman to act insane; all she has to do is act natural. Her mental characteristics are entirely inconsistent. At one moment she is in a state of exaltation and in another moment she is quiet from intense depression, and then she rises to the most supreme exhilaration."

Have you been witness to states of hysteria and madness on the part of Mrs. Judd previously?

"Yes, on many occasions. She speaks of John Robert and says she is going to see him when she dies. John Robert is the name of a child she believed she had, but he never existed."

Two more guards were brought in to watch Ruth that night at the prison. When she had returned to her cell after that day's hearing, she was quiet and waited until the matron watching her relaxed for a moment. Ruth popped a something into her mouth and began screaming that she was going to kill herself by swallowing it. When three guards wrestled her to the ground, two double-sided razor blades fell out of her mouth.

"I want to kill myself!" she shrieked. "I won't be hung! I won't be hung! You want to see me hanged to see my head flip up in the air like Eva Dugan's!"

With four guards constantly watching her, she cowered in her cell, alternately crying and screaming, hysterical and incoherent.

Arizona State Prison warden Walker took the stand the next day, testifying that he didn't want the hanging of an insane woman on his conscience. Four matrons who had watched over Ruth and the assistant warden agreed with him.

Ruth quietly watched as her mother, Carrie, testified and said simply, "There is insanity on both sides of my family. I've always felt that insanity fell on me to some extent and on Ruth even more. I want you to know that girl is insane and has been more or less insane all of her life."

Doctors who had examined Ruth for twenty or thirty minutes confirmed Dr. Judd's diagnosis of dementia praecox. She had thought they were visitors coming to see her, or newspapermen, not knowing they were there to observe her. She didn't know these men. She refused to talk, and either huddled in a corner or climbed up into her window.

She was infuriated with their testimony.

"You bullies, you cowards, you gangsters!" she screamed. "Quit torturing me! Quit taunting me!"

Two prison matrons came forward to quiet her, and one put a hand over Ruth's mouth. Ruth bit her.

Warden Walker hurried to her side and lifted her from the chair. She collapsed onto his arm and he carried her out, one foot dragging on the ground as he held her entire weight. She never stopped screaming, beating her free arm into the air.

The warden and a matron placed her on the courthouse lawn, although she could still be heard from inside. Ruth was lying in the grass, kicking her heels into the ground.

"They keep torturing me! Bullies! Cowards!" she shrieked. "Cowards! Where is Jack Halloran? Bring him here! Bring him to me! They are not going to kill me! They are not going to kill my babies!"

The warden and matron got Ruth into his car, and she finally became quiet after he drove for half an hour on dirt country roads around Florence.

When Ruth appeared before the board in a much calmer state several days later, she told them that she would try to make reparations for the mistake she had made. She begged them not to execute her.

"If you will commute my sentence," she said, "I will be good."

In closing, Ernest McFarland, one of Ruth's lawyers, stood before the jury. His plea was simple: "What we are asking for Ruth Judd is that if she is to be executed, it would be at a time when she is sane and able to ask for forgiveness."

At the Arizona State Prison, a consensus among the inmates was spreading. A letter arrived to the warden, unsigned.

"We all know Ruth Judd is insane just as we all know she is broke, so does anyone else who is sane. We are all wise as to who is behind the whole deal and whose money is paying for those fancy doctors and other witnesses against her and we have all made up our minds that if Ruth hangs those responsible will follow her to hell in short order. There are 700 of us here and we will all be free someday. We all respect Warden Walker too much to make that things tough for him but don't forget someday some way the guilty ones will have to pay after she had gone through the trap and is pronounced dead. The state will hire a preacher to preach her into heaven. If she is good enough to be preached into heaven, she is good enough to live on this earth of ours."

On her day of scheduled execution, Ruth Judd was declared insane.

Upon the announcement of the ruling, the courtroom erupted with applause.

Ruth was not there. She was coming up from the car, walking on the arm of Reverend McKinnell, her aged father. They heard the clapping as she entered the courthouse.

When she reached the courtroom and got to her chair, the applause had not abated.

Doctor Judd came to her side, his face red with emotion. He put his arm around her shoulders and told her, "You will not be hanged. Everything is all right. Do you hear? You're going to the hospital."

Ruth said nothing but stared blankly ahead of her. After a moment, a slight smile appeared, and she nodded.

⊷

The same day, the deed to 2929 North Second Street was transferred from Ethel and Frank Vance to the O'Malley Investment Company.

CHAPTER
THIRTY EIGHT

The car trip to the Arizona State Hospital took ninety-five minutes, during which Ruth was curled up in the backseat, her head resting on prison matron Mrs. Heath's lap. The first she saw of it was not the sprawling Mission-style stucco building with tall, grand windows, but the back door, where the clicks of camera shutters started as soon as the car pulled in.

Ruth was sick of cameras; that was always the first sound she heard when she arrived anywhere: a courthouse, back to prison, and now the nuthouse. Click click click.

There was a large crowd, and she was so tired. The car ride had made her sick, and her only goal right now was to make it inside the institution without vomiting.

But the clicks made her angry, set her off. Every one was a reminder of where she was and where she would be for the rest of her life. She had escaped the gallows, and she was glad, but she had just moved from one prison to another.

She took several deep breaths in the backseat before she got out of the car, clutching Egypt to her chest. She was allowed to bring her cat, Warden Walker had made sure of that. He had watched Ruth deteriorate into an almost comatose condition, and if she was going to recover, she couldn't experience any more losses. The cat was everything to her now. Walker ensured that the hospital understood this.

With one foot out of the car onto the gravel, Ruth looked up at the men waiting to grab an image of her, FRESHLY ESCAPED FROM DEATH, MURDERESS CHANGES ADDRESSES.

"I never saw such a bunch of morbids!" she shouted at them. But it didn't stop them. Photos of an angry killer were worth more than those of a complacent one and would land the image most precisely on the front page of any paper.

"It's fine Ruth, we're almost in," Mrs. Heath said, rubbing Ruth's arm with one hand as she held it with her other. "Just a couple more steps to go."

"Look at them," Ruth hissed, hiding her face with the hand not holding Egypt. "They've made a shell out of me and they are not going to take any more pictures of a corpse. They can't taunt me anymore. They can't take any more pictures of me."

Ruth's new room was a vast improvement over her death row cell. There were no bars on the window, but there was a metal screen beyond the glass. The room was filled with light and she would be allowed to open the window for air and freshness. She would be allowed a supervised walk around the grounds for an hour a day.

She would be under constant watch due to the suicide threats.

Her only permitted visitors were her parents, who were too feeble to make regular trips to see her until they moved to Phoenix, and Dr. Judd, who had already admitted himself to the Sawtelle, a disabled veterans' hospital in Los Angeles, the day before, suffering complications from diabetes.

Her attorney Ernest McFarland was also able to visit his client, but he came not as a lawyer, but as a friend.

"Maybe you don't think I was listening," she told him. "But you made a great speech to the parole board that day."

"How do you know?" he asked her. "You're crazy."

Ruth laughed.

"I know a man who worked at Grunow with you," he told her. "He told me you *did* have a baby. He saw a photo of it."

"Doctor was trying to help me live," Ruth replied. "I can forgive him that."

Ruth's first months at the hospital were uneventful. She was in solitary, and someone was watching her at all times. She found interest in walking the grounds, feeling the sunshine, and dreading the summer. She asked Burton to send her a fan. He did. He had just gotten married and they were expecting a baby. Ruth was happy for them.

She hoped that when she met the other women in the ward, someone would know how to play cards. She had missed that. In her cell in Florence, she was alone and terrified, and she worked very hard not to think about it.

She missed playing bridge, rummy, hearts.

She missed having friends.

Alone in her room with guards as her "companions," Ruth asked for fabric, thread, and sewing needles. When she was deemed recovered enough to use them, she began to sew little dresses and other items of clothing.

The staff of the hospital believed them to be doll clothes.

The Arizona State Hospital for the Insane on Twenty-Fourth Street and Van Buren in Phoenix changed its name to the Arizona State Hospital in 1924, but the original name stuck. Most of the patients were transferred in from California to ease overcrowding in that state, but the population of the hospital was not limited to those with criminal pasts; more often than not, Ruth was housed with women who suffered from depression, mental illnesses, and drug addiction and women who were convicted of prostitution. And with those women came their children.

Ruth sometimes heard the sounds of children playing, but it wasn't until she emerged from observation after a year that she understood those sounds were real.

She gravitated toward them, like she did the children at La Vina.

They sang songs together—Ruth taught them the Spanish lullabies—and she made dolls for the little girls. She cradled the babies with Down syndrome whose parents had surrendered them to the hospital, and spent as much time with the children as she was allowed. She helped the nurses feed them, and looked after them during the day, surrounded by children of mothers who couldn't care for them.

Sometimes she wondered if this was where she was supposed to be after all of what happened. She provided stability, and taught them manners and how to read and write.

It was what she would have done with John Robert, she thought, every time she spooned oatmeal into a mouth, spelled out a word, or comforted a crying baby.

At night, to keep herself occupied, Ruth offered to style hair for the other patients, then staff, and then friends of theirs. By 1937, she had a thriving beauty salon operating out of the hospital, which permitted her to order supplies including henna, permanent solution, shampoo, bobby pins, nail polish, and manicure products. She was known for her expert Marcel style, which looked like finger waves but were produced with a curling iron. Her appointments from the public booked up quickly, and she had a steady clientele who flocked to have their eyebrows and eyelashes dyed by Ruth Judd, self-taught and the most popular beautician in Phoenix.

It didn't escape her that her notoriety was the reason people sought her out, but when they came back again and again, she began to feel that she really was doing something good. You only needed to have your hair done once by Ruth Judd to get a conversation started at a dinner party.

She had dreams about Sammy and Anne, some that seemed all too real and others that were fantastical. They talked to her in those dreams like it was still 1931 and they were three girls struggling to survive the Depression, listening to detective shows, and playing cards. In others, they were playing hide-and-go-seek in a field like little children. Even as the years tallied, she thought of them constantly and refused to talk about the murders, referring to them only as "my tragedy."

Ruth was trusted in the hospital, and she earned it. She got along well with patients and staff alike. She was free to walk about the grounds, but her children and business kept her busy seven days a week. Twelve- to fourteen-hour days rendered her exhausted, but to be occupied was good. It gave her no time to think about other things. That, in the hospital, she would never find John Robert. That Doctor had not come to see her since she'd been there. About Jack Halloran, who was still out there, two miles down the road, living his life with his wife and his children on Lynwood Street in his charming house that he designed, the master bedroom door adjacent to the front door for silent and quick leave, as if nothing had ever happened at all.

In 1939, enough of the beauty parlors around town had complained that Ruth was stealing their business, so the new hospital superintendent, Dr. Louis Saxe, shut Ruth down, stating that it was because she did not have a license. She was furious and felt targeted. She was just one woman in a hospital for the insane, curling hair and painting nails. Everything, she felt, would be taken away from her sooner or later.

She sent Doctor twenty dollars to come and see her. He had just been released from jail for drunk driving; he didn't have enough bail money, so he spent several weeks there. He had gone back to live at the

Sawtelle, where he had been for years. She wasn't sure if he would come or spend the money on something else.

She bought a new purple rayon dress and new shoes and stockings for his Sunday visit, along with bottles of soda.

He never came.

Her ire rose. When she confronted Dr. Saxe with being unfair about the beauty parlor, he revoked her privileges—all of them—then placed male guards outside her room and window. She was drugged with hyoscine, and was unable to distinguish the real from the imaginary.

When the guards were finally removed, Ruth decided there was nothing left to wait for.

CHAPTER
THIRTY NINE

1939

The therapy department at the hospital had arranged for a dance on a chilly October night. Ruth had other plans.

With a combination of towels, cosmetic containers, and bottles, she fashioned a dummy of herself and covered it with blankets to resemble a sleeping inmate. By midnight, she was at 1328 East Moreland Street, one of the modest brick bungalows in a working-class neighborhood. It was her parents' house.

"Ruth," her mother said firmly. "Stay the night here and go back to the hospital tomorrow morning. They will punish you if you don't go right back."

But Ruth was smarting. They had ripped her beauty parlor away from her, and her own husband couldn't be bothered to come and see her with the money she had sent him to get there. Wasn't everything already ripped from her? Why take more?

"I don't want to talk about it," Ruth said, waving her mother away. She sat down at the kitchen table and began to scribble on a pad of paper. She addressed it to Governor Robert Taylor Jones.

Governor Jones;

My husband coaxed me to surrender to the police. I did and look what happened. Dr. Saxe tortures me. I was not overcome, so I had to surrender. Only a coward would torture one helpless. I am helpless because I trusted fairness. I do not get it. Dr. Saxe says I have no privileges I did have until he came here and took them away. For 18 months I had yard parole, could sit on the yard alone and with my family. I never abused a privilege or broken trust. Tonight I am running away. I hate everyone who has forced me to do it. May God punish them. I want to be a good patient. I like you. I hope you may be governor again. You have been kind to me and I do not want anything to ever hurt you. I am desperate to see my father in the hospital. I am going to see him tonight then somehow see my husband and I will surrender to you on condition that you promise me Dr. Saxe leaves me alone. I will not run away. I do not want my freedom illegally.

Ruth instructed her mother to deliver the letter to the governor the next day.

And then she left.

⸻

The rumors flew about where Ruth Judd was headed. She was hitchhiking her way up to the California coast. She was seen in Long Beach. She had gone back to Mexico. She was in Baker, California. She was in Honolulu. She was out to settle old scores and seek revenge.

In Tempe, Arizona, not far from Phoenix, a minister saw Ruth, who had been missing for six days, in his backyard and asked her to come inside so they could talk. She stayed for three hours while the minister and his wife tried to convince her to return to the hospital. They prayed together. She agreed to go back, and she and the minister drove back to Twenty-Fourth and Van Buren. He dropped her off near the hospital, then reported it to the sheriff.

She fled instead to an orange grove that was on hospital grounds, then decided to go back to the hospital, marching into Dr. Saxe's office and announcing, "Well, here I am."

She was barefoot and her feet were bleeding and bruised. She had sprained her ankle and had fashioned a brace for it out of her girdle.

For most of the six days that she was missing, she told them, she was in the cornfield across the street.

A key to the ward door that had been lost for months was found on her. She told the minister she'd had it for years.

She was sedated and slept fitfully.

In that six days, she had written a letter to Doctor, and he received it after she had surrendered.

She wrote: "I'm lying out here in the moonlight in the desert, but there are mountains all around. I can't get out. I do want to see you. I have a new razor and will cut my head off with it if they try to take me back. It is so cold and I have a sprained ankle."

Four weeks after she had been captured, Ruth walked through the ward door again on December 3, out to Van Buren Street, then broke into a pastor's house and took a coat, a sweater, two oranges, a box of crackers, and some milk, and left a note to apologize for the theft. Bloodhounds from Florence were brought in, tracing her from the women's dormitory to a parson's residence and then to a cemetery, but lost her scent at a fish market.

Both her mother and Doctor told Governor Jones that Ruth would likely commit suicide rather than return. She'd told her mother that she had been kept in a straitjacket after her last escape.

Ruth was not in the cornfield across the street, or hiding in an orange grove. At night, she was walking the railroad tracks to Yuma, 172 miles away from Phoenix; she was hiding during the day. She drank water from irrigation ditches and had lost thirty-six pounds by the time she was spotted trying to call her husband in a Yuma drugstore two weeks later.

She was ragged, her dress filthy. During an examination after her return to the hospital, a razor blade was found in her hair affixed with chewing gum; razor blades were also found in her slippers, vagina, and rectum, where the key to the ward door was also located.

A year of solitary confinement followed her trip to Yuma. Her clothes were taken away and she was given a torn gown to wear; all furniture was removed from her room but the bed.

Her tuberculosis returned.

Doctor sold a six-part story about his life with Ruth Judd to *Intimate Detective Stories*, writing that Ruth once had a child when they lived in Mexico.

In an act of extraordinary kindness, Sheriff James R. McFadden, who extradited Ruth to Phoenix from Los Angeles after the surrender, arranged dinner for Ruth and her husband on New Year's Eve.

The hem of a red evening gown trailed out of the box as he walked out of the courthouse on his way to deliver it to her.

This time, Doctor came.

1947

Ruth was sleeping in an orange grove near the Biltmore Hotel when they found her, wearing a blue cotton dress and scuffed tan shoes. She had a flour sack containing food and clothing and had been gone for a day. Her mother, Carrie, who had been admitted to the Arizona State Hospital two years before and had been housed on the same floor as her daughter, had been moved to a different ward. She had suffered several heart attacks and was in a very fragile condition. Once again, the things in life Ruth cared about the most had been taken from her. She had left the hospital on Mother's Day, after asking to see her mother but being refused.

Doctor had died the year before; she was never told why but suspected diabetes. Burton had taken care of the arrangements. Reverend McKinnell had also died, and now it was just Ruth and her mother.

The new hospital superintendent, Dr. John A. Larson, defended his decision to refuse Ruth's request on Mother's Day, stating it was to keep Carrie McKinnell safe. Ruth had had a tantrum earlier and had given her mother a black eye. It was not the first time, he added, that Ruth had beaten her mother. Burton had been advised and had promised to come and take his mother home with him but had never done so.

Dr. Larson advised that Ruth's dementia praecox, now known as schizophrenia, was becoming worse.

CHAPTER FORTY

Ruth

February 1952

Quiet.

I have to be quiet.

Even as I twist the stolen key in the lock of the apartment door that does not belong to me, I am being hunted.

And they will probably find me. Again.

I slowly open the front door, careful not to make the protesting creak from the hinges louder than it needs to be. I glide across the carpeted floor; I am moving cautiously, deliberately. I must be silent, so silent that I don't breathe, I don't live, I don't exist. So quiet I am not even here.

There isn't much in the cupboards, and I try not to sigh with despair. It is enough.

A can of corn, a can of soup, so I grab them, along with a bread wrapper that is empty except for three slices. An apple on the counter, a bottle of milk in the icebox. I drink it down in three frantic gulps and set it on the soapstone counter, where it tings sharply because I am not being quiet enough.

I hold the bottle steady, trying to suffocate the sound of the ring as it echoes through the dark stillness in the apartment. Crackers. I find crackers in the next cupboard, and a tin of tea. I lift the tea off the shelf, then return it. I shouldn't take what I don't need.

For years, since before Papa died, Mamma didn't know me, didn't know if I was with her at all. When there was no one left to take care of her, the hospital allowed her to come and live with me. I did my best, and though it was my deepest despair, I left her.

An hour ago, I said goodbye to Mamma before I climbed out the state hospital window and onto the ladder—woven tight like a cable from yarn, rags, and iron cord—secured around the iron frame of her bed.

I lost my gaze with her as I went down. Hand over hand, foot over foot, I descended the ladder until I dangled a good seven feet off the ground. I was willing to take the chance, make the drop, and curled into myself, landing on my side. I could make ground with a dislocated shoulder, but not with a broken leg.

I hit the dirt hard.

The stillness was immaculate, breathless, until my body threw itself back into life and I felt the silky dust coating the inside of my mouth and prickling my throat as I took an involuntary, deep gasp.

I got up, checked for broken bones. Checked for the two keys in my pocket. And then I ran.

I had lost one shoe in the fall, and I kicked the other off. My feet barely flicked the soft grass springing me up and carrying me forward toward the front gate. I had the key, and I've had it for a long time. A nurse that used to work at the hospital gave it to me when I first got here, saying that she knew I hadn't done what they said I did. She told me to run away whenever I had the chance. I pulled the gate key out of my little coin purse that I had tucked into my pocket. I opened the gate, flew past the date palms in a silence that was only broken by my breath, and I escaped.

I ran through the darkest parts of Phoenix, slowed to a quick walk under the streetlights, until I made it to Broadway. It would be hours before they would discover my rope, and that the figure of me in bed was simply crumpled newspapers and bedpans. Hours before they would look at my mother's vacant face and ask futilely, "Where is she?"

I reached the apartment hours before sunrise. It was a good start.

In the bedroom, I went to the closet and found a satchel, a pair of shoes that were a little big but would do. I turned the bathroom light on, opened the medicine cabinet, and pulled out a small shaving razor I tucked in my pocket along with a bag of henna. Carefully, I scraped at my hairline, my dark curls tumbling into the sink and onto the floor, stragglers falling on my eyelashes like spiderwebs, until I had a nice even widow's peak. I rummaged through the medicine cabinet and, with the tweezers I found, plucked my eyebrows until nearly gone, then mixed the henna with water and pulled the color through my hair with a comb, like a rake through mud. While it set, I gathered gauze, tape, and a tiny bottle of iodine and added them to my collection of supplies in the satchel. My feet were the problem the last time I ran from the hospital; the desert tore them up like old paper. I found a light blanket and threw that in, too. I rinsed out my hair. It was an almost fiery red, like a cinnamon candy. My hair always took color easily. I used to be blond, but being inside so much darkened it. I didn't even recognize myself, sometimes.

I pulled the blue silk dress off of the hanger, leaving the shift from the hospital on the floor. I looked at the fur coat. I knew how much the nurse loved this coat, and how long she had saved up to buy it for herself. Probably the reason there was so little food in the house.

The desert, at night, gets cold. People don't think it does, but you've never felt the knife of a true shiver until you've spent the night in the sand and scrub, where there is barely an ounce of life to begin with. The cold is so mean it shines. It grins when it slices right through you. Straight to the bone, settling in marrow. You'll knock your teeth out shivering.

I slipped the fur coat on and carried the shoes to the door, the satchel on my arm. I moved down the stairs like a shadow, and clung as close to the wall as I could, out of reach of the overhead light. At the entry, I slid my feet into the shoes and had almost gotten to the front door when I heard the turn of a knob from the apartment on the right and a voice called out, "Betty? Is that you?"

I stopped where I was.

"Ellen?" the voice called again, and I heard hinges whine. The name floated in the air, unclaimed.

"Yes," I said lightly, mimicking Ellen's voice; I knew it well. I talked to her every day. She was a nurse at the hospital, and probably my closest friend. I stole the apartment key from her; lifted it right from her pocketbook where I knew she left it during her shift. "It's me."

"I heard you upstairs." The voice belonged to a woman, who was out in the hall and came toward me. "Ellen? Your rent is late. I can give you a couple more days, but really—"

She was closer than I thought. Suddenly, I felt a light hand on my shoulder. I moved enough into the light that she realized her mistake and gasped, deep and throaty, her hand rising to cover her mouth.

I bolted through the front door and ran down the steps, clop, clop, clop, the heels of the big shoes slapping against the sidewalk. I slowed to a walk once I rounded the corner. The milkman was out, bottles clanging. The pink light was breaking; it was still a little frosty. The city was rousing.

I needed to go.

The desert was half a mile away; I needed to get there before I could breathe right again. Before I could breathe at all.

I saw the first police car pass slowly, and I ducked into a doorway, turning my back to the street. My heart pumped soundly and deeply, I could feel it in my temples, hear it in my ears. *Ump. Ump. Ump.* To hide my face, I pulled the apple from the satchel. I chewed the apple. Took another bite, then peered over my shoulder to see that the patrol was gone.

I picked up the pace a bit, then turned into an alley behind some shops.

I was barely two steps in when I heard a man cry out, "Ruth Judd! Stop! Stop!"

I didn't stop. I saw the man's police uniform, then his partner at the end of the alley. I was hemmed in, like the seam on a pillowcase. Trapped. I turned around and faced the first officer.

"It's time you let me go," I said, my voice only a little bit raised. "I have paid my price. I have been locked up for twenty years. I did not kill those girls. I am the only one who has paid. It is unjust."

The apple dropped to the ground.

The policeman, the barrel of his gun fixed on me, came forward slowly and took my wrist.

"I did not kill those girls," I said again. "I did not cut them up!"

"Then whose arm was in your purse, Ruth?" The officer laughed as he grabbed my other wrist.

The police returned me to the hospital, and Ellen gave an interview to the newspaper. "Had I known it was Ruth Judd, I'd have let her go," Ellen said. "She is such a dear, sweet woman. My landlady was wrong to call the police on her."

It didn't matter.

I was supposed to die a long time ago. I just never did.

CHAPTER
FORTY ONE

November 1952

She was at Eleventh Street and McDowell when the police found her, hiding under a pile of clothes at the home of Fay Harvey, her nurse at the hospital. Ruth had been gone for two days, cutting across vacant lots and passing by her old apartment on Brill Street before she arrived at the home of Mrs. Harvey, who was out of town. It was a concrete block new apartment building with fancy corner metal windows.

She was wearing Mrs. Harvey's housecoat when the authorities found her and looked away so she could change back into the green dress and sweater that she had worn when she escaped.

"Why don't you leave me alone?" Ruth said as the police loaded her into the back of the patrol car. "I'm so tired of being locked up. It has been long enough. I'm going to get a job in town. Lead a normal life. Socialize with people. I am very lonely."

The newspaper reporters were already waiting at police headquarters, but she refused to pose.

"My hair is a mess," she said. "Can I have a comb?"

No one gave her one.

They took her picture anyway.

Five hospital staff members were implicated in the sixth escape of Ruth Judd.

⟨divider⟩

June 1953

Ruth had gotten word that her former attorney, H. G Richardson, had recently died. Richardson, along with Ernest McFarland, who had successfully run for a US Senate seat and was now the Democratic majority leader, had saved her life with the insanity hearing.

It was twenty years ago, Ruth told herself, but she would never be out of danger. She had heard rumors in the hospital that proceedings might be underway to transfer her back to death row in Florence. A sanity hearing was possible. And she had not suffered this long and this heavily only to have invitations to witness her death sent out again.

She had to get it back. It was safe as long as Richardson was alive, but now that he was gone, any number of things could happen if that letter was found. A letter written out of duress, by a strained, terrified young woman who believed that telling the truth was her only way to remain alive.

She needed to get that letter back.

Dear Mrs. Richardson:

Yesterday I told my attorney Mr. Harold Whitney about some legal papers of mine which Mr. Richardson was keeping from me in a safety deposit box in the bank which he told me he had instructed you to turn over to me in case of death. You will probably be hearing from Mr. Whitney in the next day or two instructing you to mail all legal papers of mine to his office period since talking to him, I believe it would be better for some member of my family to come to you personally with a note from me authorizing them to get all of my legal papers to avoid any possibility of there being lost in transit unless the papers are in a safety deposit box in a Phoenix bank. Will you kindly advise me where I can send for these papers? My guardian has several transcripts, affidavits—my attorney others and I would like to get everything together—not scattered around and destroy such as it such as is not necessary to keep and put everything else altogether. Thanking you—

Most sincerely,

Ruth Judd

Mrs. Richardson replied to Ruth, but it never arrived. Several letters addressed to Ruth had gone missing. She wrote to Mrs. Richardson again and asked her to mail the documents to Elizabeth Harvey, Ruth's guardian, instead to ensure their safe delivery.

They never came.

1954

Ernest McFarland was elected governor of Arizona, and Ruth was elated. She remembered the arguments he had given to save her life, and him visiting her in Florence and in the hospital.

She wrote him a thirty-seven-page letter promising to not escape again while he was in office.

"I don't want to put you into any more trouble," she wrote.

She kept her word.

CHAPTER
FORTY TWO

October 9, 1962

She just walked out.

Took a bag of clothes, some of her good memories from the hospital, letters from children she had helped raise there, a few of her mother's things, and she went right out the front door.

Her mother had died several years ago, and McFarland was no longer governor. Ruth went straight to a phone booth, called a friend, and they hid her at a church that had been sympathetic to her case.

The next day, the husband of Burton's daughter, Carolyn , drove her straight to San Francisco.

Arizona State Hospital superintendent Fullbright barely made a statement.

"We're not looking for her and neither are the police. She's not dangerous."

Ruth Judd was fifty-seven years old, pudgy around the middle. She wore cat-eye glasses that were a common style, bore the wrinkles and wear of a woman who had spent the last thirty years fighting for her life. She was tired. She had slept in cornfields, walked along train tracks for weeks, drunk filthy water, nearly froze to death, and had stolen from reverends and pastors to try and live a life. She wanted her freedom.

So she finally took it.

Ruth lived with Carolyn Keiser and her husband, Robert, in a suburb of San Francisco for two years, until she took a position in Piedmont as a cook and companion to a Mrs. Nichols, who was wealthy, nearly blind, and needed help around the house.

The last time Ruth had cooked anything was an omelet for Jack the night before everything went wrong, and she was rusty, remembering how to make only the chili she had learned in Mexico. She studied cookbooks at nighttime, planned out menus, and rehearsed in her head the steps she needed to take. It was something to do, and she didn't care what she did as long as she had the choice to do it.

Mrs. Nichols knew her as Marian Lane, a dignified, tidy name that had none of the weight that Ruth Judd did. Every Thursday they planned an excursion to the de Young Museum, or the Japanese Gardens, Golden Gate Park, and the wildlife museum. They ate lunch together, dainty sandwiches and tea. Mrs. Nichols had two tiny dogs that Marian took for walks through the parks and streets of their upscale neighborhood. It was a fine place to be.

For Marian, Jack Halloran never existed.

Sammy and Anne never existed.

Doctor had never sent a gun.

And Ruth Judd was dead.

Mrs. Nichols left Marian $10,000 when she died, and stipulated that Marian continue to live in the house until the estate proceedings were settled. Burton came out to visit and brought his son, Kirk, who had never met his aunt, and they talked about going back to Indiana to see the old school and church. She called relatives there to make sure she was welcome, and then bought a ticket for her first plane ride.

<hr />

Not far from Piedmont, a mother of two was found dead of extensive head injuries in Alamo. Anna Aarons had taken her two teenage children to school, returning to their home at 8:30 a.m. When her husband, psychiatrist Z. Alexander Aarons, was preparing to leave for his office, he looked out the window and saw her surrounded by blood on their patio. She was five feet from their front door, the keys still in her hand and her purse by her side. Nothing had been taken. Despite surgery, she died the next day.

It was ruled a homicide.

A stakeout at the Aarons' home was begun by the police, taking down the license plate number of every car in the area, including a 1968 Ford Sedan that belonged to Marian Lane.

A routine visit was made to Mrs. Lane, who seemed evasive and didn't want to answer too many questions. She did tell the officers her nephew, Robert Keiser, had been driving the car, and was currently under the care of Dr. Aarons. She explained that Carolyn and Robert were undergoing a divorce and Robert had sought some medical treatment from the victim's husband.

Mrs. Lane was kindly, but to the police officers, her behavior was odd. She seemed to be hiding something.

When they left, they went through the trash and secured several objects and ran the fingerprints after they returned to the station.

They had found Ruth Judd.

<hr />

"I don't know what this is all about," Marian Lane protested at the police station, where she was taken with two small dogs she refused to leave at the house.

They took her fingerprints again, and identified a scar on her left hand between two knuckles.

The Contra Costa police issued a statement that she was being held only as a fugitive, not a suspect.

Governor Ronald Regan wanted the murderess out of his state and extradited back to Arizona, but not before Ruth made a middle-of-the-night phone call to Melvin Belli, the criminal attorney who had defended Errol Flynn, Mae West, Lana Turner, the Rolling Stones, Lenny Bruce, and Jack Ruby, who had killed Lee Harvey Oswald.

"You know who this is," she said after the attorney groggily answered the phone.

"Who?" he asked.

"Winnie," she said.

"Winnie Churchill?" he replied.

"Winnie Ruth Judd" came the answer.

Belli was stunned. Throughout law school, the Judd case had been both legendary and a joke. Now he had seen it all, he thought.

Belli agreed to represent Ruth in her extradition case, figuring that thirty years in an insane asylum was punishment enough. He pointed out in her extradition case that for the past seven years, she had held a job and was a threat to no one. He also added that out of the six times she had escaped from the hospital, Ruth had returned on her own for five of them.

Belli and Ruth held a press conference in which she declared that she expected to be found sane in a hearing and then wanted to go to Paraguay to help children in a leper colony. Reporters volleyed questions about the murders again.

"I want to block out the past and live for the future," she replied.

At her extradition hearing, Belli argued that she was "as much rehabilitated as any human being can be. If not, rehabilitation is a mockery." She was now sixty-four years old, and on her way back to Phoenix again.

⟫⟪

In August 1969, an Arizona court declared Ruth Judd sane, and ordered that she be returned to the Arizona State Prison in Florence.

She remained there until December 22, 1971, when the parole board decided to grant her parole and Arizona governor Jack Williams signed her pardon after an agreement with the state of California was reached, where she would return and work for a former employer, the Blemers family, as a housekeeper.

She never went by the name Winnie Ruth Judd again, and she died in Phoenix, Arizona, on October 23, 1998, in her sleep.

She was ninety-three years old. Her obituary appeared in the *New York Times*.

A Memorial to Marian Lane

January 29, 1905–October 23, 1998

When: January 29, 1999

Time: 6:00 p.m. to 8:30 p.m.

Turkey and ham will be provided.

If you live in town, please bring a potluck dish to share before 7:30 p.m.

Share an adventure, memorabilia, or funny story you experienced by knowing Marian.

NOTES

The papers were donated anonymously to the Arizona State Archives in 2002, the remnants of the long-ago and mostly forgotten legal career of Howard G. Richardson.

He was not a legendary lawyer, he never held office, and he has not been taught in law schools as an example to follow.

To those who remember, and there aren't many left alive, he was, along with his far more famous counterpart, Ernest McFarland, a defense lawyer for Ruth Judd at her insanity hearing in 1933, which spared her from the death sentence.

Maybe it was a banker's box, maybe it was a shoebox, but it was left unbothered for twelve years in storage until someone opened it and started scanning the contents.

On the bottom of every single page was the name Winnie Ruth Judd in her elegant, looping handwriting.

Attorney H G Richardson
Florence AZ
April 6th 1933
Thursday 7:00 PM

I am writing the absolute truth of this case, in full confidence, that you will use it as you see fit in your best judgment. Mr. Richardson, I have full confidence in you and trust you.

This is my first and only confession of the case of the homicide of Anne LeRoi and Hedvig Samuelson.

Anne was used to the world, I truly was not. Jack was the only man I had gone with since my marriage. I was ashamed of things I had done. I could not openly compete with her, I was married and ashamed to. Day after day she lorded it over me, always smiling and fresh and sweet, well knowing she was hurting me with her taunts.

Many evenings Anne would kiss Jack and caress him in our presence, then after he was gone gloat over not caring a thing for him but merely working him for money . . .

Those taunts kept me awake, I could not sleep. I cried. I even prayed. I wrote my parents to please come to me. I was losing my mind. Wild ideas kept me awake. I took sleeping sedatives, Luminal. I wrote Doctor my nerves were breaking. I couldn't eat. I couldn't sleep. I loved Anne still, but those taunts. I would take more medicine to quiet my nerves, cried to please get things off my mind, to sleep.

Friday night I expected Jack. He did not come. I went to bed. Again I could not sleep. I got up, went over to Anne's house. My brain whirling. I was so excited I was panting for breath.

The Murderess

Never did I have the slightest dream of hurting Sammy. She simply never entered my mind. Except to get Anne, stop those taunts so I could sleep. Nothing more did I think of. I took the gun and a knife. How I would do it I was not sure. But I had no intention of harming Sammy. Jack was as intimate with Sammy as Anne, but it was Anne's cruel taunts that haunted me . . .

I hid in the house next door. Anne and Sammy returned to the bedroom.

After they retired, I went to the back door, laid the knife and my shoes outside the door, then crept in the unlocked front door . . . I sat down on the couch in the same dark room and soon fell to sleep clutching the gun.

I awakened, Sammy had gone to the bathroom, that insane desire, that power lead me on, I started for Anne. My stomach was turning inside out really twitching, jumping out of me, outside not a tremor, but my stomach jumping like convulsions. I retreated, curled up and went to sleep again. I went back to sleep again. Oh again and again all night I don't know how many times. Sammy kept going to the bathroom, I started for that bedroom and retreated each time so exhausted I immediately went to sleep . . .

Morning! I heard the milkman. Sammy went to the bathroom again. I started to call her, tell her I was there. I really did. Then I began shaking inside and remembered what I had come to do so this time I crept past the bathroom door, shot Anne. It was a low shot. Sammy called, What fell, Anne? I was hurrying past the door Sammy came out demanded to know what was the matter. I was limp she completely took the gun from my hands. I was non-resistant. I said, Sammy, I am crazy. I have lost my mind give me that gun and I will blow my brains out right here in this door. She held the gun and said, you get out of here right this minute . . .

I then picked up the knife and went back after her with the knife. As I grabbed for the gun, I stabbed her in the shoulder, the fight with Sammy in that breakfast room door; her own finger on the trigger when the shot went through her chest; our fight is all about as I have always related she shot me through the hand as I grabbed for the gun; the gun jammed; we fell to the floor, struggled and I finally got the gun and shot her and in my wild state I really do not remember where in the head . . .

I pulled Sammy into the bathroom. I cleaned up the floor I pulled in the trunk from the garage. It was now about 6:30 or 7 a.m. . . .

I tugged and pulled and finally got Anne from the bed into the trunk. Now it doesn't sound possible but this all took about two hours. I left for the office . . . I had pulled the trunk with Anne's body into the living room. But the trunk was unlocked. Sammy was on the bathroom floor all day Saturday . . . This all happened in the morning . . .

I stayed in my office . . . until 4 p.m. I then took the bag home with me with the gun, knife, pajamas and dress. I fed my cat and went back to the 2929 N. 2nd Street house at around 6 p.m. I really had nothing definite in my mind. No plans made . . . I pulled the trunk back into the hall tried to lift Sammy into it, but that was utterly impossible, I couldn't possibly lift her, she was too heavy her body was stiff. I then got two cheap knives from the kitchen and severed her body into portions I could lift. I was hours doing this and then inch by inch pulling the trunk back into the living room . . .

The baggage men after taking the trunk to the truck informed me it was too heavy to ship as baggage. I told them to take the trunk to 1130 Brill Street then, which they did . . . I also left the mattress from Anne's bed rolled up right there in front of these baggage men at 2nd Street, blood soaked in the living room . . .

Sunday noon, I started getting ready to go to Los Angeles again. I transferred portions of Sammy's body to the smaller trunk and suitcase . . .

The letter found in the Broadway Department Store toilet, known as the "Drainpipe Letter," October 18, 1931

Dear Dr. Moore

I am being sought for by the police and can't get any messages to my darling precious husband Dr. Judd.

355

I've got to tell him . . . so will you deliver this let . . . to it and deliver the message . . . Be kind to my poor husband . . . I do love him . . . I'm crazy . . . I . . . Mass . . . when I get tired I'm . . . worried mentally and sick mind and be . . . then finding me for my crime . . . A . . . tell Dr. Judd forgive him . . . tell him . . . to please not die of grief . . . I love him and hope he won't hate me for being wicked.

Thank you and Mrs. Moore for having been so good and sweet to me in the past. One of my hands is about shot off so I can scarcely write. Do me this favor to let Dr. Judd know what happened . . . I can't. I love him but through . . . nobody but my dear husband a . . . and parents believing me. I'm . . . ng away from the police . . . best regards and hoping you do this . . .

⋙⋘

To Doctor:

Darling: a confession I've kept from you for life because I was so happy with you and I loved you so why tell you. I am crazy only when I am very angry or too tired physically my brain goes wrong. One obsession I've always had is wanting or saying I had a baby. First when I was seven years old I wanted a baby at our house so bad I told this at school that mother had one and four days told the neighbors we had one and such cute antics it did far beyond an infant's ability. Then when I was 16 on my birthday a fellow I was going with and I had a split up. I was furious my girlfriend was the cause, curiously I liked her just as well were chums together, but this boy's cousin antagonized me by crowing that someone could take him from me. I had taken her boyfriend months before from her. The man's name was Frank Hull he wished to be friends but liked my chum Beulah. It was OK until Joey [it's not legible] I hate her always (I had taken a fellow Ronald Carpenter from her later they married). I told Frank Hull about it and asked him not to go with Beulah. I love Beulah, but hated Joey's crowing. Frank thought I was doing it for meanness, et cetera, and so finally, as so many unmarried girls in that part of the woods were having babies I conceived of stating I was and would make Frank marry me if necessary. I was 16. He was 26. Frank Hull never touched me. I never had intercourse with him or with any man until I met you. Frank, I believe is honest. He cried and cried and told Daddy he'd never touched me. He used to tell me I was crazy. I said well quit going with Beulah or I'll send you to the pen. I won't be tormented by Joey. I was going pretty good at school then my teachers loved me. I was good in English class. My stories were published in the school paper and in the city paper. The teachers all like me. I did splendid in modern history. My classmates liked me and I them but I got so worked up I quit school and said I was pregnant and swore out warrants against Frank. I made darling dresses all kinds of dainty things I later gave for little girls dolls. Frank would walk home from church with me and tell me I was crazy I said I knew it but if I started this thing I would finish it. I wanted him to go away until I went back to college then go with Beulah, but please not then. I had an insane temper. So finally after about 10 months I decided I'd have to confess a lie or do something drastic so I proceeded to hop out my window one night in cold October in my gown. I grabbed a few gunny sacks and overshoes and run away and said I'd been kidnapped. First I wrote a letter that I had a baby girl (why I don't know) then I ran away. I was going to get some clothes at my home 16 miles from there and be gone awhile and say Frank had had me kidnapped and I got away. I brought suits against him and assumed as soon as Joey moved I dropped charges and that was the end. This is the first time I've ever told this. My parents believe Frank was wicked. I did it all myself and never have told it to anyone until now. I've always wanted to tell Frank I was sorry. He was a good boy. He thought it was funny until I had him arrested for rape and kidnapping et cetera. I'm sorry to tell you this doctor. Here is a confession I should have carried to my death if I had been intimate with any man I would have told you but I didn't tell you anything to hurt you. I've wanted your respect confidence and love. There in Mazatlán or rather Tayoltita I was sick a couple of days so as Mrs. Hines had been though so thrilled over being pregnant. I decided I'd say I was. I had hoped for three weeks I might be until I became so unwell. So when you moved I wrote that I had a miscarriage. I don't know what possessed me to tell that I had a little boy. I even showed pictures of you with a baby and showed the Fords baby pictures as my baby who was with Mamma. I'm so crazy on that line. I was working so hard at Phoenix when you went to Bisbee then something went wrong in my head and I registered under an assumed name and called you up to give you a fictitious address just to hear your voice and see you, then cried all night for doing it. Then finally wanted you to soothe me and told you I was there. You know how I cried and cried. I was crazy. You said I was at the time I came back and Mr. Halloran came out the next evening he had been on the coast and he said what's the matter you look terrible you look crazy. My two doctors said I look terrible. I've written you for a month how my nerves were doing. Then Thursday Mr. Halloran brought the girls a new radio. Mr. Halloran wanted me to get some other girl and go with him out to the house. I knew a pretty little nurse who is taking sal-varsan but she has nothing contagious now. I cer-tainly am not expecting them to do wrong anyhow. We went out to the girls house. Mr. Brinkerhoff and a couple of Mr. Halloran's friends were there. The girls didn't like it so Mr. H asked us to have dinner with them. I refused so he got dinner and came over to the house. The first time he has ever done it but it was a nice clean evening I truly didn't even take a drink you can ask. The remains of their drinks are in the ice box. Next day Anne came over and we had lunch together the remains of dinner the night before. She wanted me to go home with her that night. Evelyn Nace was going. I had some histories to do and couldn't. I said if I could get through in time I'll come over and play bridge, but I stayed all night. The next morning all three of us were yet in our pajamas when the quarrel began. I was going hunting. They said if I did they would tell Mr. Halloran I had introduced him to a nurse who had syphilis. I said Anne you've *no right to tell things from the office you know that only because you saw me get distilled water and syringes ready and she isn't contagious, the doctor lets her work nursing. Well Anne, I asked Evelyn and she thinks I should tell Mister Halloran too. And he certainly won't think much of you for doing such a thing. You've been trying to make him like you and Doctor Dixon too getting him to move with you. When I tell them you associated and introduce them to girls who have syphilis won't have a thing to do with you. I said Sammy I'll shoot you if you tell that. We were in the kitchen just starting breakfast she came in with my gun and said she would shoot me if I went hunting with this friend. I threw my hand over the mouth of the gun and grabbed the bread knife she shot I jumped on her with all my weight and knocked her down in the dining room and yelled at us I fired twice I think since Anne was going to blackmail me too if I went hunting by telling them this patient of doctor McGowan's was syphilitic and would hand me over to police. I fired at her. There was no harm introducing this nurse who is very pretty to the men. One doesn't get it from contact but they were still going to kill me for introducing Lucille Moore to their friends. Anne said before Sammy got the gun Ruth I could kill you for introducing that girl to . . . and if you go hunting I will tell them and they won't think you're so darn nice anymore. I don't want to bring Mr. Halloran into this he has been kind to me when I was lonesome at the first place I worked and has trusted me with many secrets Of all he did for the girls such as caring for Anne giving her extra money and the radio and he's been a decent fellow. It would* separate he and his wife and he's been too decent. Mr. Dixon kept Anne in an apartment here in LA for several days and then got her stateroom to Phoenix and she was mad enough to kill me when he helped me move over. Part of my things are still at the girls, three hats, thermos bottle, black dress, cookbook, green scarf you got me in Mexico and a number of things. Doctor dear I'm so sorry Sammy shot me whether it was the pain or what, I got the gun and killed her. It was horrible to pack things as I did. I kept saying I've got to go I've got to go or I'll be hung I've got to go or I'll be hung. I'm wild with cold hunger pain and fear now. Doctor darling if I hadn't gotten the gun from Sammy she would have shot me again. Forgive me not forget me. Lived to take care of . . . sick doctor but i'm true to you . . . the thoughts of being away from . . . it me crazy. Shall I give up to . . . don't think so the police will hang me. It was as much a battle as Germany and the US. I killed in self defense. Love me yet doctor.

AUTHOR'S NOTE

There are some things that never age, grow tired, or become obsolete. The murders of Hedvig "Sammy" Samuelson and Agnes "Anne" LeRoi by Winnie Ruth Judd in October 1931 could not serve as a better example.

The story of the Trunk Murders, as they are known in Phoenix, Arizona, has only grown bigger, bolder, and more revealing in the nearly one hundred years since the crimes were committed. It holds all the elements an engrossing narrative needs: horror, fear, mystery, love, betrayal, lies, and catastrophe. No one comes out of this story as a hero. Tragedy embedded itself into the lives of every one of the main players in ways that were final, terrible, and unfixable.

The story is still covered on true-crime podcasts, salacious crime series, and even tours in the Phoenix area. The murder house still stands—now alone on a neighborhood street that housed families for ninety years until apartments were recently built, which surround it— and the curious still drive by it every day.

I started my writing career as a reporter, writing stories on murders, homelessness, and crack babies. I had planned on becoming an investigative journalist, but I wound up as a humor and feature writer instead; that's just the path my career took. But as much as I enjoy that genre, I've never lost the need to know the real story behind the purported story, and that is what brought me to write this book.

I began researching the case in 2014, planting myself at a long table at the Arizona State Archives, where the original luggage tags and the autopsy reports of the victims are kept, along with trial transcripts, police reports, and the lurid tale of the murders begins to unfold. From there I went to libraries, newspaper archives, online and in person, and every place anyone would go to research a subject.

It didn't take long to understand that the story of Ruth Judd that had been floating around for decades had some major holes. Many of them were filled in at the state archives, but there were many, many outstanding questions that remained and I couldn't find answers for.

Robrt Pela, a colleague and close friend, had covered the Judd story for *New Times* on several occasions, and I often called him for help to fill in the missing information. He had also done research on the story, and we came to many of the same conclusions. A confession letter written by Judd, which hadn't seen the light of day since April 6, 1933, had been unearthed by the state archives. It had been donated anonymously to the state archives in 2002 but wasn't "discovered" until 2014, and it contained a story that finally fit the evidence. Pela had written a feature on it; the discovery of the letter was big news to those who were obsessed by the crime.

That cadre of people who were also researching the murders included Sunny Worel, a friend of Robrt's and a research librarian by profession. She was also the great-niece of Sammy Samuelson, the victim who had been dismembered. She had spent most of her life diving deep into the story, and her research skills proved her to be a master, year by year building the largest collection of documentation on the case in existence, including the Arizona State Archives.

Sunny died in 2014 at the age of forty-six from colon cancer. I never had the opportunity to meet her. She was tireless in her quest to uncover everything about the case, including the murder of a psychiatrist's wife that led to the recapture of Ruth Judd in 1969. Sunny believed Ruth was responsible for that murder as well, but she ran out of time before she could prove it.

When Sunny passed, her archive remained untouched until Sunny's mother, Janet, gave it to Pela. Who, in turn, gave me access to it.

It was the equivalent of opening a trunk of gold.

Sunny had collected everything—letters from Ruth to her family, oral histories Ruth had given over the years, even the flyer that announced Ruth's, later known as Marian Lane, memorial service details. Sunny's determination to collect, collect, collect in search for every piece of the puzzle was obvious. Along with my own research, which had already filled ten storage totes, I was able to assemble the narrative of this story in the truest form I could make it.

I could not have written this book without Sunny's archive, which took decades for her to build. She had located documentation that I had never heard of, seen, or even knew existed. Along with the archive, she had assembled a timeline that was invaluable to the construction of this book.

I am betting we were bidding against each other without knowing it for original press photos of Ruth on eBay or vintage magazines that covered the Judd case. Sunny was a vital, integral part of this project, and I have made it a point to keep the narrative as close as possible to the work that she did.

While I cannot project what Sunny would have thought of this book, I have spoken to her family and relayed that I hope she would have approved, and my hope is sincere. It took Sunny most of her life to build the collection, and I have tried to honor that in this book, filling in all the holes that I could with her research and my own, and coming as close to telling the truth of this tragedy—from all perspectives—as we will ever know.

Laurie Notaro, 2024

ACKNOWLEDGMENTS

Thank you to everyone, longtime readers, new readers, my family, friends, and all who tolerated my squealing phone calls every time I found a piece of this story that I had been looking for (and my ad nauseum chatter about this case for the last decade).

Unending gratitude to:

Laura Van der Veer

Robrt Pela

Beth Pearson

Julia Sommerfeld

Janet Worel

Jeffery Spencer

Jen Lancaster

And the work of Sunny Worel

SOURCES

While researching this novel, I consulted many sources. I'm grateful
to the following outlets, which had invaluable coverage on the Winnie
Ruth Judd case, for allowing me to get as close to the story as possible.

Timeline of Hedvig Samuelson and Winnie Ruth Judd, Sunny Lynn
Worel, 2016

Sunny Worel Archive

Arizona State Library, Archives and Public Records

Morning Oregonian

Los Angeles Times

San Francisco Examiner

Los Angeles Examiner

Los Angeles Evening Express

Ruth Judd: Summary, June 25, 1947, the personal collection of
Jerry Lewkowitz

Winnie Ruth Judd: The Trunk Murders, J. Dwight Dobkins and
Robert J. Hendricks, 1973

Los Angeles Record

Phoenix Gazette

Olney Daily Mail

Arizona Historical Society

Arizona Memory Project

The Arizona Republic

"The Truth about Winnie Ruth Judd, by Her Brother," Burton
McKinnell

San Francisco News

San Francisco Call Bulletin

Los Angeles Evening Herald

Intimate Detective Stories

Anchorage Times

Pasadena Star-News

True Crime Detective

Statesman Journal

Chicago Daily Tribune

Los Angeles Herald-Express

Mine Doctor's Wife in Mexico during the 1920s, Eleanor Swent and
Marian Lane, Western Mining in the Twentieth Century Oral History
Series, University of California, Berkeley

Tucson Daily Citizen

Bisbee Daily Review

Arizona Daily Star

ABOUT THE AUTHOR

Laurie Notaro is the #1 *New York Times* bestselling author of the novels *Crossing the Horizon, Spooky Little Girl,* and *There's a (Slight) Chance I Might Be Going to Hell,* as well as essay collections and numerous works of nonfiction. A finalist for the Thurber Prize, Laurie was born in Brooklyn, New York, and spent the remainder of her formative years in Phoenix, Arizona, where she created something of a checkered past. Laurie now resides in Eugene, Oregon, has a cute dog and a nice husband, and misses Mexican food like it was her youth. For more information, visit www.laurienotaro.com.